*It was the custom then for men such as myself,
well-bred and hopelessly in debt, to perform a tour
of the Continent. . . . I wanted to sample new
pleasures, new sensations and delights. . . .*

INTERNATIONAL ACCLAIM FOR AN
ASTONISHING LITERARY DEBUT

LORD OF THE DEAD

"Elevated and elegant . . . yet happily gory and perilous."

—Patt Morrison, *Los Angeles Times*

"A classical alternative to the traditional tale, seam-
lessly weaving mordant humour, cheeky literary allu-
sions and outrageous encounters. . . . I'm sure Byron
himself would have been pleased."

—*Time Out* (England)

"An utter banquet of sex, terror and death told in the
poet's own delectable turn of phrase. . . . This is a
work of literary scholarship positively wet with vi-
brant language and sense of place, exotic in its accura-
cy and lapidary love of detail. . . . The book is really a
tour de force. . . . A beautiful, Byzantine historical
suspense novel."

—*Boston Book Review*

"Entertaining and ingenious."
—*Manchester Evening News* (England)

A Book-of-the-Month Club Main Selection

Lord of the Dead

A NOVEL

Tom Holland

POCKET BOOKS

New York   London   Toronto   Sydney   Tokyo   Singapore

Published in Great Britain under the title *The Vampyre*

POCKET BOOKS, a division of Simon & Schuster Inc.
1230 Avenue of the Americas, New York, NY 10020

ISBN: 0-671-53426-2

First Pocket Books paperback printing September 1997

10 9 8 7 6 5 4 3 2 1

POCKET and colophon are registered trademarks of
Simon & Schuster Inc.

Cover art by Vince Natale

Printed in the U.S.A.

For Sadie, my beloved

But first, on earth as Vampire sent,
Thy corse shall from its tomb be rent:
Then ghastly haunt thy native place,
And suck the blood of all thy race:
There from thy daughter, sister, wife,
At midnight drain the stream of life;
Yet loathe the banquet which perforce
Must feed thy livid living corse:
Thy victims, ere they yet expire,
Shall know the demon for their sire,
As cursing thee, thou cursing them,
Thy flowers are wither'd on the stem . . .
Wet with thine own best blood shall drip
Thy gnashing tooth and haggard lip;
Then stalking to thy sullen grave,
Go—and with Gouls and Afrits rave;
Till these in horror shrink away
From spectre more accursed than they!

LORD BYRON, The Giaour

But I hate things all fiction . . . there should always be
some foundation of fact for the most airy fabric—and
pure invention is but the talent of a liar.

LORD BYRON, LETTER TO HIS PUBLISHER

Chapter 1

The whole Memoirs would damn Lord B. to ever-lasting infamy if published.

JOHN CAM HOBHOUSE, *Journals*

𝕸r. Nicholas Melrose, who was head of his law firm and an important man, did not like to feel upset. He was not used to it, and hadn't been for many years.

"We never give the keys to anyone," he said rudely. He stared with some resentment at the girl opposite his imposingly large desk. How dare she unsettle him like this? "Never," he repeated. He jabbed with his finger, just in case there was still any doubt. *"Never."*

Rebecca Carville stared at him, then shook her head. She bent down to pick up a bag. Melrose watched her. Long, auburn hair, at once elegant and untamed, spilled over the girl's shoulders. She swept it back, glancing up at Melrose as she did so. Her eyes glittered. She was beautiful, Melrose thought, quite upsettingly so. He sighed. He ran his fingers through his thinning hair, then stroked his paunch.

"St. Jude's has always been a special case," he muttered, in a slightly more conciliatory tone. "Legally speaking." He gestured with his hands. "Surely you see, Miss Carville, that I have no choice? I repeat—I'm sorry—but you cannot have the keys."

3

Rebecca took some papers from her bag. Melrose frowned. He really was getting old, if a mere girl's silence could unsettle him like this—no matter how lovely she was, and no matter what her business was with him. He leaned across the desk. "Perhaps," he asked, "you would tell me what you hope to find in the crypt?"

Rebecca shuffled her papers. Suddenly the chill of her beauty was thawed by a smile. She handed the papers across. "Look at these," she said. "But be careful. They're old."

Melrose took them, intrigued. "What are they?" he asked.

"Letters.

"And how old is old?"

"1825."

Melrose stared at Rebecca over his glasses, then held a letter up to the desk light. The ink was faded, the paper brown. He tried to make out the signature at the bottom of the page. It was hard, in the gloom, with only the single lamp. "Thomas—what's this—Moore?" he asked, looking up.

Rebecca nodded.

"Should I be familiar with such a name?"

"He was a poet."

"I'm afraid, in my line, one doesn't have the time to read much poetry."

Rebecca continued to stare at him impassively. She reached across his desk to take the letter back. "No one reads Thomas Moore now," she said at last. "But he was very popular in his day."

"Are you an expert, then, Miss Carville, on the poets of the period?"

"I have good reasons, Mr. Melrose, for my interest."

"Ah, do you?" Melrose smiled. "Do you? Excellent." He relaxed in his chair. So she was an antiquarian, nothing more, some worthless academic. At once she seemed less threatening. Melrose beamed at her in relief, fortified again by a sense of his own importance.

Rebecca watched him, not answering his smile. "As I

4

LORD OF THE DEAD

said, Mr. Melrose, I have good reasons." She stared down at
the sheet of paper in her hands. "For instance—this letter,
which was written to a Lord Ruthven, at an address in
Mayfair—Thirteen, Fairfax Street." She smiled slowly.
"Isn't that the same house to which St. Jude's is attached?"

Rebecca's smile broadened as she watched the lawyer's
reaction to her words. The color had suddenly drained from
his face. But then he shook his head, and tried to answer her
smile. "Yes," he said softly. He dabbed at his forehead. "So
what if it is?"

Rebecca glanced at the letter again. "This is what Moore
wrote," she said. "He tells Lord Ruthven that he has what
he calls 'the manuscript.' What manuscript? He doesn't
elaborate. All he does say is that he is sending it, along with
his letter, to Fairfax Street."

"To Fairfax Street . . ." The lawyer's voice trailed away.
He swallowed, and tried to smile again, but his expression
was even more sickly than before.

Rebecca glanced at him. If Melrose's look of fear surprised her, she betrayed nothing. Instead, face calm, she
reached across the table for a second letter, and her voice,
when she spoke again, seemed bled to a monotone. "A week
afterwards, Mr. Melrose, Thomas Moore writes this. He is
thanking Lord Ruthven for his acknowledgment of the
receipt of the manuscript. Lord Ruthven had clearly told
Moore what the fate of the manuscript was to be." Rebecca
held up the letter and read. "'"Great is Truth," says the
Bible, "and mighty above all things." Yet sometimes, Truth
must be concealed and buried away, for its horrors can be
too great for mortal man to bear. You know what I think on
this matter. Bury it in a place of the dead; it is the only place
for it. Leave it hidden there for eternity—we are both
agreed on that now, I hope.'" Rebecca allowed the letter to
drop. "'Place of the dead,' Mr. Melrose," she said slowly.
She leaned forward and spoke with sudden vehemence, her
expression at once one of passion and dread. "Surely—
surely—that can only mean the crypt of the chapel of St.
Jude's?"

5

Melrose bent his head in silence. "I think, Miss Carville," he said at last, "that you should forget about Fairfax Street."

"Oh? Why?"

Melrose stared up at her. "Don't you think he may be right, your poet? That there are truths which should indeed remain concealed?"

Rebecca smiled faintly. "You speak as a lawyer, of course."

"Unfair, Miss Carville."

"Then as what are you speaking?"

Melrose made no answer. Damn the woman, he thought. Memories, dark and unbidden, were crowding his mind. He stared around his office, as though to find comfort in the gleam of its modernity. "As—as someone who wishes you well," he said at last, lamely.

"No!" Rebecca scraped back her chair and rose to her feet with such violence that Melrose almost flinched in his chair. "You don't understand. Do you know what the manuscript was, the one that Ruthven may have hidden away in the crypt?"

Melrose made no answer.

"Thomas Moore was the friend of a poet much greater than himself—much greater. Perhaps even you, Mr. Melrose, have heard of Lord Byron?"

"Yes," said Melrose softly, resting his head upon his clasped hands, "I have heard of Lord Byron."

"When he wrote his memoirs, Byron entrusted the finished manuscript to Thomas Moore. When the news of Byron's death reached his friends, they prevailed upon Moore to destroy the memoirs. Sheet by sheet, the memoirs were torn to shreds, then tossed onto a fire lit by Byron's publisher. Nothing was left of them." Rebecca stroked back her hair, as though to calm herself. "Byron was an incomparable writer. The destruction of his memoirs was desecration."

The lawyer stared at her. He felt trapped, now that he was certain why she wanted the keys. He had heard these arguments before. He could remember the woman who had made them, all those years ago, as lovely a woman as this girl was now, with the same strange, drawn look, the same urgent need.

And still the girl was talking to him. "Mr. Melrose—please—do you understand what I have been telling you?"

He licked his lips. "Do you?" he replied.

Rebecca frowned. "Listen," she whispered softly. "It is known that Thomas Moore was in the habit of copying any manuscript that he received. Only one copy of the memoirs was burnt. People have always wondered if Moore had made a duplicate. And now here"—Rebecca held up the letter—"we have Moore writing about a strange manuscript. A manuscript which he then says has been deposited in 'a place of the dead.' Mr. Melrose—please—surely now you can understand? We are talking about Byron's memoirs here. I must have the keys to the crypt of St. Jude."

A gust of rain swept against the windows. Melrose climbed to his feet, almost wearily, and locked the catches, as though barring the night. Then, still silent, he rested his forehead against a windowpane. "No," he said at last, staring into the darkness of the street outside, "no, I cannot give you the keys."

There was a silence, broken only by the sobbing of the wind. "You must," said Rebecca eventually. Her voice was so low it was almost a hiss. "You have seen the letters."

"Yes—I have seen the letters." Melrose turned. Rebecca's eyes were narrowed, like those of a cat. Her hair seemed to glow and spark in the light. Dear God, he thought, how very like that other woman she looked. It was all quite upsetting. The memories of that other time . . .

"Miss Carville," he tried to explain, "it is not that I doubt you. Indeed, quite the reverse." He paused, but Rebecca said nothing. The lawyer wondered how he could explain himself. He had never been easy with his own suspicions, and he knew that when spoken they would sound fantastic. That was why he had always kept quiet—that was why he had tried to forget. Damn the girl, he thought again, *damn*

7

her! "Lord Byron's memoirs," he muttered at last. "They were burnt by his friends?"

"Yes," said Rebecca coldly. "By his old traveling companion, a man named Hobhouse."

"Do you not feel, then, that this Hobhouse may have been wise in what he did?"

Rebecca smiled bleakly. "How can you ask me that?"

"Because I wonder what secret these memoirs contained. What secret so terrible that even Lord Byron's closest friends thought it best to destroy all records of it."

"Not all records, Mr. Melrose."

"No." He paused. "No, maybe not. And so—I am agitated."

To his surprise, Rebecca did not smile at his words. Instead, she leaned across the desk and took his hand. "Agitated by what, Mr. Melrose? Tell me. Lord Byron has been dead for almost two hundred years. What is there to be agitated by?"

"Miss Carville." The lawyer paused, and smiled, then shook his head. "Miss Carville . . ." He gestured with his hands. "Forget everything else I have been saying. Please—just listen to what I tell you now. Here is the bottom line. I am legally obliged to withhold the keys. There is nothing I can do about that. It may seem strange that the public be barred from a church, but it is the legal position nevertheless. The right of entry to the chapel belongs exclusively to the heir to the Ruthven estate, to him and to other direct descendants of the first Lord Ruthven. It is for them alone that I hold the keys to St. Jude's, as my predecessors in this firm, for almost two hundred years, have similarly held the keys. So far as I know, the chapel is never used for worship, or indeed opened at all. I could, I suppose, put forward your name to the present Lord Ruthven, but I must be frank with you, Miss Carville—that is something I shall never do."

Rebecca raised an eyebrow. "Why not?"

Melrose watched her. "For many reasons," he said slowly. "The simplest is that there would be no point. Lord Ruthven would never reply."

"Ah. So he does exist, then?"

Melrose's frown deepened. "Why do you ask that?"

"I tried to see him before coming to see you. In his house by St. Jude's—on Fairfax Street." She smiled, then shrugged. "The fact that I'm sitting here now suggests what success I had."

"He is not often in residence here, I believe. But oh yes, Miss Carville—he exists."

"You've met him?"

Melrose nodded. "Yes." He paused. "Once."

"No more than that?"

"Once was enough."

"When?"

"Does it matter?"

Rebecca nodded wordlessly. Melrose studied her face. It seemed frozen again and emotionless, but in her eyes, he could still see the deep-burning gleam. He leaned back in his chair. "It was twenty years ago, almost to the day," he said. "I remember it vividly."

Rebecca didn't blink. "Go on," she said.

"I should not be telling you this. A client has the right to confidentiality."

Rebecca smiled faintly, mockingly. Melrose knew that she could tell he wanted to talk. He cleared his throat. "I had just been made a partner," he said. "The Ruthven estate was one of my responsibilities. Lord Ruthven phoned me. He wanted to talk with me. He insisted I visit him in Fairfax Street. He was a rich and valued client. I went, of course."

"And?"

Again, Melrose paused. "It was a very strange experience," he said at last. "I am not an impressionable man, Miss Carville, I do not usually speak in subjective terms, but his mansion filled me with—well—there's no other way to put it—with the most remarkable sense of dread. Does that sound strange? Yes, of course it does, but I can't help it, that's how it was. In the course of my visit, Lord Ruthven showed me the chapel of St. Jude's as well. There, too, I was conscious of an almost physical oppressiveness, catching at my throat, choking me. And so you see, Miss Carville, it is for your own sake I am glad you won't be visiting there. Yes—for your own sake."

Rebecca smiled again faintly. "But was it the chapel," she asked, "or Lord Ruthven who unsettled you so much?"

"Oh, both I think, both. Lord Ruthven I found—indefinable. There was a grace to him, yes, a real grace, and a beauty too . . ."

"Except?"

"Except . . ." Melrose frowned. "Yes. Except . . . that in his face, like his house, there was the same quality of danger." He paused. "The same funereal gleam. We didn't talk long—by mutual consent—but in that time, I was aware of a great mind grown cancerous. Calling for help, I would almost have said, except that . . . No, no." Melrose suddenly shook his head. "What nonsense am I talking? Lawyers have no right to be imaginative."

Rebecca smiled faintly. "But was it imagination?"

Melrose studied her face. It seemed suddenly very pale. "Maybe not," he said quietly.

"What had he wanted to talk to you about?"

"The keys."

"To the chapel?"

Melrose nodded.

"Why?"

"He told me not to surrender them to anyone."

"Not even to those who were entitled to them?"

"They were to be discouraged."

"But not forbidden?"

"No. Discouraged."

"Why?"

"He didn't say. But as he talked to me, I felt a presentiment of . . . of . . . of something terrible."

"What?"

"I couldn't describe it, but it was real"—Melrose stared around—"as real as the figures on this computer screen, or the papers in this file. And Lord Ruthven, too—he seemed afraid. . . . No—not afraid, but appalled, and yet all the time, you see, it was mingled with a terrible desire—I could see it burning in his eyes. And so I took his warning to heart, because what I'd glimpsed in his face had horrified me. I hoped, of course, that no one would ask me for the keys." He paused. "Then three days later, a Miss Ruthven came to call."

Rebecca's face betrayed not a flicker of surprise. "For the keys?" she asked.

Melrose leaned back in his chair. "The same as you. She wanted to find the memoirs of Lord Byron hidden in the crypt."

Still, Rebecca's face seemed passionless. "And you gave them to her?" she asked.

"I had no choice."

"Because she was a Ruthven?"

Melrose nodded.

"And yet now you want to try and stop me."

"No, Miss Carville, it is not a matter of trying, I *will* stop you. I will not give you the keys." Melrose stared into Rebecca's narrowing eyes. He looked away, rising to his feet, crossing to a window and the darkness out beyond. "She vanished," he said at last, not turning around. He waited to hear if Rebecca would start; but there was no noise; only her presence, as insistent as before. Melrose coughed, then continued. "It was a few days after I gave her the keys. The police never found her. There was never anything, of course, to link her disappearance with Lord Ruthven, but I remembered all he had said, and what I had glimpsed in his face. I didn't tell the police—afraid of seeming ridiculous, you understand—but with you, Miss Carville, I'm prepared to risk seeming comical." He turned around to face her again. "Go away. It's getting late. I'm afraid our meeting has come to an end."

Rebecca didn't move. Then, slowly, she smoothed her hair back from her face. "The keys are mine," she said softly.

Melrose raised his arms in anger and frustration. "Didn't

you hear what I said? Can't you understand?" He slumped into his chair. "Miss Carville, please, don't be difficult. Just go, before I have to ring for you to be taken away."

Rebecca shook her head gently. Melrose sighed, and reached across his desk to press an intercom. As he did so, Rebecca took a second sheaf of papers from her bag. She pushed them across the desk. Melrose glanced at them, then froze. He took up the first page and began to skim down it, glassily, as though unable, or unwilling, to read it through. He muttered something, then pushed the papers away from him. He sighed and for a long time said nothing more. At last, though, he shook his head and sighed a second time. "She was your mother, then?"

Rebecca nodded. "She kept her maiden name." She smiled faintly. "I was four when she . . . went. I can still remember her, though."

Melrose breathed in deeply. "Why didn't you say?"

"I wanted to know what you thought."

"Well, you know. Keep away from Fairfax Street."

Rebecca stared at him, then smiled. "You're not serious," she said. She laughed. "You can't be."

"Would it make any difference if I say again that I am?"

"No. None at all."

Melrose stared at her. "So drawn," he murmured softly.

Rebecca frowned. "Drawn?"

"Your mother. I remember it quite vividly. She was just like you. Yes, drawn."

Rebecca smiled. "The love of knowledge, Mr. Melrose."

The lawyer sat staring at her in silence; then he shrugged and nodded. "Yes, of course," he muttered, "of course." He reached for a button. "I'll have the keys brought to you." He buzzed. There was no response. "Must be later than I'd realized." He frowned, rising to his feet. "If you'll excuse me, Miss Carville." Rebecca watched him as he left his office, and the doors glided shut. She began to gather her papers together. She slipped her certificates back into her bag but kept the bundle of letters on her lap. She fiddled with them; then, as she heard the doors behind her opening again, she laid her slim fingers on the edge of the desk.

"Here," said Melrose, holding out three keys on a large brass ring.

"Thank you," said Rebecca. She waited to be given them, but the lawyer, as he stood by her, still clutched the keys in his hand.

"Please," said Rebecca. "Give them to me, Mr. Melrose."

Melrose made no answer at first. He stared into Rebecca's face, long and hard, then he reached for the bundle of letters on her lap. "These," he said, holding them up, "the mysterious letters—they were your mother's originally?"

"I believe so."

"What do you mean, believe?"

Rebecca shrugged. "I was approached by a bookseller. He had been sold them. Apparently, it was well known that they had once been my mother's."

"And so then he came to you?"

Rebecca nodded.

"Very honest of him."

"Maybe. I paid."

"But how had he got them? And how had your mother lost the letters in the first place?"

Rebecca shrugged. "I think the bookseller had received them from a private collector. Beyond that, he didn't know. I didn't press."

"Weren't you interested?"

"They must have been stolen, I suppose."

"What? After your mother—disappeared?"

Rebecca glanced up at him. Her eyes glittered. "Possibly," she said.

"Yes." Melrose paused. "Possibly." He studied the letters again. "They are genuine?" he asked, looking back down.

"I think so."

"But you can't be sure?"

Rebecca shrugged. "I'm not qualified to say."

"Oh, I'm sorry, I'd assumed . . ."

"I am an Orientalist—it was my mother who was the Byron scholar. I've always read Byron, out of respect for her memory, but I have no claims to be an expert."

"I see. My mistake." Melrose stared at the letters again. "And so I suppose—this respect for your mother's memory—is that why you're so eager to track down the memoirs?"

Rebecca smiled faintly. "It would be fitting, don't you think? I never knew my mother, you see, Mr. Melrose. But I feel—what I'm doing—she would approve of it, yes."

"Even though the search may well have killed her?"

Rebecca's brow darkened. "Do you really think that, Mr. Melrose?"

He nodded. "Yes, I do."

Rebecca looked away. She stared into the darkness of the night beyond the windows. "Then at least I would know what had happened to her," she said, almost to herself.

Melrose made no answer. Instead, he dropped the letters back into Rebecca's lap. Still, though, he didn't give her the keys.

Rebecca held out her hand. Melrose stared at it thoughtfully. "And so all along," he said softly, "you were a Ruthven. All along."

Rebecca shrugged. "I can't help my blood."

"No." Melrose laughed. "Of course you can't." He paused. "Isn't there a Ruthven Curse?" he asked.

"Yes." Rebecca narrowed her eyes as she looked up at him. "There's supposed to be."

"How does it work?"

"I don't know. The usual way, I guess."

"What? Ruthven after Ruthven—generation after generation—all felled by some mysterious power? Isn't that what it is?"

Rebecca ignored the question. She shrugged again. "Lots of old families can lay claim to a curse. It's nothing. A sign of breeding, if you like."

"Exactly."

Rebecca frowned. "What do you mean?"

Melrose laughed again. "Why, that it's all in the blood, of course." He spluttered and choked, then continued to laugh.

"You're right," said Rebecca, rising to her feet. "For a lawyer, you are too imaginative." She held out her hand. "Mr. Melrose—give me the keys."

Melrose stopped laughing. He clutched the keys in his palm. "You are quite sure?" he asked.

"Quite sure."

Melrose stared deep into her eyes; then his shoulders slumped and he leaned against the desk. He held out the keys.

Rebecca took them. She slipped them into her pocket.

"When will you go?" Melrose asked.

"I don't know. Some time soon, I expect."

Melrose nodded slowly, as though to himself. He returned to his chair. He watched as Rebecca crossed the office to the doors.

"Miss Carville!"

Rebecca turned.

"Don't go."

Rebecca stared at the lawyer. "I must," she said at last.

"For your mother's sake? But it's for your mother's sake that I'm asking you not to go!"

Rebecca made no answer. She looked away. The doors slid open. "Thank you for your time, Mr. Melrose," she said, turning back around. "Good night."

Melrose stared after her with defeated eyes. "Good night," he said. "Good night." And then the doors slid shut, and Rebecca was on her own. She hurried toward a waiting lift. Behind her, the doors of the office stayed closed.

In the foyer, a bored security guard watched her as she left. Rebecca walked quickly through the doors and then down the street. It was good to be outside. She paused and breathed in deeply. The wind was strong and the air cold, but after the closeness of the office, she welcomed the night, feeling, as she began to hurry down the street again, as weightless and storm-swept as an autumn leaf. She felt very strange holding the chapel keys at last. Yes—almost giddy. She hadn't realized how much she must have wanted them. She quickened her pace. Ahead, she could hear traffic— Bond Street, a gash in the darkness of people and lights. Rebecca crossed it, then turned, back to the silence of empty mews. Mayfair seemed deserted. The high, lowering street fronts were virtually untouched by lights. Once a car passed, but otherwise there was nothing, for Rebecca kept to the narrowest streets, for the silence seemed to fill her with a strange, fevered joy. And all the time, she kept the keys in her palm, a talisman, to quicken the rhythm of blood through her heart.

By Bolton Street, she came to a halt. She realized she was shaking. She leaned against a wall. Her excitement suddenly frightened her. She remembered the lawyer's strange words. "Drawn," he had said, describing her mother. She remembered how he had appealed to her, despairingly, not to visit Fairfax Street. At the time, she had laughed at him; but now, she realized, his strange words must have affected her more than she had known. Rebecca glanced behind her. The road she was on had been the haunt of dandies once, where fortunes had been lost, lives lost, gambled away with the curl of a lip. Lord Byron had come here. Byron. Suddenly the fever in her blood seemed to sing to Rebecca, with ecstasy and a quite unexpected shock of fear. There was no reason for it, nothing she could put into words, and yet, as she stood there in the shadowed silence, she realized that, yes, she was terrified. But of what? She tried to identify the cause. She had just been thinking of something. Byron. Yes, that was it—Byron. And there it was—the same fear again. Rebecca shuddered and suddenly knew, with absolute certainty, that she would not, as she had planned to do, enter the chapel that night. She could not even take a step toward it, so paralyzed she was, and exhilarated, by a terror that felt like a dense mist enveloping her and sucking out her will, absorbing her. She struggled to break free. She turned. There was traffic moving on Piccadilly. She began to walk toward the sound of it, then to run.

"Rebecca!"

She froze.

"Rebecca!"

She spun around. Sheets of paper, caught by the wind, were fluttering across an empty street.

"Who's there?" Rebecca called.

Nothing. Rebecca tilted her head. She couldn't hear the traffic now. There was only the screaming of the wind and a signboard, rattling, at the end of the street. Rebecca walked down toward it. "Who's there?" she called out again. The wind moaned as though in answer, and then suddenly, just faintly, Rebecca thought she heard laughter. It hissed, rising and falling with the wind. Rebecca ran toward it, down a further street, so dark now that she could barely see ahead. There was a noise, a tin kicked, clattering over tarmac. Rebecca glanced around, just in time to see, or so she thought, a flitting silhouette of black. But even as she stepped toward it, it was gone, melted so totally that she wondered if she had seen anything at all. There had seemed something strange about the figure, something wrong but also familiar. Where had she seen such a person before? Rebecca shook her head. No, there had been nothing. It was hardly surprising, she thought. The wind was so strong that the shadows were playing tricks on her.

She felt breath on her neck. Rebecca could smell it as she spun around—acrid, chemical, prickling her nostrils—but even as she turned and held out her arms to ward off the attacker, she could see that there was nothing there to fend away. "Who are you?" she called out into the darkness, angry now. "Who's there?" Laughter hissed on the wind again, and then there was the sound of footsteps, hurrying away down a narrow lane, and Rebecca began to run, chasing after them, her heels echoing, her blood thumping like a drum in her ears. So deep it pulsed, she felt quite distracted by the sound. But no, she told herself, ignore it, listen for the footsteps. They were still ahead of her, down a very narrow lane now, and then suddenly they were gone, faded on the air, and Rebecca stopped to recapture her bearings and her breath. She looked around. As she did so, the clouds overhead became ragged and frayed, and were then scattered altogether on a gusting shriek of wind. Moonlight, death-pale, stained the street. Rebecca looked up.

Above her loomed a mansion-front. Its grandeur seemed quite out of proportion to the alley, otherwise narrow and blank, in which Rebecca found herself. In the moonlight, the stone of the mansion was cast maggot-white; its windows were pools of darkness, sockets in a skull. The impression given by the whole was that of something quite abandoned by time, a shiver of the past conjured up from death by the light of the moon. The wind began to scream again. Rebecca watched as the light faded, then was lost. The mansion, though, remained, revealed now as something more than just an illusion of the moon, but Rebecca was not surprised; she had known full well that it was real. She had called at these mansion gates before.

She did not bother this time, however, as she had done on her previous, fruitless visit, to climb the steps and knock at the door. Instead, she began to walk down the mansion-front, past the railings that speared up from the pavement to guard the mansion from the passer-by. Rebecca could smell the acid again, just faint on the wind, but bitter as before. She began to run. There were footsteps behind her. She glanced around, but there was nothing, and she felt the terror return, descending on her like a poisonous cloud, choking her throat, burning her blood. She stumbled and staggered forward. She fell against the railings. Her fingers clutched at a tangle of chains. She lifted them up. There was a single padlock. It barred the way to the chapel of St. Jude's.

Rebecca shook out the keys. She fitted one into the padlock. It scraped rustily and didn't turn. Behind her, the footsteps came to a halt. Rebecca didn't look around; instead, in a wave so intense that it was almost sweet, terror coursed through her veins, and she had to steady herself against the gate, as fear possessed her, fear and strange delight. Her hands shaking, she tried a second key. Again, it scratched against rust, but this time there was movement, and the lock began to shift. Rebecca forced it; the lock opened; the length of chain slithered to the ground. Rebecca pushed at the gate. Painfully, it creaked ajar.

Now Rebecca turned. The acrid smell had faded; she was quite alone. Rebecca smiled. She could feel her terror sweet in her stomach, lightening her thighs. She stroked back her hair, so that it flew in the wind, and smoothed down her coat. The wind had blown the gate shut again. Rebecca pushed at it, then walked in toward the chapel door.

It was approached down a flight of steps, mossy and cracked. The door itself, like the railing gate, was locked. Rebecca felt for her keys again. As gentle as the fall of a dying breeze, her terror arced and was gone. She remembered Melrose again, his fear, his warnings to avoid St. Jude's. Rebecca shook her head. Inside were the memoirs of Lord Byron, presumed lost for two hundred years, soon to be hers, held in her hands. Such a discovery could not be delayed. "No," she whispered to herself, "no, I am myself again." A memory of her mother, the only one she could recall, bending low over her face to kiss her, rose before Rebecca's eyes. She shook her head again. What had ever possessed her, to think that she could wait? She turned the key.

Inside the chapel, the darkness was total. Rebecca cursed herself for not having brought a torch. Feeling her way along the wall, she reached some shelves. She ran her finger along them. There were matches, and then, on the shelf below, a candle box. She took one of the candles and lit it. Then she turned to see what the chapel contained.

It was almost bare. There was a single cross, at the end of the room. It had been carved and painted in the Byzantine manner. It represented Cain, sentenced by the Angel of the Lord. Waiting below them, more vivid than both, was Lucifer. Rebecca peered at the cross. She was struck by the representation of Cain. His face was beautiful, but twisted in the most terrible agony, not from the mark that had been burned onto his brow but from some deeper pain, some terrible loss. From his lips came a single trickle of red.

Rebecca turned. Her footsteps echoed as she crossed the bare floor. At the far end of the chapel, she could see a tomb, built into the floor, marked by an ancient pillar of stone. Rebecca knelt down to look for inscriptions on the tomb, but there was nothing to read, just a strip of faded brass. She glanced up at the headstone; the candle flickered in her grip, and shadows danced over faint patterns and marks. Rebecca held the candle up closer. There was a turban, carved into the top of the stone, and then lower down, scarcely legible, what seemed like words. Rebecca peered at them. To her surprise, she saw that the script was Arabic. She translated the words: verses from the Koran, mourning the dead. She shook her head in puzzlement. A Muslim grave, in a Christian church? No wonder it was never used for worship. She knelt down by the tomb again. She scanned it for further inscriptions. Nothing. Then a gust of wind blew, and her candle flickered out.

As she lit it again, she saw, in the spurt of the match's flame, a rug stretched out behind the tomb. It was beautiful—Turkish, Rebecca guessed—and, like the headstone, clearly very old. She pulled it back, tenderly at first, and then with a sudden thrill of excitement, frantically. Below it was a wooden hatchway, padlocked and hinged. Rebecca pushed the carpet away, then fitted the third and final key. It turned. Rebecca tugged the padlock off, then breathed in deeply. She heaved at the hatchway. Slowly it lifted. With a burst of strength that she hadn't known she possessed, Rebecca pulled the hatchway up until it toppled and fell, with an echoing thud, onto the flagstones behind. She stared at the opening she had uncovered. There were two steps, then nothing beyond them but a yawning blank. Reaching for more candles, Rebecca slipped them into her pocket and took a careful first step. Suddenly she breathed in. The fear had returned, in every corpuscle of her blood, lightening her until she thought she would float, and the fear was as sensual and lovely as any pleasure she had known. The terror possessed her and summoned her. Obeying its call, she began to walk down the steps, and the opening to the chapel was soon just a glimmer, then was gone.

Rebecca reached the final step. She halted and lifted up her candle. As she did so, the flame seemed to leap and expand, to meet the gleam of oranges and yellows and golds that met Rebecca's glance wherever she looked. The crypt was wondrous—no moldy place of the dead, but a pleasure chamber from some eastern harem, bedecked with beautiful things—tapestries, carpets, silver, gold. From the corner came a soft bubbling. Rebecca turned and saw a tiny fountain, with two couches, exquisitely carved, on either side. "What is this place?" she whispered to herself. "What is it doing here?" And the memoirs—where were they? She held the candle up high again and glanced around the room. There were no papers she could see. She stood, rooted, wondering where to start. It was then that she heard the scrabbling.

Rebecca froze. She tried not to breathe. Her blood was suddenly deafening in her ears, but still she held her breath, straining to hear the noise again. There had been something, she was sure. Her heart was thumping so loudly now that it seemed to be filling the room. There was no other noise. Eventually she had to gasp for air, and then, as she breathed in greedily, she heard it again. The scrabbling. Again, Rebecca froze. She lit a second candle and held them both above her head. In the far end of the room, raised and central like an altar in a church, was a beautiful tomb of delicate stone. Beyond it was a doorway in the Arabic style. Slowly, Rebecca walked toward the tomb, candles held out in front of her. She strained her ears as the scrabbling returned. It was rasping but feeble. Rebecca stopped. There couldn't be any doubt. The scratching was coming from within the tomb.

With a numb sense of disbelief, Rebecca reached out to touch the side. The scrabbling seemed frantic now. Rebecca stared down at the lid of the tomb. She could just make out words buried beneath the dust. She blew the dust away, and read the lines that had been hidden underneath.

> *Mixed in each other's arms and heart in heart,*
> *Why did they not then die? They had lived too long*
> *Should an hour come to bid them breathe apart.*

Byron. Rebecca recognized the poetry at once. Yes, Byron. She read the lines again, softly sounding the words, as the scrabbling grew and the candles began to flicker, despite the heaviness of the dull crypt air. Suddenly, like vomit, horror rose up in Rebecca's throat. She staggered forward and leaned against the tomb. She lowered the two candles to the floor, then began to push at the covering slab, like an amputee scratching at her bandages, desperate to face the absolute worst. The lid shifted, then began to move. Rebecca pushed even harder as it slid across. She lowered her candles. She stared into the tomb.

A thing was looking up at her. Rebecca wanted to scream, but her throat was dry. The thing lay still, only its eyes alive, gleaming yellow from socket pits, everything else withered, lined, incalculably old. The thing began to twitch its nose, just a layer of skin over splintered bone. It opened its mouth greedily. As it sniffed, the thing began to move, its arms, furrowed twists of dead meat on bone, struggling to reach for the side of the tomb, its nails, sharp like talons, scraping at the stone. With a rattling shudder, the creature sat up. As it moved, a haze of dust rose from the furrows in its skin. Rebecca could feel it in her mouth and eyes, a cloud of dead skin, choking her, blinding her, dizzying her brain. She turned, arms over her eyes. Something touched her. She blinked. The thing. It was reaching for her again, its face twitching eagerly, its mouth a gash of jaws. Rebecca heard herself scream. She felt flakes of dead skin in the back of her throat. She retched. The crypt began to spin, and she fell down to her knees.

She looked up. The creature sat on the edge of the tomb like a bird of prey. Its nose still sniffed at her, its mouth grinned open wide. But it was holding tightly to the edge of the tomb, and seemed to be shuddering, as though reluctant to make the leap to the ground. Rebecca saw that the creature had shriveled breasts like calluses, which tremored against a hollowed chest. So the thing had been a woman once. And now? What was it now?

Rebecca realized that her horror had ebbed away. She looked up at the creature again, but could scarcely make it out, her eyes felt so heavy with ease. She wondered if perhaps she were not asleep. She tried to sit up, but her head felt thick, as though with opiates; she couldn't move, except to tilt her head fractionally until it came to rest. She was lying in someone's arms. A soft pain was welling from her throat. Blood, in a warm stain, felt heavy on her skin. A finger stroked the side of her neck. The pleasure it gave her was wonderful. Whose finger was it? she asked herself vaguely. Not the creature's—she could see it, still perched above, a dim and shadowy form. Then Rebecca heard a voice. "This one. You promised me. This one! And look—look at her face!" Rebecca struggled to stay awake, to listen further, but the words began to fade into the dark. The dark was satin, and delicious to the touch.

But Rebecca never swooned wholly into unconsciousness. She was aware of herself, all the time, of the blood inside her veins, of the life inside her body and soul. She lay in that place of the dead she knew not how long. She did recognize, when it happened, that she was rising to her feet, but only remembered being led up the steps and out across the church once the wind from the London night had blown cold across her face. Then she began to walk, down endless dark streets. Someone was beside her. She began to shiver. She felt cold inside, but her skin was hot, and across her neck the wound burned like liquid gold. She stopped, and stood still. She watched as the figure from beside her walked on, just a silhouette in a long black coat. Rebecca looked around. To her right flowed the Thames, its waters greasy with the dark and cold. The storm had died to a preternatural hush. Nothing living disturbed the calm.

Rebecca clutched herself and shuddered. She watched the figure ahead of her walk along the Embankment sweep. He was limping, she saw, and carried a cane. She felt her wound. The pain was already beginning to chill. She looked for the figure again. He had gone. Then Rebecca saw him again, crossing over Waterloo Bridge. The silhouette reached the far bank. It disappeared.

Rebecca wandered through London's depeopled streets. She had lost all sense of time or place. Once, someone tried to stop her, pointing at the wound to her neck and asking to help, but Rebecca brushed him aside, not even pausing to glance into his face. Morning broke slowly, and still Rebecca walked. She grew aware of traffic, and the faint songs of birds. Streaks of red light began to touch the eastern sky. Rebecca found herself walking by the Thames again. For the first time that night, she glanced at her watch. Six o'clock. She realized with a shock how light-headed she felt. She leaned against a lamppost and stroked at the pain that stretched across her neck.

Ahead of her, she could see a crowd of people by the riverside wall. She walked toward them. Everyone was peering into the waters below. There were policemen, Rebecca saw. They had dredging hooks. They began to pull on them, and a limp dripping bundle was hauled up the embankment face. Rebecca watched as it was rolled over the wall and fell with a damp thud onto the paving stones. A policeman bent down to peel some rags away. He made a face and shut his eyes. "What is it?" Rebecca asked the man in front of her. He said nothing, just stood aside. Rebecca looked down at the bundle. Dead eyes met her own. The face was smiling, but wholly white. There was a terrible gash across the dead man's neck.

"No," said Rebecca softly to herself, "no." Like the sound of a stone dropped into a well, comprehension of what she was seeing had come slowly. And broader comprehension, of what or who could have done such a thing, to the corpse and to herself, seemed impossibly beyond her reach. She felt tired and sick. Turning, she hurried from the scene. Instinctively, she muffled herself in her coat, so that no one should see the wound on her own neck. She began to climb the bridge that led to Charing Cross.

"Rebecca!"

The same voice, the one she had heard outside St. Jude's. She spun around in horror. A man was standing behind her, a leer on his face.

"Rebecca!" The man's grin broadened. "Surprise, surprise! Remember me?"

Rebecca turned her face. The smell of acid on the man's breath was foul. He chuckled softly, as she looked at him again. He was young and well-dressed, almost dandyish, but his long hair was tangled in greasy knots and his head lolled strangely as though the neck had been twisted around. Yes, she remembered him. The silhouette on the Mayfair street. And seeing him in the light, she knew why he had seemed familiar even then. "The bookseller," she whispered. "You brought me the letters. The ones from Thomas Moore."

"Oh good," he wheezed, "it's all coming back again, I see. Nothing less flattering for a fellow than to be forgotten by a pretty girl." He leered again, and again Rebecca had to hold her breath and look away. The man seemed unoffended. He took Rebecca's arm, and when she tried to shake him off, he gripped her until she could feel his nails gouging deep into her flesh.

"Come on," he whispered, "move those lovely legs!"

"Why?"

"I am a humble worm, I crawl and obey."

"Obey what?"

"Why, the unspoken wishes of my master and lord."

"Lord?"

"Lord." The man spat out the word. "Oh yes, we all love a lord—don't we?" Rebecca stared at him. The man was muttering to himself, and his face seemed contorted by bitterness and loathing. He met her glance and bared his teeth in a grin. "I speak now as a medical man," he said suddenly. "You have a most intriguing wound across your throat." He stopped her, holding her hair and yanking back her head. He sniffed at her wound, then licked it. "Mmm," he said, breathing in, "salty and sanguinary—a splendid mix." He hissed a chuckle, then pulled her along by her arm again. "But we must hurry now, so come along! People might notice."

"Notice what?"

The man muttered to himself again under his breath, dribbling now.

"I said, notice what?"

"Oh, for fuck's sake, you stupid bitch!" the man yelled suddenly. He pointed back at the crowd around the corpse. "Your wound!" he shouted, wiping saliva from his lips. "It's the same. But the bastard, the fucking bastard, he killed that other one, but not you, the bastard, he didn't kill you." His head began to twitch and loll on its twisted neck. "Bastard," he muttered again, "bastard," and his voice trailed away.

Rebecca stopped. "You know who did that terrible thing?" she asked, pointing back across the bridge.

"Oh yes!" The man began to chant. "Oh yes, oh yes, oh yes!"

"Who?"

The man winked. "You should know."

Without thinking, Rebecca stroked at her neck. "Lord Ruthven? Is that who you mean? Lord Ruthven?"

The man tittered to himself, then stopped, and his face was a twitching mask of hate. Rebecca struggled suddenly, managing to break free. "Leave me alone," she said, backing away.

The man twisted his neck about. "I'm sure he'd want to meet you again."

"Who?"

"You know."

"I don't. I don't. It's impossible."

The man reached out to take her arm again and stare into her face. "Fuck me," he whispered, *"fuck me,* but you're gorgeous. Quite the most gorgeous I've ever sent. He will be pleased." Again, the man's smile was livid with hate. He began to pull her along the bridge. "Now, now, no more struggling. You'll bruise your pretty skin."

Numbly, Rebecca followed him. "Lord Ruthven," she whispered, "who is he?"

The man cackled. "You surprise me, you being such an educated girl."

"What do you mean?"

"That you should know who Lord Ruthven was."

"Well, I know of *a* Lord Ruthven. . . ."

"Yes?" The man grinned encouragingly.

"He was the hero of a—"

"Yes?"

"Of a short story."

The man nodded and chuckled. "Very good. And what was it called?"

Rebecca swallowed. " 'The Vampyre.' But—but that was just fiction. . . ."

"Really? Fiction? Is that so?" The man twisted his mouth into a leer of sudden, terrible bitterness. "And who wrote it, this fiction?"

"A man called Polidori."

The man grinned again. He pressed his face close to Rebecca's, the acid as thick as ever on his breath. "And this Polidori," he whispered, "who was he?"

"The personal physician to . . ."

"Yes? Yes?"

"To Byron. Lord Byron."

The man nodded slowly. "So he would have known what he was talking about, don't you think?" He held Rebecca's cheeks. "That was what your mother thought, anyway."

Rebecca stared at him. "My mother?" she whispered.

The man pulled on her arm, so that she almost fell. "Yes, your mother, of course, your mother. Come on," he muttered, "you bitch, come on." Again, Rebecca struggled and managed to break free. She began to run. "Where are you going?" the man screamed after her. Rebecca made no answer, but still the sound of the man's laughter pursued her across the bridge. She joined the road, then glanced behind her. Traffic and blank crowds, nothing else. She hailed down a taxi. "Where'd you want?" the driver asked. Rebecca swallowed. Her mind seemed empty—and then she knew. "Mayfair," she whispered as she climbed into the back. "Thirteen, Fairfax Street." She clutched herself, and shivered, as the taxi pulled away.

Chapter 11

The Vampire superstition is still general in the Levant. The Romaic term is, "Vardoulacha." I recollect a whole family being terrified by the scream of a child, which they imagined must proceed from such a visitation. The Greeks never mention the word without horror.

LORD BYRON, NOTES TO *The Giaour*

Jt is, of course, dangerous to walk too close to a
vampire."

The same beautiful voice Rebecca had heard in the crypt.
She would have braved any peril to hear it. She understood
what it was to hear the sirens' song.

"But you realize that, of course. And still you have
come." The voice paused. "As I hoped—and feared—you
would."

Rebecca walked across the room. From the shrouded
gloom, a pale hand flickered in a gesture at her. "Won't you
sit down, please?"

"I would prefer some light."

"Of course, I forget—you don't see in the dark."

Rebecca pointed toward the curtains, and London's distant hum. "Can I draw them?"

"No, you will let in the winter." Rebecca watched as the
figure rose to his feet and limped across the room. "The
English winter—ending in June, to start in July. You must
excuse me—I can't even bear to glimpse it. I have been too
long a creature of sunnier climes." There was the spurt of a

match, and Rebecca recognized the back of the man she had watched on the Embankment that night. Light, in a golden wash, flickered across the room. The figure stayed bent as he tended the flame. "I hope you don't object to the lamp," he said. "I brought it back from my first trip abroad. There are times when electricity just doesn't seem right, don't you think?"

The vampire laughed and turned, and held the lamp up to his face. Slowly, Rebecca sank back into her seat. There could be no doubt who she was staring at. The dark curls of his hair set off the ethereal paleness of his skin; so delicate were his features that they seemed chiseled from ice; no flush of color, no hint of warmth touched the alabaster of his skin, yet the face seemed lit by some inner touch of flame. This was not the man who had died in the Missolonghi swamps, bald and overweight with rotting teeth. How had it happened, that he was standing here now, miraculously restored to the loveliness of his youth? Rebecca drank in the sight of him. "That beautiful pale face," she murmured to herself. And beautiful it was, inhumanly so—the face of an angel cast from another world.

"Tell me how it is possible," said Rebecca at last.

Lord Byron lowered the lamp and returned, limping, to his seat. As he did so, Rebecca thought she heard movement from the room behind her. She turned around, but the darkness was impenetrable. Lord Byron smiled. He whistled softly. Out of the shadows padded a large white dog. It stared at Rebecca, then yawned, and sank down at Lord Byron's feet. Lord Byron stroked the dog's head while on his other hand he rested his chin. He stared at Rebecca. His eyes glittered, and a faint smile curled his lip.

Rebecca stroked back her hair. "My mother," she wanted to scream, "my mother, did you kill her?" but she dreaded the answer she might receive. She sat in silence for a long while. "I came to find the memoirs," she said at last.

"There are no memoirs."

Rebecca frowned with surprise. "But I was given the letters, from Thomas Moore . . ."

"Yes."

"So what happened to the copy he had made, the one he writes about to you?"

"It was destroyed."

"But . . ." Rebecca shook her head. "I don't understand. Why?"

"For the same reason as the original was destroyed. It contained the truth."

"Then why was I shown Moore's letters? Why was I tricked into visiting the crypt?"

Lord Byron raised an eyebrow. "Tricked?"

"Yes. The bookseller. I assume he works for you."

"For me? No. Against me, eternally, and always for himself."

"Who is he?"

"Someone to avoid."

"Like you? And like that thing, that creature below?"

Lord Byron's brow darkened, but his voice, when he spoke, was as calm as before. "Yes, she is a creature, and so am I a creature, who has already fed on you tonight." He licked his teeth with the tip of his tongue, and the dog stirred, growling faintly from his chest.

Rebecca struggled not to lower her eyes before the vampire's gaze. Again, the question she wanted to ask died on her lips. "Why haven't you killed me, then?" she murmured eventually. "Why haven't you drained me like you drained that poor man by Waterloo Bridge?"

Lord Byron's face seemed frozen into ice. Then, faintly, he smiled once again. "Because you are a Byron." He nodded. "Yes, indeed a Byron." He rose to his feet. "Because you have my blood in your veins. Mine and another soul's."

Rebecca swallowed. "So did my mother," she said at last. Her voice sounded distant and frail in her ears.

"Yes."

33

"She too—once—she came looking for your memoirs."

"I know."

"What happened to her?"

Lord Byron made no answer. In his eyes, pity and desire seemed mingled as one.

"What happened to her? Tell me! *What happened to her?*"

Still Lord Byron did not reply. Rebecca licked her lips. She wanted to repeat her question in a howl of anguish and accusation, but her mouth was dry and she couldn't speak. Lord Byron smiled as he stared at her. He glanced at her throat lingeringly, then rose and limped across the room. He held up a bottle. "You are thirsty. Can I offer you wine?"

Rebecca nodded. She glanced at the label. Château Lafite Rothschild. The best, the very best. She was offered a glass—she took it and sipped, then gulped the liquid down. Never had she tasted anything half so good. She glanced up. Lord Byron was watching her expressionlessly. He drank from his own glass. No sign of pleasure crossed his face. He sat back in his own chair, and although his eyes glittered as brightly as before, Rebecca could see now how behind the gleam the eyes seemed dead.

"Even now," he said, "I could almost wish you hadn't come."

Rebecca stared at him in surprise. "The bookseller said . . ."

"The bookseller. Forget the bookseller."

"But . . ."

"I have told you—forget him."

Rebecca swallowed. "He said that you had been waiting for me."

"Yes. But what does that mean? It is the torture we desire which is the cruelest of all."

"And the bookseller knew this?"

Lord Byron smiled faintly. "Of course. Why else would he have sent you to me?"

His lassitude seemed suddenly terrible. He closed his eyes, as though to avoid the sight of Rebecca. The dog stirred and licked at his hand, but Lord Byron stayed motionless, a mockery of his own seeming loveliness and youth.

"What were you hoping for tonight?"

"Hoping for?"

"Yes." Rebecca paused. "By the tomb, tonight. You had been waiting for me. What had you been hoping for?"

A look of terrible pain crossed Lord Byron's face. He paused, as though waiting for the murmur of some answer from the dark. He was staring beyond her, Rebecca realized, into the blackness from which the dog had come. But there was no movement from there now, nothing but stillness, and Lord Byron suddenly frowned and shook his head. "Whatever I hope for," he said, "seems not quite ready to happen yet." He laughed, and of all the sounds she had listened to that night, Rebecca had heard nothing that did more to strike cold into her blood. "I have existed for over two centuries," Lord Byron said, staring at Rebecca, but again, it seemed, still speaking to the darkness beyond. "Never have I felt further from the life I once possessed. Each year, each day, has forged a link in the chain—the weight of my own immortality. That burden, now, I find insupportable."

He paused, and reached for his wine. He took a sip, very delicately, and closed his eyes, as though in mourning for its forgotten taste. His eyes still shut, he drained the glass, and then slowly, without a trace of passion, dropped it so that it shattered on the floor. The dog stirred and growled; from the far corner of the room, several birds rose and fluttered in the air. Rebecca had not seen them before—she wondered what other creatures lurked, waiting in the darkness behind her chair. The birds settled; silence returned; once again, Lord Byron opened his eyes.

"It is singular," he said, "how soon we lose our memories, how soon their luster fades. And yet, seeing you here now, I remember how existence was fresh once."

"And is that so great a torture?"

"A torture and delight. Both the greater for their intermingling."

"But they are rekindled now, aren't they—these lights of your memory?"

Lord Byron inclined his head gently. There was a flicker of movement from his lips.

"Can you bear to extinguish them again?" Rebecca asked. "Or is it not better now to tend their flame?"

Lord Byron smiled.

Rebecca watched him. "Tell me," she said.

"Tell you?"

"You have no choice."

The vampire laughed suddenly. "But I do. I could kill you. That might allow me to forget for a while." There was a silence. Rebecca knew that Lord Byron was staring at her throat. But still she waited, strangely distanced from her fear. "Tell me," she repeated softly. "Tell me how it happened. I want to know." She paused, thinking of her mother. She sat frozen. "I deserve to know."

Lord Byron raised his eyes. Slowly he began to smile again. "Yes, you do," he said, "I suppose you do." He paused, and again stared past Rebecca into the darkness beyond. This time, she thought, there was a faint sound, and Lord Byron smiled again, as though he had heard it too. "Yes," he said, still staring through Rebecca, "it should be done this way. You are right. Listen, then, and understand."

He paused, and folded his hands. "It happened in Greece," he said. "On my first journey there. The East had always been the most fertile island of my imagination. And yet my imaginings had never even skirted the truth, never even dared draw vaguely close to it." His smile faded, as the blankness of lassitude returned again. "For I believed, you see, that if a doom were to fall upon me, it lay dormant already within my own blood. My mother had warned me that the Byrons were cursed. She hated them, and loved them, for what my father had done. He had charmed her, married her, then bled her of her wealth—a vampire in his own way, and therefore I suppose, though I never met him, a true father to me. Left penniless, my mother would often warn me against the inheritance that flowed in my blood.

Each Lord Byron, she would say, had been more wicked than the last. She told me of the man I was to inherit the title from. He had murdered his neighbor. He lived in a ruined abbey. He tortured cockroaches. I had laughed at that, to my mother's rage. I vowed that when I became Lord Byron, I would put my patrimony to more enjoyable use."

"And you did." Rebecca didn't ask, merely stated a fact.

"Yes." Lord Byron nodded. "Indeed, I fear I became quite dissipated. I loved the abbey, you see, and the shivers of romantic gloom it sent up my spine, for, on the whole, I was then so far from being gloomy or misanthropical that I found my fear merely an excuse for revelries. We had dug up the skull of some poor monk, and used it as a drinking bowl—I would preside in my abbot's robes, while, with the help of assorted village maidens and nymphs, we lived in the style of the monks of old. But the pleasures even of sacrilege can fade—I grew satiated with my dissipations, and boredom, the most fearful curse of all, began to dull my heart. I felt a longing to travel. It was the custom then for men such as myself, well-bred and hopelessly in debt, to perform a tour of the Continent, long seen by the English as the most suitable place for the young to take rapid steps in the career of vice. I wanted to sample new pleasures, new sensations and delights—everything for which England was too narrow and tight, and which I knew, abroad, would be easy to procure. It was decided—I would leave. I felt little regret for England as her white cliffs slipped away.

"I traveled with my friend Hobhouse. Together, we crossed Portugal and Spain, and then on toward Malta, and beyond that, Greece. As we neared the Greek shore, a purple band glimmering across the blue of the sea, I felt a strange presentiment of longing and fear. Even Hobhouse, who was seasick, paused in his vomiting to look up. The gleam, though, was soon lost, and it was raining as my feet touched the soil of Greece. Preveza, our port of arrival, was a wretched place. The town itself was ugly and drab, while of its inhabitants, we found the Greeks servile and their Turkish masters savage. Yet even in the drizzle, my thrill of excitement never wholly died, for I knew, riding through the dismal streets below the minarets and towers, that we had left our old lives far behind, and stood now on the rim of a strange untested world. The West had been abandoned—we had crossed into the East.

"After two days spent in Preveza, we were happy enough to leave. It was our intention to visit Ali, the Pasha of Albania, whose daring and cruelty had won him power over Europe's most lawless tribes, and whose reputation for savagery was respected by even the most bloodthirsty of the Turks. Few Englishmen had ever penetrated Albania; yet for us, the lure of so dangerous and poetical a land was all the greater for that very cause. Yanina, Ali's capital, lay far to the north, and the road that led to it was mountainous and wild. We were warned, before we left, to beware of the *klephti,* Greek mountain bandits, and so we took, with our manservant and our guide, a bodyguard of six Albanians, all armed with pistols, long guns, and swords. When we at last set off, it was, as you can imagine, in a most romantic state of mind.

"We had soon left all traces of habitation behind us. This, we were to find, was not strange in Greece, where a man could often ride for three, sometimes four days, and never find a village able to feed himself and his horse, so wretched was the state to which the Greeks had been reduced. But what we lacked in human intercourse was made up for by the grandeur of the landscape and the beauty of our route, which was soon winding high and mountainous. Even Hobhouse, generally as capable of being moved by such things as a tobacco bung, would sometimes rein in his horse to admire the peaks of Suli and Tomaros, half-robed in mist, clothed in snow and purple streaks of light, across which the eagle soared, and from whose distant jagged crags we could sometimes hear the howling of the wolf.

"It was as the afternoon began to darken with a gathering storm that I first mentioned to Hobhouse that I was afraid we might be lost. He nodded and glanced around. The road had narrowed until the rocks above us were precipitous; no other traveler had passed us now for almost three hours. Hobhouse spurred his horse forward and rode up to the guide. I heard him ask where our shelter was to be for that night. The guide assured us both that we had nothing to fear. I gestured at the storm clouds massing above the peaks, and shouted at him that it wasn't fear, merely a desire to avoid a drenching, that made us eager to reach some sheltering place. The guide shrugged, and muttered again that we had nothing to fear. This, of course, at once persuaded us to send three of our Albanians ahead, while the others were dropped behind to cover our rear. Fletcher, the manservant, began to mutter up his prayers.

"It was as the first heavy drops of rain began to fall that we heard the crack of a gunshot. Hobhouse swore violently at the guide, asking him what the devil it could be. The guide stammered some nonsense, then began to shake. Hobhouse swore again, and drew a pistol out. Together, the two of us spurred our horses and galloped down the defile ahead. Around a sharp outcrop of rock, we saw our three Albanians, their faces white as chalk, shouting amongst themselves, struggling to rein in their nervous steeds. One of them was still holding a gun; it was evidently he who had fired the shot. 'What is it?' I called to him. 'Are we under attack?' The Albanian said nothing, but pointed, and his two companions both fell quiet. Hobhouse and I turned to look. In the cliff's shadow was a grave of earth. A rough stake had been hammered into it; nailed to the wood hung a blood-boltered head. Its features were remarkably pale, but at the same time quite fresh.

"Hobhouse and I dismounted.

"'Extraordinary,' said Hobhouse, staring at the head as though it were some interesting antiquity. 'A peasant superstition, I suppose. I wonder what it means?'

"I shivered, and drew my cloak around close. It was dark now, and the rain was starting to fall hard. Hobhouse, whose belief in spirits began and ended with brandy punch, was still staring at the damnable head. I pulled him by the shoulder. 'Come on,' I said. 'We should leave this place.'

"Behind us, the Albanians had been screaming at the guide. 'He has tricked you,' they told us. 'This is not the way. This is the way to Aheron!'

"I glanced at Hobhouse. He raised an eyebrow. We both recognized the name. Aheron—the river believed by the ancients to take the damned to Hell. If it did lie just ahead, then we had strayed a long way indeed from the Yanina road.

" 'Is this true?' I asked the guide.

" 'No, no,' he whined.

"I turned to the Albanian. 'How do you know that we are close to the Aheron?'

"He pointed to the stake, then spoke a single word I didn't understand: *'Vardoulacha.' "* Lord Byron paused. He repeated the word slowly, sounding the syllables. *"Vardoulacha."*

Rebecca frowned. "What did it mean?" she asked.

Lord Byron smiled at her. "As you can imagine, I asked the guide the very same question. But he was too crazed with fear to make any sense. He just kept repeating the same word over again: *'Vardoulacha, vardoulacha, vardoulacha.'* Suddenly, he screamed at me. 'My Lord, we must turn, go back!' He stared wildly at his companions, then began to gallop back up the road.

" 'What the devil's the matter with them?' asked Hobhouse, as the other two Albanians followed the first around the outcrop of rock. 'I thought the beggars were meant to be brave.'

"There was a distant rumble of thunder, and then, over the jagged silhouette of Mount Suli, we saw the first fissure of lightning stab. Fletcher started to cry. 'Damn it,' I muttered. 'If we wanted to be tourists, I knew we should have gone to Rome.' I wheeled my horse. 'You,' I said, pointing at the guide, 'don't move from here.' Hobhouse was already riding hard back up the path. I followed him, then galloped on ahead. For almost ten minutes we rode hard through the rain.

"The darkness now was virtually impenetrable. 'Byron,' shouted Hobhouse, 'those other three . . .'

" 'Which other three?'

" 'Those other three guards—where are they gone, do you think? Can you make them out?'

"I peered into the rain, but could scarcely see as far as my horse's nose.

" 'Damnedest thing,' muttered Hobhouse. He wiped at his nose. 'Still—something to tell the fellows back home, I suppose.' He paused, and glanced at me. 'If we manage to get home to tell them, that is.'

"At that moment, my horse stumbled, then reared up, whinnying in fear. Lightning lit the path ahead. I pointed. 'Look,' I said.

"We trotted slowly up to where three bodies lay. Their throats had all been cut. There was no other mark on them. I reached for the cliff and took a handful of earth. I leaned from my saddle and scattered the soil over the corpses, then watched as the soil was washed away.

"Dimly, through the thudding of the downpour, we heard a scream. It rose and pitched, then faded into the rain. We pressed our horses forward. I almost trampled a fourth corpse, and then, down the path, we found the final two members of our bodyguard. As with their companions, their throats had been cut. I dismounted, and knelt beside one to touch the wound. Thick purple blood slipped over my fingertips. I looked up at Hobhouse. 'They must be out there,' he said, gesturing vaguely with a sweep of his hand, 'somewhere.' We both stood and listened. We could hear nothing but the beating of the rain upon the rocks. 'Quite a scrape,' said Hobhouse. 'Yes,' I agreed.

"We rode back to where we had left Fletcher and the guide. The guide had vanished, of course; Fletcher was offering bribes up to his god. Hobhouse and myself, already quite convinced enough of the Almighty's hostility to us, were agreed that we had no choice but to ride on through the storm, and hope to find shelter before a knife found us.

We headed toward Aheron, while angry clouds poured the vengeance of the skies upon us, and lightning gilded the torrents and spray. Once, a shepherd's hut seemed to loom out from the dark, but when we cantered forward, we saw that it was only a Turkish tomb, with the Greek word for freedom, *eleutheria,* chiseled across its face. 'Perhaps it's lucky we still have our foreskin,' I shouted out to Hobhouse. 'Perhaps,' he nodded back. 'But I feel now they are all savages, the people of this hellish land. I wish we were in England.'" Lord Byron paused and smiled at the memory. "Of course, Hobby never was a good traveler."

"While you were?" Rebecca asked.

"Yes. I never sought out strange lands, and then complained because they weren't like Regent's Park."

"But that night . . ."

"No." Lord Byron shook his head. "Maybe it was odd, but agitation of any kind always gave a rebound to my spirits and set me up. Dullness, that was what I feared. But up on the mountains, peering through the storm for the bandit's dagger—yes—the excitement of that took a long time to fade."

"But it did fade?"

"Yes." Lord Byron creased his brow. "Yes, it did at last. The fear remained, but it was no longer an agitation, merely a dullness, and Hobhouse was affected by it in just the same way. The further we rode, the more physical it seemed to become, as though it were something like the rain, through which we had to force ourselves to go. It was ahead of us, an emanation of something, whatever it was, draining away our spiritedness. Fletcher began muttering his prayers again.

"Then Hobhouse reined in his horse. 'There's someone up ahead,' he said. He pointed into the drizzle of the dying storm. 'See?' I looked. I could just make out figures, but nothing more. 'Where are you going?' Hobhouse called, as I spurred my horse down the track.

"'What choice have we got?' I shouted back. I cantered

through the rain. 'Hello!' I shouted. 'Is anyone there? We need help! Hello!' There was no answer, except for the drizzle pattering on the rocks. I stared around. The figures, whatever they were, had disappeared. 'Hello!' I called again. 'Please, hello!' I reined in my horse. Ahead of me now, just faintly, I could hear a rumbling sound, but nothing else. I slumped in my saddle, and felt fear, like paralysis, numbing every limb.

"Suddenly, someone seized my horse's reins. I looked down, startled, and reached for my gun, but before I could cock it, the man by my stirrups had raised up both his hands and called out the Greek words of welcome. I answered him, then sat back in my saddle and laughed with relief. The man watched me patiently. He was old, with silver mustaches and a straight back, and his name, he told me, was Gorgiou. Hobhouse joined us—I explained to the old man who we were and what had happened to us. He seemed unsurprised by the news, and when I had finished talking, said nothing at all at first. Instead he whistled and two other figures stepped forward from behind the rocks. Gorgiou introduced them as his sons, Petro and Nikos. Petro I liked at once; he was a large, weatherbeaten man, with strong arms and an honest face. Nikos was clearly much younger, and seemed slight and frail beside his brother. He wore a cloak over his head, so that it was impossible for us to see his face.

"Gorgiou told us that he and his sons were shepherds— we asked him if he had a shelter nearby. He shook his head. Then we asked if Aheron was far. He made no reply to this, but looked startled, then took Petro to one side. They began to whisper urgently. Several times we overheard the word our bodyguard had spoken, *'vardoulacha, vardoulacha.'* At last Gorgiou turned back to us. He explained that Aheron was dangerous; they were traveling there because Nikos was sick, but that we, if we could, should find somewhere else. We asked if there were any other villages nearby. Gorgiou shook his head. Then we asked why Aheron was dangerous.

Gorgiou shrugged. Were there bandits, we asked, robbers? No, there were no bandits. Then what was the danger? Just danger, Gorgiou said with a second shrug.

"Behind us, Fletcher sneezed. 'I don't care how dangerous it is,' he muttered, 'just so long as there's a roof over our heads.'

" 'Your valet is a philosopher,' said Hobhouse. 'I absolutely agree.'

"We told Gorgiou that we would accompany him. The old man, seeing that we were determined, did not protest. He began to head on down the path, but Petro, instead of walking with him, reached out for Nikos. Would I carry the boy on my horse? he asked. I said that I would be happy to, but Nikos, when his brother tried to lift him, flinched away. 'You are ill,' Petro told him, as though reminding him, and Nikos, reluctantly, allowed himself to be lifted up onto the horse. I caught the gleam of dark girlish eyes from beneath the shadow of his hood. He wrapped his arms around me; his body against mine felt slim and soft.

"The path began to descend. As it did so, the roaring I had heard earlier became more thunderous, and Gorgiou reached up to touch my arm. 'Aheron,' he said, pointing toward a bridge ahead of us. I cantered gently down toward it. The bridge was stone and clearly centuries old. Just beneath its span, waters boiled and hissed as they split from a wave-worn precipice into the river far below, and then slipped black and silent between two barren cliffs. The storm had almost died, and a pale twilight was staining the sky, but no light caught the Aheron as it flowed through the gorge. All was dark, deep and dark. 'In old times,' said Gorgiou, standing by my side, 'it is said a ferryman carried the dead to Hell from here.'

"I looked at him sharply. 'What, this very place?'

"Gorgiou pointed toward the gorge. 'Through there.' He glanced up at me. 'But now, of course, we have the Holy Church, to guard us from evil spirits.' He turned hurriedly, and walked on. I glanced again at the dead waters of the Aheron, then followed him.

"The ground now was flattening out. The rocks were starting to be replaced by scrubby grass, and looking ahead I could see faint lights. 'The village?' I asked Gorgiou. He nodded. But it was no village, our destination, scarcely even a hamlet, just a mean straggle of shacks and a tiny inn. I saw a crossroads beyond the inn.

" 'Yanina,' said Petro, pointing down the second road. There was no sign by the crossroads, but I could see a forest of stakes, very like the one our soldiers had found by the mountain road. I trotted past the inn to look at them, but Nikos, seeing the stakes, held my arms. 'No,' he whispered fiercely, 'no, turn back.' His voice was enchanting, musical and soft like a girl's, and it acted on me like a charm. But before I wheeled my horse around, I was relieved to see that the stakes were unadorned.

"Inside the inn, our rooms were wretched, but after our ordeal on the mountainside and the grim spectacle of the Aheron, I welcomed them as though they were paradise. Hobhouse grumbled, as he always did, about hard beds and rough sheets, but agreed reluctantly that it was better than a grave, and tucked in well enough when supper came. Afterward, we went to find Gorgiou. He was sitting by the fire, sharpening his knife. It was a long, cruel blade, and at once I remembered the sight of our soldiers dead in the mud. Gorgiou, however, I liked, and Petro too, for being as stern and upright as the mountains themselves. Yet both men seemed nervous; they stayed by the fire, their knives by their sides, and though everything between us soon seemed hiccups and friendliness, their eyes kept straying to the windows. I asked them once what they were looking for; Gorgiou said nothing; Petro laughed and muttered about the Turks. I didn't believe him—he didn't seem the man to be scared of other men. But of what else, if not the Turks, was there to be afraid?

"Outside in the yard, a dog began to howl. The innkeeper hurried to the door and unslid the bolts. He peered out. We could hear hooves approaching us through the mud. I left Gorgiou and walked across to the door. I watched the landlord as he hurried out into the road. Thin wisps of mist, stained in the twilight a watery green, had risen from the earth and obscured all but the outline of the mountain peaks, so that I might almost have been staring out at the dead waters of Hell, and it would not have been a surprise to see the ferryman, old Charon, piloting his bark of specters through the descending night.

" 'You must be careful here,' said a girl's voice from beside me.

"I turned around. It was not a girl at all, but Nikos." Lord Byron paused. Again, he stared past Rebecca into the dark. He bowed his head, and then, when he looked up again, he gazed deep into Rebecca's eyes.

"What is it?" she asked, disconcerted by his look.

Lord Byron shook his head.

"Tell me."

Lord Byron's smile was twisted and strange. "I was thinking, as poets do, how beauty must always pass away."

Rebecca stared at him. "Not your own, though."

"No." His smile faded. "But Nikos was lovelier by far than me. Looking at you just now, I remembered him, as he stood by me in that inn, with a sudden utter clarity. His hood had been thrown back, not so far that it revealed his hair, but sufficient to display the beauty of his face. His eyes, I saw, were black as death, his lashes the same hue. He lowered them, and I stared into their silk shadow, until Nikos blushed and looked away. But he stayed by my side, and when I walked out into the mist, he followed me. I could sense that he wanted to take my arm.

"Two travelers had arrived. One was a woman, one a priest; both were dressed in black. The woman was escorted past us into the inn: her face was pale and I could see that she had been crying. The priest stayed outside, and when the innkeeper re-emerged back into the road, he shouted some orders and walked toward the crossroads. The inn-keeper followed, but before he joined the priest, he untethered a goat from the side of the inn, and then carried it with him as he walked down the road toward the forest of stakes.

" 'What are they doing?' I asked.

" 'They are trying to lure the *vardoulacha* with the smell of fresh blood,' Nikos said.

" '*Vardoulacha*—I keep hearing this word, *vardoulacha*. What is it?'

" 'It is a dead spirit that will not die.' Nikos glanced up at me, and for the first time since I had made him blush, our eyes met. 'The *vardoulacha* drinks blood. It is an evil thing. You must beware of it, for it prefers to drink from a living man.'

"Hobhouse had joined us. 'Come and see this, Hobby,' I told him. 'It might give you something to scribble in your journal.' Together, the three of us walked down the road. The priest, I saw, was standing by a trench; the innkeeper held the goat over it. The animal was bleating with fear; the innkeeper, with a sudden movement of his arm, silenced the goat's screams, and blood began to pump into the trench. 'Fascinating,' said Hobhouse, 'quite fascinating.' He turned to me. 'Byron—the *Odyssey*—you remember it—Odysseus does the same thing when he wants to summon up the dead. The ghosts of the underworld can only feed on blood.'

" 'Yes.' I remembered the passage well. It had always chilled me, the thought of the hero, waiting for the ghosts of Hades to come. I peered through the mists at the road that led back to Aheron. 'And he would have come to this very place, I suppose—to the river of the dead—to summon them.' I imagined the spirits, the sheeted dead, squeaking and gibbering as they flocked down the road.

" 'Why,' I asked Nikos, 'if the *vardoulacha* is so dangerous, do they want to summon him?'

" 'It was once a woman's husband. The priest has come to destroy it.'

" 'The woman in the inn?' asked Hobhouse. 'The woman who has just arrived?'

"Nikos nodded. 'She is from a village near to ours. Her husband has been buried for months now, but he is still seen, walking as he always did when alive, and the villagers are afraid.'

"Hobhouse laughed, but Nikos shook his head. 'There can be no doubt,' he said.

"'How?'

"'When he was alive, his leg was withered, and now when he is seen, he limps in the same way he used to do.'

"'Ah, well,' said Hobhouse, 'that proves it. Better kill him off quick.'

"Nikos nodded. 'They will.'

"'But why have they come here?' I asked. 'To this spot?'

"Nikos looked at me in surprise. 'Because this is Aheron,' he said simply. He pointed at the road we had come down that evening. 'This is the way that the dead come from Hell.'

"We stared into the trench. The blood had almost drained now from the corpse of the goat, and lay black and viscous inside the earth. Beside the trench, I saw, a long stake lay prepared. The priest turned to us, and gestured that we should return inside. We needed little encouragement. Gorgiou and Petro both seemed relieved when we joined them again by the fire. Petro rose to his feet and took Nikos in his arms; he spoke to him in a low urgent whisper, and seemed to be scolding him. Nikos listened impassively, then shrugged himself free. He turned to me. 'Don't mock us for what I have told you, My Lord,' he said softly. 'Tonight, bar your windows.' I promised that I would. Nikos paused; then he felt inside his cloak and drew out a tiny crucifix. 'Please,' he said, 'for my sake—keep this by your side.'

"I took the cross. It seemed made of gold, and was beautifully worked with precious stones. 'Where did you get this from?' I asked in surprise—its value seemed far in excess of anything that might be owned by a shepherd boy.

"Nikos brushed my hand. 'Keep it, My Lord,' he whispered. 'For who knows what things may be abroad tonight?' Then he turned and was gone, like a girl suddenly embarrassed that her lover might be admiring her.

"When I retired to bed, I did as Nikos had advised, and locked the windows shut. Hobhouse chaffed me, but as I pointed out to him, he failed to open them up again. We both fell straight asleep, even Hobhouse, who usually lay in his bed waiting to complain about the sharpness of the fleas. I had placed the crucifix on the wall above our heads, hoping that it would give us a dreamless night, but the air was filthy and close, and I slept badly. Several times I woke, and I noticed that Hobhouse too was sweating and tossing on his sheets. Once I dreamed that there was scratching on the wall outside. I imagined that I woke and saw a face, bloodless and with a look of imbecilic savagery, staring in at me. I fell back to sleep and dreamed again, this time that the creature was scratching at the bars, his nails like talons making a hideous sound, but when I awoke there was nothing, and I half-smiled to think how powerfully Nikos' tale had affected me. A third time I fell asleep, and a third time I dreamed, and now the creature's nails were slicing through the bars, and the stench of carrion on his breath seemed to be carrying some foul pestilence into our room, so that I grew suddenly afraid that unless I opened my eyes we would never wake again. I sat up in a violent sweat. Again, the window was empty, but this time I walked across to it, and saw, to my horror, that there were gouges sliced across the bars. I gripped them, until my knuckles were white, and leaned my forehead against the central bar. The metal felt cool against my feverish skin. I stared out into the night. The mist was thick, and it was hard to see far beyond the road. Everything seemed still. Then suddenly, I thought I saw movement—a man, or at least something resembling a man, running with extraordinary pace, but also with what seemed a lurch, as though one of the legs had been damaged in some way. I blinked, and the creature was lost. I peered desperately into the mists, but everything was still again, stiller perhaps, I thought with a grim half-smile, even than death itself.

"I reached for the pistols that I always slept with under my pillow, and threw on my traveling cloak. I walked stealthily through the inn. To my relief, I saw that the doors were still barred; I opened them, and crept outside. In the far distance, a dog was howling; all else was silent and motionless. I walked down the road a small way, toward the clump of stakes. The crossroads was swathed in mist but everything there seemed as still as at the inn, and so I turned and made my way, as you can imagine, thoughtfully back. When I reached the inn, I barred the doors, then, as quietly as before, I crept back toward my room.

"The door, when I reached it, was hanging open. I had left it shut, I was certain. As silently as I could, I approached it, and walked into the room. Hobhouse lay as I had left him, sweating on his filthy sheets, but bending over him, head almost touching his naked chest, was a figure muffled in an ugly black cloak. I aimed my pistol; the cocking of the weapon made the creature flinch, but before it could turn, the barrel of the pistol was buried in its back. 'Outside,' I whispered. Slowly, the creature rose. I nudged it with the gun, and prodded it back into the corridor outside.

"I pulled it around, and tore the cloak back from its face. I stared at it and then I began to laugh. I remembered what had been said to me earlier that evening. I repeated the words. 'Who knows what things may be abroad tonight?'

"Nikos did not smile. I gestured with the pistol that he should sit down. Reluctantly, he sank onto the floor.

"I stood over him. 'If you wanted to rob Hobhouse—and I presume that's what you were doing in our room—why wait until now?'

"Nikos frowned in puzzlement.

"'Your father,' I explained, 'your brother—they were the *klephti* who killed our guards yesterday?'

"Nikos made no answer. I prodded my pistol into his back. 'Did you kill my guards?' I asked again.

"Slowly, Nikos nodded his head.

"'Why?'

"'They were Turks,' he said simply.

"'Why not us as well?'

"Nikos looked at me angrily. 'We are soldiers,' he said, 'not bandits.'

"'Of course not. You are all honest shepherds—I was forgetting.'

"'Yes, we are shepherds,' said Nikos with a sudden explosion of fury, 'just peasants, My Lord, animals, the slaves of a Turkish *vardoulacha!*' The word was spat at me without irony. 'I had a brother, My Lord, my father had a son—he was killed by the Turks. Do you think slaves cannot take their revenge? Do you think slaves cannot dream of freedom, and fight for it? Who knows, My Lord, perhaps the time will come when Greeks do not have to be slaves.' Nikos's face was pale, and he was shaking, but his dark eyes gleamed with defiance. I reached out to calm him, to hold him in my arms, but he leaped to his feet and pressed himself against the wall. Suddenly, he laughed. 'Of course, you are right—I am a slave, so why should I care? Have me, My Lord, and then give me the gold.' He reached up to take my cheeks. He kissed me, his lips burning, with anger first, and then, I knew, with something more, a long, long kiss of youth and passion, when heart and soul and sense move in sudden concert, and the sum of what is felt can no longer be reckoned.

"Yet the despairing mockery of his words stayed in my ears. Without sense of time, I still knew that I had to break from the kiss. I did so. I took Nikos by the wrist, then dragged him back into my room. Hobhouse stirred; seeing me with the boy, he groaned and turned his back on us. I reached across him for a bag of coins. 'Take it,' I said, tossing the bag to Nikos. 'I enjoyed your tales of vampires and ghouls. Take it as a reward for your inventiveness.' The boy stared back at me in silence. His inscrutability only made him seem all the more vulnerable. 'Where will you go?' I asked him, more gently than before.

"The boy spoke at last. 'A long way off.'

"'Where?'

"'To the north perhaps. There are free Greeks there.'

"'Does your father know?'

"'Yes. He is sad, of course. He had three children—one is dead, and I must flee, and tomorrow there will only be Petro left to him. But he knows I have no choice.'

"I stared at the boy, as slim and frail as a beautiful girl. He was, after all, just a boy—and yet I regretted the thought of losing him. 'Why do you have no choice?' I asked.

"Nikos shook his head. 'I can't say.'

" 'Travel with us.'

" 'Two foreign lords?' Nikos laughed suddenly. 'Yes, I could travel very inconspicuously with you.' He glanced down at the bag I had given him. 'Thank you, My Lord, but I prefer your gold.'

"He turned, and would have left the room had I not held his arm. I reached back to the wall and unhooked the cross. 'Take this as well,' I said. 'It must be valuable. I won't need it now.'

" 'But you do!' said Nikos in sudden fear. He reached up to kiss me. From the road outside came the muffled sound of a shot being fired. There was a second shot. 'Keep it,' said Nikos, pressing the cross back into my palm. 'Do you really think I could invent such things!' He shivered, then turned and hurried from me. I watched him run down the corridor. When I woke the next morning, it was to find that he had already gone."

Lord Byron sat in silence, his hands clasped, his eyes staring into the flickering dark.

"And Nikos?" Rebecca asked, her voice sounding distant in her own ears. "Did you see him again?"

"Nikos?" Lord Byron looked up, then slowly shook his head. "No, I never saw *Nikos* again."

"And the shots—the two shots—you heard in the night?"

Lord Byron smiled palely. "Oh, I tried to convince myself that it could only have been the innkeeper firing at some creeping thief. A useful reminder, if we'd needed it, that there were robbers in the mountains less scrupulous than Gorgiou. A warning, that was what we had heard—to be careful at all times."

"And were you?"

"Oh yes, in one sense—we reached Yanina without further difficulty, if that is what you mean."

"And the other sense?"

Lord Byron hooded his eyes. The faintest curl of mockery played on his lips. "The other sense," he repeated softly. "When we left in the morning, we saw the corpse of a man half-tumbled into the innkeeper's trench. The man had been shot twice in the back; the priest's sharpened stake had been driven through his heart. The priest himself stood watching as a grave was dug by the forest of stakes. A woman, the same we had seen the night before, stood weeping by his side.

" 'So they caught their vampire,' said Hobhouse cheerily. He shook his enlightened head. 'The things these people believe. Extraordinary. Quite extraordinary.'

"I said nothing. We rode on until the hamlet could no longer be seen. Only then did I point out the coincidence, that the corpse had had a withered leg."

Chapter III

LUCIFER: *What are they which dwell*
   So humbly in their pride, as to sojourn
   with worms in clay?
CAIN: *And what are thou who dwellest*
   So haughtily in spirit, and canst range
   Nature and immortality—and yet
   Seem'st sorrowful?
LUCIFER: *I seem that which I am;*
   And therefore do I ask of thee, if thou
   Wouldst be immortal?

LORD BYRON, *Cain*

ℱor as long as we remained on the mountain track, our memories and imaginings together bred unmentionable fears. But we reached the Yanina road without mishap, and from then on progressed with such good speed that the superstitions we had pretended to mock amongst the mountains we now felt able to deride with quite genuine contempt—even I, who lacked my companion's faith in skepticism, could discuss the *vardoulacha* as though we were back in London sipping tea. Yet our first glimpse of Yanina was enough to remind us that we were still far from Charing Cross, for the domes and minarets, glittering through gardens of lemon trees and groves of cypress, were as picturesque—and unlike London—as we could possibly have hoped. Not even the sight of a human trunk, hanging from a tree by its single arm, could dampen our spirits, for what might have seemed in a remote village a great horror, now appeared, as we galloped down toward the gates of an oriental city, merely a pleasing touch of barbarism, romantic fodder for Hobhouse's notes."

"So you were made welcome?"

"In Yanina? Yes."

"That must have been a relief."

Lord Byron smiled faintly. "Yes, it was rather. Ali Pasha—I think I told you—had a rather ferocious reputation, but though he was off slaughtering the Serbs when we arrived, he had left orders for us to be met and entertained. Rather flattering. We were welcomed at the gates, and then led through the narrow, crowded streets, with their endless swirl of color and noise, while over everything, in almost visible clouds, hung the stench of spices and mud and piss. Crowds of children followed us, pointing and laughing, while from shopfronts, and hashish dens, and the latticed balconies where women sat behind their veils, eyes pursued us unceasingly. It was a relief, at last, to feel the sunlight against our faces again, and a cooling breeze, as we were led along a lakefront road toward the caravanserai that Ali Pasha had set aside for us. It was open and airy, in the Turkish style, with a wide courtyard that led down to the lake. Not all the rooms around the court had been given to us: two Tartar soldiers stood on guard by an opposite gateway, and there were horses tethered in the stable yard. But there was no one else to be seen, and in the quiet of our rooms, even the hum of the city behind us seemed stilled.

"We both slept. When I woke again, it was to the distant wail of the muezzin, summoning the faithful to evening prayers. Hobhouse, like a true infidel, snored on oblivious, but I rose and crossed to the balcony. The lake outside was dyed crimson, and beyond it, the mountains that rose abruptly from its far bank seemed washed in blood. Yanina itself lay behind me all unseen, and only a small boat, crossing from an island in the lake, reminded me that such a thing as man could still exist. I turned, shoved Hobhouse, then wandered out into the court.

"The house and lakefront were as hushed as before. I glanced around, looking for some sign of human movement, and saw the boat, which just a few minutes previously had been in the center of the lake, now moored and rocking gently at my feet. It must have crossed the water with almost impossible speed. I could see the pilot sitting hunched in the prow, but when I called to him, he didn't look up. I called again, and reached out to shake him by the arm. He was swathed in black rags, greasy and damp to the touch, and when he looked up his face was that of a lunatic, flesh and eyes dead, mouth open wide. I took a step back, then heard Hobhouse thumping his way outside, and so I turned and hurried up the road toward the house. The sun's last rays were disappearing behind the courtyard roof. I paused and glanced over my shoulder, to watch the lake, and then, at the very moment when the reds on the water shimmered and died, I saw someone else."

Lord Byron paused. He was gripping the sides of his chair, Rebecca saw. He had closed his eyes.

There was a long silence. "Who was it?" Rebecca asked.

Lord Byron shook his head. "I didn't recognize him. He was standing where I had been just a minute previously, a tall man, head shaved in the Turkish style, but with a curling white mustache and neatly trimmed beard, such as an Arab might have worn. His face was thin and unnaturally pale, yet even obscured by the darkness, he excited in me an admixture of revulsion and respect that I found hard to explain, so powerfully and immediately it affected me. His nose was hooked; his lips tight; his expression mocking and predatory—yet there were suggestions as well of great wisdom and suffering in his face, not constant, but passing like the shadows of clouds across a field. His eyes, which had glittered at first like those of a snake, appeared suddenly deep and incandescent with thought; staring into them, I felt certain that this was a man of a kind I had never seen before, a compound, unbalanced, of spirit and clay. I bowed to him; the figure smiled, his lips curling sensuously to reveal his gleaming white teeth; then he answered my bow. He swept back his cloak, which had hung around him like desert robes, and walked past me toward the Tartar guards. They saluted him respectfully; he made no response. I watched him as he entered the house and disappeared.

"At the same time, we heard men's voices from the road,

and saw a deputation approaching us. It was from the Vizier, come to greet us and bring us the flattering news that although Ali was not in residence in Yanina, we were invited to join him in Tapaleen, the town of his birth, some fifty miles further along the road. We bowed, and expressed our profoundest thanks; we swapped courtesies; we praised the beauties of Yanina. Then, having exhausted our stock of pleasantries, I asked about the man who was sharing the courtyard with us, explaining that I would like to pay him my respects. There was a sudden silence; the members of the delegation all glanced at each other, and the leader looked embarrassed. The man I had seen, he muttered, was a pasha from the southern mountains; the leader paused, and then added with sudden insistence, as though the idea had just come to him, that since the Pasha was only staying for the one night, it might perhaps be best to leave him undisturbed. Everyone else nodded and agreed, and then a sudden flood of pleasantries rolled out over us. 'Near as damn drowned me,' as Hobhouse put it later. 'Almost as though they'd had something to hide.'

"Well, Hobby always had a genius for sniffing out the obvious. The next day we rode out to view the countryside, and I asked our guide, a soft, fat Greek named Athanasius, a scholar assigned to us by the Vizier, what our hosts might possibly have wanted to conceal. Athanasius had flushed slightly at the mention of the Pasha, but then he composed himself and shrugged.

"'It is Vakhel Pasha who is staying opposite you,' he explained. 'I imagine the Vizier's servants were frightened of his reputation. They did not want any unpleasantness. If you were to make complaints against them to Ali Pasha, then, well, of course—it would be bad for them.'

"'Why, what unpleasantness are you talking about? What is Vakhel Pasha's reputation?'

"'He is said to be a magician. He is said by the Turks to have sold his soul to Eblis, the Prince of Hell.'

"'I see. And has he?'

"Athanasius glanced at me. I noticed, to my surprise, that

he hadn't smiled. 'Of course not,' he muttered. 'Vakhel Pasha is a scholar, indeed a great scholar, I believe. That is a rare enough among the Mussulmen for it to excite rumor and suspicion. They are all pigs, you see, our lords and masters, all ignorant pigs.' Athanasius glanced over his shoulder. 'But if Vakhel Pasha is not ignorant—well then— it is that which makes him dangerous. Only Turks and peasants could believe he was truly a demon—but he is a strange man, all the same, and the subject of strange tales. I would do as you have been advised, My Lord, and keep away from him.'

"'But Athanasius, you make him sound quite unmissable.'

"'Perhaps that is why he is so dangerous, then.'

"'You have met him yourself?'

"Athanasius nodded.

"'Tell me,' I asked.

"'I have a library. He wished to consult a manuscript.'

"'On what topic?'

"'As I recall,' said Athanasius in a thin voice, strange from one so fleshy, 'it was a treatise on the Aheron, and its role in ancient myth as the river of death.'

"'I see.' The coincidence was enough to make me pause. 'What was his interest in the Aheron, do you remember that?'

"Athanasius didn't answer. I looked into his face. It was waxy and pale. 'Are you well?' I asked.

"'Yes! yes.' Athanasius shook out his reins, and cantered ahead. I joined him, so that we were riding side by side again, but didn't press my guide, who remained nervous and withdrawn. Suddenly though, he turned to me. 'My Lord,' he whispered, as though confessing a secret, 'if you must know, Vakhel Pasha is the ruler over all the mountains around Aheron. His castle is built on a cliff above the river. It is that, I'm sure, which explains his interest in its past— but please, do not press me on this topic any more.'

"'No, of course not,' I said. I had already grown accustomed to the cowardice of the Greeks. Then I remembered

Nikos. He had been brave. He had also hoped to flee a Turkish lord. Had the lord been Vakhel Pasha? If it had been, then I was afraid for the boy. That night at the inn—I nodded to myself—yes, Nikos had been wild and beautiful, he deserved to be free. 'What is Vakhel Pasha doing in Yanina, do you know?' I asked casually.

"Athanasius stared at me. He began to shake. 'I don't know,' he whispered, then spurred his horse on. I let him ride ahead for a while. When I rejoined him, we neither of us mentioned Vakhel Pasha again.

"We passed the day among the ruins of an ancient shrine. Hobhouse prodded at stones and made interminable notes; I sat in the shade of a toppled column, poeticizing. The beauty of the sky and mountains, and the mournful reminders of decay all around, were pleasantly profound; I scribbled, and dozed, and followed my thoughts. It grew increasingly hard for me to know, as day darkened into the purples of evening, whether I was awake or asleep; everything around me began to grow impossibly vivid, so that I felt that I was seeing the true stuff of life for the very first time, the beat of existence in flowers and trees and in the grass, even in the land itself, the rocks and soil, which seemed to me like flesh and bone, something like myself. A hare sat watching me; I could hear the pulsing of its heart in my ears, and feel the warmth of its blood. Its life smelled rich and beautiful. It began to run, and the pumping of its blood, through its muscles and arteries, and heart, its beating heart, washed the landscape red and stained the sky. I felt a scorching thirst in the back of my throat. I sat up, clutching at my neck, and it was then, as I stared after the disappearing hare, that I saw Vakhel Pasha.

"He too was smelling after the animal. He was standing on a rock, against which he slowly lowered himself, so that he was crouching like some beast of the mountains, a wolf perhaps. The hare was gone; but still the Pasha lay crouched, and I realized that he was smelling after something far richer and more precious than the hare. He turned to look at me. His face was deathly pale, and smooth with

LORD OF THE DEAD

an extraordinary calm. His eyes seemed to be staring at me from within my own head; they gleamed with the knowledge of all that I was and desired. He turned, and smelled the air again, and smiled, and then his features were suddenly dimmed, and where before there had been stillness, there was now only envy and despair, and yet the show of wisdom in his face was none the less remarkable for its disfigurement. I stood up to join him, and felt myself wake. When I looked at the rock, Vakhel Pasha was gone. Just a dream—yet I continued to feel troubled, and on our journey back from the ancient site, the memory of what I had seen oppressed me as though it had been somehow more than a dream.

"Athanasius too seemed uneasy. The sun was setting. The further it sank behind the mountaintops, the more he glanced over his back to watch its descent. I asked him why he was troubled. He shook his head and laughed, but played with his reins like a nervous child. Then the sun was lost behind the mountain range, and at once we heard hoofbeats, pounding behind us down the valley road. Athanasius reined in his horse, then reached over to pull in mine, as a squadron of cavalry thundered past. The horsemen were Tartars, dressed like the guards outside Vakhel Pasha's rooms. I looked for the Pasha among them, to my relief in vain. 'What were they after?' I asked Athanasius, gesturing at the disappearing cavalry.

"'What do you mean?' he answered in a hoarse whisper.

"I shrugged. 'Oh, just that they seemed to be searching for something.' Athanasius made a choking noise, and his face twitched horribly. Without saying a further word, he spurred his horse onward down the Yanina road. Hobhouse and I were happy to follow him, for it was growing very dark."

"But the Pasha," Rebecca interrupted, "when you saw him on the rock—had it really been a dream?"

Lord Byron stared at her coldly. "We stayed in Yanina five more days," he said, ignoring her question. "So too, across the courtyard, did the Tartar guards! And I assumed that Vakhel Pasha, despite what the Vizier's servants had told us, remained in Yanina as well. I never saw him, however; instead"—and here he stared hard at Rebecca again—"I dreamed of him, not as we normally dream, but with the clarity of wakefulness, so that I could never be wholly sure that I was not awake after all. The Pasha would visit me wordlessly, a pale livid form, by my bed, in my room, or sometimes on the streets or on the mountainside, for I found now that I was sleeping at strange times, almost as though someone else was dreaming me. I would struggle against these fits of slumber, but always succumb, and it was then that the Pasha would appear, breaking through my dreams like a thief into a room."

Lord Byron paused, and closed his eyes, as though trying to glimpse the phantom's image again.

"I felt the same!" said Rebecca with a sudden nervous insistence. "In the crypt, when you held me in your arms. I felt that you were dreaming me."

Lord Byron raised an eyebrow. "Really?" he asked.

"And the Pasha came like that to you?"

He shrugged.

"Or did you meet him in the end?"

Rebecca stared into the gleam of the vampire's eyes. "Sleep hath its own world," he murmured. "A boundary between the things misnamed—death and existence." He smiled sadly, and stared into the flickering of the candle flame. "There was a monastery," he said at last. "We visited it on the evening before our departure. It was built on the island in the lake." Lord Byron looked up. "The same island from which, on my first night, I had seen a boat rowed across. I had wanted to see the monastery earlier, for that reason alone. According to Athanasius, however, such a visit had been impossible to arrange. One of the monks had been found dead, he explained—the monastery had had to be purified. I asked him when the monk had died. On the day of our arrival in Yanina, he replied. Then I asked what had killed the monk. But Athanasius shook his head. He didn't know—monks were always secretive. 'But at least the monastery is open now.'

"We landed. The jetty was empty, and the village beyond it as well. We walked into the monastery, but when Athanasius called out, there was no answer, and I saw our guide frown. 'In here,' he said without conviction, opening the door to a tiny side chapel. Hobhouse and I followed him; the chapel was empty, but we paused to study the walls. 'The Last Judgment,' said Athanasius unnecessarily, pointing at one gruesome fresco. The representation of Satan in particular struck me; he was both beautiful and terrible, perfectly white except for a mottling of blood around his mouth. I caught Athanasius watching me as I studied it; he turned hurriedly and called out again. Hobhouse joined me. 'Looks like that Pasha fellow,' he said. 'This way,' said Athanasius hurriedly, as though in response. 'We must go.' He led us into the main church. At first I thought that it too was empty, but then I saw, bent over a desk by the far wall, a shaven-headed figure clad in flowing robes. The figure stared around at us, then rose slowly to his feet. Light from a window illumined his face. I saw that where before I had remembered only pallor, Vakhel Pasha now had a flush of color in his cheeks.

"*'Les milords anglais?'* he asked.

"'I am the lord,' I told him. 'This is Hobhouse. You may ignore him. He is a mere commoner.'

"The Pasha smiled slowly, then greeted us both with formal elegance. He did so in the purest French, in an accent that was impossible to place, but charmed me, for it sounded like the rustling of silver in a wind.

"Hobhouse was asking him about his French. The Pasha told us that he had visited Paris, before Napoleon, before the Revolution, a long time ago. He held up a book. 'My thirst for learning,' he said, 'it is that which took me to the city of light. I have never visited London. Perhaps one day I should. So great it has become. I can remember a time when it was nothing at all.'

" 'Then your memory must be long-lived indeed.'

"The Pasha smiled and bowed his head. 'The wisdom we have here, in the East, it is long-lived. Is that not so, Monsieur Greek?' He glanced at Athanasius, who stammered something unintelligible, and began to shake in rippling folds of fat. 'Yes,' said the Pasha, watching him, and smiling with slow cruelty, 'we in the East understand much that the West has never possessed. You must remember that, *milords,* as you travel in Greece. Enlightenment does not only reveal. Sometimes also, it can blot truth out.'

" 'Such as what, Your Excellency?' I asked.

"The Pasha held up his book. 'Here is a work I have waited a long time to read. It was found for me by the monks of Meteora and brought to me here. It tells of Lilith, Adam's first wife, the harlot princess, who seduces men in the streets and fields, then drains them of their blood. To you, I know, this is superstition, the merest nonsense. But to myself, and yes, to our Greek friend here as well—it is something more. It is a veil that both conceals and suggests the truth.'

"There was silence. In the distance, I could hear the tolling of a bell. 'I am intrigued,' I said, 'to know what truth does lie in the tales of blood-drinkers we hear.'

" 'You have heard other tales?'

" 'Yes. We stayed in a village. We were told there of a creature named the *vardoulacha.'*

" 'Where was this?'

" 'Near the River Aheron.'

" 'You know, perhaps, that I am the Lord of Aheron?'

"I glanced at Athanasius. He was glistening like moist lard. I turned back to Vakhel Pasha and shook my head. 'No, I didn't know that.'

"The Pasha stared at me. 'There are many tales told of Aheron,' he said softly. 'For the ancients, too, the dead were drinkers of blood.' He glanced down at his book, and held it close to his chest. He seemed on the verge of telling me something, a look of fierce desire suddenly flaming across his face, but then it froze, and the death-mask returned, and when Vakhel Pasha did speak, there was only a sullen contempt in his voice. 'You must ignore anything a peasant tells you, *milord*. The *vampire*—that is the word in French, I believe?—yes, the vampire, it is man's oldest myth. And yet in the hands of my peasants, what is it become, this vampire?—just a shuffling idiot, a devourer of flesh. A beast, dreamed up by beasts.' He sneered, and his perfect teeth gleamed white. 'You need have no fear of this peasants' vampire, *milord*.'

"I remembered Gorgiou and his sons, their friendliness. Wishing to defend them, I described our experiences at the Aheron inn. I noticed, as I told my story, that Athanasius had virtually melted into sweat.

"The Pasha too was watching our guide, his nostrils twitching as though he could smell the fear. I finished, and the Pasha smiled mockingly. 'I am glad you were so well looked after, *milord*. But if I am cruel, then it is only to prevent them being cruel to mc.' Hc glanced at Athanasius. 'I am not only here in Yanina, you see, to consult the manuscripts. I am also hunting a runaway. A young serf I brought up, cared for—loved—as my own. Have no worries, *milord*—I hunt this serf more in sorrow than in rage; no harm will befall the serf.' Again, he glanced at Athanasius. 'No harm will befall the serf.'

"'I think, My Lord,' whispered our guide, almost tugging at my sleeve, 'I think perhaps that it is time to leave.'

"'Yes, leave,' said the Pasha with sudden rudeness. He sat down again, and opened up his book. 'I still have much to read. Go, please go.'

"Hobhouse and I bowed with studied formality. 'Will we see you again in Yanina, Your Excellency?' I asked.

"The Pasha looked up. 'No. I have almost achieved what I came here to do.' He stared at Athanasius. 'I leave tonight.' Then he turned to me. 'Perhaps, *milord*, we shall meet again—but in some other place.' He nodded, then returned to his book, and Hobhouse and myself, almost pushed by our guide, walked back out into the afternoon sun.

"We turned down a narrow road. The bell was still

tolling, and from a small church at the end of the track, we could hear the sound of chanting.

"'No, My Lord,' said Athanasius when he saw that we intended to enter the church.

"'Why not?' I asked.

"'No, please, please,' was all that Athanasius could wail.

"I shrugged him off, tired of his perpetual cowardice, and followed Hobhouse into the church. Through clouds of incense, I could make out a bier. A corpse lay on it, garbed in the black of a priest, but the robes drew attention, not to the dead man's office, but to the ghastly pallor of his face and hands. I stepped forward, and saw, over the mourners' heads, how flowers had been arranged around the dead monk's neck.

"'When did he die?' I asked.

"'Today,' whispered Athanasius.

"'So he is the second man to die here this week?'

"Athanasius nodded. He looked around, then whispered in my ear. 'My Lord, the monks are saying there is a devil loose.'

"I stared at him in disbelief. 'I thought devils were only for Turks and peasants, Athanasius.'

"'Yes, My Lord.' Athanasius swallowed. 'Even so, My Lord'—he pointed at the dead man—'they are saying that this is the work of a *vardoulacha*. See how white he is, drained of his blood. I think, My Lord, please—we should go.' He was almost on his knees now. 'Please, My Lord.' He held the door open. 'Please.'

"Hobhouse and I smiled at each other. We shrugged, and followed our guide back out to the jetty. There was a second boat moored next to ours that I had failed to notice on our landing, but recognized now at once. A black-swathed creature sat in the prow, his idiot's face as dead and bleached as before. I watched him growing smaller as we slipped across the lake. Athanasius was watching the creature too.

"'The Pasha's ferryman,' I said.

"'Yes,' he agreed, and crossed himself.

"I smiled. I had only mentioned the Pasha to watch our guide shake."

Lord Byron paused. "Of course, I should not have been cruel. But Athanasius had saddened me. A scholar—intelligent, well read—if freedom for the Greeks was to come from anywhere, then it was from men like him. So his cowardice, although we laughed at it, also filled us with something like despair." Lord Byron rested his chin on his fingertips, and smiled with faint self-mockery. "He parted for good after our return from the monastery. We called on him before we left the next day, but he wasn't at home. Sad." Lord Byron nodded his head gently. "Yes, very sad."

He lapsed into silence. "So you went on to Tapaleen?" asked Rebecca eventually.

Lord Byron nodded. "For our audience with the great and notorious Ali Pasha."

"I remember reading your letter," Rebecca said. "The one you wrote to your mother."

He looked up at her. "Do you?" he asked softly.

"Yes. About the Albanians in their gold and crimson, and the two hundred horses, and the black slaves, and the couriers, and the kettle drums, and the boys calling the hour from the minaret of the mosque." She paused. "I'm sorry," she said at last, seeing how he stared at her. "But I always thought it was a wonderful letter—a wonderful description."

"Yes." Lord Byron suddenly smiled. "No doubt because it was a lie."

"A lie?"

"A sin of omission, rather. I neglected to mention the stakes. Three of them, just outside the main gates. The sight of them, the smell—they rather polluted my memories of arrival in Tapaleen. But I had to be careful with my mother—she never could bear too much reality."

Rebecca ran a hand through her hair. "Oh. I see."

"No, you don't, you can't possibly. Two of the men were dead—shredded hunks of carrion. But as we rode beneath the stakes, we saw from the third a faint stirring. We looked up; a thing—it was no longer a man—was twitching on its stake, even as the movement drove the wood higher into its guts, so that it screamed, a terrible, inhuman, degraded sound. The poor wretch saw me staring at him; he tried to speak, and then I saw the caked black filth around his mouth, and understood that he had no tongue. There was nothing I could do—I rode on through the gates. But I felt horror, knowing that I shared clay with the creatures that could do such things, and suffer them as well, without meaning, without hope. I saw that I was nothing, that I must die, a thing which would come as much without my act or choice as birth, and I wondered if perhaps we had not all sinned in some old world, so that this one was nothing but Hell after all. If that was true, then the best was that we would die—and yet still, that night in Tapaleen, I loathed my mortality, and felt its constriction tight about me as though it were a shroud.

"That night Vakhel Pasha returned to my dreams. As when I first saw him, he was pale like death, yet also mightier, and the blaze of his eyes was both sad and stern. He beckoned me; I rose from my bed and followed him. I trod on the winds and didn't sink; below me Tapaleen, above me the stars; all the time, around my hand, a grip of ice. His lips never moved, and yet I heard him speak. 'From the star to the worm, all life is motion, leading only to the stillness of death. The comet wheels, destroying as it sweeps, and then is lost. The poor worm winds its way upon the death of other things, but still, like them, must live and die, the subject of something which has made it live and die. All things must obey the rule of fixed necessity.' He took my other hand, and I saw that we were on a mountainside, among the shattered statues and opened graves of some ancient town, now abandoned, left to silence and the pallid moon. Vakhel Pasha reached out to stroke my throat. '*All* things must obey, did I say? *All* things must live and die?' I felt his nail, which was sharp like a razor, skim my throat. A soft cravat of blood muffled my neck, and I felt a tongue lapping at it gently, as a cat would lick his mistress's hand. I heard the voice again from inside my head. 'There is a knowledge which is immortality. Follow me.' Still the lapping at my throat. 'Follow me. Follow me.' As the words faded, so too did the ruined town, and the stars above my head, and even the touch of lips against my skin, until at last there was nothing but the darkness of my swoon. I struggled to break free of it. 'Byron, Byron!' I opened my eyes. I was still in our room. Hobhouse was leaning over me. 'Byron, are you well?' I nodded. I felt my throat; there was a faint pain. But I said nothing; I felt too exhausted to speak. I closed my eyes, but as I drifted towards sleep, tried to reach for images of life with which to guard my dreams. Nikos. Our kiss—lips on lips. His slender warmth. Nikos. I dreamt, and Vakhel Pasha did not return.

"The next morning I felt faint and unwell.

"'God, but you look pale,' said Hobhouse. 'Shouldn't you stay in bed, old fellow?'

"I shook my head. 'We have our audience this morning. With Ali Pasha.'

"'Can't you miss it?'

"'You must be joking. I don't want to end up with my anus on a stake.'

"'Yes,' Hobhouse nodded, 'good point. Shame there's no liquor here. That's what you need. God, this damnable country.'

"'I have heard that in Turkey, paleness of skin is a sign of breeding.' There was no mirror, but I knew that a pallor suited me. 'Don't worry, Hobhouse,' I said, leaning on his arm. 'I'll have the Lion of Yanina eating from my hand.'

"And I did. Ali Pasha was delighted with me. We met in a large, marble-paved room, where we were served coffee and sweetmeats, and were profusely admired. Or rather, I was, for Hobhouse was too red, and his hands too large, for him to be afforded the praises that my beauty won—a beauty which, as Ali told Hobhouse endlessly, was an infallible sign of my superior rank. He announced at last that I was his son, and a most charming parent he made, for with us he had the appearance of anything but his real character, behaving throughout with the most delightful *bonhomie*.

"Lunch was brought. We were joined by Ali's courtiers and followers, but we were given no chance to meet them, for Ali kept us entirely to himself. He continued paternal, feeding us almonds and sugared fruit as though we were little boys. The lunch was finished—and still Ali kept us by his side. 'Jugglers,' he ordered, 'singers'—they performed. Ali turned to me. 'Is there anything else you would like to see?' He didn't wait for my answer. 'Dancers!' he said. 'I have a friend here—he is staying with me—and he has the most extraordinary girl. Would you like to see her perform?'

"Of course, we both politely said that we would. Ali turned on his couch to look around the room. 'My friend,' he called out, 'your girl—could she be sent for now?'

"'Naturally,' said Vakhel Pasha. I twisted around, in something like horror. The Pasha's couch lay just behind my own—he must have been there unnoticed by us for the length of the meal. He sent a servant scurrying from the hall, then nodded politely to Hobhouse and myself.

"Ali asked the Pasha to join us. He did so in terms of the utmost respect—I was surprised, for Ali, we had thought, respected no one but himself, yet with Vakhel Pasha, he seemed almost afraid. He was interested—and worried, I felt—to discover that we knew the Pasha already. We described to him our meeting in Yanina, and all the circumstances surrounding it. 'Did you find your escaped boy?' I asked Vakhel Pasha, dreading his reply. But he smiled and shook his head. 'What made you think that my serf was a boy?'

"I blushed, as Ali collapsed into paroxysms of delight. Vakhel Pasha watched me with a lazy smile. 'Yes, I caught my serf,' he said. 'Indeed, it is she who will shortly be performing for us.'

"'Beautiful she is,' said Ali with a wink, 'like the peris of Heaven.'

"Vakhel Pasha inclined his head politely. 'Yes—but she is

headstrong too. I almost think, if it weren't that I loved her as my own child, I would have let her escape.' He paused, and his pale brow was shaded by an expression of sudden pain. I was surprised—but had no sooner caught the shadow than it had passed from his face. 'Of course'—his lip curled faintly—'I have always enjoyed the thrill of a chase.'

" 'Chase?' I asked.

" 'Yes. Once she had broken from Yanina.'

" 'That was what you were waiting for?'

"He stared at me, then smiled. 'If you like.' He stretched his fingers as though they were claws. 'I had known all along that she was there, of course, hiding. So I had my guards patrol the roads, while I waited'—he smiled again—'studying in the monastery.'

" 'But if you had to wait for her to break, how did you know she was there in the first place?' Hobhouse asked.

"The Pasha's eyes gleamed like sun on ice. 'I have a nose for such things.' He reached for a grape, and delicately sucked the juices out. Then he looked up at Hobhouse again. 'Your friend,' he said casually, 'the fat Greek—it appears that she had been hiding in the cellar of his house.'

" 'Athanasius?' I asked in disbelief.

" 'Yes. It is strange, isn't it? He was clearly a great coward.' The Pasha took another grape. 'But it is often said that the bravest men are those who first have to conquer their fear.'

" 'Where is he now?' I asked.

"Ali giggled with sudden delight. 'Outside,' he hissed cheerfully, 'on a spike. He did very well—only died this morning. That was very impressive, I thought—the fat are usually the quickest to go.'

"I glanced at Hobhouse. He had turned as white as a corpse—I was relieved that I had no more color to lose. Ali seemed oblivious to our sense of shock, but Vakhel Pasha, I could see, was watching us with a bitter smile on his lips. 'What happened?' I asked him, as lightly as I could. 'I hunted them down,' Vakhel Pasha replied. 'By Pindus—a rebel stronghold—so they almost got away.' Again, I saw a faint shadow cross his face. 'Almost—but not quite.'

" 'The fat Greek,' said Ali, 'he must have known a lot of useful stuff—about the rebels, and so on. But he wouldn't talk. Had to rip his tongue out in the end. Annoying.' He smiled benignly. 'Yes, a brave man.'

"There was a sudden flutter of sound from the musicians. We all looked up. A girl in red silks had come running into the hall. She approached us: her face was concealed behind flowing veils, but her body was beautiful, slim, and olive-brown. There was a rustle of bells from her ankles and wrists as she prostrated herself; then, at a snap of the fingers from Vakhel Pasha, she rose to her feet. She waited, in a posture to which she had clearly been trained; there was a crash of cymbals; the girl began to dance."

Lord Byron paused, then sighed. "Passion is a rare and lovely thing, the true passion of youth and hope. It is a pebble dropped into a stagnant pond—it is the striking of an unheard bell. And yet just as ripples die, and echoes fade, so too is passion a fearful state—for we all know, or we soon find out, that happiness remembered is the worst unhappiness of all. What can I tell you? That the girl was as pretty as an antelope?—pretty and graceful and alive?" The vampire shrugged faintly. "Yes, I can, but it means nothing. Two sleepless centuries have passed me by since I watched her dance. She was lovely, but you will never picture her as she was, while I . . ."—he stared at Rebecca, frowning, his eyes blazing cold, and then he shook his head—"while I have become the thing you see." He closed his eyes. "Understand, however, that my passion was *furious*. I was in love before I even knew who my goddess was. Slowly, veil by veil, she revealed her face. If she had been pretty before, she now grew painfully beautiful." Again, he stared at Rebecca, and again, he frowned, his features stamped with disbelief and desire. "Auburn hair, she had." Rebecca touched her own. Lord Byron smiled. "Yes," he murmured, "very like yours, but hers was braided and woven with gold; her eyes were large and black; her cheeks the color of the setting sun; her lips red and soft. The music ended; the girl fell in a sensual movement to the floor, and her head bent low just before my feet. I felt her lips touch them, the lips that had met my own before, when we had embraced in the inn at Aheron."

Lord Byron stared past Rebecca into the dark. Almost, she thought, as though he were making an appeal, as though the darkness were the centuries that had borne him on their flow, far from that shiver of happiness.

"It was Nikos?" she asked.

"Yes." He smiled. "Nikos—or rather, the girl who had pretended to be a boy named Nikos. She raised her head, and tossed back her hair. Her eyes met mine; there was no sign of recognition in them, only the dulled indifference of the slave. How clever she was, I thought, how brave and strong-willed! And all the time, of course, yes, all the time"—he glanced at Rebecca again—"how beautiful! It was no wonder that I began to feel a tumult in my blood, and turmoil in my thoughts, and feel as though I were in an Eden, being offered the fruit of a forbidden tree. This was the poetry of life I had traveled to find! A man, I thought, cannot always cling to the shores. He must follow where the ocean takes him, or what is life?—an existence without passion, sensation, or variety—and therefore, very much like death."

Lord Byron paused and frowned. "That is what I believed, anyway." He laughed hollowly. "And it was true enough, I suppose. There *can be* no life without tumult or desire." He sighed, and glanced up at Rebecca again. "And if I tell you all this, it is so you can understand, both my passion for Haidée, and why I acted on it; for I knew—and even now, even here, I think I was right—that to smother an impulse is to kill the soul. And so when Vakhel Pasha, leaving Tapaleen with his serf in tow, requested us to stay with him in Aheron, I accepted. Hobhouse was furious, and swore he wouldn't go; even Ali frowned mysteriously, and shook his head—but I wouldn't be persuaded. And so it was agreed, that I would travel with Hobhouse down the Yanina

road, and then we would separate, Hobhouse to tour
Ambracia, and myself to stay in Aheron. We would meet
again, after three weeks, in a town on the south coast named
Missolonghi."

Again Lord Byron frowned. "All most romantic, you
see—and yet, if it was quite true that I was sick with
passion to an extent I scarcely understood myself, that was
not everything." He shook his head. "No, there was another
reason for my visit to Aheron. On the night before Vakhel
Pasha's departure, I had dreamed again. For the second
time, I was amongst ruins, not of a small town now, but of a
great city, so that wherever I looked, there was nothing but
decay, the shattered steps of thrones and temples, dim
fragments cast pale by the moon, tenanted by nothing but
the jackal and the owl. Even the sepulchers, I saw, lay open
and bare, and I knew, amongst all this vast expanse of
wreckage, there was no other living man but me.

"I felt the Pasha's nails across my throat again—felt his
tongue as he lapped at my blood. Then I saw him ahead of
me, a pale form luminous amid the cypress and stone, and I
followed him. Incredibly ancient, he seemed now—as ancient as the city he led me through, possessed of the wisdom
of centuries, and the secrets of the grave. Ahead of us
loomed the shadow of some titanic form. 'Follow me,' I
heard whispered; I approached the building; I walked
inside. There were staircases, stretching and twisting impossibly; up one of them the Pasha walked, but when I ran to
join him, the staircase fell away, and I was lost in a vast
enclosure of space. Still the Pasha climbed, and still, in my
head, I heard his call: 'Follow me.' But I could not; I
watched him, and felt a thirst more terrible than any
longing I had ever known, to see what lay at the summit of
the stairs, for I knew that it was immortality. High above
my head, a dome arched, jeweled and glowing; if only I
could reach that, I thought, I would understand, and my
thirst would be slaked. But the Pasha was gone, and I stood
abandoned to crimson shadow. 'Follow me,' I could still

hear as I struggled to wake, 'follow me,' but I opened my eyes, and the voice bled away on the morning light.

"I imagined sometimes, during the next few days, that I heard the whisper again. Of course, I knew it was fancy, but even so, I was left feeling restless and disturbed. I found myself desperate for Aheron."

Chapter IV

'Tis said thou holdest converse with the things
Which are forbidden to the search of man;
That with the dwellers of the dark abodes,
The many evil and unheavenly spirits
Which walkest the valley of the shadow of death,
Thou communest.

LORD BYRON, *Manfred*

obhouse, as we had agreed, parted from me on the Yanina road. He rode on south; I turned back to the mountains, and the winding track to Aheron. We rode hard the whole day—I say we, for with Fletcher and myself came a single guard, a faithful rogue named Viscillie, lent to me, in a signal show of favor, by Ali Pasha himself. The crags and ravines were as lonely as ever; crossing through the desolate wilds a second time, I couldn't help but remember how easily my six guards had been picked off before. Yet I never felt truly worried—not even when we passed the site of the ambush, and I caught a glint of bone in the sun. I was costumed like an Albanian pasha now, you see, all crimson and gold, very *magnifique,* and it's hard to be a coward when you're dressed like that. So I twirled my mustaches, and swaggered in my saddle, and felt myself the equal of any bandit in the world.

"It was late when we heard the waterfall's roar, and knew that we had reached the Aheron. Ahead of the bridge, the road forked: one path led down, toward the village where I had stayed before; the other ever up. We took the second path; it was steep and narrow, winding through crags and littered boulders, while to our right, a chasm of blackness, yawned the gorge through which the Aheron flowed. I began to feel nervous, ridiculously, wretchedly nervous, as though the waters below me were chilling my soul, and even Viscillie, I noticed, seemed ill at ease. 'We must hurry,' he muttered, glancing at the red-lined mountain peaks to the west. 'It will be nightfall soon.' He drew out a knife. 'Wolves,' he said, nodding at me. 'Wolves—and other beasts.'

"Ahead of us, in an unclouded blaze of light, the sun was disappearing fast. But even after it was gone, its heat remained, oppressive and thick, so that as the twilight deepened into night, the stars themselves seemed like prickles of sweat. The track began to wind more sharply upwards, through a forest of dark cypresses, their roots twisting and clutching at the rocks, their branches shadowing our path in black. Suddenly, Viscillie reined in his horse and held up his hand. I couldn't hear anything, but then Viscillie pointed, and I saw, through a break in the trees, a gleam of something pale. I rode forward: ahead of me was an ancient archway, its marble cast white by the moon, but crumbling, on either side of the path, into rubble and weeds. There was an inscription, barely legible just above the arch: 'This, O Lord of Death, is a place sacred to you . . .'—nothing more could be read. I glanced around: everything seemed still. 'There's nothing here,' I said to Viscillie, but he, whose eyes were trained to the night, shook his head and pointed up the path. Someone was walking there, his back to us, in the shadow of the rocks. I spurred my horse forward, but still the figure didn't look around, just continued walking with a relentless stride. 'Who are you?' I asked, wheeling in my horse to confront the man. He said nothing, just stared ahead, and his face was shadowed by a coarse black hood. 'Who are you?' I asked again, then leaned down to flick the hood back from the man's face. I stared—and laughed. It was Gorgiou. 'Why didn't you say?' I asked. But still Gorgiou said nothing. Slowly, he looked up at me, and his eyes seemed without sight, glazed and torpid, sunk deep into his skull. No flicker of recognition crossed his face; instead, he turned, and my horse whinnied in sudden fear and backed away. Gorgiou crossed the path and went into the trees. I watched him disappear, his pace the same slow stride as before.

"Viscillie joined me, and his horse too seemed coltish and afraid. Viscillie kissed the blade of his knife. 'Come, My Lord,' he whispered. 'These ancient places are haunted by ghosts.'

"Our horses continued nervous, and it was only with an effort that we could force them to carry on. The path was widening now, as the rocks on one side began to fall away, while on the other a sheer cliff rose high above our heads. This was a promontory, I realized, jutting out between us and the Aheron; I stared up at it, but its summit was just a line of black against the silver of the stars, blotting out the moonlight so that we could scarcely see ahead. Reluctantly, our horses picked their way along the path, until the cliff grew less sheer and the moonlight returned. Ahead of us, the path rounded its way past an outcrop of rock—we followed it, and there, built up the mountainside, were the ruins of a town. The path snaked upwards, to a castle built on the peak. It too seemed ruined, and I could see no light shining from its battlements. Nevertheless, staring at the jagged form the castle made against the stars, I was certain that we had reached our journey's end, and that there, inside its walls, Vakhel Pasha would be expecting us.

"We began to ride through the town. There were churches, open to the moon, and shattered pillars submerged by weeds. In one ruin, I saw a small shack, built between the columns of some abandoned hall, and then, as I rode on up the path, I saw more houses, wretched like the first, huddled like squatters amongst the wreckage of the past. This was the village, I realized, from which Haidée must have fled, but there was no sign of her now, nor of any living thing, save for a dog, which barked wildly, then came running up to us wagging its tail. I reached down to stroke it; the creature licked my hand, and followed us as we rode on up the path. Ahead was a great wall, guarding the castle, with two open gates. I paused beneath them to look back at the village. I remembered Yanina and Tapaleen, the scenes of life that had greeted us there, and I shivered now, despite the unbearable heat, to see the wretched stillness of the hovels below. As we turned and rode on through the gates, even the dog whined and slunk away.

"The gates slammed shut—and still there was no one to be seen. There were more walls, I could see now, between us and the castle, which seemed built from the very mountain, so sheerly its battlements rose up from the cliffs. The only path to the castle was the one we were following now—and the only route of escape, I thought suddenly, as a second pair of gates swung shut behind our backs. But I could see torches now, bobbing on the walls, and I was grateful for the signs of life—I began to think of food, and a soft bed, and all those pleasures you have to be a traveler to earn. I pressed my horse forward through a third and final gate, and as I did so, looked behind me to see that the entire road was lit by torches now. Then the third pair of gates swung shut, and all was stillness again, and we were alone. Our horses whinnied with fear, and the striking of their hoofs echoed off the stone. We were in a courtyard; ahead of us, steps led up to an open doorway, very ancient, I realized, decorated with the statues of monstrous things; above us towered the castle wall. All was lit by the blazing silver of the moon. I dismounted and crossed the courtyard towards the open door.

"'Welcome to my home,' said Vakhel Pasha. I had not seen him appear; but there he was, waiting for me, at the top of the steps. He held out his hands and took mine; he embraced me. 'My dear Lord Byron,' he whispered in my ear. 'I am so glad you have come.'

"He kissed me, fully on the lips, then stood back to stare into my eyes. His own gleamed more brightly than I remembered from before; his face too was as silver as the moon, its border luminous, like crystal against the dark. He took my arm and led me. 'The journey here is hard,' he said. 'Come and eat, and then take your well-earned rest.'

"I followed him through courtyards, up stairways, past countless doors. I realized that I was more tired than I had known, for the architecture of the place seemed like that of my dreams, endlessly extending and diminishing itself, full of impossible junctures and blendings of styles. 'Here,' said the Pasha at last, brushing aside a curtain of gold, and beckoning me to follow him. I looked around; pillars, in the style of an ancient temple, framed the room, but above me, in a glittering mosaic of golds and blues and greens, rose a dome so airy it seemed made of glass. The light was faint, there being only two large candlesticks in the form of twining snakes, but even so, I could make out words, in Arabic, around the edge of the dome. The Pasha must have been watching me: 'And Allah created man,' he whispered in my ear, 'from clots of blood.' He smiled lazily. 'It is a quotation from the Koran.' He took my hand, and gestured me to sit down. There were cushions and silks set around a low table of food. I took my place, and obeyed my host's invitation to eat. An ancient servant-woman kept my glass filled with wine, and the Pasha's too, although I noticed he swallowed it without apparent pleasure or taste. He asked me if I was surprised to see him drinking wine; when I agreed that I was, he laughed and said that he obeyed no god's command.

"'And you,' he asked me, his eyes glittering, 'what would you dare defy for the sake of pleasure?'

"I shrugged. 'Why, what pleasures are there,' I asked, 'beyond drinking wine and eating dead pig? I follow a sensible religion, which allows me to indulge in both of those pursuits.' I raised my glass, and drained it. 'And so I avoid damnation.'

"The Pasha smiled softly. 'But you are young, *milord,* and beautiful.' He reached across the table, and took my hand. 'And yet your pleasures truly end with the consumption of pork?'

"I glanced down at the Pasha's hand, then met his eyes again. 'I may be young, Your Excellency, but I have learned already that on every joy there is a proportionate tax.'

" 'You may be right,' said the Pasha evenly. A film of blankness seemed to curtain his eyes. 'I must admit,' he added, after a tired pause, 'that I can scarcely remember what pleasure is, I feel so dulled by the passage of the years.'

"I glanced at him in surprise. 'Forgive me, Your Excellency,' I said, 'but you do not strike me as being a voluptuary.'

" 'Do I not?' he asked. He took his hand from my own. I thought at first that he was angry, but when I looked into his face, I saw only a look of terrible melancholy, passions turned to ice like the waves of some frozen pond. 'There are pleasures, *milord,*' he said slowly, 'of which you have not even dreamed. Pleasures of the mind—and of the blood.' He looked at me, and his eyes now seemed deep as space. 'Is that not why you have come here, *milord?* To sample these pleasures for yourself?'

"There was compulsion in his stare. 'It is true,' I said, failing to lower my eyes before it, 'that although I hardly know you, I feel already that you are as extraordinary a man as I have ever met. You will laugh at me, Your Excellency— but in Tapaleen, I had dreams of you. I imagined that you came to me, and showed me strange things, and hinted at hidden truths.' I laughed suddenly. 'But what will you think of me, saying I came here at the prompting of a few strange dreams? You will be offended.'

" 'No, *milord,* I am not offended.' The Pasha rose to his feet, taking my hands, then embracing me. 'You have had a hard day. You deserve to sleep dreamlessly tonight—the sleep of the blessed.' He kissed me, and his lips felt cold to the touch. I was surprised, for they had not done so outside, in the moonlight. 'Wake fresh and well, *milord,*' the Pasha whispered; he clapped his hands; a veiled slave girl came in through the curtain. The Pasha turned to her. 'Haidée, show our guest to his bed.'

"My thrill of surprise must have been evident. 'Yes,' said the Pasha, watching me, 'she is the one I brought back from

Tapaleen, my pretty runaway. Haidée'—he waved with his hand—'remove your veil.' Gracefully, she did so, and her long hair spilled free. She was lovelier even than I had remembered her, and I was filled with sudden disgust to think of her serving as Vakhel Pasha's whore. I glanced at the Pasha as he stared at his slave, and saw a look of such hunger and desire cross his face that I almost shivered, for his lips were parted and his nostrils flared, almost as though he were smelling the girl, and his desire seemed transfused with a terrible despair. He turned and saw me watching him; the same look of hunger pinched his face as he stared into my own, and then it was gone, and his expression was as frozen as it had been before. 'Sleep,' he said dismissively; he waved his hand. 'You need your rest—you will have much to occupy you in the days to come. Goodnight, *milord.'*

"I bowed and thanked him, then followed Haidée. She led me up a stairway; when we had reached the top, she turned round and kissed me, long and lovingly, and I, who needed no encouragement, took her in my arms, and met her lips as well as I could. 'You came for me, my dear sweet Lord Byron'—she kissed me again—'You came for me.' Then she broke away from my embrace, and took me by the hand. 'This way,' she said, leading me up a second flight of steps. There was no trace of the slave about her now; instead, she seemed bright with passion and excitement, prettier than ever, with a kind of fierce joy that warmed my own blood, and quickened up my spirits most entertainingly. We ended in a room that reminded me, much to my surprise, of my old bedroom in Newstead—thick pillars and heavy archways, Venetian candlesticks, all the familiar Gothic stuff. I could almost imagine myself back in England—certainly, the room was no place for Haidée, so natural was she, so loving—so Greek. I held her; she raised her lips to kiss me again, and it was as burning and sweet as that first kiss in the inn, when she had dared to believe that she might be free.

"And then, of course, I remembered she was not. Slowly,

I parted my lips from hers. 'Why has the Pasha left us alone?' I asked.

Haidée stared up at me, her eyes wide. 'Because he hopes that you will deflower me,' she said simply.

" 'Deflower?'—and then, after a pause—*'Hoping?'*

" 'Yes.' Her brow darkened with sudden bitterness. 'I was unlocked tonight, you see.'

" 'From where?'

" 'From nowhere.' Despite herself, Haidée laughed. She crossed her hands chastely in front of her. 'Here,' she said. 'What lies here—it is my master's, after all, not mine. His to do with as he pleases.' She raised her hands, then lifted up her skirts—around both her wrists and ankles were delicate rings of steel, not bracelets as I had thought before, but fettering bands. Haidée clasped her hands again. 'The chains can be fitted to lock up my thighs.'

"I paused. 'I see.'

"She stared at me, her wide eyes unblinking, then pulled me tight against her. 'Do you, though?' she asked, reaching up to comb the curls of my hair. 'I cannot—will not—be a slave, My Lord—and not *his* slave, no, not *his.'* She kissed me softly. 'Dear Byron—help me—please help me.' Her eyes blazed suddenly, with fury and tortured pride. 'I *must* be free,' she whispered on a single breath. *'I must.'*

" 'I know.' I held her tight. 'I know.'

" 'Do you swear?' I could feel her shaking as she pressed against me. 'Do you swear you will help me?' I nodded. Such passion, like a tigress's, combined with the prettiness of a goddess of love—how could I fail to be stirred? How, indeed? I glanced across at the bed. And yet, as before, the same uneasy prompting in my mind—*why* had we been left alone?—the Pasha scarcely seemed the man who would take kindly to the bedding of his favorite slave by a guest. And I was high in the mountains, in a strange land, virtually alone.

"I remembered what Haidée had said before. 'The Pasha,' I asked slowly, 'he truly hasn't made love to you?'

"She looked up at me, and then away. 'No, never.' There

was distaste in her voice, but also, unmistakeably, a sudden hint of fear. 'He has never used me for—that.'

" 'Then for what?'

"She shook her head gently, and closed her eyes.

"I pulled her round to face me again. 'But why, Haidée—I still don't understand—why has he left you unchained with me?'

" 'You really don't see?' She looked up at me with sudden doubt in her eyes. 'Surely you do? How can a slave have love?—slaves are whores, my Byron. Do you want me to be your whore, my Byron, my sweet Lord Byron, is that what you want me to become?' God, I thought, she's going to cry, and I almost took her there and then, but no, she had the strength and passion of a mountain storm, and I couldn't do it. If she'd been some drab, some London bitch, well—I was rake enough already to know that a woman cried generally just to lubricate herself—I would have pressed her. But Haidée—she had the beauty of her land—but she also had more, something of the spirit of old Greece, which I had waited for so long to find, and now, in this slave girl, I held it, rays of that light which had led the Argonauts, and inspired her ancestors at Thermopylae. So beautiful, so wild—a creature of the mountains, restless almost to death in her cage. 'Yes,' I whispered in her ear, 'you will be free, I promise it.' Then, under my breath: 'And I won't even make love to you until you want me to.'

"She led me across to a balcony. 'So we are agreed, then?' she asked. 'We will escape together from this place?'

"I nodded.

"Haidée smiled happily, then pointed up at the sky. 'We must wait,' she said. 'We cannot leave while the moon is full.'

"I looked at her in surprise. 'Whyever not?'

" 'Because it isn't safe.'

" 'Yes, but why not?'

"She raised a finger to my lips. 'Byron, trust me.' She shivered, despite the heat. 'I know what has to be done.' She shivered again, and glanced over her shoulder. I followed her stare, and saw a tower jagged against the moon, a red light glowing from its very top. I crossed to the balcony edge, and saw how the tower rose sheer from the promontory edge. Far below flowed the Aheron, its thick waters unstained by the moon; I peered over my own balcony's side, and saw that the drop into the chasm below was as sheer as that along the rest of the walls. Haidée held me, and pointed. I looked up again; the red light from the tower had disappeared. 'I must go,' she said.

"At that moment, there was a knock on the door. Haidée fell on her knees to unlace my boots. 'Yes,' I called.

"The door opened, and a creature came in. I say creature, for although the thing had the form of a man, there was no sign of intelligence in its face, and its eyes were more dead than a lunatic's. Its skin was leathery, covered in tufts of hair; its nose was rotted; its fingernails curved like claws. Then I remembered that I had seen it before, the same creature, slumped at the oars of the Pasha's boat. It was dressed now as then, in greasy black, and it held a tub of water in its hands.

"'Water, master,' said Haidée, her head bowed. 'For you to wash.'

"'But where is my own servant?'

"'He is being taken care of, master.' Haidée turned to the creature, and gestured to him to lower the tub. I saw her stifle a look of horror and disgust. She bent down, to remove my boots, then rose and waited, her head bowed again. 'Will that be all, master?' she asked.

"I nodded. Haidée glanced at the creature; again, the same stifled expression of shock. She crossed the room, and the creature followed, then passed her, shambling onto the stairway outside. Haidée brushed past me. 'Visit my father,' she whispered. 'Tell him I am alive.' Her finger stroked my hand; then she was gone, and I was left alone.

"I felt so agitated, and my spirits so confused by desire and doubt, that I was certain I would never sleep. But I must have been more tired from my journey than I had realized, for I only had to lie on my bed that night and I was deep in slumber. No nightmares visited me, not even the breath of a dream; instead, I slept without break, and it was late in the morning when I finally awoke. I crossed to my balcony; far below me, black as before, was the Aheron, but all other colors, the tints of the earth, the hues of the sky, seemed dyed with the beauty of paradise, and I thought how strange it was, in this land formed for the gods, that man should have marred it with such tyranny. I glanced up at the tower, as jagged against the morning sky as it had been against the stars; in this spot at least, I thought, gazing at the beauty of the landscape again, it is as though the fiend has prevailed against the angels, and fixed his throne in a heaven, to rule it as though it were Hell. And yet, I thought—and yet—why *did* Vakhel Pasha fill me with such dread, that I could call him a demon, and feel it to be more than just an idle word? It was other people's fear, I thought—the rumors I had heard—his own loneliness and mystery—all these things—the blighted marks of his dark command. Had it not always been claimed, after all, and I known for sure, that the Devil was an aristocrat?

"I dreaded, and anticipated, having to meet him again. Yet when I descended to the domed room of the night before, there was only the old servant-woman waiting for me. She handed me a note; I opened it. 'My dear Lord Byron,' I read, 'you must forgive me, but I am unable to join you today. Please accept my profoundest apologies, but I am caught up in business which I cannot drop. The day is yours; I will see you tonight.' The signature was scrawled in Arabic.

"I asked the servant-woman where the Pasha was; but she began to shake, and seemed so nervous as to be incapable of speech. I asked about Haidée; then about Fletcher and Viscillie; but she was too scared even to understand me, and all my inquiries were in vain. At last, to her relief, I allowed her to serve me breakfast; having eaten it, I dismissed her, and was left alone.

"I wondered what to do—or rather, what I would be allowed to do. The disappearance of my two followers was disturbing me more and more; the absence of Haidée gave rise, if possible, to even darker thoughts. I decided that I would explore the castle, the vast extent of which I had been given some impression of the night before, to see what traces of them, if any, I might find. I left the domed hall, and began to walk down a long vaulted passageway. Arch after arch seemed to lead off from it, opening out only to yet further passageways, and yet further series of arches, so that there seemed no end to them, and no way back or out. The passageways were lit by vast braziers, whose flames rose high along the sides of the walls, and yet which gave off no heat, and only the dimmest light. My imaginings began to crowd me; the thought of the colossal weight of rock above my head, and the flickering gloom of the maze itself, was convincing me that I was lost forever in some vast sealed crypt. I called out—my voice scarcely echoed in the musty air. I called out again; and then again; for even as I felt myself to be alone in this prison, so also I had the sense of eyes, unblinking, observing me. Into the pillars of some of the arches, statues had been carved, very ancient, their form Greek and yet their faces, where these had survived, ones of extraordinary horror. I stopped by a pillar, to try to understand in what this horror lay, for there was nothing apparent, nothing monstrous or grotesque, about the statue's face, and yet just to look at it made me feel ill with disgust. It was the blankness, I realized suddenly, which with remarkable skill had been combined with an expression of desperate thirst; at once, I saw that the statue reminded me of the Pasha's servant, the creature in black who had come to my room the night before. I looked around—then stumbled on. I began to imagine that I could see other such creatures in the shadows, watching me with their dead man's eyes. Once, I was so certain of their presence that I called out, and thought I saw a creature slipping away, but when I followed it through an archway, there was nothing ahead of me but torchlight and stone.

"Yet the light seemed deeper than it had done before, and when I walked on through the archways, the stonework winked as though inlaid with gold. I studied the walls, and saw that they were decorated with mosaics, done in the Byzantine style, but long since defaced. The eyes of the saints had been chiseled out, so that they too had the familiar stare of the dead. A naked Madonna clutched a Christ; the infant smiled with cunning malignance, while the Virgin had been given a face so seductive I could scarcely believe it was mere artwork on a wall. I turned away, then felt drawn to glance back, at the same whorish smile, the same glint of hunger in the Madonna's eyes. I turned away a second time, forcing myself not to glance round again, and hurried on through a further arch. The light was richer now, a deeper red. Ahead of me was a brocade curtain, screening my way. I brushed it aside, and walked on, then stopped, to gaze at what lay all above and around.

"I was in a vast hall, empty and domed, its far end so distant from me that it was shrouded in dark. Colossal pillars, obtruding from the walls, loomed like shadowed titans; archways, of the kind I had just come through, seemed openings onto night. Yet the hall was lit—as in the passageway, braziers burned without heat, their flames rising in a pyramid to the very pinnacle of the dome. Directly below this point, in the center of the hall, I glimpsed a tiny altar made from black stone—I walked toward it, and saw that it was the only thing standing in that whole colossal place. All else was bare, and there was no sound in the hall's lofty, heavy emptiness but the ringing of my feet.

"I reached the altar—and saw that I had misjudged its size, so far away from it had I originally been. It was no altar at all, but a small kiosk, of the kind Mohammedans sometimes build in their mosques. I couldn't read the Arabic script carved around the kiosk door, but I recognized it from the evening before—'And Allah created man from clots of blood.' Yet if the kiosk had indeed been built by a Mohammedan—and I could see no other possible explanation for its presence there—then the other decorations on its walls left me uncertain and surprised. It is forbidden in the Koran to represent the human form—and yet there, carved on the stone, were the figures of demons and ancient gods. Directly above the doorway was the face of a beautiful girl, as whorish and cruel as the Madonna's had been. I stared up at it, and felt the same strange prickings of disgust and desire as I had done before the mosaic. I felt that I could stare into the girl's face forever— and it was only with an effort that I was able to break my glance away, and cross the doorstep into the darkness beyond.

"I thought I heard movement. I looked into the shadows, but could see nothing. Directly ahead of me were steps, leading down into blackness; I took a pace forward, and then heard the movement again. 'Who's there?' I called out. There was no answer. I took another step forward. I was starting to feel conscious of a terrible fear, worse than any I had experienced before, rising almost like incense from the blackness ahead and clouding my nerves. But I forced myself to walk on, toward the steps. I took my first pace down. There was a foot-tread behind me, and I felt dead fingers holding my arm.

"I swung round, raising my cane. A ghoulish creature, blank-eyed and slack-jawed, was behind me. I struggled to free my arm, but the grip was implacable. I could feel the creature's breath, thick with the smell of dead flesh, on my face. Desperate, I swung my cane down on the monster's arm, but he seemed not to feel it, and pushed me so that I stumbled and fell outside the kiosk door. Furious, I picked myself up and swung at the creature again; it shuffled back, but then, as I moved towards the flight of steps, it bared its teeth, cracked and black but jagged as a mountain range. It hissed, a loathsome sound of warning and thirst, and at the same time, from the blackness of the steps, I felt a fresh cloud of terror swirling at my nerves. Now, I've always held myself a brave man, but I realized then, confronted by the darkness of the steps and their hideous guard, that even the bravest should know when to retreat. So I withdrew and the creature at once lapsed into his torpor again. I breathed in deeply, and brought my terror under control. Yet I had been a coward—and knew it. As is ever the case in such situations, I longed for someone else to blame.

" 'Vakhel Pasha!' I called out. 'Vakhel Pasha!'

"No answer came but the sound of my own voice, echoing round the vastness of the hall. I could see now, obscured by the shadows of a distant wall, a creature like the thing in the kiosk, and the one who had brought the water to my room—it was bent on its hands and knees, scrubbing at the flagstones, oblivious to me. I crossed to it. 'You,' I said, 'where is your master?' The creature didn't look up. In my anger, I sent its tub of water flying with my cane, then reached down to pull at the creature's black rags. 'Where is the Pasha?' I asked. The creature stared at me, slapping its lips together wordlessly. 'Where is the Pasha?' I yelled. The creature didn't blink, and began to smile with a dumb animal thirst. I loosed my hold, controlling myself, and stared around the hall again. I saw a staircase, winding up one of the colossal pillars; another creature, on its hands and knees like the first, was scrubbing it. I followed the stairway's curl, and saw how it left the pillar and arced away, through the flames of the torches, along the side of the dome, before dropping into nothingness. I looked at other pillars, and again, up at the rim of the dome; I saw what I had not done before, that there were stairways everywhere, patterns of them, a lattice of futility, soaring high, leading only at last into empty, hopeless space. On each stairway, like lost souls in some prison of the damned, hunched figures were scrubbing at the stones, and I remembered my dream, how I too, seeking to climb impossible steps, had found myself lost and abandoned on them. Was this to be my fate, then, to join these creatures in their mindless bondage, and never to scale that dark realm of knowledge which had been hinted at to me? I shuddered, for at that moment I felt to the depths of my soul a certainty of the Pasha's hidden wisdom and power, and knew for sure, what previously I had said without understanding, that he was a being of a kind I had never met before. But what? I remembered that single Greek word, never uttered but in a low whisper of horror—*vardoulacha*. And was it possible—truly possible—that I was now the prisoner of such a thing? I stood there, in that monstrous hall, and felt my fear becoming violent rage.

"No, I thought—I couldn't surrender to the terror of the place. In my dream, I had been abandoned, but the Pasha had still found a stairway to climb. And so I looked up at the dome of the great hall again, at the drop of the steps into nothingness, at each one—and then I saw it—the single stairway that did not drop away. I hurried towards it, and began to climb. Up and up it wound—a narrow flight of steps carved out from the pillar, and then soaring out around the edge of the dome. There was no one else—nothing else—to pass on the way—no hunched thing in black: I was alone. Just ahead of me, the stairway disappeared into the wall. I looked down at the great hall below me, at its dizzying expanse of stone and space, and felt a sudden repugnance at the thought of entering a passageway as narrow as that which lay ahead of me now. But I bowed my head and entered it, and then, in virtual darkness, climbed up and up.

"I felt a strange excitement of anger and doubt. The stairway seemed endless; I was climbing the tower, I realized, the one I had seen lit red the night before. At last, I reached a door; 'Vakhel Pasha!' I shouted, rapping on it with my cane. 'Vakhel Pasha, let me in!' There was no answer; I pushed at the door, my pulse throbbing, my heart pounding with dread at what I might find inside. The door opened easily. I walked into the room.

"There were no horrors. I looked around. There was nothing but books—in shelves, on tables, in piles on the floor. I picked one up and looked at the title. It was in French: *Principles of Geology*. I frowned: this wasn't what I had been expecting to find at all. I crossed to a window: there was a beautiful telescope, of a make I had never seen before, aimed at the sky. I opened a second door; it led into a further room, full of glasses and tubes. Bright-colored liquids bubbled inside them, or flowed through glass pipes, like blood through transparent veins. Jars full of powders were ranged along shelves. There was paper everywhere; I picked up one of the sheets, and glanced at it. It was covered in scribblings which I couldn't read; one phrase, though, written in French, I could make out: 'Galvanism and the Principles of Human Life.' I smiled. So the Pasha was a natural philosopher—a student of the Enlightenment—while I—I had been wallowing in the most stupid superstitions imaginable. *Vardoulachas,* I thought—vampires! How could I have believed in such stuff, even for a moment? I walked to a window, shaking my head. I needed to get a hold on myself. I stared out at the clear blue sky. I would ride, I decided, get away from the castle—and see if I couldn't somehow spring-clean the phantoms from my brain.

"Not that I felt myself suddenly to be free from danger—far from it. A man can be a man, and not be any the less a monster—the thought that I might be the Pasha's prisoner still filled me with doubt and rage. Yet down in the stables, there was no one to prevent me from saddling my horse; the gates in the castle walls were open; when I passed the Tartar guards whose torches I had evidently seen the night before, they stared, but they didn't follow me. I galloped hard down the mountain road—it felt good to have the wind in my hair, the sun on my face. I rode out under the archway with its inscription to the ancient Lord of Death; as I did so, the heaviness that had been weighing down my spirits seemed to melt, and I felt the richness of life, its beauty and joy. I was almost tempted to gallop on down the mountain road, and never return; but I remembered my duty to Viscillie and Fletcher, and above all else, above all, my promise to Haidée. I only had to contemplate it, even for a second, to know how unbearable it would be to abandon her—there was my honor at stake, yet, of course, but that wasn't it; what was honor but a word? No, I had to admit it—something I was not accustomed to admitting—I was shamelessly, painfully, cravingly in love. A slave girl's slave—and yet how unfair that was to Haidée, for a slave must know herself to be so, or she is no such thing. I reined in my horse, and stared out at the wild beauty of the mountains, and thought how true a daughter she was of such a land. Yes, she would be free—only just now, hadn't I left the castle without hindrance of any kind, and wasn't it clear, after all, that the Pasha was nothing but a man? He was to be feared—but not as a vampire; no peasant dread of demons was going to hold me back. Steeled by such resolute philosophy, I would be hero enough, I was sure, to brave the Pasha's worst. As the sun began to sink, so the more my spirits rose.

"I remembered the promise I had made Haidée, to visit her father. We would need supplies for our escape—food, ammunition, a horse for Haidée herself. Who better to provide such things than her family? I began to make my way back to the village. I didn't hurry—the darker it was, the less chance I stood of being seen. It was almost twilight by the time I reached the village, and rode up a track that was as empty as before; I could see eyes, though, watching me, full of suspicion and fear. There was one man, sitting amongst the wreckage of a mighty basilica, who rose when I passed; it was the priest, the one who had killed the vampire by the inn; I rode up to him, and asked for directions to Gorgiou's house. The priest stared at me, wild-eyed, then pointed. I thanked him, but he still made no answer, and slid back at once into the shadows. I rode on up the track, and the village continued as deathly as before.

"Outside Gorgiou's house, though, there was a man on a bench. It was Petro. I scarcely recognized him, so drawn and preoccupied he looked. When he saw me, though, he called out and raised a hand in greeting.

"'I need to see your father,' I said. 'Is he in?'

"Petro narrowed his eyes, then shook his head.

"'I have news for him,' I said, 'a message.' I leaned down in my saddle. 'From his daughter,' I whispered.

"Petro stared at me. 'You'd better come in,' he said at

9 8

last. He stood holding my horse's reins while I dismounted, then showed me into his house. He sat me down by the door, while an old woman, his mother, I guessed, brought us both a cup of wine. Then Petro asked me to tell him all I had to say.

"I did so. At the news that Haidée was still alive, Petro's vast frame seemed to swell and become light with relief. But when I asked him for supplies, the color drained from his cheeks again, and when his mother, overhearing me, pressed him in support of my request, he shook his head and made a gesture of despair.

"'You must know, My Lord,' he said, 'that we have nothing in this house now.'

"I felt inside my cloak, and drew out a bag of coins. 'Here,' I said, tossing it into Petro's lap. 'Go where you have to—be as secret as the grave—only get us those supplies. Otherwise, I am afraid, your sister will be damned.'

"'We are all damned,' said Petro simply.

"'What do you mean?'

"Petro stared at his feet. 'I had a brother,' he said at last. 'We were *klephti* together. He was the bravest of the brave— but he was captured at last, by the Pasha's men, and put to death.'

"'Yes.' I nodded slowly. 'I remember being told.'

"Petro continued to stare at his feet. 'We felt such agony and rage. Our attacks grew more daring. My father especially—he waged war against the whole race of the Turks. I helped him.' Petro glanced up at me, and half-smiled. 'You saw an example of our handiwork yourself.' His smile faded. 'But now it is finished—and we are all damned.'

"'Yes, so you keep saying, but how?'

"'The Pasha has decided it.'

"'It is rumor, nothing more,' the mother interrupted.

"'Yes, but where does the rumor come from,' Petro asked, 'if not from the Pasha himself?'

"'He could destroy us with his horsemen if he wanted to,' the mother said, 'like a boy swatting a fly. I don't see them, though. Where are they?' She hugged her son tightly. 'Be brave, Petro. Be a man.'

"'A man?—yes! But it is not a man we are fighting against!'

"There was a silence. 'What does your father think?' I asked eventually.

"'He has gone into the mountains,' Petro said. He looked up, staring at the peaks as they swallowed the sun. 'He wouldn't rest. His hatred for the Turks drives him on and on. He has been gone for ten days now.' Petro paused. 'I wonder if we shall see him again.'

"At that moment, the sun disappeared at last; and Petro's eyes began to bulge. He stood up slowly, and walked to the door. He pointed; his mother joined him. 'Gorgiou,' she whispered, 'Gorgiou! He is back!'

"I looked out through the doorway. It was indeed Gorgiou who was coming up the road. 'May the Lord have mercy on us,' whispered Petro, staring at the old man horror-struck. Gorgiou's face was as pale as I remembered it from the night before, his eyes as dead; he walked with the same relentless stride. He brushed us all aside as he came in through the door; then he sat down, in the darkest corner of the house, and stared at nothing, until a wolfish smile began to curl along his lips.

"'Well,' he said, in a harsh, distant voice, 'this is a fine welcome.'

"No one answered at first. Then Petro stepped forward. 'Father,' he said, 'why do you cover your neck?'

"Slowly Gorgiou looked up at his son. 'No reason,' he said at last, his voice now as dead as his eyes.

"'Then let me see it,' said Petro, reaching down to uncover his father's neck. Gorgiou bared his teeth suddenly, hissing, and reached up in turn for his son's neck, gouging his nails into the flesh of the throat, squeezing tightly so that Petro began to choke.

"'Gorgiou!' his wife screamed, throwing herself between him and her son. Other members of the family, women, small boys, hurried into the room, and helped pull Petro from his father's grip.

"Petro himself breathed in deeply, staring at his father, then reached to take his mother's arm. 'It has to be done,' he said.

" 'No!' his mother screamed.

" 'You know we have no choice.'

" 'Please, Petro, no!' His mother threw herself, sobbing, around his knees, as Gorgiou began to chuckle. Petro turned to me. 'My Lord, please go!'

"I bowed my head. 'If there is anything I can do . . .'

" 'No, no, there is nothing. I will see that you have your supplies. But please, My Lord, please—you can see—just go.'

"I nodded, and pushed my way out to the door. Mounted on my horse again, I waited; there was only a low wail coming now from inside the house. I glanced in through the door. Petro's mother was sobbing, held in the arms of the son; Gorgiou sat motionless as before, his eyes staring at nothing. Then suddenly, he rose to his feet. He crossed to the door, and my horse backed away, up the path towards the castle gates. I reined him in with effort, then wheeled him round again. Gorgiou was walking down the pathway, back towards the village, just a silhouette now in the gathering dark. I saw Petro come out, standing on the track to watch his father leave. He began to run after him; then stopped; and his whole body seemed to slump. I watched him walk slowly back into his house.

"I shivered. It really was getting late—I shouldn't be out in such dark. I spurred my horse on, and rode through the gates. Slowly, they slammed shut behind me. I heard them being bolted. I was locked inside the castle walls."

Chapter V

A change came o'er the spirit of my dream
The Wanderer was alone as heretofore,
The beings which surrounded him were gone,
Or were at war with him; he was a mark
For blight and desolation, compass'd round
With Hatred and Contention; Pain was mix'd
In all which was served up to him, until,
Like to the Pontic monarch of old days,
He fed on poisons, and they had no power,
But were a kind of nutriment; he lived
Through that which had been death to many men,
And made him friends of mountains: with the stars
And the quick Spirits of the Universe
He held his dialogues; and they did teach
To him the magic of their mysteries;
To him the book of Night was open'd wide,
And voices from the deep abyss reveal'd
A marvel and a secret.

LORD BYRON, *"The Dream"*

J am trying very hard, Your Excellency,' I told the Pasha that evening, 'not to feel like a prisoner here.'

"The Pasha stared at me, his eyes wide, then slowly began to smile. 'A prisoner, *milord?*'

"'My servants—where are they?'

"The Pasha laughed. His spirits had been excellent the length of the meal. Running up his cheeks there was even a delicate trellis of capillaries. He reached out to take my hand, and the touch of his fingers, I noticed, felt much less cold than before.

"'Your Excellency,' I repeated, 'my servants?'

"The Pasha shook his head. 'They weren't needed here. So I sent them away.'

"'I see.' I breathed in deeply. 'To where?'

"'To—where is it you are meeting Mr. Hobhouse?—yes, to Missolonghi.'

"'And I will find them there?'

"The Pasha raised his hands. 'Whyever would you not?'

"I smiled mirthlessly. 'And myself? How am I to cope?'

"'My dear Lord Byron'—the Pasha took my other hand,

and stared into my eyes as though wooing me—'you are here as my guest. Whatever I have in this place, it is yours. Believe me—there is so much here for you to discover, so much to be revealed.' He leaned over, his mouth slightly parted, and kissed me softly on the neck. My blood seemed to ripple at the touch of his lips. The Pasha ran his fingers through my hair, then reclined again among the cushions on his couch. He waved his hand disdainfully. 'Don't fret about your servants. I have given you Yannakos.'

"I glanced across the room. Yannakos, the creature who had brought me water the night before, stood against the far wall, quite motionless apart from the twisting of his neck, as though strung up on a hangman's rope.

"'He's not—how can I put it?—' I glanced back at the Pasha, 'very lively, is he?'

"'He is a peasant.'

"'You have others like him too, I saw.'

"The Pasha bowed his head noncommittally.

"'In your great hall,' I continued, 'they all seemed like Yannakos. Somehow mindless—dead behind their eyes.'

"The Pasha laughed shortly. 'I don't want philosophers scrubbing my floors. Nothing would ever get done.' He laughed again, then sat in silence, and watched me through narrowed eyes. 'But you must tell me, *milord*—what did you think of the hall?'

"'I thought it stupendous. Stupendous—and blood-chilling.'

"'It was I who had it built, you know.'

"I stared at him in surprise. 'Really?' I paused. 'How strange. It gave me the impression of being much older.'

"The Pasha made no answer, and his eyes were like glass. 'You saw the rest of the castle too?' he asked eventually. 'You saw the labyrinth?'

"I nodded.

"'That, *milord,* is truly ancient. I had it repaired, but its foundations date back to long before my time. You have heard of Thanatopolis, perhaps?—the City of Death?'

"I frowned, and shook my head.

" 'It is not surprising,' the Pasha said. 'I have found almost no reference to it in any of the ancient sources, yet that it existed—well—you have seen the evidence yourself. This mountain was believed to be the gateway to the underworld, and a temple was built here to Hades, Lord of the Dead. The labyrinth led into the sacred precinct—to symbolize in stone, I suppose, the mysteries of Death.'

"I sat in silence. 'How fascinating,' I said at last. 'I have never heard of a temple to Death.'

" 'No.' The Pasha narrowed his eyes, and stared into the wash of the candle flame. 'It was abandoned, you see, and forgotten. And then a Byzantine town was built here, and then a Venetian fort. You will have seen the range of architecture this castle contains. And yet neither settlement lasted here for more than a generation at most.' The Pasha smiled. 'Strange, that they should both have disappeared so soon.'

" 'What happened to them?'

" 'No one can be sure.'

" 'You have no theory yourself?'

"The Pasha shrugged. He looked into the candle flame again. 'There are stories,' he said at last. 'So far, in the ancient sources themselves, there is only one legend that I have been able to find. In that account, it is said that the damned rose back from Hades, and seized the temple for themselves. Oddly, the peasants today have a folktale that is much the same. They say that the dead inhabit this place. All who build here, all who live here, soon must join the ranks of the damned. They talk of demons—in fact, I believe you mentioned the word to me in Yanina—they talk of the *vardoulacha.*'

"I smiled faintly. 'Amusing.'

" 'Yes, isn't it?' The Pasha bared his teeth into a grin. 'And yet . . .'

" 'Yet?'

" 'Yet—those settlements *did* collapse.'

" 'Yes,' I smiled, 'but there must be a more likely reason

for that than all the settlers becoming demons.' My smile broadened. 'Surely?'

"The Pasha made no answer at first. 'The castle,' he said eventually, staring into the shadows, 'is far vaster than you would ever believe.'

"I nodded. 'Yes, I've seen something of its size.'

"'Even so—you can have no idea. There are depths to it that I have scarcely fathomed, miles of unlit stone, and what lives in such blackness—I would not like to say.' The Pasha leaned over, and pressed my hand again. 'But there are rumors, glimpses of dark things. Can you believe that, *milord?*'

"'Yes, Your Excellency—yes, I can.'

"'Ah!' The Pasha raised an eyebrow.

"'In the labyrinth, I can't be sure, but I think I caught a glimpse of something.'

"The Pasha smiled. 'The *vardoulacha?*'

"'I wouldn't like to say.'

"'What was it like?'

"I stared straight into the Pasha's eyes, then glanced across at Yannakos. 'Very like him, Your Excellency.' The Pasha's grip tightened, and his face, I noticed, seemed pale again. 'We mentioned the slaves, who scrub in your hall. Very like them as well.'

"The Pasha let go of my hand. He stared at me, stroking his beard, and a smile, like a livid bloom, slowly touched the paleness of his lips. 'What an—imagination—you have, *milord,'* he whispered.

"I bowed my head. 'I have seen so many things here that really, I would have to be very dull not to wonder about them a little.'

"'Is that so?' The Pasha's smile faded again. He glanced at a watch on a low table by his side. 'I think, perhaps, it is time we were retiring to bed.'

"I didn't move. 'Your Excellency,' I asked, 'in the great hall, I saw a kiosk. In the Arabic style. Did you build that?'

"The Pasha stared at me. He pointed to the watch. *'Milord,'* he said.

" 'Why did you have it built? And in such a blasphemous way—with a woman's head above its door?'

"A look of anger crossed the Pasha's face. 'I have told you, *milord,* I am not bound by any petty laws of religion.'

" 'But why then did you build it?'

" 'If you must know'—the Pasha paused, then hissed— 'to mark the most sacred spot in the ancient temple to the underworld. The point believed by the ancients to be the entranceway to Hades. I built the kiosk out of respect—for the past, and for the dead.'

" 'So Hades, then, is a greater god than Allah, in your view?'

" 'Oh yes.' The Pasha laughed softly. 'Oh yes.'

" 'There are steps inside the kiosk.'

"The Pasha nodded.

" 'I would very much like to see what lies beyond them.'

" 'Impossible, *milord,* I am afraid. You forget that the underworld is only for the dead.'

" 'So have you entered it yourself, Your Excellency?'

"The Pasha's smile was as cold as ice. 'Good night, *milord.'*

"I bowed my head. 'Good night, Your Excellency.' I turned, and walked towards the staircase that led to my room. Immediately, Yannakos shuffled after me. I turned around again. 'Oh, I was just wondering—the slave girl, Haidée—where is she tonight?' The Pasha stared at me. 'Only I noticed,' I went on, 'she wasn't serving us. I was afraid, perhaps, that she might not be well.'

" 'She was a little feverish,' said the Pasha at last.

" 'Nothing serious, I hope?'

" 'Nothing at all.' His eyes gleamed. 'Good night, *milord.'*

" 'Good night.'

"I climbed to my bedroom. Yannakos followed me. I locked the door, of course, but I knew that he was outside, guarding, waiting. All most awkward. I lay down to sleep, then felt something under my pillow. I reached beneath it, and drew out Haidée's crucifix. There was a note attached to it: 'My dearest Byron, keep this next to you. I am well. Be

brave, whatever happens.' She had signed it *'Eleutheria'*—
Freedom. I smiled, and lit a candle. I paused—then lit as
many candles as I could find. I placed them around my bed,
so that they formed a wall of light, then burned the note
over one of the flames. I watched it turn to ash. As I did so,
my eyelids began to droop. I felt a terrible weariness. Before
I even knew it, I had fallen asleep.

"He came to me in my dreams. I couldn't move; I
couldn't breathe; there was no sound but the rhythm of
blood in my ears. He was on me, a loathsome thing of
darkness, heavy and taloned like a bird of prey, but as he fed
on me, drinking from my chest, his lips felt as soft as
leeches, fat and full with blood. I struggled to open my eyes;
I had thought they were already open, but there was no sign
of the candle flames, nothing but darkness, and it was
suffocating me. I looked up and thought I saw the Pasha's
face. He smiled at me, a pale faint smile of desire, but then,
when I looked into his eyes, there was nothing in the
sockets, only pits of emptiness. I seemed to be falling into
them. Darkness was eternal and everything. I screamed, but
made no sound, and then I too was a part of the darkness.
There was nothing else.

"I was feverish all the next day. I slipped in and out of
consciousness, so that I could never be certain what was
real, and what was not. I thought that the Pasha appeared by
my bed. He was holding the crucifix in his hands, and
laughing at me. 'Really, *milord*—I am disappointed! If I
have contempt for my own religion, why should I show any
respect for yours?'

"'You believe in a world of spirits, don't you?'

"The Pasha smiled and turned away. I reached out after
him. 'You believe in it, don't you?' I asked again. 'You
believe—in this castle—that the passageways are walked by
the dead?'

"'That is a quite different matter,' said the Pasha in a
calm voice, turning back to me.

"'Why?' I was sweating violently now. The Pasha sat
down beside me, and stroked my arm. I wrested it free. 'I

don't understand,' I told him. 'Last night—I was visited by a spirit. You know that, don't you, or is it just that I am delirious?' The Pasha smiled and said nothing, his eyes like silver water. 'How can there be such things, then,' I asked, 'and yet there be no God? Please, tell me, I am fascinated! I want to know. How can it be?'

"The Pasha rose to his feet. 'I do not say there is no God,' he said. His face seemed darkened suddenly, by a frown of melancholy and haughty despair. 'A God may exist, *milord*—but if he does, then he has no interest in us. Listen—I have passed through horrors, and made myself familiar with Eternity. I have plumbed the interminable ` realms of space, and the infinity of endless ages; I have spent long nights in strange sciences, and measured the secrets of both spirits and man. World by world, star by star, universe by universe, I have sought for a God.' He paused, and snapped his fingers in my face. 'I have found nothing, *milord.* We are alone, you and I.' I struggled to say something, but he cut me short with a gesture of his hand. He bent low beside me, and I felt his lips brush my cheek. 'If you would share my wisdom,' he whispered softly in my ear, 'then you must dive, as I have done, into the caves of death.' I felt him kiss me again. 'Sorrow is knowledge, *milord,*' he whispered, and his breath was as soft as a breeze across my skin. 'You must remember only this'—his lips caressed my own, so that his words were like a kiss—'the Tree of Knowledge is not that of Life.'

"He was gone—and I slipped back into the swamp of my dreams. Time had no meaning for me, and hours, days perhaps, passed in a feverish haze. But Yannakos was always there, and whenever I returned to consciousness, I would see his cold eyes watching me. I began to recover. I saw, to my horror, that a thin wound ran across my chest; sometimes I tried to get up, to find Haidée, to confront the Pasha, but Yannakos would stand between me and the door, and I felt too weak to confront him yet. Once, I almost made it past him, but his hands clutched me, and they were so cold and dead that I felt a shiver of fever running through my blood. I crawled back to my couch; tiredness was pressing on my eyelids again; I was asleep almost before I had reached the rugs.

"In my dream, I was in the Pasha's tower. He didn't speak, but led me across to his telescope. I looked through it: I saw stars and galaxies, spinning away into eternity, and then it seemed that we were treading space ourselves, a dark wilderness of interminable air. The Pasha smiled, and pointed; I looked; behind us was a small blue dot, and as we moved onwards like sunbeams, it grew tinier and tinier, gathering a halo of light around it, so that it seemed like all the other stars, and then it disappeared, and there was nothing but a mass of innumerable lights. Our world is so little, I thought, stunned and intoxicated by all I was being shown. Onward we swept through space, through a universe of endless expansion, and my soul ached, to see how beautiful it was, and unimaginable. The Pasha turned to me again, and his white hair was crowned by the blaze of countless stars; he smiled; I felt his fingers brush my own, and then his touch was gone.

"At once, I was in darkness. The air about me now was fetid and dull. I was lying on my back. I struggled to sit up—I could just make out an archway in front of me, and see the vaulted roof above my head. I was in the labyrinth—I tried to scrabble to my feet, but the roof was too low, and so I began to crawl, until the weight of stone was pressing me flat. I felt something brush at my side, and for the first time, I realized I was naked. Fingers were holding my arm; I looked round and saw Yannakos. His white lips were like maggots. I tried to brush him away, but he began to feed on me, and then I felt other lips against my skin, and it was as though I were walled up in a pit of the dead, with nothing but corpses ahead of me, behind me, blocking out my breath. And all the time, there were the creatures' lips, feeding with the greedy pleasure of grave worms on a living thing, and they were soft, and cold, and damp with my blood. I tried to move; the weight was too suffocating. I tried to scream; a creature's tongue was coiling in my mouth. I prayed for death; and as the horrors began to fade, I half believed I had been offered it.

"I woke up weak, and staring down my body, saw that there were bruises all over my flesh. But I felt purged of fever, and when I opened my bedroom door, Yannakos did not stand in the way. He followed me, of course; I ate, served by the old servant woman, and read, and occasionally dabbled in a bit of verse. I did not go near the labyrinth, and I did not see the Pasha or Haidée. Once, I tried to saddle my horse, but Yannakos, seeing this, made his views on my intentions very clear by starting to throttle me. I stumbled back from the horse; Yannakos loosed his grip; at once, I turned around and punched him as hard as I could. I had boxed for Harrow; Yannakos staggered and almost fell. Almost—but not quite. Instead, he came back at me, and I, picking up a set of spurs, slashed with them across the monster's throat. To my horror, the wound had no effect, except to stain my best shirt with the creature's blood. All that day, I was in despair. How was I ever to escape such a thing?—a thing that could not be killed? That night, I saw it on my balcony, staring at the moon—it turned around to face me, and I saw that its throat was completely healed. I shuddered—and glanced up at the moon myself. It was crescent now, and I wondered if Haidée could see it too. The time was approaching we had agreed on for our escape—but was she even alive? And would I be alive for much longer myself?

"Each night, you see, I would feel the same drowsiness, and each night, my attempts to fight it would be in vain. The Pasha would show me strange wonders—the history of the earth, or the eons of space, seeming to pass before my very eyes—but then I would find myself abandoned in the darkness of the labyrinth, and I would wake up with bruises across my skin. But as the moon waned, so also I noticed that the bruises grew less, and I wondered what Haidée had known, when she had warned me to escape beneath a moonless sky. At last, there was nothing of the moon but a sliver of light; and that night, when I slept, the Pasha did not appear to me in his tower. Instead, I dreamed that I was alone; above me stretched the dome of the colossal hall; in front of me, the kiosk, with its steps down into the dark. All was silent; I heard no voices inside my head, whispering of immortality, and yet I knew that the Pasha was summoning me, that I had to join him, in whatever it was that lay beyond the steps. I took a pace forward; still nothing stirred. My sense of calm deepened, and I knew that I was near some great secret, some key, perhaps, to the riddles of life—yes, I thought, and maybe of death as well. For surely I was entering the depths of which the Pasha had spoken before, out of which grew the Tree of Knowledge, and its forbidden fruit? I began to hurry; there was a door, wide open, at the bottom of the steps; I would pick the apple, and eat of its flesh!

" 'Byron. My Byron.'

"I stirred.

" 'My Byron!'

"I opened my eyes.

" 'Haidée.' I sat up to kiss her. She held me tight in her arms, then rose to her feet. She was more beautiful than ever, but pale, deadly pale. 'I must go back to him,' she whispered, 'but tomorrow—tomorrow we leave.'

" 'Have you been—are you all right?'

" 'Yes.' She smiled, then kissed me again urgently. 'The supplies,' she asked, still kissing me, 'are they ready yet?'

" 'Your brother has them.'

" 'You must tell him, tomorrow morning, that we are leaving at midday.'

" 'I'll do my best, but there's a problem—a slight obstruction.' Then I paused, and stared at her in sudden surprise. 'You got past Yannakos,' I said.

"Haidée glanced at the door. 'Yes,' she said. She bent down and picked up the crucifix. 'Kill him,' she said without emotion, handing it to me.

"I took the cross. 'I've tried before. He seems to survive any wound I can inflict on him.'

"'In the heart,' whispered Haidée. She walked across to the door. 'Yannakos,' she called softly. 'Yannakos.'

"Like a shambling bear, the creature answered her call. Haidée sang to him, stroking his cheeks as she gazed into his eyes. A faint look of bewilderment creased the blankness of the creature's stare. A single tear fell, down Haidée's cheek and onto Yannakos's hand. He stared at it. Then he looked up at Haidée again, and he tried to smile, but it was as though his muscles had atrophied. Haidée nodded to me; she kissed the creature on either cheek, and then I stabbed him with the crucifix deep into the heart.

"Yannakos screamed, a terrible and unearthly sound, as a fountain of blood sprayed the balcony. He fell to the floor, and there, before our very eyes, began to decompose, the flesh shriveling off the muscles and bones, the intestines melting into a hideous soup. I watched, revolted. 'Now,' said Haidée softly, 'throw him into the river.' Holding my breath, I wrapped the corpse up in a tapestry; then I flung it over the balcony into the Aheron. I turned back to Haidée. 'What was he?' I asked. 'Who was he?'

"She looked at me. 'My brother,' she said at last.

"I stared at her appalled. 'I'm sorry,' I said at last. 'So sorry.' I held her in my arms; I felt a single shudder pass through her body, then she looked up at me, and walked across to the door. 'I must go,' she said in a distant voice.

"'Tomorrow,' I asked, 'where shall I see you?'

"'In the village—you know the ruin of the old church?'

"'The great basilica?—yes.'

"'There—have the supplies sent there—and I will be with you by midday. We must escape in the sunlight.' She raised my hand to her lips. 'And then, dearest Byron—we must pray to Liberty, and hope that she will smile on us.' She kissed my hand again, then turned, and before I could hold her, she had disappeared. I didn't follow her; there seemed nothing I could say or do to help. Instead, I walked back across to the balcony. All my tiredness was gone. Over the eastern mountains, the first pinks of dawn were touching the snows.

"As soon as it was day, I slipped out to the stables, and then down the road. The three gates were open, and no one tried to stop me; I reached the village without being seen. I tethered my horse outside Gorgiou's house, then walked inside and called out Petro's name. A small boy stared at me from a corner of the room. His face looked pinched and white with hunger; I offered him a coin, but he didn't move, didn't even blink. 'Is your father here?' I asked. I bounced the coin up and down in my palm, and suddenly the boy darted across the room to snatch it from me. As he took the coin, one of his nails scratched my hand; he froze at once, as a tiny trickle of blood welled up from the scratch, and I licked it with my tongue. 'Your father?' I asked him again. The boy continued to stare, then tried to seize my hand; I smacked him lightly across the head, and I almost thought that he was going to bite me back. But then Petro walked in; he shouted at the boy, and the child ran into the shadows of another room.

"Petro watched him leave, then turned back to me. 'My Lord?' he asked. His voice sounded strange, almost distant, but his eyes gleamed as brightly as they had ever done. I told him what I had come to say. Petro nodded, and promised that everything would be ready for us.

" 'In the old basilica?' I checked.

"Petro nodded again. 'In the old basilica. The far corner, by the ruined tower.' I thanked him for his efforts; Petro bowed with a stiffness I hadn't remembered from before. I asked him if his father was well. Petro nodded. 'Very well,' he muttered. I could see that he wanted to be left alone.

" 'Good,' I said, backing through the door. 'Please give him my regards.' Petro nodded again, but said nothing more, as I mounted my horse and rode on down the path. Petro watched me go; I could almost feel his eyes in my back.

"I remembered, as though understanding it for the first time, that Yannakos had been her brother. Had Petro known the truth? I hoped not. What could be more terrible, I thought, than to see your own flesh and blood transformed

1 1 6

into such a thing? Better by far to have believed that he was truly dead. And yet Haidée had known—Haidée had lived by that creature day after day—and she a woman, and a Greek, and a slave. Yes, I thought, freedom burns brightest amongst dungeon walls—and the spirit is chainless which soars highest despite the weight of chains. I would pray to Liberty, as Haidée had told me to do—but the face of that goddess would be Haidée's own.

"I rode down the mountain track, to make certain there was nothing which might obstruct our escape. All seemed clear; ahead, in the far distance, there was a wisp of black cloud, but otherwise the sky was azure with light. I glanced up at the sun. It was high above me now—midday already, I thought. I rode back to the village, and into the basilica. Through the main doorway, there was nothing but an empty shell; my horse's hooves echoed among the ruin. I saw the tower immediately: fifteen or twenty steps beyond a bare expanse of rubble and weeds, where once the altar had stood. No one else was there. I pulled out my watch—not quite yet twelve. I waited in the tower's shade, but still no one came, and I began to grow anxious, as the minutes passed away, and the silence seemed to shimmer like the heat before my eyes. 'Damn it,' I swore. 'Not even the supplies have come.' I climbed up into my saddle again, and rode to Petro's house. I rapped on the door. There was no answer. I walked inside, and called out Petro's name—still no answer. I looked around in desperation. Had the Pasha found out about our plans? Had Petro been arrested, and all his family? Outside, tethered to a post, I found a horse, a beautiful animal which Petro could only ever have bought with my gold. I untied it, then led it back to the basilica tower. I tethered it again in the shade of the steps, then pulled out my watch. It was now almost two. I climbed quickly back onto my horse, and rode as hard as I could up the castle road.

"Again, it was empty. Not a living thing stirred, for the heat now was unbearable, and hung thick over the white rocks of the mountainside. Before I walked through the castle door, I glanced behind me; the horizon was bruised a deep purple, and along the margins of the coming storm was the gleam of electricity. We would have to hurry, I thought. Darkness, like some stealthy predator, was rising slowly to swallow the sun.

"I hurried down endless, empty corridors. 'Haidée!' I shouted, 'Haidée!' But I knew, even as I called out, that there would be no answer—and every room, every passage-way, was as empty as the last. I found myself in the labyrinth.

"I stopped to check my pistol, then hurried on, calling out as before, while I felt desperation rising in my throat, and fear, that familiar, numbing fear, which seemed to breed in the air of the labyrinth, and drain all who dared to enter it. Yet I saw nothing in the shadows this time—no sudden flickers of movement as I had done before. I found myself by the mosaics of the demoness and her Christ-like child; I tried not to look at it, and stumbled on, through the awning and into the hall. I stopped again, and looked around. Above me rose the vast dome; around me were the pillars and the colossal dungeon walls. I looked at the stairways; they were empty. I looked across the stone floor; that too was empty of the hunched forms I had seen before. 'Hai-dée!' I yelled. 'Haidée!' I gazed in despair at the pyramid of fire, my eyes rising with the flames to its crown. Then my shoulders slumped; I lowered my eyes. I was staring at the kiosk in the middle of the hall.

"Slowly, deliberately, I cocked my pistol; I glanced around again; then I walked with measured steps toward the entranceway. I stepped inside it—and waited. But nothing happened—there was no creature there—no one to stop me from walking on down the steps. I stared at what lay ahead of me—as before, the steps disappeared into darkness. I began to walk down them, and with each step I took, my grip on my pistol grew tighter, and yet more tight. The blackness seemed as close as the stale dead air; I paused, to see if my eyes could adjust to it, but I had no choice, in the end, but to feel my way on. 'The underworld, *milord,* is only for the dead.' The Pasha's words seemed to rise and echo in my ears. At that very moment, I felt something ahead of me; I raised my pistol; then I breathed in deeply, and lowered it again. I was by a door; I felt for the catch; I opened it. Beyond the door, the stairway wound on; but it was lit now by a dim light, flickering ruby-red, and I saw, painted on the walls, frescoes done in the Arabic style. The paintings seemed to illustrate the story of Adam and Eve; yet Eve stood on one side, pale and white as though drained of blood, while Adam was held in a second woman's arms, and she was feeding on him, and her face, I saw, was the same as the woman's above the kiosk door. I walked on, and the flickerings of the shadows across the stonework were growing higher now, and ever deeper red, so that I wondered if the ancients had been right, and I was indeed on steps that led to Hell. Then I saw them finish, and beyond them, there seemed to be a chamber of stone, and I realized, so deep inside the earth, that this could only be a burial place. I raised my pistol, ready to fire; then I walked through the doorway, and into the crypt."

Lord Byron paused. Rebecca, having sat in silence for so long, was reluctant to speak, to hurry him on. So she sat motionless, watching the vampire, who seemed to be staring, not at her, but at whatever it was he had found those long years ago, in that chamber of stone. He stroked his chin with his fingertips, and his face was expressionless; yet his eyes seemed to gleam with a mysterious smile.

"There were flames," he said at last. "Flames from a chasm at the far end of the room, and in front of the flames, an ancient altar stood, with inscriptions to Hades, the Lord of Death. Haidée was by the altar. She lay on her back, lovely and desolate, her veils ripped, her tunic torn away from her breasts, and the Pasha was feeding on them, like an infant drawing on its mother's milk. Sometimes he would seem to pause, and stroke the girl's breast with his cheeks and his lips, and I realized he was toying with the flow of her blood. Haidée stirred and moaned, but she couldn't rise, for the Pasha was holding her wrists with his arms, and she was weak, of course, very weak. Yet how tenderly the Pasha drank from her; again, he stroked the side of her breast with his cheek, and he dyed her nipple red with the blood on his tongue. Haidée gasped suddenly, and her fingers tore at air; she clenched her legs around the Pasha's own. I shook. Steadying my arm, I raised my pistol; I took a step forward; I placed the pistol against the Pasha's head.

"He turned slightly, to look at me. His eyes gleamed silver; his cheeks were fat and full; dabblings of blood flecked his lips and mustache. He smiled, baring his sharp, white teeth at me, and I thought he was about to spring at my throat. Yet when I pushed the pistol harder against the side of his head, he teetered and fell, like a bloated tick being knocked off its host, and then I realized—of course—that such an image was nothing less than the literal truth. The Pasha lay on his side, ruddy, swollen, gorged on blood—and when he tried to lift himself, he could only rest his head on the altar's base. It was as though he were drunk, I realized, so intoxicated that he could barely move.

"'Kill him,' Haidée whispered softly. She had risen to her feet, but had to lean upon my arm. 'Kill him,' she said again. 'Shoot him through the heart.'

"The Pasha laughed. 'Kill me?' he said scornfully. Yet his voice sounded remarkably beautiful in my ears, and even Haidée seemed almost entranced by it. But then she crossed into the shadows, and I saw her pick up a sword. She must have left it there earlier, ready for just such a moment as this.

"'A bullet bites deeper,' I said. 'Please, Haidée—put it down.'

"The Pasha laughed again. 'You see, my pretty slave?— your dashing liberator will never kill me—he's far too greedy for all I could reveal.'

"'Kill him,' said Haidée. She screamed suddenly. 'Kill him now!'

"My hand on the pistol stayed as steady as before. 'The

basilica,' I whispered, 'the ruined tower—wait for me there.'

"Haidée stared at me. 'Do not be tempted.' She reached up to stroke my cheek, then whispered in my ear. 'Do not betray me, Byron, or you will be damned in Hell.' She turned, and crossed to the steps. 'The ruined tower, then,' she said—and was gone. The two of us, the Pasha and I, were left alone. I crossed to him. 'I will kill you,' I said, still aiming the pistol directly at his heart. 'Do not delude yourself, Your Excellency, that I will not.'

"The Pasha smiled lazily. 'Delude myself?'

"I stared at him, and my hand began to shake. I steadied it again. 'What are you?' I asked. 'What kind of—thing?'

"'You know what I am.'

"'A monster—a *vardoulacha*—a drinker of human blood.'

"'I must drink blood—yes.' The Pasha nodded. 'But I was a man once—much like you. And as for now, my dear Lord Byron—I own the secret of immortality—as you well know.' He smiled at me, and nodded again. 'As you well know.'

"I shook my head. 'Immortality.' I stared at him with disgust. 'But you're not alive. You are a dead thing. You may feed on life, but you don't have it yourself—don't ever think that—you are wrong—you *are* wrong.'

"'No, *milord.*' He raised a hand to me. 'Do you not see? Immortality lies in a dimension beyond life. You must clear your body of clay, and your mind of mortal thoughts.' He brushed my fingers, and I felt the pulse of something warm and living in his touch. 'Do not be afraid, *milord.* Be young and old; be human and divine; be beyond life, and beyond death. If you can be all these things together in your being and your thoughts, then—then, *milord*—you will have discovered immortality.'

"I stared at him. His voice had the sweetness and the wisdom of an angel. My arm fell to my side. 'I don't understand,' I said helplessly. 'How can this be true?'

" 'Do you doubt me?'

"I didn't answer him. But I continued to stare as his eyes grew deeper, and they seemed like the waters of some beautiful lake, rising to cool my revulsion and fear. 'Long ago,' the Pasha said softly, 'in the city of Alexandria, I was a teacher of the sciences. I studied chemistry, medicine, philosophy; I read the ancient sages, the Egyptians and the Greeks; I made myself the master of buried wisdoms and long-forgotten truths. I began to dream that death might be conquered. I dreamed of discovering the very elixir of life.' He paused. 'A fateful ambition—and one that was to decide my destiny. It came on me in the three hundred and ninety-ninth year of the Muslim era, during the reign of the Khalif al-Hakim—by the Christian reckoning, in the year one thousand and twenty-one.'

"I could feel myself drowning in his eyes. I had to cling to my skepticism. I had to believe he was lying to me. But I could not. 'So you found it, then,' I said, 'the elixir of life.'

"But the Pasha shook his head. 'No,' he said. 'Not then, not since, although I search for it in the modern sciences as I searched for it in the old.' He shook his head again. 'If it exists at all, then so far it has eluded me.'

"I gestured at him with the pistol. 'Then how . . . ?' My voice trailed away.

" 'Can you not guess?'

"I could, of course. I said nothing, but yes—I could guess.

"The Pasha reached for my hand again. He pulled me down close beside him. 'I was seduced,' he whispered. 'For a year in Alexandria, the cry had been going up: "Lilith is come! Lilith the blood-drinker is come!" Bodies had been found, drained white, abandoned by the crossroads and in the fields. People had come to me—my reputation was great—they were afraid. I told them to keep up their courage, that there was no Lilith, no harlot-princess who might drink their blood. And yet even as I told them this, I knew otherwise, for I was being visited by Lilith myself—shown, as I have shown you, the heights of immortality.' He gripped my arm. 'These heights, *milord,* they are real. If I tell you now, what happened to me, it is only so you may comprehend all it is that I am offering you—the wisdom, the delight, the unearthly power. Have you heard of Lilith? Do you know who she truly is? In Jewish legend, she was Adam's first wife—but men have worshipped her since the dawn of time. In Egypt, in Ur, among the Canaanites, she has been known as Queen of the Succubi, the queen of all those who—like myself—have the wisdom that comes from drinking blood.' He stroked my throat, then ran a finger down the front of my shirt. 'Understand this, then, *milord*—I do not offer you life—I do not offer you death—but I offer you something as ancient as the rocks themselves. Prepare yourself for it. Prepare, *milord,* and be grateful.'

"He kissed me savagely. I felt his teeth against my lip, and tasted the scent of blood in his mouth. Haidée's blood. I flinched, and the Pasha must have felt it, for he grappled me, and tried to hold me down, but I pulled myself free and rose back to my feet. The Pasha stared up at me. 'Do not be afraid, *milord,*' he said. He reached out to stroke my boot. 'I too fought my seduction—at first.' He raised his finger, slowly, up my leg; I aimed my pistol; the Pasha saw me and laughed, a cold sneer of greed and contempt. Suddenly, like a wild creature, his jaws open, he sprang at my throat. I fired, and in the confusion, I missed my aim, but the bullet caught him in the abdomen. The Pasha held his wound, watched the blood as it slipped out over his hand, then looked up at me in astonishment. I fired again; this time, I hit the Pasha in the chest, and the impact hurled him back against the altar stone. 'I choose life,' I said, standing over him. 'I reject your gift.' I aimed at his heart, I fired; his chest disappeared into a mess of bone and blood. The Pasha moaned and his whole body twitched; he raised his hand as though reaching for me; then the arm dropped back down and the body was still. I touched it with the edge of my boot, then brought myself to feel its pulse—there was nothing, no trace of life. I stared at the Pasha one second more, as he lay with his head against the altar to Hades; then I turned and left him—a dead thing at last in that shrine to the dead.'"

Chapter VI

*If I could explain at length the real causes which
have contributed to increase this perhaps natural
temperament of mine—this Melancholy which hath
made me a bye-word—nobody would wonder—but
this is impossible without doing much mischief.—I
do not know what other men's lives have been—but
I cannot conceive anything more strange than some
of the earlier parts of mine—I have written my
memoirs—but omitted all the really consequential
& important parts—from deference to the dead—to
the living—and to those who must be both.—*

LORD BYRON, *Detached Thoughts*

The sky over Aheron had changed to a terrible darkness, as though in mourning for the castle's dead lord. My horse whinnied with fear as I climbed onto him, and spurred him down the winding road. I saw guards on the battlements with flaming torches, and I heard them shout at me as I galloped through their open gates. I glanced back at them; they pointed to the village, and shouted again, what seemed words of warning, but the wind screamed across the crags, and their voices were lost. I galloped on, and had soon left the battlements behind; I reined in my horse; ahead of me, ghostly white beneath a heavy green sky, the village lay.

"It was as deserted as ever, but for some reason, the state of my nerves perhaps, or some presentiment, I drew out my pistol again, and looked into the empty ruins, as though afraid of what I might see in them. But there was nothing—and so I spurred my horse on toward the basilica. But as I passed Petro's house, I saw a small form standing motionless by the side of the road. 'Lord Byron!' he called out, in a high, piping voice. I reined in my horse to stare at him. It was Petro's son, the small boy with the pinched face, who had taken the coin from me that morning. 'Please, Lord Byron, come inside,' he said. I shook my head, but the boy pointed to the house, and said a single word—'Haidée.' And so then, of course, I dismounted and followed him.

"I walked into the house. All was dark inside—no candles, no fire. I heard the door swinging shut behind me, and then a bolt being drawn. I looked around, startled—but the boy stared up at me, his solemn face gleaming pale in the dark, and pointed again toward a second room. I walked toward it. 'Haidée,' I called out. 'Haidée!' There was no answer. But then I heard giggling, soft and high-pitched, coming from the room ahead of me. Three or four childish voices began to sing: 'Haidée, Haidée, Haidée!' There was more giggling, and then silence. I pushed open the door.

"Four wide pairs of eyes stared up at me—three girls, and a tiny boy. Their faces were as pale and solemn as their brother's; then one of them, the prettiest of the girls, smiled at me, and her childish face seemed suddenly the cruelest and most depraved thing I had ever seen. She bared her teeth; her eyes gleamed silver; her lips, I could see now, were red and whorish. Then I realized that they were dyed with blood; all four of the children were crouched over a woman's body, and when I took a step forward, I could see that their meal was Petro's mother, her face frozen in a death agony of indescribable horror. Unthinkingly, I bent down beside her; I reached out to stroke her hair; and then she too suddenly stared at me, her eyes burning, and she rose up, her teeth gleaming as she hissed with thirst. All the children giggled with delight as their grandmother reached up to slash at my throat—but she was slow. I stepped back, aimed my pistol and sent a bullet through her chest. Then I felt nails against my back—the fifth child, the one who had guided me in, was trying to climb onto me. I shook him off, and then, instinctively, as he fell against the floor, I fired a bullet into him as well. His skull was shattered, and the other children shrunk back; but then, to my horror, the grandmother began to stir again, and then the child, and all of them began to stalk me, and I didn't know which was worse, the sight of the boy staring at me with his head half-blown away, or the hunger in the eyes of the other children, all of them still so young and beautiful. The smallest boy ran at me; I cuffed him with my hand, then stumbled back, closing the first door behind me, and then, as the *vardou-lachas* opened it again, pushing at the door that led out onto the street. It was barred—damn it, I thought—I had forgotten about that. I struggled with the bolt, and as I fumbled with it, the children were running at me again, their tiny mouths open, a gleam of triumph in their eyes. One of them scratched me; but then the door was open at last, and I fell out through it, slamming it shut again before they could follow me. I leaned against the door, feeling their small bodies as they pushed against it; then I moved, as fast as I could, and climbed onto my horse before they could cross to me. I galloped down the road; I glanced back over my shoulder, and saw the children staring after me, sobbing, a strange animal sound of frustrated desire. I did not look around a second time—I had to reach the basilica. I had to find out if Haidée was still alive.

"Ahead of me, I saw a glow of flame. I cantered up to the basilica arch; a figure stood in front of me, his arms uplifted, silhouetted against the orange of the fire. He laughed, a cruel sound of mockery and triumph; he stared at me, and laughed again; it was Gorgiou. He leapt at me as I passed, but my horse's hoof caught him on the side of the head, and he was sent stumbling back. I rode as hard as I could across the basilica floor. Dark figures turned to look at me; I recognized the priest; he, like all the others, had the silver gleam of death in his eyes. The creatures were gathered in a mob at the far end of the church, around the ruined tower. I rode toward them, crushing those ahead of me, brushing away the others as they reached up to pull me down.

"'Byron!' I heard Haidée's scream. She was standing on the highest step, dressed in the costume of a servant boy. She held a flaming torch in either hand, and in front of her blazed the fire she had lit. She ran past it down the steps;

one of the monsters leapt at her, but I aimed my pistol and fired, and he staggered back, a bullet in his chest. I looked for her horse; then I saw it, dead, its blood still being drained by thirsty human leeches.

"'Jump!' I shouted to Haidée; she leapt and almost fell, but she clutched onto my horse's mane, and as I rode on, I was able to pull her up until she was safely in the saddle, and my arms. I couldn't see now where we were riding; we were stumbling across rocks and past olive trees, and I knew, if we were to escape, that we had to find the road. Then suddenly, forking above the jagged mountain peaks, a crackle of lightning lit up the sky.

"'To the right!' Haidée shouted.

"I nodded and looked. I could see the road now, winding down from the castle, and then, in a second flash of lightning, I saw something else, an army of black wraiths, drifting aimlessly out through the battlement gates and scattering like leaves before the roar of the storm. As we reached the road, they seemed to smell our blood, and we heard their squeakings above the wind, but they were far behind us, and the road ahead was clear. We had soon lost them around the mountain bend.

"I began to think we were safe. But then, as I rode beneath the archway that had marked the ancient limit of the town, I felt something heavy leap onto my back, and I was pulled from the saddle down into the dust. There was breath against the back of my neck; it smelled rotten and dead. I tried to twist around, struggling in the grip of my assailant, whose nails felt like claws as they dug into my arms.

"'Don't let him bite you!' Haidée screamed. 'Byron, don't let him draw your blood!'

"The creature seemed distracted by the sound of her voice; he glanced around, and as he did so, I was able to slip free, and look up, and see the thing that had been holding me. It was Petro—but how changed! His skin now was as waxy as a newly dead corpse's, but his eyes gleamed like those of a jackal, and when he saw me free, they blazed red, and he leapt at me again. I reached for his throat and tried to push him away, but he was too strong, and I smelled the corpse breath again as his jaws came closer and closer to my throat. The stench was so overpowering I thought I would faint.

"'Petro!' I heard Haidée shout. 'Petro!'

"Then I felt saliva dripping on my face, and I knew that I couldn't hold him off anymore. I prepared for death—or rather, the living death that had been the village's fate. But then there was a thud—and a second thud. Petro rolled off my body. I looked up. Haidée stood there with a heavy stone. It was wet with blood and matted hair. Petro lay still at her feet; then he began to stir again, clawing with his fingers toward her, and Haidée drew out the crucifix from underneath her cloak, aimed at her brother's heart, and drove it in as hard as she could. Petro screamed, as his brother had done; a soft fountain of blood welled and bubbled up from his chest. Haidée pulled the crucifix out from the corpse; she lay down beside it; she began to weep, in racking, tearless sobs.

I held her; then, when her tears began to flow at last, I took her gently by the arm and led her back toward the horse. I said nothing—what could I have said?

"'Ride hard,' Haidée whispered, as I shook out the reins. 'Leave this place behind us. Leave it forever.' I nodded; I spurred the horse; we began to gallop down the mountain road."

There was a brief pause; Lord Byron gripped the sides of his chair, and breathed in hard.

"And did you leave it?" Rebecca asked impatiently. "Forever, I mean?"

Lord Byron smiled faintly. "Miss Carville, please—this is my story. You have been very good so far, allowing me to tell it as I wish. Don't let's spoil things."

"I'm sorry . . ."

"But?"

Rebecca smiled in acknowledgment. "Yes—*but*—you

haven't said what happened to the village. At least tell me about that."

Lord Byron raised an eyebrow.

"How could they all have changed so soon, I mean? Was it the Pasha? Was it Gorgiou?"

Lord Byron smiled faintly again. "Those were questions—you can imagine—that weren't too distant from my own mind at the time. I didn't want to press Haidée—didn't want her thinking—remembering—what had happened to her family. But then again, as the storm grew worse, I was also desperate to find some shelter—I needed to know if it would be safe, or whether we should continue to ride on through the night."

"Your horse—if he was carrying both of you—he must have started to flag, I suppose?"

"No. We met someone, you see—by the same bridge where we had met Gorgiou before—we were riding over it, when suddenly a horseman loomed out of the rain, a second horse in tow, and called out to me by name. It was Viscillie. He had been waiting for me. 'Desert you, My Lord?' he asked, grinning beneath his huge mustache. 'Just because a *vardoulacha* bribed me to?' He spat, and abused the Pasha gloriously. 'Didn't he know,' Viscillie asked, 'that a bandit loves his honor as a priest loves gold and boys?' He launched into another volley of abuse, then pointed to a shelter he had built among the rocks. 'We'll ride at dawn, My Lord, but for now—the girl needs rest. There's fire, and food'—he winked—'yes, and raki too.' How could I argue with him?—it was hard enough, just thanking him. Remember—look to a robber if you want a good-hearted man.

"Even Haidée seemed to revive, once we were camped around the fire. She still hardly spoke, but after our meal, I began to ask her about our prospects for escape—would the creatures in the village pursue us, did she think? Haidée shook her head. Not if the Pasha were indeed destroyed, she said. I asked her what she meant. She paused, then, in a halting voice, began to explain: the Pasha, when he made a *vardoulacha* from a man, created monsters that seemed to have no existence at all beyond their thirst for human blood. Some of these creatures were mere zombies, dependent entirely upon the Pasha's will; others were transfused with animal ferocity, infecting those they drank from with a craving as desperate as their own. She supposed . . . and then she paused, and Viscillie handed her the raki flask. Haidée drank from it. She started again. She supposed, she said, swallowing, that her father had been made a creature of the second kind. She looked up at me. Her eyes were gleaming with passionate hate. '*He* would have known what would happen, then. *He* would have done it quite deliberately—to inflict a living death on my father, on my family, on all the village. But Byron—if you did kill him—then the creatures he made will start to die as well, and we are safe from them. *If* you killed him.'

"'What do you mean, *if?* I shot him; I saw him die.'

"Viscillie grunted. 'You shot him through the heart, My Lord?'

"'Yes.'

"'You are certain of that, My Lord?'

"'Damn you, Viscillie, I can split a walking-stick at twenty paces; how would I miss a human heart at two?'

"Viscillie shrugged. 'Then we have only the Tartars to fear.'

"'What, the Pasha's guards? Why would they be bothered chasing us?'

"Viscillie shrugged again. 'To avenge the death of Vakhel Pasha, of course.' He looked up at me, and smiled. 'Loyalty is something they share with bandits, you see.'

"'*Share?* No—they couldn't approach such loyalty.'

"Viscillie grinned at the compliment, but he had clearly not been bogging it, and so his warning disturbed me. 'Surely,' I asked, 'the dead things will have fed on the guards as well?'

"'Let us hope so.' Viscillie took out his knife, and stared at it. 'But if I was a Tartar, I would have torched the village, and then waited for dawn.'

" 'The sun can kill those creatures?'

" 'That is what we are taught, My Lord.'

" 'But I've seen the Pasha in the light of day.'

" '*He* can survive anything,' said Haidée suddenly, clasping her arms around herself. 'He is older than the mountains, and more deadly than the snake—are a few rays of sun going to threaten *him?* But it is true, nevertheless—the sun does weaken him, and he is feeblest of all when there is no moonlight to restore him to his strength.' She took my hands, and kissed them with sudden passion and exhilaration. 'That is why we must travel at first light tomorrow—travel as hard as we have never done before.' She nodded. 'Then we will win our liberty.' She smiled at me. 'Did you pray to the goddess, Byron, as I asked you to?'

" 'Yes.'

" 'And is she with us?'

" 'Of course,' I whispered. I kissed her lightly on her brow. 'How could she not be?' I told her to sleep.

"Viscillie, who seemed made of rock, spent the night on watch. I tried to stay awake with him, but I was soon nodding, and before I knew it, he was whispering in my ear that it was almost dawn. I looked out at the sky; the storm had long blown over, and the early morning air was soft and clear.

" 'The sun should be hot today,' whispered Haidée, joining me in the road.

"I looked at her. Her cheeks seemed as fresh as the dawn in the east, and her eyes gleamed with the light of the coming day. I could see that at last, through all the horror of her memories, she was glimpsing a freedom only dreamed of until now. 'We'll make it,' I said, squeezing her hand. She nodded shortly, then stepped up into her saddle. She waited until Viscillie and I were ready in our own; then she shook out her reins, and cantered down the track.

"We rode as hard as we could, while the sun grew hotter, and rose higher in the sky. Occasionally, Viscillie would dismount and climb up the sides of cliffs or ravines; when he rejoined us, he would smile and shake his head. But around midday, as he clambered down hurriedly from the top of a crag, we saw that he was frowning, and when he joined us he muttered that he had seen a cloud of dust, a long way off, but moving.

"'This way?' I asked.

"Viscillie shrugged.

"'Would they be riding faster than us?'

"Viscillie shrugged again. 'If they were Tartars, they might be.'

"I swore softly, staring at the road ahead of us, then looking back over my shoulder at the cloudless blue sky. 'Where do we have to get to, Viscillie?' I asked slowly. 'To be safe?'

"'The limits of the pashalik. They wouldn't dare pursue a noble foreign lord beyond that—not when he is a friend of the great Ali Pasha.'

"'You are certain of that?'

"'Yes, My Lord.'

"'Where is this limit?'

"'The Missolonghi road. There is a small fortress there.'

"'And how long will it take us to reach it?'

"'A couple of hours. One and a half, maybe—if we ride hard.'

"Haidée glanced up at the sky. 'It's almost midday. From then on, the sun starts to sink.' She looked back at me. 'We must ride more than hard. We must ride as though the Devil is at our back.'

"And so we did. An hour passed, and we heard nothing in the stillness of the heat but our horses' hooves, pounding the white dust of the track, carrying us ever nearer to the Missolonghi road. We paused by a brook, a pleasant spot of green among the rocks and crags, to allow our horses to drink; Haidée dismounted, but then, as she filled her water bottle, she glanced around and saw a faint cloud of dust rising in the distance.

"'Is that what you saw?' she asked Viscillie. We both looked.

"'They're getting nearer,' I said.

"Viscillie nodded. 'Come on,' he said, raising his horse's head from the brook. 'We still have a way to go.'

"The cloud of dust, though, however hard we rode, could not be shaken off. Just the reverse—it grew thicker all the time, so that soon it seemed to be overshadowing us. And then I heard Haidée gasp; I looked around, and saw a glint of metal, a horse's bit, and heard the distant thud of hooves. We rounded an outcrop of rock, and our pursuers were lost, before we could even be certain they had spotted us. But the road was descending now, straightening as the rocks and cliffs fell away, and we would easily be seen on the open plain.

"'How far?' I shouted at Viscillie. He pointed. I could just make out, in the far distance, the white line of a road, and guarding it, a small fort.

"'Castle of Ali Pasha,' shouted Viscillie. 'We must reach there. Ride, My Lord—ride!'

"Our pursuers had rounded the cliff now, and seen us. I heard their howls of triumph, and looking around, saw them start to spread out as they hunted us across the plain. I heard a shot fired, and my horse almost stumbled and fell, and I swore as I struggled to reach for my pistols from my bag.

"'Just ride, My Lord!' shouted Viscillie, as another shot was fired. 'Tartars cannot aim!' But they could ride; even as Viscillie was shouting at me, three of them broke from the others, and began to gallop toward us. One of them reached Haidée, and laughed as she swung vainly at him with a dagger. He toyed with her, feinting and wheeling, and as he did so, I managed to find my pistol at last. I had loaded it before; I prayed it would fire. The Tartar took Haidée by the hair; she clung on desperately to her reins as he yanked at her. The Tartar broke, then closed in again, and this time, took Haidée's arm. He laughed—and then I fired, and the Tartar rose up high in his saddle, as though he were giving a salute, only to topple backward, and be dragged by his ankles back along the road. As the startled horse galloped through their ranks, our pursuers paused, and I could feel my spirits rise now, for we could see the gates of the fortress being opened to us. The Tartars must have seen them too, for suddenly we heard yells of fury and derision, and the sound of their horses now was almost in our ears. I glanced around; was the Pasha with them? I couldn't see him. I glanced around again. He wasn't there. Of course not—he was dead, I had seen him die.

"'My Lord, ride!' shouted Viscillie. Bullets whistled past us—and then there was an answering crackle of fire from the fortress wall, and some of the Tartars fell back. Most, though, did not, and I thought, as we galloped up toward the open gates, that we would not make it. I felt a hand on my arm. I looked around; a Tartar was grinning in my face. He reached for my throat, but as he did so, I dodged his grip, and my horse knocked his own, and the Tartar was sent crashing from his saddle. I looked around for Haidée; she had reached the gates.

"'My Lord, quick, quick!' shouted Viscillie from ahead of me. I spurred my exhausted steed; the horsemen behind me fell away; as I rode past them, the fortress gates swung shut.

"We were safe, for a while at least. But even behind walls, we felt uncomfortable. The commander of the garrison was surly and suspicious. How could he not have been, for our arrival and appearance had been strange enough, but there had also been the fury with which the Tartars had given us chase. I told the commander that they had been *klephti*—he gave me a look of frank disbelief. But he grew more polite when I emphasized that I was a close friend of Ali Pasha, and when he saw the letter of proof I bore, he grew almost Greek in his servility. But I didn't trust him—and after a short break to refresh ourselves and make certain that the Tartars had indeed returned to the hills, we pressed on with our journey through the afternoon. The Missolonghi road, although scarcely crowded, seemed a veritable thoroughfare after the loneliness of the mountain track, and being in better condition as well, it enabled us to make fairly good speed. Of course, we kept a careful watch on the distance we had crossed, but we saw no clouds of dust rising up in the sky, and after a while, we started to feel more secure. We spent the night in Arta, a pleasant enough place, and where we were able to hire soldiers, ten of them, to guard us on the journey that still lay ahead. Now I felt almost confident. We didn't start again until late in the morning, for Haidée was exhausted and slept for almost twelve hours. I didn't choose to wake her. Platonism too, then, continued undisturbed.

"Yet how could I blame Haidée for reserving herself in this way, until that moment when she could know herself to be truly free?" Lord Byron paused; his eyes widened; he stared into the darkness as though it were the vanished past. "Her purity . . ." He paused, looking back into Rebecca's eyes. "Her purity," he whispered, "had been as fierce and untamed as the passion in her soul—a flame of hope tended through the long years of bondage, and if I loved her then as I have loved nothing else since—well—it was because this flame had illuminated her—touched her wild beauty with immortal fire. I had no wish to steal what would scorch me—for all that my own blood seemed like lava in the veins—and so I waited. We pressed on to Missolonghi, and I knew, for as long as Haidée kept herself from me, that she could still not be certain that the Pasha was in his grave.

"On the third afternoon of our journey, we reached the shores of Lake Trihonida. We paused here, for the lake was near Viscillie's native village, and he suggested adding to our bodyguard with his own countrymen. He had to ride into the mountains; so in his absence, we sheltered in a cave, where the air was heavy with the scent of wild roses, and the lake's blue crystal could just be seen through the trees. I held Haidée in my arms, pulling away her pageboy's cap so that her long hair spilled free. I stroked it, and she ran her fingers through mine, and we lay in loving solitude, as though there were no other life beneath the heavens but our own.

"I stared out at the mountains across the lake, and felt my spirits blaze with hope and joy. I turned to Haidée. 'He can't reach us,' I said. 'Not here. He is dead.'

"Haidée stared at me, her eyes large, languishingly dark. Slowly, almost imperceptibly, she nodded her head.

"'He told me once that he loved you. Was that true, do you think?'

"Haidée said nothing, but lay her cheek against my heart. 'I don't know,' she said at last. 'It may be.' She paused. 'Love, though?—no, it couldn't have been love.'

"'What, then?'

"Haidée lay still on my chest. She could hear my heart, I knew, beating for her. 'Blood,' she said at last. 'Yes. The taste of my blood.'

"'Blood?'

"'You saw—saw what it did to him. He was intoxicated by it. I don't know why. It never happened when he drank from other people.' She sat up suddenly, clasping her knees. 'Only when he drank from me.' She shivered. 'Only me.'

"She reached for me again. She kissed me. I could feel her body shaking. 'Byron,' she whispered, 'is it true? Am I really no longer a slave?' She kissed me a second time, and I felt her tears on my skin. 'Tell me I am free,' she said, stroking her cheeks against mine. 'Show me I am free.' She rose to her feet; her cloak fell away; she tugged at her sash, so that her breasts were no longer concealed by her shirt. One after another, her clothes fell, and lay scattered at her feet. She bent low and her eyes gleamed dark—our lips drew near—they clung into a kiss. Haidée's arm clasped my shoulders, while mine, arcing around her head, was half-buried in the tresses it held. We were all in all to each other now—I had no feeling, no thought, but of Haidée—of her tongue's velvet touch—of the soft warmth of her nakedness against my own. We loved—and were beloved—drinking the other's sighs—until they ended in broken gasps, and I thought that if souls could die of joy, then ours would surely perish now, and yet it was not death, no, not death at all—

not as we shuddered and melted in the other's arms—it was not death. At last, by degrees, our senses were restored, only to be overcome and dashed on again, so that sounding against my chest, Haidée's heart felt as though it would never beat apart from mine again.

"Outside now, the afternoon was darkening. Haidée slept. So beautiful she was—so fierce in love before, now stirless, trusting, gentle. The solitude of love and of the night was filled with the same tranquil power; in the distance, the shadows of the rocks were advancing across the lake; in my arms, Haidée stirred and whispered my name, but she did not wake, and her breathing was as soft as the twilight breeze. I watched her, pillowed on my chest. Again, in that silent place, I felt how utterly alone we were, alone with the plenitude and richness of life. I gazed at Haidée, and knew Adam's wonder at the gift of Eve, with the whole world mine, a paradise I believed would never be lost.

"I looked up. It was almost night now. The sun must have set, and the mountains were blue silhouettes against the stars. Above one peak gleamed the moon, waxing again—and then, just for a moment, I thought I saw a dark form pass in front of it. 'Who's that?' I whispered softly. No answer broke the stillness of the night. I stirred, and Haidée looked up at me, her eyes suddenly wide and bright. 'What have you seen?' she asked. I said nothing, but pulled on a cloak and reached for a sword. Haidée followed me. We walked outside. No sound, no movement, broke the calm.

"And then Haidée pointed. 'There,' she whispered, clutching my arm. I looked—and saw a body lying among the flowers. I bent down and rolled it over. The wide eyes of one of the guards stared up at me. He was dead. He seemed drained of blood, and a look of unbearable terror disfigured his face. I looked up at Haidée, then rose to my feet to hold her in my arms. At that moment, ahead of us, there was the spurting of a torch, and then another, until there was an arc of flames ringing us, and I saw, behind each one, a Tartar face. None of them spoke. I raised my sword. Slowly, the line parted. A figure, cloaked in black, stepped out from the dark.

"'Put up your sword,' said the Pasha.

"Dumbly, I stared at him. Then I laughed, and shook my head.

"'Very well.' The Pasha pulled aside his cloak. His wounds, where I had shot him, were still damp with blood. He drew a pistol from his belt. 'I thank you for the opportunity,' he said. 'I owe you this.'

"He cocked the pistol. The stillness, in that brief instant, was like ice. Then Haidée threw herself in front of me, and I pushed her aside, and as I heard the pistol shot explode in my ears, so also I felt a pain that knocked me to the ground. I clutched at my side—it was wet. Haidée called out my name, but as she ran to me, she was held by two of the Tartar guards, and at once she froze, not sobbing, but pale and stern, so that her face seemed chilled by the kiss of death.

"The Pasha stared at her. Then he gestured, and a third guard stepped forward. He held what looked like sacking in his hand. The Pasha lifted his slave girl's chin. I watched his lip quiver, and then it was fixed again, as though sorrow or disdain forbade him to smile. 'Take her,' he said.

"Haidée glanced at me. 'Byron,' she whispered. 'Goodbye.' Then she went with the guards, and I saw her no more.

"'How touching,' hissed the Pasha, close to my face. 'So it was for her—for *her, milord*—that you spurned all I had to offer you?'

"'Yes,' I said softly. I twisted my neck, so that I could stare into his eyes. 'It was not her fault. I took her. She never wanted to come with me.'

"The Pasha laughed. 'Such nobility!'

"'It's the truth.'

"'No.' The Pasha's smile faded. 'No, *milord,* it is not. She is as guilty of treachery as you. For both of you, then—punishment.'

"'Punishment? What will you do to her?'

"'We have a penalty in this part of the world, an amusing

one, for faithlessness. It will do quite well enough for a slave. But I would forget about her, *milord*—it is your own fate that should be disturbing you.' He reached over to my side, and dabbled his fingers in my blood. Then he licked them, and smiled. 'You are dying,' he said. 'Would you welcome that—death?' I said nothing. The Pasha frowned, and suddenly his eyes gleamed as though lit by red fire, and his face was darkened by rage and despair. 'I would have given you immortality,' he whispered. 'I would have had you share eternity with me.' He kissed me, brutally, his teeth cutting my lips. 'And instead—betrayal!' He kissed me again, and his tongue licked at the blood in my mouth. 'So pale you are already, *milord*—so pale and beautiful.' He stretched across me, so that his wound touched and blended with mine. 'Shall I let it rot, your beauty?—drink out your mind?—set you to scrubbing my castle floors?' He laughed, and tore away my cloak, so that I lay naked beneath him. He kissed me again and again, pressing himself tight against me, and then I felt his fingernail stroke across my throat. Blood, in a thin line, welled up from the scratch. The Pasha lapped at it, while with his nails he tore delicate ribbons from my chest. My heart was beating loudly in my ears; I looked up at the stars, and the sky seemed to be pulsing like some tortured living thing. I felt the Pasha's lips, drinking from my wounds, and when he looked up at me again, his mustache and beard were matted with gore, my gore, and he smiled at me. He bent down close, to whisper in my ear. 'I give you knowledge,' he said. 'Knowledge and eternity. I curse you with them.'

"Then there was nothing in my ears but the pulsing of my blood. I screamed: my chest was being ripped apart, but even as the pain seared my every nerve, I felt the quickening I had known with Haidée, the shiver of passion. The delight and the pain both rose until I thought they could rise no more, and yet still they rose, up and up, like twin themes of music soaring into the night—and then, somehow, I was above them both. Feelings remained—and yet it wasn't I who was feeling them. The blood beat on—and the Pasha's tongue now was against my living heart. A great calm descended on me, as the blood slipped thick and barely felt from my veins. I looked at the trees, the lake, the mountain peaks—all were dyed red. I looked up at the sky; my blood seemed splashed across it. As the Pasha drank on, I felt myself drawn into him, and then beyond him, and I felt myself become the world. The beating thickened and slowed. My blood across the sky was growing dark. A final pulse—and then stillness. There was nothing. All was dead—the lake, the breeze, the moon, the stars. Darkness was the universe.

"And then—then—from that motionless silence—a pulse again—a single beat. I opened my eyes—I could see. I looked down at myself. I seemed stripped of all my skin, so naked that there was nothing but flesh, and organs, and arteries and veins, shimmering in the moon, viscous and ripe. And yet, although I was flayed like an anatomist's corpse—I could move. As I stirred and rose, I felt a terrible strength start to flow through my limbs. My heart was quickening. I looked around—the night seemed touched with silver, and the shadows were blue and deep with life. I moved toward them; my feet touched the ground; each blade of grass, each tiny flower, filled me with pleasure, as though my nerves were harp strings to be brushed against, and as I moved, the rhythms of life hung rich in the air, and I felt a great hunger for them. I began to run. I didn't know what I hunted, but I moved like the breath of the wind, through woods and over mountain passes, and all the time, the hunger inside me grew more and more desperate. I bounded up a cliff of rocks, and smelled something golden and warm ahead of me. I had to have it. I would have it. I shouted my need to the sky. But no human voice came out from my throat. I listened to my cry—the howling of a wolf.

"A flock of goats looked up, startled. I pressed myself flat against the rock. One of the goats stood just below me. I could smell it—the blood in its veins and muscles, animating it, giving it life. The tiniest corpuscle would seem like a fleck of gold. I leapt. With my jaws, I ripped at the goat's neck. Blood, in a thick warm spray, washed my face. I drank it, and it was as though I had never understood what taste could be before. Speed I had too, and eyesight, and understanding. I would observe the wide eyes of a terrified kid, and almost pause with delight that such a thing could exist—how delicate it was, how intricate! When I held the creature, the beat of its life beneath my claws filled me with an exquisite joy. And then I would drink—and feel the joy quickening through my own veins. How many of the flock did I kill? I couldn't tell. I was drunk on them—the pleasure of killing left me with no time for thought. There was only sensation, pure and distilled. There was only life, all around and inside me again."

Rebecca, who had been staring at the vampire, her eyes wide with horror, slowly shook her head. "Life?" she asked softly. "Life? But it wasn't yours. No. You had passed beyond life now . . . hadn't you?"

Lord Byron looked at her, and his eyes were like glass. "The pleasure, though . . ." he whispered. "The pleasure of that hour . . ." Slowly, he hooded his eyes, and laced his fingers together in remembrance.

Rebecca watched him, afraid to speak. "Even for that hour, though," she said quietly at last, "for all the life you had drunk—you were not alive."

Lord Byron opened his eyes. "I slept until the rising of the sun," he said abruptly, ignoring Rebecca's words. "The touch of its rays filled me with dizziness. I tried to climb to my feet—I couldn't. I looked at my hand—it was my own again. It was sticky with slime. I stared down over my naked body. I was lying in a pool of effluent, of foul waste, and then, as I stirred again and felt the unaccustomed lightness in myself, I knew what the stuff was—my living matter—excreted by my body as something alien to itself. The filth was already starting to bubble and rot in the heat.

"I crawled to my hands and knees. Carcasses were scattered all over the rocks—a mess of goat hair, and bone, and drying blood. I felt disgust, yes, and revulsion—but no nausea—instead, looking at the black blood on the rocks and on myself, I felt a glowing strength that rose up through my body and limbs. I stared at my side; there was no sign of my wound, not even a scar. I noticed a stream—I crossed over to it and washed. Then I began to walk. Out of the water, the sun hurt my skin. Soon, it was unbearable. I looked around for shelter. Ahead, over the brow of the hill, was an olive tree. I hurried toward it. I crossed the brow, and there, below me, stretching away, lay the blue stillness of Lake Trihonida. I stared at it from under the tree. I remembered the last time I had seen it—when I had been alive. And now?"—Lord Byron stared at Rebecca, and nodded—"Yes, now—this was when I understood—*fully* understood—that I had passed beyond life—that I had been transformed into a quite different order of being. I began to shake. What was I? What had happened? What was this thing the Pasha had made me into?—a drinker of blood—a tearer of throats . . . " He paused. "A *vardoulacha . . .*" He smiled faintly, and clasped his hands. Silence, for a few moments, shrouded him.

"I stayed beneath the olive tree all day," he said at last. "The strange powers I remembered from the night seemed dulled in the sun—only hatred for my creator blazed as undimmed as before, while noon, and then afternoon, slowly passed. The Pasha had escaped me before, but now, a creature like him, I understood what would have to be done. I laid my hand across my chest. My heart, beating slowly, felt heavy with blood. I longed to feel the Pasha's own heart between my fingers, to pinch it slowly until it burst. I wondered about Haidée, and the punishment that her master had whispered about. Would it leave her alive?— leave her for me? And then I remembered again what I had been made into, and I felt a sick despair, and my loathing for the Pasha redoubled itself. Oh, how I welcomed my hatred, how I cherished it—my only pleasure that whole long first day.

"The sun began to set, and the western peaks seemed touched with blood. I found my senses returning to me. Once again, the air grew rich with the scents of life. The twilight gathered—and the darker it became, the more I could see. Out on the lake, I noticed fishing boats. One of them in particular caught my eye. It was being rowed out into the center of the lake; it anchored there; two men raised a weight in a sack, and threw it overboard. I watched as the ripples spread out and died, and then the lake was as glassy as before. The waters were crimson now, and staring at them, I felt my longing for blood reborn. I left the shelter of the olive tree. The darkness was like skin against my own. It filled me with strange desires, and feelings of power.

"I reached the cave where the Pasha had taken me. There was no sign of him, nor of anyone else. I found my clothes scattered as I had left them—I pulled them on. Only my cloak was ruined—torn and stiff with blood—so I searched for Haidée's instead, and found it discarded at the back of the cave. I remembered how she had dropped it the night before. I wrapped myself in it, and sat in the cave's mouth. I stared at its black folds, falling around me, and buried my head in my hands with despair.

"'My Lord!'

"I looked up. It was Viscillie. He was running through the olive grove up toward me. 'My lord!' he called out again. 'My Lord, I had thought you were dead!' Then he looked into my face. He stammered something; he froze where he was. Slowly, he looked up again. 'My Lord,' he whispered, 'tonight . . .'

"I raised an eyebrow in inquiry.

"'Tonight, My Lord—you can have your revenge.' He paused. I nodded. Viscillie fell to his knees. 'It is our one chance,' he explained in a hurried voice. 'The Pasha is journeying through the mountains. If you don't delay, we can capture him.' He swallowed and fell silent again. How curiously delicate he smelled—I had never noticed it before. I studied him, and watched how his brown face turned pale.

"I rose to my feet. 'Haidée—where is she?'

"Viscillie bowed his head. Then he turned and beckoned someone, and I smelled another man's blood. 'This is Elmas,' said Viscillie, gesturing at a ruffian as massive as himself. 'Elmas—tell the Lord Byron what you saw.'

"Elmas looked up into my face, and I saw him frown, then blanch just as Viscillie had done.

"'Tell me,' I whispered.

"'My Lord, I was by the lake . . .' He looked up at me again, and his voice trailed away.

"'Yes?' I said softly.

"'My Lord, I saw a boat. In it were two men. They had a sack. Inside the sack was . . .'

"I lifted my hand. Elmas fell silent. Blankness passed before my eyes. I had known already, of course, when I saw the boat myself, but I hadn't then been willing to acknowledge it, not the hidden meaning of that scene. I fingered the edge of Haidée's cloak. When I spoke, my voice was like the splintering of ice in my ears. 'Viscillie,' I asked, 'where does the Pasha ride tonight?'

"'Through the mountain passes, My Lord.'

"'We have men?'

"Viscillie bowed his head. 'From my village, My Lord.'

"'I need a horse.'

"Viscillie smiled. 'You will be given one, My Lord.'

"'We ride at once.'

"'At once, My Lord.'

"And so we did. The crags and ravines echoed to our speed. Iron hooves clattered over the rocks; foam streaked the sides of my raven horse. We reached the pass. In a gully above it, I wheeled and paused, standing in my stirrups to gaze into the distance, trying to smell my foes drawing near. I looked up at the sky—still red, blood-red, but deepening into black. Winters of memory rolled over me; in that drop of time, I seemed to glimpse my own eternity. I felt a dread, and then hatred settled in its place. 'They are coming,' I said. Viscillie looked. He could see nothing, but he nodded and gave the words of command. 'Kill them all,' I said. 'All.'

I grasped my sword and drew it, so that its steel flushed red with the light of the sky. 'The Pasha, though,' I whispered, 'he is mine.'

"We heard the clash of men on horseback coming down the ravine. Viscillie grinned; he nodded to me and raised his arquebus. Then I saw them—the squadron of Tartar cavalry, and at their head, his pale face gleaming among the shadows of the rocks, the monster, my creator. I tightened my grip around the hilt of my sword. Viscillie glanced at me; I held my sword poised; I lowered it. Viscillie fired, and the foremost Tartar bit the ground. Vakhel Pasha looked up—no expression of fear or surprise crossed his face. But all around him, as gunfire crackled out, there was chaos; some men sheltered behind their horses and tried to answer back; others fled into the rocks, where they were finished off by the knife. I felt the lust for blood on me. I spurred my horse forward, so that I stood silhouetted against the western sky. All across the ravine, there was a sudden fall into silence. I stared at the Pasha; he met my look impassively. But from one of his horsemen there was a sudden wail. 'It's him, it's him! See how pale he is—it's him!' I smiled; I spurred my horse down; with the shrieks of Viscillie's men in my ears, I rode into the pass.

"It was littered with corpses now, as men fought hand to hand. Alone among the carnage, the Pasha sat and waited on his horse untouched. I rode to face him. Only then, slowly, did he smile. 'Welcome to eternity, *milord,*' he whispered.

"I shook my head. 'Haidée—where is she?'

"The Pasha stared at me, startled, then he threw back his head and laughed. 'You can truly be bothered with her?' he asked. He reached out to touch me. I flinched back. 'You have so much to learn,' said the Pasha softly. 'But I will teach you. We shall be together, for all time, and I will teach you.' He held out his hand. 'Come with me, *milord.*' He smiled. He beckoned with his hand. 'Come with me.'

"For a moment, I sat frozen. Then my sword swung down. I felt it bite through the bone of the Pasha's wrist.

The hand, still seeming to beckon, arced upward, then dropped into the dust. The Pasha stared at me in horror, but he seemed to feel no physical pain, and this infuriated me all the more. I swung at him blindly. My sword rose and fell, cutting deep, until the Pasha slumped from his horse's back. He stared up at me. 'You are going to kill me,' he said. A look of puzzlement and disbelief crossed his face. 'So soon. You are truly going to do it.' I stepped down from my horse, and placed the sword's point above his heart.

" 'This time,' I whispered, 'I will not miss.'

" 'No!'; the Pasha screamed suddenly. He struggled with the sword, his single hand cutting itself as he tried to push away the sword's edge.

" 'Goodbye, Your Excellency,' I said. I pushed the sword down. I felt it puncture the soft sack of his heart.

"The Pasha shrieked. Not a human cry, but a terrible unearthly wail of pain and hate. It echoed through the pass, across the ravines, and everything was stilled by it. A fountain of blood spouted up into the sky, bright scarlet against the deeper reds of the horizon, and then it began to pour down upon my head, like rain from a bloated crimson cloud. It fell as softly as a blessing, and I raised my face to welcome it. The shower ended at last, and when I moved, I realized that my skin beneath my clothes was wet with blood. I looked down at the Pasha. He lay in the stiffness of his death agony. I reached for dust, and scattered it over his face. 'Bury him,' I said. 'Bury him, so that he never walks again.' I found Viscillie, and told him I would wait for him in Missolonghi. Then I mounted my horse and without looking around, left the pass, that place of death.

"I rode through the night. I felt no tiredness, only the most extraordinary desire for experience. The shower of blood had cooled my thirst, while my powers, my senses, my sensations, all seemed heightened to an extraordinary degree. I reached Missolonghi at dawn. The light gave me no pain now. Instead, the colors, the interplay of the sky and the sea, the beauty of the sun's first ray all ravished me. Missolonghi was not a beautiful place, just a straggling town perched on the marsh's edge, but to me it seemed the most wondrous place I had ever been. As I cantered across the mudflats, staring in amazement at the streaks of color to the east, it was as though I had never seen a dawn before.

"I entered Missolonghi and found the tavern where Hobhouse and I had agreed to meet. The tavern keeper, after I had woken him up, stared at me with horror—I was wild-eyed, and my clothes, of course, were still caked with blood. I ordered fresh linen, and hot water, and the pleasure of my freshness, once I had washed and redressed, was again like nothing I had ever known. I clattered up to Hobhouse's room. I picked up a pillow and threw it at him. 'Hobby, get up, it's me. I'm back.'

"Hobhouse opened a bleary eye. 'Damn it,' he said. 'So you are.' He sat up and rubbed his eyes. 'Well, old fellow, what have you been up to?' He smiled. 'Nothing interesting at all, I suppose?'"

Chapter VII

He had a fancy for some oriental legends of pre-existence, and in his conversation and poetry took up the part of a fallen or exiled being, expelled from heaven, or sentenced to a new avatar on earth for some crime, existing under a curse, predoomed to a fate really fixed by himself in his own mind, but which he seemed determined to fulfill. At times, this dramatic imagination resembled a delusion; he would play at being mad, and gradually get more and more serious, as if he believed himself to be destined to wreck his own life and that of everyone near him.

LORD BYRON'S GRANDSON, *Astarte*

What did you tell him, then?" Rebecca asked.

Lord Byron looked up at her. He had been staring into the darkness, a half-smile playing on the edge of his lips. He frowned. "Tell?" he asked.

"Hobhouse—did you tell him the truth?"

"The truth?" Lord Byron laughed. "What was the truth?"

"About your transformation."

"Into a vampire?" Lord Byron laughed again, and shook his head. "Hobhouse had caught the sun, you know, while he'd been away from me. He'd always been red-faced, but now he was puce. Then, that evening, he had indigestion as well. Spent the whole night glowing in the dark, groaning and farting. And Hobby was never the most credulous of people, not at the best of times. So no, Miss Carville, I did not tell him—the man was practically afloat on his own wind. Not the moment to make a dramatic revelation."

"But even so, he must have guessed."

"Yes, that something had happened, of course. But what exactly?—I wasn't sure of that myself. Hobhouse was so damned *alive,* you see." Lord Byron smiled, and for a brief second, something like fondness seemed to warm his eyes. "No—a couple of hours with Hobby, grumbling and scratching and complaining about his wind, and it was hard to believe in vampires at all. Even harder, of course, to believe that I could have become one myself. I began to doubt everything that had happened to me—wonder if I hadn't dreamed the whole thing—except that all the time, quite indisputably, there was the numbness in my heart, the numbness of an aching sense of loss. I was alone, and Haidée was not with me; I was alone, and Haidée was murdered, drowned beneath the waters of Lake Trihonida. And something—*something*—*had happened to me*—something strange—for my senses, as I've told you, no longer seemed my own, but like some spirit's, some angel's, so that I could feel things which mortals have never felt. Just the breath of air on my face, the merest whisper, and sensations would flood me, passions of extraordinary beauty and strength. Or I would stroke the skin of my arm—hear the scraping of a chair—smell the wax of a candle, stare for hours at its flame—tiny things, but they ravished me—yes—gave me a pleasure that was . . ."—he paused, then shook his head—"indescribable." He smiled again, and stroked his forearm, reliving the memories. "Everything seemed changed," he whispered softly, "changed utterly. And so I wondered what had happened—to the world—or to me—to give birth to such a state of mystery."

Rebecca stared into his face, so pale, and beautiful—and melancholy. "But you knew," she said.

Lord Byron slowly shook his head.

"But—you must have known." Instinctively, Rebecca reached for her neck, to stroke the puncture marks. "How could you not have done?" She realized that Lord Byron was staring at her scars, his eyes as brilliant and cold as jewels, and she lowered her arm. "The blood lust," she asked quietly. "I don't understand. What had happened to it?"

"I didn't feel it," said Lord Byron after a pause.

"But you'd felt it before—on the mountains—you said you did."

Lord Byron nodded imperceptibly. "But it was that," he said softly, "which I came to believe had been a fantasy. I would smell the life all around me, in humans, creatures, even the flowers—yes, and be intoxicated—but still have no hunger. Once, riding by the Gulf of Lepanto, I saw an eaglet flying above us, and I felt the rush of desire then—the mountains on one side of us, the still waters on the other, and this beautiful living thing between. I felt the aching lust for blood—not for its own sake, though, but because I too wanted to soar and be free like the bird—because I wanted it to be a part of me, I suppose. I had a gun with me. I shot the eaglet, and watched it drop. It was only wounded, and I tried to save it, its eye was so bright; but it pined, and died in a few days; and I felt a terrible sickness at what I had done. It was the first creature I had killed since the death of the Pasha; and since then, I have never attempted—and hope I never will attempt—the killing of another animal or bird."

"No." Rebecca shook her head. "I just don't understand." She remembered the body of the tramp, laid out by Waterloo Bridge; she remembered the soft flow of her own blood. "An eagle? Why feel remorse for an eagle?"

"I explained," said Lord Byron, a coldness in his voice now. "I wanted it to be a part of me—it was so alive—and in killing it, I destroyed what attracted me."

"But isn't that what you have done throughout your whole existence?"

The vampire bowed his head. "Perhaps," he said softly. His face was shadowed; Rebecca couldn't tell how angry he might be. But when he looked up again, his face was impassive; and then, as he talked, it seemed gradually to lighten and grow almost warm. "You must believe me," Lord Byron said. *"I felt no thirst.* Not in those first months. There were only sensations—desires, whole universes of them, hinting at still further delights, far beyond my dreams. At night, when the moon was full and the air

ghostly with the scent of mountain flowers, eternity would
seem all about me. I would feel a calm that was also a fierce
joy in my veins, just from the delight of having consciousness, of knowing myself to exist. My nerves were sweet to
the touch—the faintest experience would brush them, and
send shivers of pleasure out through my flesh. Sensuality
was in everything—the kiss of a breeze, the scent of a
flower, the breath of life in the air and all around."

"And Haidée?" Rebecca tried not to sound caustic, but
failed. "Amid all this unalloyed happiness—what about
her?"

Lord Byron rested his chin on his fingertips. "Misery," he
said at last, "can sometimes be a fine and pleasant thing. A
dark drug. The joy least likely to betray its faithful addicts."
He leaned forward. "I still mourned Haidée, yes, of
course—but rather in the way that I would take a lengthy
bath. It disturbed me, this inability to feel true pain—I
sensed, I think, that it was a mark of how much my
humanity was altered, and yet at the same time, for all that I
tried to weep, I could not regret it. That was to change, of
course . . ." He paused. "Yes—that was to change." He
studied Rebecca, almost, she imagined, as though pitying
her. She stirred uneasily, and as she did so, found herself
caught again in the ice of his stare. Lord Byron reached out
a hand, as though to touch her cheek, or stroke her long
hair—then he too froze. "The time was to come," he
whispered, "when I would grieve cruelly enough for Haidée.
Oh yes—the time was to come. But not then. The joy of my
new state could not be fought. It was a madness. It drowned
all else." He smiled. "And so even my misery enchanted
me."

He nodded. "It was in such a mood that I became a poet.
I had started a poem that was something quite new—not
like the satires I had written in London, but wild and
restless, full of romantic despair. It was called *Childe
Harold's Pilgrimage.* In England, it was to make me famous,
and a byword for melancholy, but in Greece, where I wrote
it, the gloom it expressed gave me nothing but delight. We

were riding at this time past the mountain of Parnassus, on our way to Delphi. I wanted to visit the oracle of Apollo, the ancient god of poetry—I offered him a prayer, and the next day, we saw a flight of eagles, soaring high above us past the snow-clad peaks. I took it as an omen—the god had blessed me. I stared at the mountains, and thought of Haidée, and my wretchedness grew ever more splendid and poetical. I had never felt half so elevated before. Hobhouse, of course, being Hobhouse, claimed that the eagles had been vultures, but I damned him cheerfully, and rode on, gloomy in my poetry, exultant within myself.

"It was late in the year now—but we continued to travel—and on Christmas Day, from a rugged mountain track, we had our first glimpse of Athens. It was a glorious sight—the Attic plain, the Aegean, and the town itself, surmounted by the Acropolis, all bursting upon our eyes at once. But it wasn't the archaeology which delighted me— Athens had charms far more vital and fresh than dead rock. We took rooms with a widow, a Mrs. Tarsia Macri—she had three daughters—they were all lovely, but the youngest, Teresa, was a pouting little houri fresh from paradise. She served us our first meal, and she smiled and blushed as though she had been trained to it. That evening, we settled with the widow for a stay of several months.

"Later, in the dead of night, I fell on Teresa like a thunderbolt. Had I forgotten Haidée?—no—but she was dead—and my desire for Teresa seemed to have risen suddenly like a fountain from a desert, so powerfully that it almost frightened me. Love, constant love?"—Lord Byron laughed and shook his head—"no—not even for Haidée— though I swear to you, I did all I could. I walked in the yard, to cool my blood, but the soft little whore was waiting for me, and promising myself still that I wouldn't consent—I consented, of course. There was no help for it—none at all—she was far too delicious and alive. The veins beneath her skin were so delicate, and her bare neck and breasts so inviting to kiss—and the pleasure—when I fucked her— was like the rush of a drug. We crushed winter flowers beneath us, while above gleamed the impassive sky, and the spectral marble of the Parthenon. Teresa moaned with exultation, but there was terror as well in her eyes, and the emotions, I could sense, were inextricable. I explored inside her, felt the deep warmth of her life. My sperm smelled of sandalwood—she, of wild roses. I took her again and again, until morning rose behind the Acropolis.

"Nothing else in Athens was to compare with that night. Yet our stay in the city passed delightfully enough, and winter began to melt into spring. Hobhouse ranged around the countryside after antiquities; I rode my mule, haunted by the mythic beauty of the land, but making no notes, asking no learned questions. Instead, I gazed at the stars, and ruminated, and felt my dreams take wing until they seemed to fill the sky. But profundity could be tiring—and then I would return to more voluptuous pursuits. My Maid of Athens was insatiable—fortunately, for she needed to be—my own need for pleasure raging in my blood like a disease. At last, though, I grew tired of Teresa—I looked around, and took her sisters instead, apart at first, then *en famille*—and still my desire prickled endlessly. Something was missing—some pleasure that I hadn't contemplated yet. I took to wandering the streets of Athens by night, as though searching for it, the fulfillment, the *to kalon,* as the Greeks would say. I haunted the squalid alleyways of the modern town, and the pale relics of the glory that was lost, shattered marble, altars to forgotten gods. Nothing. And then I would return to the Macri sisters' bed, and wake them, and make them perform again. But still that hunger—for something—but for what?

"One evening, early in March, I was to find out. Friends of ours, both Greeks and fellow travelers, had come to dine with us. The evening started off silent, then talky, then disputatious, then drunk—and for the final hour, all seemed happiness. My three pretty concubines danced attendance on me, and the wine cast a rosy veil across my thoughts. Then, gradually, through its warmth, the hunger began to scream at me again. All of a sudden, I was shaking,

at the nakedness of Teresa's throat, and the glimpse of the
shadow that marked out her breasts. She must have seen my
expression, for she turned away coyly, and flicked back her
hair in a way that made my stomach clench. Then she
laughed, and her lips were so moist and red, that I rose
unthinkingly, and reached out to take her arm. But Teresa
laughed again, and danced back, and then she slipped, and
the bottle of wine she had been carrying was shattered on
the floor. There was a silence. Everyone turned to look at
her; Teresa slowly raised up her hands and we all saw that
they were wet with blood. Again, in my stomach, I felt the
clenching of desire. I walked across to her and held her in
my arms, as though to comfort her. She held up her hands to
me, and I took them—and suddenly, with a naked thrill of
certainty, I knew what my hunger had been for. My mouth
was watering; my eyes were blind. But I lifted Teresa's
hands to my lips, and I kissed them gently, and then I
licked. Blood! The taste . . ." Lord Byron swallowed. "What
can I say?—the taste was that of the food of paradise. *Blood.*
I licked again, and felt lightness and energy in a wash of
radiant gold, staining my soul with its purity. Greedily, I
began to drink from the deepest wound. With a sudden
scream, though, Teresa pulled her hand away, and at once,
there was silence across the room again. Teresa looked for
her mother and ran to her, but everyone else was staring at
me. I wiped at my mouth. My hand, when I pulled it away,
was smeared with blood. I brushed it on my shirt—then I
touched my lips again. They were still damp. I licked them,
and stared around the room. No one met my eyes. No one
said a word.

"Then Hobhouse—my dearest, best friend Hobhouse—
rose and took me by the arm. 'Damn it, Byron,' he said, in a
loud, ringing voice, 'damn it, but you're drunk.' He led me
from the room; as I walked out, I heard voices behind me
starting to murmur again. I stood on the steps that led up to
my room. The realization of what I had done struck me
afresh. My legs seemed like flowing water. The taste of the
blood came back to me—and I staggered, and fell into

Hobhouse's arms. He helped me upstairs, and left me in my room. I slept at once—the first time for over a month—but it was not an easy sleep. I dreamed that I had never been a living thing at all, but instead a creature manufactured by the science of the Pasha. I saw myself laid out on a dissecting table, exposed to lightning at the summit of his tower. I had no skin. I was wholly naked to the Pasha's touch. He was creating me. I longed to kill him, but I knew that whatever I did, I would always be his thing. Always, always . . .

"When I woke at last, it was to find myself lying in a putrid stench of matter. The sheets were caked with my own filth, just as the rocks had been by Lake Trihonida. I leaped to my feet, and stared down at the stuff which had once formed my living self. How much residue was there left in me? And when it had all gone—what would I be then?—alive or dead?—or neither, perhaps? It had been the blood, I knew, the blood I had drunk, it was that which had made my body sweat like this. I began to shake. What was happening to me? I didn't care to pause and think. Instead, I washed and dressed, then ordered Fletcher to burn the sheets. I woke Hobhouse. 'Get up,' I told him. 'We're leaving now.' Hobhouse, to my surprise, didn't grumble once—just nodded, and staggered out of bed. We left Athens like thieves. Above us, as we reached Piraeus, the dawn was bleeding across the sky.

"We took a ship across the Aegean Sea. The captain was an Englishman, whom we had met a few days before, and he saw to it that we both had our private berths. I kept to mine, for the thirst was starting to plague me again, and I was afraid of what it might lead me to do. In the evening, Hobhouse joined me; we got ragingly drunk; for a second night, he saw me to bed. But I didn't sleep; instead, I lay on my couch, and remembered the forbidden, golden taste of blood. The craving grew worse; at last, just before dawn, I reached for a razor, and sliced my own arm. Only a thin line of blood rose up from the wound, but I drank it greedily, and the taste was as rich and delicious as before. Then I slept, and dreamed, and imagined I was a creature of the Pasha again, a mass of skinless limbs beneath his anatomist's knife. In the morning, my bedclothes were stiff with the familiar filth.

"We reached Smyrna on the afternoon of our second day at sea. My stay there was torture. I felt a restlessness and disquietude that I had never known before, and a terror at the thought of what might be happening to me. The proofs of that, both within my body and inside my mind, seemed terrible and full—and yet still I couldn't bear to believe the truth. And if I could not confess it to myself, then to whom else could I turn for help and advice? Hobhouse, as ever, was a devoted friend; and yet he was so solid, and generous, and down-to-earth—I couldn't stand it. I didn't want sympathy or reasonableness. I had darker dreams. I wanted—no—I tried not to think about it—and yet all the time, of course, I could think of nothing else.

"So I continued silent and desperate. At last, my thirst grew so terrible, I thought I was turning mad. Hobhouse, seeing how black my mood had grown, and ever the sportsman, advised me to take some exercise"—Lord Byron smiled—"as though boxing, or a game of cricket, would have helped me then." He smiled again, and shook his head. "Sadly, neither of those activities being ready to hand, it was agreed instead that we should make a tour. Two days' ride away lay the ruins of Ephesus—and so we set out for them, accompanied only by a single janizary. The road was wild and desolate, surrounded by bleak marshes, from which the croaking of frogs was deafening. At last, we had left even the frogs behind; and only the odd Turkish tombstone hinted that life had ever existed in that wasteland. Otherwise, not a broken column or roofless mosque disturbed the bleakness of the wilderness—nothing at all; we were wholly alone.

"I could feel the thirst starting to consume me now. I looked desperately across the dreary plain, searching for any glimpse of life, but there was only a cemetery ahead of us, a shattered, empty city of the dead. My breath was starting to rattle now—my lungs felt as though they were shriveling away. I raised my hand to wipe my brow, but as I did so, I checked myself, and stared in horror at what my fingers had become—gnarled twists of blackened bone. I stared down at my arm—again, it was black and dry; felt my face—it was withered to the touch; tried to swallow—but my tongue seemed thick with fiery dust. I scratched a sound out from my throat, and Hobhouse looked round. 'My God,' he whispered. I had never seen such a look of revulsion before. 'Byron. My God, Byron.' He rode back to me. I was so dry. I could smell the blood in Hobhouse's veins. It would be cool and fresh, and as moist as dew. I needed it. I had to have it. I reached out for his throat. I clutched at air. I tumbled from my horse.

"With our janizary's help, Hobhouse bore me to the cemetery. He laid me beneath the shade of a cypress tree, and I leaned back against one of the tombs. I stripped my shirt away. My whole body was black, I could see now, and my flesh was burning on the bone, so that I seemed a virtual skeleton. Hobhouse knelt by my side. 'Drink,' I managed to hiss, 'must drink.' I raised a finger to point at our janizary, then stared greedily back at Hobhouse, trying to make him understand.

"He nodded. 'Yes, of course, old chap.' He turned to the janizary, who had been watching me, a look of terror in his eyes. *'Suleiman, verban su!'* Hobhouse yelled—'Fetch water!' The janizary bowed, and scampered away. I groaned with frustrated need. 'Come on, old fellow,' said Hobhouse, wiping my brow, 'you'll have your water soon.' I stared at him with fury, and longing for his blood. I scraped feebly with my fingers against the tomb, but my nails flaked away, and I was afraid that my scratchings might expose the bone. I lay helplessly where I was.

"Time went by—five minutes, ten, then quarter of an hour. I could feel my stomach collapsing in, and imagined my intestines shriveled like dry grapes. Hobhouse was looking more and more desperate as he watched me burn away. 'Damn him!' he screamed suddenly. 'Damn him, what the devil is he at?' He rose to his feet. 'Suleiman!' he yelled. 'Suleiman, that water, we need it *now!*' He looked back down at me. 'I'm going to find him,' he said. 'Byron.' He tried to smile. 'Byron, just—just—don't . . .' I thought he was about to cry, but he turned his face and started to run, hurrying through the weeds and shattered tombs, until I could see him no more. I lay as he had left me. I felt my consciousness evaporate before the black thirst in my veins.

"I passed out—but not beyond the reach of my agony— and I woke again, and prayed for death. Then suddenly—in the desert of that pain—I felt a startling coolness. It was a hand—laid against my brow. I tried to mouth Hobhouse's name.

"'No. Not Hobhouse,' said a man's voice I didn't recognize. 'Rest your tongue. We shall have time enough to talk.' I struggled to look up. I felt a second hand tilt my head. I was staring into a face of striking handsomeness. Long golden hair framed features that seemed both pale as death, and yet also light with the pleasures of life—it was an aristocrat's face, amused, faintly cruel, touched by animal grace. The strange man smiled at me, then kissed me on the lips. 'A maggoty greeting,' he said. 'Kissing shall be better, I think, when you are prettier again.' He laughed with delight, but his eyes, I could see now, gleamed like sunlight on a lake of ice. They reminded me of the Pasha's—and then, at once, I understood: I was lying in the arms of a creature like myself.

"The vampire rose to his feet. 'You have an itching inclination, I think, to drink some blood,' he said. 'Obey it. For blood is the finest cordial of all. It begets wit, good humor, and merriness. It restores health to our bodies when they are shriveled like old paps. It banishes all those heavy thoughts which make existence seem unkind.' He laughed. 'Sweeter than wine, sweeter than a maiden's ambrosia—it is your only draft. So come.' He took my hand. 'Come and drink.'

"I tried, but I couldn't rise. 'Trust yourself,' hissed the vampire, a hint of scorn in his voice. He took my other hand. 'You are dangerous as the plague, and evil as the Devil. Do you really think you are still the slave of your flesh? Damme sir, I tell you, you are not. Have faith in your powers—and follow me.'

"I tried to lift myself—and suddenly, I could. To my surprise, I found that I had risen to my feet without ever seeming to move. I took a step forward—and it was as though I were nothing but a whisper of air. I took another step, and found that I had passed across the tombs, and was standing on the road. I looked back toward the cypress tree where I had been lying. A body was still slumped there, twisted and black. It was my own.

"'Am I dead?' I asked, and my voice, in my ears, was like the wailing of a storm.

"My guide laughed. 'Dead? No—undead! You will never be dead, so long as there is life!' He laughed again, with a libertine's glee, and pointed down the road. 'I passed him on the way,' he said. 'Have him. He is yours.'

"I moved, like a black gale, with a speed I could scarcely recognize as being speed at all. The janizary's blood smelled wonderfully fresh. I could see him now ahead of me, galloping back to Smyrna, and his horse's flanks were white with foam. The janizary glanced around—and I stood still where I was, a silhouette against the sky, savoring his blank-faced look of shock. His horse whinnied and stumbled. 'No!' the janizary screamed, as he was thrown to the ground. 'No, no, Allah, please, no!' I felt a sudden detachment from my own thirst. I watched, intrigued, as the janizary tried to recapture his horse. He didn't have a chance—surely he understood that? The janizary was sobbing now—and suddenly the thirst was back inside me again. I moved—I leaped—the janizary screamed—my teeth bit against the skin of his neck. I felt the incisors extend from my gums; the skin gave—blood, in a soft silken spurt, filled my mouth. I felt a shuddering delirium, as the blood was pumped by the dying man's heart, and rain flooded out across my parched skin and throat.

"I drained my victim white. When I had finished, his gore in my blood felt heavy like a drug.

"'Pleasant to meet a fellow drinker on the road.' I looked around. The vampire had been watching me. Amusement glittered in his eyes. 'Are your thirsty veins restored?' he asked. I nodded slowly. 'Excellent,' the vampire smiled. 'Believe me, sir, 'tis purple nectar. There is nothing more salutiferous than your bumper of fresh blood.' I stood up, to kiss either side of the handsome, moonstone face, then pressed my lips against the vampire's own. He narrowed his eyes, tasting the janizary's blood in my mouth before breaking free to bow with an extravagant sweep. 'I am Lovelace,' he said, bowing a second time. 'Like yourself, I believe, an Englishman, and a peer of the realm. That is, sir, if I am correct in addressing you as the notorious Lord Byron?'

"I raised an eyebrow. 'Notorious?'

"'Why, yes sir! notorious! Did you not, at some dinner party or rout, feed in public on your Athenian whore? Do not be surprised, *milord*, if such scrapes provoke wonder and discussion among the common herd.'

"I shrugged. 'I had no intention of causing a scandal. She cut herself. I was surprised by my own desire when I saw her blood.'

"Lovelace stared at me, intrigued. 'How long, *milord*, have you been of the fellowship?'

"'Fellowship?'

"'The aristocracy, sir, the aristocracy of the blood, by which you—and I—are made doubly a peer.' He reached up to stroke my cheek. His nails were sharp, like crystal to the touch. 'You are a virgin, are you not?' he asked suddenly. He gestured at the slaughtered janizary. 'That was your first kill?'

"I bowed my head coldly. 'In a manner, I suppose.'

"'A pox on't, sir, I could tell you were a virgin from your blackened state back there.'

"'How do you mean?'

1 6 5

" 'You must be young in blood indeed, to have permitted yourself to decline in such a way.'

"I stared at him. 'If I don't drink, you mean'—I gestured back toward the cemetery—*'that* will happen to me again?'

"Lovelace bowed shortly. 'I do, sir. And I am mightily surprised that you have endured for so long since Athens without blood. That is why I wished to know, when did you join the fellowship?'

"I tried to remember. Haidée in the cave—the Pasha's teeth against my chest. 'Five months,' I said at last.

"Lovelace stared at me, a look of stunned surprise on his handsome face; then he narrowed his eyes. 'Why sir, if this be true, then you are like to prove the choicest drinker I have met with yet.'

" 'I don't understand your surprise,' I said.

"Lovelace laughed, and pressed my hand. 'I once survived dry for upward of a month. *Two* months has been heard of—but more than that, never. And yet you, sir, the freshest, greenest recruit to our ranks—five months, sir—*five,* you say.' He laughed again, and kissed me on the mouth. 'Oh, *milord*—what entertainments we shall have, what routs and kills! How glad I am that I followed you!' He kissed me again. 'Byron—let us be wicked together.'

"I bowed my head. 'There is clearly much I need to be taught.'

" 'Yes, there is,' said Lovelace, with a simple nod of his head. 'Believe me, sir—I have sampled a century and a half of libertinage. I speak as a courtier of the second King Charles. We were not a canting, mewling, puritan age—no sir, we understood what pleasure could be.' He whispered in my ear. 'Whores, *milord*—fine wines—refreshing drafts of blood. You will find eternity a welcome thing.' He kissed me, then paused to wipe blood from my mouth. He glanced down at the janizary's corpse. 'Was it good?' he asked, tapping the dried-out body with his foot. I nodded. 'There will be better,' said Lovelace shortly. He took my hand. 'For now, though, *milord,* we must both return to our corporeal forms.'

" 'Corporeal?'

"Lovelace nodded. 'Your friend will believe you dead.'

"I touched myself. 'It seems very strange,' I said. 'The pleasures I have drunk in seem bodily enough. But how do I feel them, if I am nothing now but spirit?'

"Lovelace shrugged contemptuously. 'I leave such quibbles to wranglers and diviners.'

" 'But it is not a quibble. If I have no body, then what is it that I am feeling now, here, inside my veins? Is the pleasure real? It seems unbearable to think of it as just a fantasy.'

"Lovelace reached for my hand. He drew it inside his shirt and over his chest, so that I could feel the muscles beneath the skin. 'We are in a dream,' he whispered, 'one we share between us. We rule it and form it. You must understand, sir, that we have this power, to make the stuff of our dreams a reality.'

"I stared into his eyes. I could feel his nipple hardening at my touch. I glanced down at the janizary. 'And him?' I asked. 'Did I only dream that I fed on his blood?'

"Lovelace smiled, a faint smile of amusement and cruelty. 'Our dreams are a canopy, *milord,* into which we draw our prey. Your Turk is dead—and you, sir, are whole once again.' He took my hand. 'Come. We must return you to your grieving friend.'

"We went, and once we had reached the cemetery, I left Lovelace on the road, and walked back through the tombs. Ahead of me, past the turbaned gravestones, I made out Hobhouse. He was sobbing inconsolably over my blackened corpse. It was a pleasant sight. What can be finer than to know you will be missed by your friends when you are gone? And then I felt sorrow to think that I had caused my dear Hobhouse pain, and I returned, like a shiver of light, into my flesh. I opened my eyes—and felt blood start to flow through my withered veins." Lord Byron closed his eyes. His smile had the ecstasy of memory. "As though they had been freed from the grip of a vise, my limbs returned to life. Champagne after soda water, sunlight after mist; women after a monastery—all seem to offer a hint of resurrec-

tion. But they do not. There is only one true resurrection—
and that is blood after a drought of the flesh."

"So you draw blood by dreaming?" Rebecca asked,
interrupting him. "That is how it happens?"

Lord Byron stared at her. "You should remember," he
said softly. He stared at Rebecca's neck. "You have been
caught in the web of my dreams."

Rebecca shivered, and not just from fear. "But you drank
from Teresa," she said.

Lord Byron bowed his head.

"So you don't have to dream to drink blood?"

"No." Lord Byron smiled. "Of course not. There are
many ways of tasting it. Many arts."

Rebecca stared at him, fascinated and appalled. "Arts?
What do you mean?" she asked.

"Lovelace, that first evening, tempted me by hinting at
them."

Rebecca frowned. "Why tempt?"

"Because I didn't want to hear them. Not at first."

"But you said—the pleasure you'd had—you've been
describing it."

"Yes." Lord Byron's lip curled faintly. "But I was satiated
on the blood I had drunk, and that evening, in the village
outside Ephesus, I suffered the self-disgust that follows all
great pleasures. I had killed a man—I had drained him—I
was only surprised that I wasn't more revolted with myself.
But there was another reason, too, for ignoring Lovelace's
blandishments. It was the property of blood, I discovered,
that it heightened all other experiences. The food and drink
that night were delicious in a way I had forgotten they could
be. I had no time for whisperings about secret arts or fresh
victims."

"Lovelace wanted to kill again?"

"Oh, yes. Very much so." Lord Byron paused. "He
wanted Hobhouse."

"Hobhouse?"

Lord Byron nodded, then smiled. "Lovelace was an
admirer of breeding, you see. 'I must have him,' he told me

that night. 'For months now, Byron, I have had nothing but peasants and vile-smelling Greeks. Faugh, sir, I am a true-bred Briton; I cannot survive on such trash. And Hobhouse, you say, is a Cambridge man? Why then, sir, he *must* be mine.'

"I shook my head, but Lovelace only pressed me the more eagerly. 'He must die,' he hissed. 'Apart from all else, he saw you expire and resurrect.'

"I shrugged. 'Medicine isn't Hobby's strongest suit. He thinks it was heatstroke.'

"Lovelace shook his head. ''Tis no matter.' He stroked my arm, and his eyes were pinpricks of eager fire. I shuddered, but Lovelace mistook my disgust for thirst. 'Red blood is fine,' he whispered in my ear, 'but blue blood, sir—why, there is no drink on this earth which compares with that.'

"I told him to go hang. Lovelace laughed. 'You seem not to understand what you have become, *milord.*'

"I stared at him again. 'Not a thing like you, I hope.'

"Lovelace gripped my arm. 'Do not deceive yourself, *milord,*' he hissed.

"I stared at him coldly. 'I wouldn't presume to try,' I said at last.

"'But I think you do.' Lovelace grinned evilly. 'You are a creature wicked as sin. To deny that is vile hypocrisy.' He let go of my arm, and started to walk down the moon-white path to Ephesus. 'Your body has a thirst, *milord,*' he shouted out, as I stood watching him go. He paused, and turned around to face me. 'Ask yourself, Byron—can a thing such as you afford to have friends?' He smiled, then turned again, and disappeared. I stood where I was, trying to banish the echoes of his question from my mind. I shook my head—then returned to the room where Hobhouse was asleep.

"I kept watch over him through the night. My body stayed pure and unstained throughout. This was the first time that I had drunk blood and not sweated out filth the next night. I wondered what this portended. Had Lovelace been right? Were the changes to me now indeed irrevocable? I clung to

Hobhouse's company as though he were a charm. The next day we visited the ruins of Ephesus. Hobhouse poked at inscriptions in his usual way; I sat on the mound which had once been the temple of Diana, and listened to the mournful wailing of the jackals. It was a melancholy sound, as melancholy as my thoughts. I wondered where Lovelace had gone. I couldn't sense him among the ruins, but my instincts and powers were dulled by the sun, and I knew that he couldn't be far away. He would surely be back.

"That night, he was. I had sensed his approach as he drew near to us, and I watched unseen as he crossed to Hobhouse's bed. He bent low over my friend's naked throat, and I saw the gleam as he bared his razor teeth. I took his wrist; he struggled silently, but couldn't escape; I pulled him out from the room to the stairs. There, Lovelace broke free. 'You shitten salt-arse,' he snarled, 'let me have him.' I blocked his way. Lovelace tried to push me aside, but I took his throat and as I tightened my grip around it, I felt strength flood me in a rush of joy. Lovelace started to choke; he struggled again and I enjoyed his fear; at last, I let him drop, and Lovelace swallowed painfully, then looked up at me again.

"'God's wounds, sir, but you have a mighty strength,' he said. ''Tis pity you are such a mope-eye about your friend.'

"I inclined my head politely. Lovelace continued to stare at me, rubbing at his neck, and then he rose to his feet. 'Tell me, Byron,' he said, frowning, 'who created you?'

"'Created?' I shook my head. 'I was not created, I was transformed.'

"Lovelace smiled faintly. 'You were created, sir,' he said.

"'Why do you ask?'

"Lovelace stroked at his neck again, and breathed in deeply. 'I saw you at Ephesus today,' he whispered. 'I have been a vampire for a century and a half. I am deep in blood and experience. Yet I could not have stood the glare of that sun, not as you did, sitting in that open place. So I wonder, sir. I am sore perplexed. Who gave you his blood, that you can have such power?'

"I paused—then spoke the name of Vakhel Pasha.

"I caught a flicker of amusement in Lovelace's eye. 'I have heard of Vakhel Pasha,' he said slowly. 'A mage, is he not? An alchemist?'

"I nodded.

"'Where is he now?' Lovelace asked.

"'Why?'

"Lovelace smiled. 'Because he seems to have taught you so little, *milord.*'

"I said nothing, just turned and walked back up the stairs. But Lovelace ran after me and held my arm. 'Did you kill him?' he whispered. I shook my arm free. 'Did you kill him?' Lovelace bared his teeth in a grin, and held my arm again. 'Did you kill him, sir, so that his blood rose up, and fell on you in a shower, like the fountains that play in St. James's Park?'

"I turned around. My spine seemed made of ice. 'How did you know?' I asked.

"Lovelace laughed. His eyes sparkled with delight. 'There were rumors, *milord.* I heard them by Lake Trihonida. I was filled at once with a desire to establish their truth. And so here I am.' He drew his face close to mine. 'You are damned indeed, Byron.'

"I stared into his pitiless eyes. I felt hatred and anger flow through me like lava. 'Get away,' I hissed.

"'And would you banish your own urgings as well, *milord?*'

"I took him by the throat again and squeezed; then I flung him back. But Lovelace still smiled evilly. 'You may have the strength of a mighty spirit, *milord,* but doubt not, you are fallen, as Lucifer, son of the morning, is fallen—as we are all fallen. Creep back to your ditch-water friend. Enjoy him—he is mortal—he will die.'

"'Destroy him, Lovelace—'

"'Yes?'

"'Destroy him—and I will destroy you.'

"Lovelace bowed mockingly. 'You do not know the secret, Byron, do you?'

" 'Secret?'

" 'It hasn't been revealed to you.' Lovelace didn't ask; he merely stated a fact. I took a step back toward him; Lovelace melted toward the door.

" 'What secret?' I asked again.

" 'You are damned—and you will damn all who are close to you.'

" 'Why?'

"Lovelace smiled mockingly. 'Why, that, sir, is the secret.'

" 'Wait.'

"Lovelace smiled again. 'You are journeying to Constantinople, I believe?'

" 'Wait!' I shouted.

"Lovelace bowed—and was gone. I ran to the door, but there was no sign of him. On the night breeze, though, I thought I heard his laugh, and his whisper seemed to echo in my thoughts. 'You are damned—and you will damn all who are close to you.' From far off, a cock crew. I shook my head. I turned and walked—alone—back up to the room where Hobhouse lay asleep."

Chapter VIII

. . . even the society of his fellow-traveller, though with pursuits so congenial to his own, grew at last to be a chain and a burden on him; and it was not till he stood, companionless, on the shore of the little island in the Aegean, that he found his spirit breathe freely.

THOMAS MOORE, *Life of Lord Byron*

On what authority does Tom say this? He has not the remotest grasp of the real reason which induced Lord Byron to prefer having no Englishman immediately and constantly near him.

JOHN CAM HOBHOUSE,
NOTE WRITTEN IN THE MARGIN OF THE ABOVE

read hung over my thoughts like a mist for the next few days. Lovelace himself seemed to have melted with the cockcrow, but his mocking reference to a 'secret' haunted me. What had he meant, that I was doomed to destroy all those dearest to me? I stayed close to Hobhouse, and studied my feelings carefully—yet my blood lust seemed tamed, and my affection for my friend was as undimmed as before. I began to relax—and then to revel in the powers that my meal of blood had heightened for me. We set sail for Constantinople. Once again, my emotions grew thrillingly poetical. We were caught in a storm off the Dardanelles. We visited the legendary plain of Troy. Most exhilarating of all, I swam the Hellespont—four miles against an icy tide, from Asia across to the European shore—to prove, as the legends had always claimed, that the hero Leander could have achieved the feat. Leander, of course, had probably not had the benefit of a draft of fresh blood, but for all that, I was mightily impressed with myself.

"Constantinople we reached in the teeth of a gale. We anchored with difficulty below a sheer cliff. Above us stood the Seraglio, the Sultan's palace, yet the darkness all around us seemed like that of the open sea. However, I could sense the flow of the great city on the shore; and the wailings from the mosques, carrying faintly to us over the choppy waves, seemed like summonings to strange and exotic joys. The next day, a small boat ferried us along the Seraglio cliff. I stared up at it, and imagined the silken delights that lay within the palace walls. Then suddenly, I smelled blood—fresh blood. I stared across at a narrow terrace between the wall and the sea; dogs were growling over carcasses. I watched fascinated as one of them stripped the flesh from a Tartar's skull, much as a fig is peeled when the fruit is fresh. 'Refractory slaves,' muttered the captain of our boat, 'tossed from the walls.' I nodded slowly, and felt a dull ache of thirst in my bones again.

"As Europeans, we stayed in the quarter reserved for us. This was modern, and full of travelers like ourselves—I hated it. I had traveled to escape my countrymen, but now I felt doubly removed from them. There was a wild music in my veins singing of darkness and the pleasures of the night, which I knew marked me out as a thing apart. Across the waters of the Golden Horn, Constantinople was waiting—cruel, ancient, rich in forbidden delights. I haunted the narrow streets. The close air was spiced with blood. Around the gateway to the Seraglio severed heads were exposed on display; butchers draining carcasses let the blood flow through the streets: dervishes, as they screamed in mystic climax, would slash themselves until the courtyards ran red. All these things I watched silently—but I did not drink. I imagined, surrounded as I was by these delicious fruits, that I would not feel the need to pluck my own. Instead, in the hashish dens, or in the taverns where painted dancers writhed in the sands, I sought other joys—and hoped, by sampling them, to dull my deeper thirst.

"Yet I could feel it gradually parching me again. I began to loathe myself. The pleasures of the city only intensified my disgust, and I found that I was tiring of Constantinople, for its cruelties revolted me the more they reminded me of myself. In desperation, I returned to the society of my countrymen. I avoided Hobhouse—I was still afraid of what Lovelace's 'secret' might be—but with other Englishmen, I tried to behave as though I were no different from them. At times, I found this easy enough—at others, the pretense would seem unbearable. Whenever I felt my thirst for blood grow, I would conceal my longing behind displays of coldness or rage—I would argue over minor points of etiquette, or cut acquaintances when I passed them in the street.

"One afternoon, it happened that I met with a man who had been the victim of just such a mood. I had turned my back on him at the Ambassador's, and seeing him again, I was filled with a sudden remorse—the man had always been polite to me. He was a resident in Constantinople— and so, knowing it would flatter him, I asked him to show me the city's curiosities. I had seen them all before, of course, and endured my guide's company as a form of penance. At last, we ended up beneath the Seraglio walls.

"My companion glanced at me. 'You know,' he asked, 'that in three days' time, we are to be granted an audience with the Sultan himself? So sad—don't you think, Byron?—that we will see only a fraction of the palace's delights.' He pointed up at where the harem lay. 'A thousand women . . .' He tittered nervously, then glanced at me again. 'They say that the Sultan is not even that way inclined.' I nodded shortly. The perfume of blood was in the air—on dunghills before the Seraglio walls, headless corpses were being gnawed at by dogs. I felt sickened and aroused. 'Are you—fond—of women?' my companion asked. I swallowed and shook my head without understanding him, then wheeled my horse around, and cantered away.

"It was evening now, and the minarets were pricking a blood-red sky. I felt dizzy with unacted desires. I asked my companion to leave me, and then I rode alone by the great city walls, which for fourteen hundred years had loomed massive above the city of Constantine. But they were moldering now, and deserted, and I had soon left all human settlements behind; instead, I was surrounded by burial grounds, wild with ivy and cypress trees, and quite empty, it seemed. Then I heard a rustling, and saw two goats scamper through the bushes ahead of me. The smell of their fear hung delicious in the air. I paused, and dismounted. The fever was on me. The scent of blood lay rich and heavy in the shadows. I glanced up at the moon. It was full, I noticed for the first time, glimmering palely over the waters of the Bosporus.

"'I say, Byron . . .'

"I looked around. It was my companion from the Seraglio. He saw my face, and stammered something, then fell into silence.

"I stared at him, dizzy with desire for his blood. 'What do you want?' I whispered slowly.

"'I . . . I was wondering if . . .' He fell silent again. I smiled. Suddenly, I recognized what I had chosen to ignore all day, his longing for me, intermingled now with a paralyzing terror which he barely understood. I crossed to him. I stroked his cheek. My nail drew blood. I opened my mouth. Nervously, and then with a sudden desperate sob, the man reached up to kiss me. I took him in my arms, felt his heart beating against my chest. I tasted the blood from his scratched cheek, opened my mouth a second time—and then pushed him violently back onto the path.

"'Byron?' he quavered.

"'Get away,' I said coldly.

"'But . . . Byron . . .'

"'Get away!' I screamed. 'If you value your life—for God's sake, get away!'

"The man stared up at me, then scrabbled to his feet. It seemed he couldn't bear to look away from my eyes, but he hurried backwards all the same, as though struggling to break from the spell of my face; finally, reaching his horse, he mounted it and galloped down the path. I breathed in deeply; then cursed under my breath. My veins, disappointed in their expectation of blood, seemed to be pulsing and shuddering; my very brain seemed dry with thirst. I mounted my own horse, and spurred it forward. If I rode fast enough, I would surely catch my prey before he left the tombs.

"Then suddenly, a flock of goats ran out in front of my path. I had smelled the shepherd's blood before I heard his cry; he came running past me, shouting after his goats, and he barely had time to give me more than a glance. I wheeled my horse around and followed him. Then the shepherd did pause and look back at me; I slid down from my saddle, and walking over to him, sought to trap him, as I had almost trapped the other man, with the power of my stare. The shepherd stood paralyzed—then he wailed and fell down to his knees; he was an old man; I felt a terrible sorrow for him, as though it wasn't myself who was to be his murderer. I almost turned away; but then the moon came out from behind a cloud, and touched by its light, my thirst seemed to scream at me. I bit into the old man's throat; his skin was leathery, and I had to tear at it twice before the blood came pumping out. Its taste, though, was as rich as before, and the fullness it gave me even more violent and strange. I looked up from the husk of my prey, and saw anew how the moonlight was silver with life, and the silence haunted by beautiful sounds.

"'Egad, sir, there is no law which states you must kill in a cemetery.'

"I glanced over my shoulder. Lovelace was sitting on a shattered column. Despite myself, I smiled. It was good, after so many weeks alone, to see a creature like myself.

"Lovelace rose to his feet, and wandered over to me. He looked down at my kill. 'The one you let go was handsomer.'

"'He was English.'

"Lovelace smiled. 'Damn you, Byron, I never imagined it—a patriot.'

"'Just the opposite. But I thought his absence would be noticed more readily.'

"Lovelace shook his head mockingly. 'If you say so,

milord.' He paused. 'But I thought he was a dull cod's head of a guide, for all that.'

"I looked up at him suspiciously. 'What do you mean?'

"'Why, sir, I was watching you both all day. You were by the walls of the harem, and then you broke away. 'Tis like resting content with the merest glimpse of a strumpet's drawers.'

"'Oh?'

"Lovelace winked. 'What lies inside, *milord,* that is the treasure.' His bright eyes glittered. 'In the Turk's Seraglio wait a thousand caged whores.'

"I stared at him, a faint smile of disbelief on my lips. 'You're offering to lead me into the Sultan's harem?'

"Lovelace bowed. 'Why naturally, sir.' He stroked my hand. 'On a condition.'

"'I thought there might be.'

"'Your friend, Hobhouse . . .'

"'No!' I interrupted with sudden fury. 'And I warn you again . . .'

"Lovelace swished contemptuously with his hand. 'Sir, calm yourself, there are morsels here much daintier than your friend. But, Byron'—he smiled at me—'you must persuade him to leave for England at once.'

"'Oh? Why?'

"Lovelace reached out to stroke my hand again. 'So that we may be alone together,' he said. 'You will give yourself up to me, Byron, that I may teach you the arts.' He glanced down at the shepherd's corpse. 'It seems to me you are in need of them.'

"I stared at him. 'Abandon Hobhouse?' I said at last. Lovelace nodded. Slowly, I shook my head. 'Impossible.'

"'I will show you the delights of the Seraglio.'

"I shook my head again, and climbed up into my saddle. 'You told me of a secret, Lovelace—a secret that would threaten all those dearest to me. Well, I defy it. I will not abandon Hobhouse. I will never abandon those I love.'

"'Secret?' Lovelace seemed surprised by my mention of

it. Then he smiled, as though remembering. 'You need not worry, *milord*. It is not Hobhouse you threaten.'

"'Then who?'

"'Stay with me in the Orient, and I will teach you all I know.' His lips parted slightly. 'So much pleasure, Byron. I know you are a man who delights in it.'

"I stared at him with sudden contempt. 'I know we are both killers,' I said, 'but it does not give me any joy. I have told you before—I have no wish to be a creature like you. I have no wish to share in the knowledge you possess. I have no wish to be your pupil, Lovelace.' I inclined my head coldly. 'And so—I bid you good night.'

"I shook out the reins of my horse. I rode past the still graves. I rejoined the path by the city walls. The moon burnt brightly, and lit my way.

"'Byron!' I glanced around. 'Byron!' Lovelace stood where I had left him, a thing of spectral beauty among the ivy-clad tombs. His golden hair seemed touched by fire, and his eyes blazed. 'Byron,' he shouted with sudden ferocity, 'I tell you—it is the way of things! Here, in these peaceful gardens, dogs gorge on their prey—the gentle birds must feed on the worms—there is nothing in nature but eternal destruction! You are a predator—no longer a man, no longer what you were. Do you not know that the greater will always feed on the lesser?' Suddenly, he smiled. 'Byron,' I heard him whisper in my mind, 'we *shall* drink together.' I shivered, and my blood seemed turned to quicksilver, as brilliant as the moon. When I looked up for him, Lovelace had disappeared.

"I did not see him again for three days. His words had disturbed me—and excited me too. I began to relish the splendor of what I had become. Hadn't Lovelace merely spoken the truth?—I *was* a fallen being, and it *was* a fearsome and romantic state. Hobhouse, who was as satanic as a kipper, began to infuriate me—we quarreled endlessly and I started to wonder if we shouldn't separate after all. So when Hobhouse duly mentioned that he was thinking of returning home, I didn't discourage him—and neither did I pledge myself to doing the same. Yet the thought of what Lovelace's pleasures might be still filled me with dread—I was afraid, more than anything, that I might relish them, and find yet crueler desires awoken in me. So I reserved my opinion, and waited for Lovelace to approach me again. But all the while, I hoped, deep in my soul, that his temptations would be sufficient to encourage me to stay.

"The day came for our audience with the Sultan. Twenty of us, all English, suffered this excruciating privilege—my guide of three days before was with us, and so also, arriving at the last moment, was Lovelace. He saw me with my guide, and smiled, but said nothing. He stood just behind me, though, as we waited in the Sultan's presence-chamber, and later, when the whole tedious affair was at an end, he hovered within earshot of Hobhouse and myself.

"My guide came over to us, his eyes bright with excitement. 'You had a signal effect on the Sultan,' he told me. I inclined my head politely. 'Yes, yes, Byron,' he explained, 'the splendor of your dress, and your striking appearance, made him single you out as a particular object of attention. Indeed . . .'—here, the man paused and giggled, then flushed bright red.

"'What is it?' Hobhouse asked.

"The man giggled again, and turned back to me. He stammered, swallowed, and composed himself. 'The Sultan said that you were not a man at all.'

"My brow darkened, and I flushed cold; I glanced at Lovelace, who grinned back evilly. 'Not a man,' I said slowly. 'What did he mean?'

"The man's blush deepened. 'Why, Byron,' he tittered, 'the Sultan thought you were a woman dressed in man's clothes.' I breathed in deeply—then smiled with relief. My guide beamed eagerly. Lovelace's smile, I noticed, was the broadest of all.

"He came to me later that night, when Hobhouse was asleep. We stood together, on the roof of my house, and bathed our faces in the light of the moon. Lovelace took out his dagger. He stroked its thin, cruel blade. 'The Great Turk was a maggoty pimp, do you not think?' he asked.

"'Why?'

"Lovelace bared his teeth. He tested his thumb on his dagger's edge. 'To mistake you for a whore, of course.'

"I shrugged. 'Better that than to be recognized as what I am.'

"'Why sir, I would demand some revenge on him for his arrant impudence!'

"I stared coldly into Lovelace's gleaming eyes. 'I am not averse to people finding me beautiful.'

"Lovelace grinned. 'Are you not, sir?' he whispered. He turned, to gaze across the waters at the Seraglio, then slid his dagger back into his belt. 'Are you not?'

"He began to hum a tune from an opera. He bent down, and drew several bottles from a bag. He uncorked one. I smelled the golden perfume of blood. 'The salubrious juice,' said Lovelace, handing the bottle to me. 'I have mixed it with the finest Madeira known to man. Drink well, Byron, for tonight we need all our strength.' He raised a second bottle. 'A toast.' He smiled at me. 'To the rare sport we shall have tonight.'

"We grew drunk on the cocktails of wine and blood. No—not drunk—but my senses seemed richer than they had ever been, and I felt a violent joy rise like fire in my blood. I leaned on the wall, and stared at the dome-haunted skyline of the ancient city; the stars behind the Seraglio seemed to blaze with the fierceness of my own eager cruelty, and I knew that Lovelace was winning my soul. He held me in his arms, humming an aria under his breath, then speaking in my ear. 'You are a creature of great power,' he whispered. 'Would you care to see what you are capable of?' I smiled faintly. 'It will drain you, Byron, but you have the strength for this—young though you are in experience and blood.'

"I stared out at the waters of the Golden Horn. 'We are going to cross naked air,' I whispered. Lovelace nodded. I frowned, realizing how distant my memories had become.

'In my dreams, long before, I followed the Pasha. He showed me the miracles of time and space.'

"Lovelace grinned. 'A pox on the miracles of time and space.' He glanced across at the Seraglio. 'I want whores.'

"I laughed, from the depths of my stomach, helplessly. I was exhausted by my laughter. Lovelace held me, stroking the curls of my hair. He pointed across to the Seraglio. 'Look at it,' he whispered, 'imprison an image of it within your eye. Make it yours. Make it rise and come to you.'

"I stopped laughing abruptly. I stared into the cold depths of Lovelace's eye—then did as he had said. I saw the sky bend. The minarets and domes seemed to flow like water. My brow felt the touch of the palace's kiss. 'What's happening?' I whispered. 'How am I doing this?'

"Lovelace pressed a finger to my lips. He bent down for a final bottle, and uncorked it. 'Yes, that's good,' he nodded, 'breathe in its scent. Smell its richness. All your existence is contained within this. You are a creature of blood. You can flow like it out across the sky.' Suddenly he flung the bottle upward, and I saw blood in a crimson arc spattered over the city and the stars. 'Yes. flow with it!' Lovelace cried. I rose. I felt my disembodied self leave my flesh, like blood slipping from an open wound. The air was still thick. I was moving with it. Constantinople was stained, dark as the night, crimson as the blood I could hear summoning me. I saw it all, spinning, the city, the sea and the sky—and then suddenly, ahead, there was nothing but the Seraglio, distorted and disappearing from me, as though reflected in an endless series of mirrors, and I followed it, deep into the darkening heart of the vortex, and then I felt cool air on my face, and saw that I was standing on the harem wall.

"I turned. My movements seemed strange. I walked, and it felt to me as though I were a breeze skimming a dark-watered lake.

"'Byron.' The voice was a stone dropped into the depths. The two syllables rippled away. Lovelace smiled at me, and his face seemed to swim and change before my eyes. I imagined he was sinking beneath the lake's dark waters.

The ghostly pallor of his face was dimmed; his body shrunk; it was as though he had the form of a negro dwarf. I laughed, and the sound in my brain was refracted and strange. 'Byron.' I looked down again. Lovelace still had the shape of a dwarf. He smiled horribly, and his lips began to move. 'I am the eunuch,' I heard him say; 'you shall be the Sultan's slave.' He leered at me again, and I laughed drunkenly, but there were no ripples now, for the darkness was still like a crystal pool. Suddenly, conjured up from the whorls of my memory and desire, glimmering in the crystal, I saw Haidée. I gasped, and reached out to touch her. But the image spread, escaping me, and then I felt it lapping my skin, and I could no longer see Haidée, and everything seemed to be melting away. I placed my fingers over my eyes. The strangeness seemed even more bewitching than before. When I opened my eyes again, I saw that my nails were painted gold, and my fingers slim.

" 'Beautiful,' said the dwarf. He laughed, and pointed. 'This way, lovely infidel maid.'

"I followed him. Like the shadows of a storm, we passed through the harem gates. Long passages stretched away from us, rich in amethyst and green and yellow faience. All was silent, save for the footfalls of black dwarfs guarding elaborate doors of gold. As we passed them, they would frown and look around, but they did not see us until, outside the most beautiful gate of all, Lovelace drew his dagger and slashed its sentry's throat.

"I pressed forward eagerly at the smell of blood. Lovelace shook his head. 'Why drink water when there's champagne inside?' He held me back, and his touch on my body was sweet and strange. I looked down. I saw the truth of what I had imagined to be a dream—my body was that of a beautiful girl. I touched my breasts; raised a slim arm to stroke my long hair. I felt no surprise, only the heightening of a cruel and erotic joy. I walked forward, and for the first time was aware of the swirl of thin silk against my legs, and heard the tinkling rustle of ankle bells. I looked around me. I was in a spacious chamber. Couches were ranged along the wall. All was silent and dark. I began to glide past the couches down the center of the hall.

"Women were asleep on every couch. I breathed in the dizzying scent of their blood. Lovelace stood beside me. His grin was hungry and lecherous. 'Gad,' he whispered, 'but this is as sweet a room of strumpets as I've ever seen.' He bared his teeth. 'I must have 'em.' He glanced up at me. 'I shall have 'em.' He moved forward, like a mist across the sea. He stood by a girl's bed, and as the shadow fell across her dreams, she moaned and raised her arm as though to ward the evil away. I heard Lovelace's soft chuckle, and then, not wanting to see any more, I turned and walked on down the center of the hall. Ahead was another ornate door of gold. It was slightly ajar. I could hear a faint sobbing. I brushed my veil back from my ears. I heard a crack, and then the sobbing again. With a rustle of bells, I passed into the room beyond.

"I looked about me. Cushions were spread across a marble floor. Along the room's edge stretched a blue-watered pool. A single flame burned within a golden lamp. Standing in its wash was a naked girl. I studied her. She was wonderfully beautiful, but her bearing was imperious, and her face seemed equally voluptuous and cruel. She breathed in deeply, then raised the cane and swung it down hard. It bit into the back of the slave girl at her feet.

"The girl sobbed, but didn't break her posture of submission. Her mistress stared down at her handiwork, then glanced up suddenly into the shadows where I stood. Her bored, spoiled features seemed to lighten with interest; she narrowed her eyes; then the look of satiation returned to her face, and she sighed, dropping her cane onto the ground. She shouted at the girl and turned her back; the girl, still sobbing, began to pick up fragments of glass. When they had all been gathered, the slave girl bowed low in obeisance, and scurried from the room.

"The Sultan's Queen, for such she clearly was, threw herself onto the cushions. She held one of them tight, screwing it around and around, then hurled it violently back onto the floor. As she did so, I saw that her wrists were gashed with damp blood; the queen stared at them, and touched a wound, then rose to her feet again. She called for her maid; there was no response. She called again, and stamped her feet; then she picked up her cane, and walked toward the door. As she did so, I stepped out from the shadows. The Queen turned to look at me. She frowned when she saw that I did not lower my eyes.

"Slowly, the frown became a stare of surprise, and a strange tumult seemed to flash across her face. Command struggled with voluptuousness—and then she snapped her fingers, and was imperial again. She shouted something in a language I didn't understand, then pointed to the spot where her maid had smashed the glass. 'I am bleeding,' she said in Turkish, holding out her wrists. 'Call the physician, girl.' I smiled slowly. The Queen flushed—and then disbelief darkened into a passion of rage. She brought the cane stinging down on my back. The pain was like fire, but I stood where I was. The Queen stared deep into my eyes— then she choked, and dropped the cane, and stumbled back from me. She sobbed noiselessly. I watched as her shoulders rose and fell. She buried her face in her hands. In the golden light, the blood on her wrists gleamed like jewelry.

"I crossed the marble floor to her, and held her in my arms. The Queen looked up, startled; I placed a finger on her lips. Her eyes and cheeks were soft now with tears; I brushed them away, then gently stroked the wounds on her wrists. The Queen flinched with pain, but when she met my eyes, her agony seemed forgotten, and she reached up to hold me and stroke my hair. Nervously, she held my breasts; then she whispered something in my ear, words I didn't understand, and her fingers started to loosen my silk. I knelt, kissing her hands and wrists, tasting the fresh blood that welled from her cuts; when I was as naked as she, I kissed her on the lips, touching them with the rouge of her own blood, then leading her across to the stillness of the bath. Softly, the waters enveloped us. I felt the Queen's gentle fingers stroke my breasts and stomach; I opened my legs. She touched me, and I reached for her; she moaned, and tossed her head back; light caught the water on her throat and made it seem flushed with gold. The Queen shook; the warm water rippled gently, and I felt my blood seem to move with its flow against my skin. I licked her breasts, then gently, I bit; as my teeth pierced her skin, the Queen stiffened and gasped, but she did not scream, and her breathing deepened with eagerness. Suddenly, she shuddered; her body shook and she fell back against the tiles; once again, her throat was touched by gold. I seemed beyond self now, beyond consciousness, to have nothing but desire. Without thought, I slashed across my lover's neck, and as her blood spilled out into the waters of the bath, I felt my own thighs turn to water and join with the flow.

"Still the Queen hadn't screamed. She lay in my arms, lapped by her own blood as her breathing grew fainter and I drank from her wounds. She died without a sigh, and the waters were cloudy with her departed life. I kissed her softly, then slipped from the bath. I stretched—my smooth limbs seemed oiled and refreshed by her blood. I stared at the Queen, floating on her purple bier, and saw how her dead lips smiled back at me."

Lord Byron paused, and smiled himself. "You are disgusted?" he asked Rebecca, noticing how she stared at him.

"Yes, of course." She clenched a fist. "Of course I am. You enjoyed it. Even once you'd killed her, you felt no disgust."

Lord Byron's smile faded. "I am a vampire," he said softly.

"Yes, but . . ." Rebecca swallowed. "Before—before you had defied Lovelace."

"And my own nature."

"So he had won you?"

"Lovelace?"

Rebecca nodded. "You felt *no* remorse?"

Lord Byron hooded his burning eyes, and said nothing for what seemed a long, long time. Slowly, he ran his fingers through his hair. "I found Lovelace wet with blood, squatting like an incubus on his victim's chest. I told him that I had killed the Sultan's Queen. His amusement was quite immoderate. I didn't laugh with him, but no . . . I felt no remorse. Not until . . ." His voice trailed away.

Rebecca waited. "Yes?" she asked at last.

Lord Byron's lip curled. "We fed until dawn—two foxes in a chicken coop. Only with the muezzin's first call to prayers did we leave the chamber of odalisques. We passed, not into the passageway outside, but into a further room, set aside for the slave girls to adorn themselves. The walls were lined with mirrors. For the first time, I saw myself. I stopped—and froze. I was looking at Haidée—Haidée, whom I had not seen since that fatal night in the cave. But it was not Haidée. Haidée's lips had never been wet with blood. Haidée's eyes had never glittered so coldly. Haidée had never been a damned and loathsome vampire. I blinked—and then saw my own pale face staring back at me. I screamed. Lovelace tried to hold me, but I brushed him away. The pleasures of the night seemed suddenly transformed into horrors. They bred like maggots on my naked thoughts.

"For three days I lay exhausted and feverish in my bed. Hobhouse nursed me. I don't know what he heard me say in my delirium—but on the fourth day, he told me we were leaving Constantinople, and when I mentioned Lovelace's name, his face darkened and he warned me not to ask after him again. 'I have heard strange rumors,' he said, 'impossible rumors. You will leave with me on the ship I have booked. It is for your own safety and good. You know that, Byron, so I will hear no arguments.' And nor did he. We sailed that day, on a ship bound for England. I left Lovelace neither message nor address.

"But I knew that I couldn't go back home with Hobhouse. As we neared Athens, I told him I was going to stay in the East. I had thought my friend would be furious—but he said nothing, just smiled strangely, and handed me his journal. I frowned. 'Hobby, please,' I said, 'save your scribblings for your audience back home. I know what we did; I was with you, if you recall.'

"Hobhouse smiled again, a twisted smile. 'Not all the time,' he said. "The entries marked Albania—study them.' He left me.

"I read the passages at once. Then I wept—Hobhouse had changed the record of what he had done, so that it seemed as though we had never been apart—my time with Vakhel Pasha was quite obliterated. I found Hobhouse, and held him tight, and wept again. 'I do love you, Hobby,' I told him. 'You have so many good qualities, and so many bad ones, it is impossible to live with or without you.'

"The next day we parted. Hobhouse divided a small nosegay of flowers with me. 'Will it be the last thing we ever share?' he asked. 'What will happen to you, Byron?' I didn't answer. Hobhouse turned and boarded the ship again, and I was left alone.

"I headed on to Athens, and stayed briefly again with Widow Macri and her three lovely nymphs. But I was not made welcome, and though Teresa embraced me enthusiastically enough, I could still glimpse the fear that waited in her eyes. I began to feel the fever again, and reluctant to create a second scandal, I left Athens behind and journeyed on across Greece. Stimulation, sensation, novelty—I had to have them—the alternative was restlessness and agony. God, I was relieved that Hobhouse was gone. In Tripolitza, I stayed briefly with Veli, Ali Pasha's son, who entertained me as though I were a long-lost friend; I could see that he wanted me in his bed. I let him take me, of course—why not?—the pleasure of being used as a whore was a momentary thrill. Then, in return for my services, Veli passed on news of Albania. It seemed that Vakhel Pasha's castle had been burnt to the ground and quite destroyed. 'Would you believe it?' Veli asked, shaking his head. 'The mountain people thought that the dead had risen from their graves.' He laughed at the thought of such hapless superstition. I listened with amusement—then asked about Vakhel Pasha himself. Again, Veli shook his head. 'He was found near Lake Trihonida,' he said.

" 'Dead?' I asked.

"Veli nodded. 'Oh yes! very dead indeed, *milord.* A sword had been driven deep through his heart. We buried him by his castle on the mountainside.'

"So he was gone. Dead in truth. I realized I had half-believed he might still be alive. But now I could be certain—and the knowledge, somehow, served to liberate me. Everything seemed changed—I was free of my creator—and at last I accepted the truth of what I was. Above the Gulf of Corinth, as I fed on a peasant boy, I was discovered by Lovelace. We embraced warmly, and neither of us mentioned my flight from Constantinople.

" 'Shall we be wicked?' Lovelace asked me.

"I smiled. 'Wicked as sin,' I replied.

"We returned to Athens. Cloaked as we were in our mutual pleasures, dread and guilt became forgotten words—two such libertines had never existed, Lovelace assured me, not since the days of the Restoration rakes. New worlds of delight were opened up to me, and I grew drunk on companionship, sex, and fine wines. And blood, of course—yes—always blood. The fires of joy seemed to have burned away my shame. My cruelty now seemed a beautiful thing—I loved it, I found, in the same way that I loved the blue skies and landscapes of Greece, as an exotic paradise I had made my own. My old world seemed impossibly distant from me now. With Lovelace's encouragement, I began to think of it as forever gone.

"Yet sometimes—after I had bathed perhaps, and was sitting on some lonely rock, gazing at the sea—then I would hear its call again. Lovelace, who scorned such moods as hypocrisy, would damn me roundly for my gloom, and lead me out on fresh revelries—yet often, at these moments, it was his very encouragements which most discomforted me. Sometimes, when I felt the call of home, he would hint again at secrets, dark truths, threats that in England might betray me.

" 'And in Greece?' I would ask.

" 'Why no, sir,' Lovelace answered once. 'Not if you have wrapped your tizzle in a good sheath of pig-gut.' I pressed him to explain, but he laughed. 'No, Byron, your soul is not yet flinty enough. The time shall come, when you are steeped in blood. Then go back to England, but for now—egad, sir, 'tis almost the night—let us venture out and twatscour the town.' I protested, but Lovelace held up his hands. 'Byron—I beg you—let us have an end on't, please!' And straightaway, he gathered up his cloak and hummed an opera tune, and I knew he was relishing his power over me.

"But the conversation didn't worry me for long—nothing worried me—there were far too many pleasures to learn. Much as a lover is instructed by a courtesan, so I was taught the arts of drinking blood. I learned how to enter a victim's dreams, how to master my own, how to hypnotize and generate illusions and desires. I learned how vampires could be made, and the various orders into which a victim might be transformed—the zombies, whose dead eyes I had seen in the Pasha's castle, the ghouls, such as Gorgiou and his family had become, or, most rarely, the masters—the lords of death—the order of creatures to which I belonged.

"'But be careful who you choose for that honor,' Lovelace warned me once. 'Know ye not, in death as in life, there must be aristocracy?' He smiled at me. 'You, Byron, might almost have been chosen as a king.'

"I shrugged off Lovelace's flattery. 'I damn all kings to Hell,' I said. 'I am not a vile Tory like you. If I could, I would teach the very stones to rise against tyranny. I kill—but I shall not enslave.'

"Lovelace spat with contempt. 'What distinction is that?'

"I stared at him coldly. 'One that is clear enough, I would have thought. I need to drink blood or I die—you have said it, Lovelace, we are predators, we cannot defy what is natural in us. But is it ever natural to make our victims slaves? I hope not. I will not be like my creator, that is what I mean—surrounded by mindless serfs, beyond the redemption of love and hope.'

"'Why? You think you are not already?' Lovelace smiled cruelly at me but I ignored his mocking questions, his familiar hinting at some dark mystery. For I felt powerful now, and knew that I had passed beyond his authority—I doubted that Lovelace had a secret at all. I thought I understood the thing I had become—I had no self-disgust, only joy and strength. And so I also felt free—free in a way I had never dreamed might be possible—and I trusted myself to this sense of freedom, which rolled as boundless and untamed as the sea.

"Or so I imagined." Lord Byron paused—and for a long moment, stared into the shadows of the candle flame. Then he poured himself a glass of wine, and with a single gulp, emptied it. When he spoke again, his voice sounded dead. "One evening, I was passing down a narrow, crowded street. I had drunk recently; I felt no thirst, only a pleasant richness suffusing my veins. But suddenly, above the stenches of the street, I smelled the purest scent I have ever known. I cannot describe it"—he glanced at Rebecca—"even if I could put the perfume into words, since it was something a mortal could never understand. Golden, sensual—perfect."

"It was blood?" Rebecca asked.

"Yes." Lord Byron nodded. "But . . . blood? No—it was more than that. It gave me a craving that seemed to hollow out my bones—my stomach—my very mind. I stood where I was, in the center of the street, and breathed in deeply. Then I saw it—a baby, held in a woman's arms—and the scent of the blood was coming from that child. I took a step forward—but the woman slipped away, and when I crossed to where she had been standing there was no sign of her. I breathed in again—the scent was fading—and then, as I stumbled desperately on down the street, I saw the woman ahead of me, just as she had been before—and then a second time, she seemed to fade into the air. I pursued her, but soon even the scent of blood was gone and I was left in the grip of agonies. I searched for that baby all night. But his mother's face had been cloaked beneath a hood and the baby had looked much like any other child of his age and so at last I despaired and abandoned my search.

"I rode hard out from Athens. There was a temple perched on a cliff above the sea where I was in the habit of going to order my thoughts—but that night, its calmness seemed a taunt, and I felt nothing but my hunger still gnawing at me. Always, in my nostrils, there was the perfume of that blood. I knew, with the certainty of revelation, that I would never have true happiness until I had tasted it, and so I rose, and untethered my horse, and prepared myself to return and track the infant down. It was then that I saw Lovelace. He was standing between two columns, and the dawn behind him was the color of blood. He walked across to me. He stared deep into my eyes—then suddenly, he smiled. He slapped me on the shoulder. 'Congratulations,' he said.

" 'On what?' I asked slowly.

" 'Why, sir, on your child, of course.'

" 'Child, Lovelace?'

" 'Yes, Byron—child.' He slapped me on the shoulder again. 'You have fathered some bastard on one of your whores.'

"I licked my lips. 'How do you know?' I asked slowly.

" 'Because, Byron, I have seen you running around town all night like some damn bitch on heat. 'Tis the infallible sign, sir, among our kind, that a child has been born.'

"I felt a ghastly coldness creeping over me. 'Why?' I asked, staring for some sign of hope in Lovelace's eyes. But there was none.

"I think, sir, now, there can be no denying you the fateful truth.' He laughed. 'Fateful, I call it, though to me, of course, 'tis not worth a Tom-turd collector's cuss.' He grinned. 'But you, sir, despite what you are, have still not wholly lost your principles. Presumptuous of you, I call it, Byron—in the circumstances, damn presumptuous.'

"Slowly, I reached for him, and gripped him around the throat. 'Tell me,' I whispered.

"Lovelace choked, but I did not loosen my grip. 'Tell me,' I whispered again. 'Tell me that what you hint at isn't true.'

" 'I cannot,' panted Lovelace. 'I would have kept this from you yet longer,' he said, 'seeing how feebly your soul is touched by vice, but there is no helping it, you must be told the truth. Know then, Byron,' he whispered, 'it is the doom of your nature'—he paused and grinned—'that those who share your blood are most delicious to you.'

"'No.'

"'Yes!' shouted Lovelace with enthusiasm.

"I shook my head. 'It cannot be true.'

"'You smelled the blood. 'Tis a wondrous scent, is it not? Even now, it hangs in your nostrils. It will drive you mad; I have seen it all before.'

"'So you—you have known it too?'

"Lovelace shrugged, and twirled a mustache. 'I was never much fond of children.'

"'But . . . your own flesh and blood . . .'

"'Mmmm . . .' Lovelace slapped his lips together. 'Believe me, Byron—the little bastards make for a most unparalleled draft.'

"I took him by the throat again. 'Leave me,' I said. Lovelace opened his mouth, to make some further jeering comment, but I met his eyes and slowly he was forced to lower them, and I knew, despite my agony, that my strength was undimmed. But what help was it to know that?—my powers would serve merely to compound my doom. 'Leave me,' I whispered again. I threw Lovelace back, so that he staggered and fell—then, with the sound of his horse's hooves fading in my ears, I sat myself alone on the edge of the cliff. All day I wrestled with my thirst for the blood of my child.'

"He had told you the truth?" Rebecca asked softly. "Lovelace?"

Lord Byron gazed at her. His eyes glittered. "Oh yes," he said.

"Then . . ."

"Yes?"

Rebecca stared at him. She clutched at her throat. She swallowed. "Nothing," she said.

Lord Byron smiled at her faintly, then hooded his eyes, and stared far, far away. "Everything was changed by what Lovelace had told me," he said. "That evening, staring into the waves, I imagined I saw a bloody hand, fresh severed from its limb, beckoning me. I raved at it—yet I knew then that I was far more like the Pasha than I had ever dared fear. I returned to Athens. I found Lovelace. I hadn't smelled my child's blood again, but I dreaded, and longed for it, all the time. 'I must go,' I told Lovelace that night. 'Leave Athens at once. There can be no delay.'

"Lovelace shrugged. 'And will you leave Greece as well?'

"I nodded.

"'Then where will you go?'

"I thought. 'To England,' I said at last. 'I must raise money—sort out my affairs. Then, when that is done, I will leave again, far from anyone who shares my blood.'

"'You have family in England?'

"'Yes.' I nodded. 'A mother.' I thought. 'And a sister—a half-sister.'

"''Twill make small difference. Avoid them both.'

"'Yes, of course.' I buried my head in my hands. 'Of course.'

"Lovelace held me in his arms. 'When you are ready,' he whispered, 'join me again, and we will renew our sport. You are a rare creature, Byron. When your soul is black with vice, you will be a vampire like none I have ever known.'

"I looked up at him. 'Where will you be?' I asked.

"Lovelace began to hum an opera tune. 'Why, sir, in the only place for fun—in Italy.'

"'I will join you,' I said.

"Lovelace kissed me. 'Excellent!' he cried. 'But Byron—come quickly. Do not delay in England. Stay there too long, and you will find it hard—perhaps impossible—to leave.'

"I nodded. 'I understand,' I said.

"'There is a girl I know in London. She is of our kind.' He winked. 'The damndest pair of bubbies you ever saw. I will write to her. She will guide you, I hope.' He kissed me again. 'Guide you, while you are apart from me.' He smiled. 'Do not delay, though. It has taken me a long time, Byron, to find a companion as agreeable as you. Zounds, sir, together

again, what riots we shall have. And now'—he bowed—
'God's speed to you. We shall meet again in Italy.'

"With that, he left me—and a week later, I too had left
Athens behind. The voyage, as you can imagine, was not a
pleasant one. Not a day went by when I did not contemplate
leaving the ship—setting up in some foreign city—never
returning to England again. Yet I needed money—and I was
homesick—for my friends—for my home—for a final
glimpse of my native land. I was homesick too for my
mother and for Augusta, my sister—but those, of course,
were thoughts I tried to banish from my mind. At last, after
a voyage of a month, two years of travel, and the utter
transformation of my life, I felt English soil beneath my feet
once again."

Chapter IX

It happened that in the midst of the dissipations attendant upon a London winter, there appeared at the various parties of the leaders of the "ton" a nobleman, more remarkable for his singularities, than his rank. He gazed upon the mirth around him, as if he could not participate therein. Apparently, the light laughter of the fair only attracted his attention, that he might by a look quell it, and throw fear into those breasts where thoughtlessness reigned. Those who felt this sensation of awe could not explain whence it arose: some attributed it to the dead gray eye, which, fixing upon the object's face, did not seem to penetrate, and at once glance to pierce through to the inward workings of the heart; but fell upon the cheek with a leaden ray that weighed upon the skin it could not pass. His peculiarities caused him to be invited to every house; all wished to see him, and those who had been accustomed to violent excitement, and now felt the weight of ennui, were pleased at having something in their presence capable of engaging their attention. In spite of the deadly hue of his face, which never gained a warmer tint, either from the blush of modesty, or from the strong emotion of passion, though its form and outline were beautiful, many of the female hunters after notoriety attempted to win his attentions, and gain, at least, some marks of what they might term affection: Lady Mercer, who had been the mockery of every monster shewn in drawing-rooms since her marriage, threw herself in his way, and did all but put on the dress of a mountebank, to attract his notice . . .

DR. JOHN POLIDORI, *The Vampyre*

J had to be in England before I truly understood how cursed I had become. I was my mother's only son—for two years, she had been running Newstead, my home, for me—I knew how deeply she had longed for my return. Yet I couldn't even visit her. I remembered the golden scent from Athens too well, and I knew that to breathe it again would be fatal, to my mother, and to myself. So instead, I traveled to London. I had business to sort out, friends to meet. One of them asked if I had written any poems while abroad. I gave him the manuscript of *Childe Harold's Pilgrimage*. My friend came back to me a day later, full of excitement and praise.

"'Please, don't be insulted,' he said, 'but you must pretend that this Childe Harold is a portrait of yourself.' He narrowed his eyes, as he studied me. 'A pale, beautiful wanderer, gloomy with thoughts of decay and death, bringing wretchedness on all who come close to him. Yes, it's going to work, you could really do it.' He studied me again, and then he frowned. 'Do you know, Byron, there *is* something strange about you, something almost—well—

201

unsettling. I never noticed it before.' Then he grinned, and slapped me on the back. 'So just play it up, all right?' He winked. 'It's going to sell this poem, and make you very famous indeed.'

"I laughed, when he had gone, to think how little he or anyone knew. Then I wrapped myself in my cloak, and left my rooms to stalk the London streets. I did this almost every night now. My thirst seemed to have become unsatisfiable. It ached all the time, a promise of delight that made all other pleasures seem like dust. Yet even as I fed, I knew that I was denying myself the sweetest joy of all. As the moon started to wax, so too did the craving for my mother's blood continue to grow. Several times, I ordered a carriage to take me up to Newstead—only to cancel it at the last moment, and seek out other, lesser, prey. Yet I knew the temptation would defeat me in the end; it could only be a matter of time. And then, almost a month after my return, came news that my mother had fallen ill. My resolve snapped—I ordered a carriage—I set out at once. The horror and desire I felt cannot be described. I seemed to be melting with anticipation. I would kill my mother—drain her—I *would* do it—I would feel her golden blood filling up my veins. I was shaking, even before I had left London— and it was on the outskirts of London that the servant found me, with his message that my mother was dead.

"I was numbed. For the whole journey I felt nothing at all. I reached Newstead. I stood by my mother's corpse, and began to sob, and laugh, and kiss her icy face. To my surprise, I realized that I felt no frustration—it was almost as though, with her death, my knowledge of how her blood would have tasted was dead as well. So I mourned her as any son would mourn his mother, and for a few days, I savored the forgotten pleasure of a mortal's grief. I was alone in the world now—alone save for my half-sister, Augusta, and she I hardly knew. She wrote to me, a kind letter of condolence, but she did not come and stay at Newstead, and I was happy to realize that I did not want her to. If I smelled her blood, I knew that the craving would return—but I felt none of the temptation I had suffered with my mother, to search her out. Instead, I vowed that our lives would continue separate. A week after my mother's death, I went hunting in the Abbey woods. I drank with a delight I had almost forgotten. The pleasure seemed as profound as it had ever been—as profound as before that fatal afternoon, when I had paused in the Athens street, and first smelled the golden blood of my child. Might it really be possible, I wondered, that the memory of that scent had died with my mother? I prayed that it had, and as the months passed, began to believe that it was indeed dead.

"Yet even so, things were not as they had been before. The creature I had been in the East, so free, so in love with the freshness of his crimes, was gone—instead, in England, my thirst seemed crueler, more impatient with a world too dull to recognize it. I sheathed my soul in guarded coldness, and moved, a restless hunter, through the uncomprehending mortal crowds. More and more, I understood what it was to be a thing apart—a spirit among clay, a stranger among scenes that had once been my own. Yet I felt a pride in my desolation, and longed to soar, like a wild-born falcon, high and boundless above the limiting earth. I returned to London, that mighty vortex of all pleasure and vice, and climbed the giddy circles of its delights. In the dark places of the city, where misery bred nightmares far worse than myself, I became a whispered rumor of horror, stalking the drunk and the criminal; I fed with a greedy compulsion, glutting my hunger where it could not be witnessed, cloaked in the filthy mists of the slums, yet I had no wish to skulk forever in the city's underworld, living like a rat in the foulest recesses—I was a vampire, yes, but I was also a creature of mighty, of terrifying power, and I knew that all of London was mine to subdue. And so I rose, and entered the bright salons of Society, that glittering world of great mansions and balls—I passed through it—and as I did so—so also I conquered it.

"For my friend had been right about *Childe Harold*. I awoke one morning, and found myself famous. The whole world seemed suddenly stark-mad about the poem—and about me, its author, madder still. I was courted, visited, flattered, and desired—there was no other topic of conversation but myself, no other object of curiosity or praise. But it was not my poetry that had won me such fame—no—I never for a moment presumed to think that. It was the spell of my eyes which had prostrated London—the spell of my nature, which subdued duchesses and viscounts as easily as peasant boys. I had only to enter a ballroom to sense its surrender to me. I would gaze around at the wealth and beauty swirling on the floor, and at once, a thousand eyes would turn to admire my face, a thousand hearts would beat faster at my stare. Yet this fascination people felt was something they barely understood—for what could they know of the vampire, and his secret world? But I understood—and witnessing my empire, I felt anew what it meant to be a lord of the dead.

"Yet, for all this—all these manifold proofs of my power—I was not happy. Among the poor, I fed on blood; among the aristocracy, on their hapless worship. Both served to calm my restlessness, which tortured me now, as though it were a fire in the very core of my being, which would consume me unless it was constantly fed. Yet as I sought to appease these flames, so also I felt my soul wither all the more—and I began to long again for mortal love, to redeem me, perhaps, and fall like cooling rain on my heart. But where could I find such a love? My eyes, now, could only win me slaves—and those I despised, for they loved me as birds love a rattlesnake. I could scarcely blame them; the stare of a vampire is deadly and sweet. Yet sometimes, when my thirst for blood was satiated, I loathed my own powers, and felt how strongly—how painfully—my own mortal longings still survived in me.

"It happened, at the height of my fame, that I went to Lady Westmoreland's ball. The usual crowds of women came flocking up to me, begging for a word or even a glance—but among the throngs was one woman who looked away. I asked for an introduction—it was refused. Naturally enough, I was intrigued. A few days later, I saw the same woman again—and this time, she graciously acknowledged me. Her name, I learned, was Lady Caroline Lamb; she was married to the son of Lady Melbourne, whose house in Whitehall was the most fashionable in town. The new morning, I called on Lady Caroline—I was ushered to her room—and found her waiting for me, dressed as a page.

" 'Byron,' she drawled, 'lead me to your carriage.' I smiled, but said nothing, and did as she asked. 'The docks,' she told my coachman. Her lisp was quite captivating. Physically, she was a little on the bony side, but in her pageboy's uniform, she reminded me of Haidée, and I had decided already I would have her if I could. Lady Caroline, it seemed, had made her mind up too. 'Your face,' she told me in a dramatic whisper, 'I think it is my fate.' She gripped my hand. 'How icy your touch is. How cold.' I smiled faintly, disguising my frown—and Lady Caroline shuddered with delight. 'Yes,' she said, kissing me suddenly, 'I think your love will be pollution. It will destroy me utterly!' The idea seemed to arouse her even more. She kissed me again violently, then leaned out of the carriage. 'Faster,' she yelled at the coachman, 'faster! Your master is keen to wreak his evil way on me!'

"I did so, in a foul-smelling tavern by the edge of the docks. I used her once, casually, up against the wall, then had her a second time, in her pageboy's suit—Caro adored it both ways around. 'How awful it is,' she gasped happily, 'to be the object of your intemperate lusts. I am shamed, ruined, oh, I shall kill myself.' She paused, then kissed me again with wild abandon. 'Oh, Byron, what a fiend you are—what a black-souled monster!'

"I smiled. 'Flee me then,' I whispered mockingly. 'Do you not know, my touch is deadly?'

"Caro giggled and kissed me—then suddenly, her face grew solemn. 'Yes,' she said softly, 'I rather think it is.' She slipped from my embrace, and ran from the room—I dressed unhurriedly, then followed her out, and together we rode back to Melbourne House.

"How much had she understood when she had called me a fiend, an angel of death? Had she suspected the truth? I doubted it—but I was sufficiently captivated to want to find out. The following day, I visited her again. I gave her a rose. 'Your ladyship, I am told, likes all that is new and rare for a moment.'

"Caro stared at the rose. 'Indeed, My Lord?' she whispered. 'I had imagined that to be truer of you.' She laughed hysterically, and began to tear the petals from the flower. Then, her taste for melodrama seemingly satisfied, she took my arm and led me into Lady Melbourne's hall.

"It was crowded, but the moment I had walked into the room, I knew there was another vampire there. I breathed in deeply, and looked around—and then the feeling was gone. But I was certain that my senses hadn't lied to me. I remembered Lovelace's promise, that he would write to a girl of our own kind, to help and advise me while I stayed in London. I glanced around the salon again. Caro was watching me, with her violent, burning eyes—Lady Melbourne herself was watching me—the whole room was watching me. And then, in the corner, I saw someone sitting on her own who was not.

"She was a young girl, radiant and grave. Suddenly, I felt tears prick my eyes. The girl was as much like Haidée as a gem is like a flower—and yet in her face there was the same hint of sublimity, all youth but with an aspect beyond time. She felt my eyes on her, and glanced up. There was a great depth in her stare, and a sadness too—but it was a sadness for another person's crime—and that person, I realized with a sudden shock, was myself. She sat as though guarding the gateway to Eden, mourning for those who could return no more. She smiled again, then turned away, and however piercingly I continued to stare at her, she did not look up a second time.

"But later in the evening, when I was standing alone, she came up to me.

"'I know you for what you are,' she whispered.

"I stared at her. 'Indeed, miss?' I asked.

"She nodded gently. How young she was, I thought, and yet how profound was her look, as though her soul were embracing boundless thoughts. I opened my mouth, to mention Lovelace's name—and then suddenly, I realized something strange, and paused. For if she were the creature I had presumed her to be—where was the cruelty in her face?—the ice of death?—the hunger in her eyes?

" 'You *can* feel nobly, My Lord,' the strange girl said. She paused, as though in sudden confusion. 'But you discourage your own goodness,' she said quickly. 'Please, Lord Byron—never believe that you exist beyond hope.'

" 'You have hope yourself, then?'

" 'Oh, yes.' The girl smiled. 'We all have hope.' She paused, and glanced down at her feet. 'Goodbye,' she said, looking up again. 'I trust we shall become friends.'

" 'Yes,' I said. I watched as she turned to leave, and felt a sudden bitterness curl my lip. 'Perhaps we shall be,' I whispered softly to myself, and then I laughed mirthlessly and shook my head.

" 'Has my niece been amusing you, My Lord?'

"I glanced around. Lady Melbourne was standing behind me. I bowed politely. 'Your niece?' I asked.

" 'Yes. Her name is Annabella. The daughter of a frigidly provincial elder sister of mine.' Lady Melbourne glanced at the door through which her niece had disappeared. I followed her stare. 'She seems an extraordinary girl,' I said.

" 'Indeed?' Lady Melbourne turned to stare at me. Her eyes glinted with a touch of mockery, and her smile was cruel. 'I hadn't thought she was the type of girl to attract you, My Lord.'

"I shrugged. 'She is perhaps a little encumbered by virtue.'

"Lady Melbourne smiled again. She really was a most attractive woman, I realized—dark-haired, voluptuous, with eyes that glittered as brightly as my own. It was impossible to believe she was sixty-two. She rested her hand gently on my arm. 'Beware of Annabella,' she said softly. 'Too much virtue can be a dangerous thing.'

"For a long while, I made no answer—just stared into the death-like paleness of Lady Melbourne's face. Then I nodded. 'I am sure you are right,' I said.

"At that moment, I heard Caro shouting my name. I glanced over my shoulder. 'Call your carriage,' she yelled at me, in a voice which carried across the room. 'I want to leave, Byron. I want to leave now!' I saw her husband stare darkly at me, then look away. I turned back to Lady Melbourne. 'I wouldn't worry,' I told her. 'I doubt I'll have the time to be distracted by your niece.' I smiled faintly. 'I think your daughter-in-law will see to that.'

"Lady Melbourne nodded, but she didn't answer my smile. 'Again, My Lord,' she whispered, 'be careful. You are powerful, but young. You do not know your strength. And Caroline is passionate.' She squeezed my hand. 'If things turn wrong, dear Byron—it can be good to have a friend.'

"She stared deep into my eyes. How unearthly her beauty was, I thought, how strange and fierce—how very like Lovelace's. And yet she was too old to be the girl he had known. I glanced across at Caro, then back at Lady Melbourne as she walked away from me. I called after her.

"She raised a single eyebrow as she turned around. 'My Lord?' she asked.

"'Lady Melbourne . . .' I laughed, then shook my head. 'Forgive me—but I must ask . . .'

"'Please,' she said. She waited. 'Ask.'

"'Are you what you seem to be?'

"She smiled softly. 'That you ask me the question surely answers you.'

"I bowed my head.

"'We are so few,' she whispered suddenly. She took my hand again. 'We who have chosen to kiss the lips of death.'

"'Chosen, Lady Melbourne?' I stared at her. 'I never chose.'

"A sad half-smile played on Lady Melbourne's lips. 'Of course,' she said. 'I was forgetting.' She turned, and when I reached after her, she brushed my hand away. 'Please,' she said, staring back at me, 'I beg you—forget what I have just said.' Her eyes glittered with sudden warning. 'Do not press me on it, dear Byron. Anything else—ask—and I will help you. But not the causes that led me to . . . to become what you see. I am sorry. The fault was mine. I never intended to refer to it.' A shadow of bitterness passed across her face— and as though reminded by something, she glanced across at her daughter-in-law. 'Be kind to her,' she whispered. 'Do not unbalance her mind. She is mortal—you are not.' Then, with a sudden smile, she was once again the urbane hostess. 'Now,' she said, dismissing me, 'I mustn't keep you to myself.' She kissed me farewell. 'Off you go and seduce my son's wife.'

"I did so, that night. I paid little attention to Lady Melbourne's requests. Naturally—for it was my immortal nature which I most longed to forget; I had no other motive for falling in love. I had been craving a woman such as Caro—a tameless spirit, a lover without restraints, whose desire would be equal to the greed of my own. For a few weeks, our passion burned madly, with a desperate fever which infected us both, torching our every thought which was not of our love, so that for a while, even my restless lust for blood seemed dimmed. But the fever passed—and I realized that I had only another slave—like all my slaves— save that Caro's wildness made her bondage to me even more complete. I had not drained her, as the vampire normally does, but—far crueler—I had infected her with a scorching, remorseless desire, so that her mind grew ever more frantic and unhinged. I realized for the first time how deadly a vampire's love can be—that the drinking of blood is not the only way to destroy. For I had enveloped Caro in the full glare of my passion—and like the sun, it was too bright for a mortal's mind to bear. My own love was soon spent, very soon spent—but it was Caro's doom never to be cured of me.

"Soon, her indiscretions became insufferable—and it was I, the vampire, who was haunted by her. She sent me presents, letters, came at midnight to my rooms, followed my carriage in her pageboy disguise. I sent her brutal dismissals—I took a second mistress—in desperation, I even contemplated killing her. But Lady Melbourne, when I suggested such a plan, laughed and shook her head. 'The scandal is already quite damaging enough.' She stroked my hair. 'Dearest Byron, I did warn you—you must be more restrained. Draw less attention to yourself. Be discreet—as I am—as all our breed are.'

"I looked up at her. I thought about the girl that Lovelace had known, and who had not yet come to me. 'There are others, then,' I asked, 'like us, here in London?'

"Lady Melbourne tilted her head. 'Doubtless,' she said.

"'But surely you know?'

"She smiled. 'As I said—we are mostly discreet.' She paused. 'We also, Byron, it is true to say, lack your power—it makes you extraordinary—but dangerous as well. You have genius and fire—and so—for those very reasons—*you must be careful.*' She held my arms, stared into my face. 'Do you doubt that the law, if it finds us, would seek to destroy us? Your fame is something terrible—your exposure could serve to annihilate us all.'

"'I do not care to skulk,' I said lazily; but her urgency had impressed me, and I was careful, this time, to heed her words. I did not kill Lady Caroline—merely redoubled my efforts to keep her at bay. I did nothing that would draw attention to myself—in other words—I seduced, drank, gambled, talked politics—like any other London gentleman—and above all, I spent time with Hobhouse—that single fixed point my life still possessed. Hobby had never asked me about my year alone in Greece, and I never told him. Instead, like the true friend he was, he fought hard to keep me out of scrapes, and I trusted him in a way I found hard to trust myself. Only late at night, when we had returned from a party or a gaming club, did I shrug him off. Then I would slip into the dark, and resume an existence that Hobhouse couldn't check, and for a few brief hours, I would be true to myself. But even among the docks and the foulest slums, I remembered Lady Melbourne's plea—and I was discreet. My victims, once selected, never escaped.

"One night, though, my thirst grew more than usually sharp. Caro had created a scene—arriving at my house, very late, in her pageboy's disguise—demanding an elopement. Hobhouse, as ever, had been a pillar of strength, and Caro had been bundled out at last—but I was left feeling feverish with cruelty, and a loathing of the need to disguise what I was. I waited till Hobhouse was gone—then I left for the darkness of the Whitechapel slums. I walked through the loneliest, dimmest streets. My need for blood was desperate. Suddenly, I could smell it, both ahead of me and behind. But I was in no mood now for carefulness. I walked on, into a foul, mud-filled lane, and my footsteps were the only noise to be heard. The smell of blood was very rich now. Then I sensed someone stepping out from behind me. I turned around, and saw an arm coming down—I caught it—I twisted it—I forced the mugger to the ground. He looked into my face, and he screamed, and then I slashed across his throat, and there was silence, save for the sweet, sweet washing of his blood against my face. I drank long and deep; holding the dead man's throat to my lips. At last I was full—I dropped the withered corpse into the mud—and then—I paused. I could smell the perfume of another person's blood. I looked up. Caro was watching me.

"Slowly, I wiped the blood from my mouth. Caro said nothing, just stared with her wild, desperate eyes, as I rose and walked across to her. I ran my finger through her hair; she shuddered; I thought she was about to break away. But then she began to shake, her thin body racked by tearless sobs, and she reached for my lips, kissing me, smearing the blood across her mouth and face. I held her. 'Caro,' I whispered, deep within her thoughts, 'you have seen nothing tonight.' Wordlessly, she nodded. 'We must leave,' I said, glancing at the corpse where it lay in the mud. I took Caro's arm. 'Come on,' I said. 'It isn't safe for either of us here.'

"Caro was dumb in the carriage. On the way back to Whitehall, I made love to her, tenderly, and still she didn't speak a word. At Melbourne House, I escorted her in, and we parted with a kiss. As I left, I caught sight of myself in a mirror. The soul of passion seemed stamped on every feature. My face was pale with haughtiness and bitter contempt; yet there was an air as well of dejection and woe, which softened and shaded the fierceness of my looks. It was a terrible face, beautiful and wretched—it was my own face. I shuddered, as Caro had done, and saw distress struggling with malignity, till everything was cold and solemn as before. Impassive once again, I swept my cloak about me, and returned into the night.

"The next day, Caro came to my rooms, forcing her way past my servants and shouting at my friends to leave us alone. 'I love you,' she said, when we were alone. 'I love you, Byron, with all my heart, my everything—my life. Take that, if you won't have me.' Suddenly, she ripped open her dress. 'Kill me!' she screamed. 'Feed on me!'

"I stared at her, long and hard. Then I shook my head. 'Leave me in peace,' I said.

"But Caro seized my arm, and flung herself at me. 'Let me be a creature like you! Let me share in your existence! I will surrender everything!'

"I laughed. 'You don't know what you say.'

"'I do!' Caro screamed. 'I do, I do! I want the kiss of death on my lips! I want to share this darkness you have risen from! I want to taste the magic of your blood!' She began to sob. She fell on her knees. 'Please, Byron! Please, I cannot live without you. Give me your blood. Please!'

"I stared at her, and felt a terribly pity, and a temptation as well. To let her share my existence with me—yes—to ease the burden of my loneliness . . . But then I remembered my vow, never to create another creature like myself, and I turned my back on her. 'Your vanity is ridiculous,' I told her, as I rang the servant's bell. 'Exert your absurd caprices upon others.'

"'No!' Caro wailed, beating her head against my knees. 'No, Byron, no!'

"A servant came in. 'Find her ladyship decent clothing,' I ordered. 'She is leaving now.'

" 'I will reveal your secret,' she screamed. 'I will see you destroyed.'

" 'Your love of theatricals is notorious, Lady Caroline. Who has ever believed a thing you say?' I watched as she was led by my servant from the room. Then I took out ink and paper, and wrote a note to Lady Melbourne, warning of all that was happening.

"We both agreed that Caro should be sent away. Her madness now was growing desperate. She sent me a gift of her pubic hair, matted with gore—with it came a note, asking again to be given my blood. She followed me endlessly; she screamed at me in the street; she told her husband she was marrying me. He shrugged coldly at this news, and said he doubted I would have her—as Lady Melbourne had instructed him to. At last, through our combined efforts, we persuaded Caro to leave with her family for Ireland. But already, as she had threatened to do, she had been talking wildly about my taste for blood. The rumors became so dangerous that I even contemplated marrying, as the only way of answering them. I remembered Annabella, Lady Melbourne's niece—she had been suitably virtuous—ideal, I thought. But Lady Melbourne had only laughed, and when I made her write with my proposal to her niece, Annabella herself turned me down. I was neither hurt, nor greatly surprised by this rejection—I had admired Annabella—and knew she merited a better heart than mine. My matrimonial ambitions began to fade. Instead, to quieten the rumors, I followed a plan only scarcely less enervating: I abandoned London, and went to Cheltenham.

"There I lay low. My affair with Caro had left me wretched and dull. I had loved her—truly loved her—but I had also destroyed her, and been confronted once again by the nature of my doom. I could have no ties—enjoy no love—and so I grew feverish again for travel, to escape England for Italy, as I had always intended to do. I sold Newstead—the money was swallowed up at once by bills; I tried to sort out my finances—the months dragged by. The thought of the eternity to which I was an heir began to numb me. I found it more and more impossible to stir myself. How true Lovelace's warning had been, not to tarry and delay. Almost every week I would sketch out my plans to go abroad, yet futilely, for my resolution and energy seemed gone, and my existence lacked the tumult that would have stirred them up again. I needed some action, some new great delight, to thrill my blood and reawaken me. Nothing happened—dullness endured. I gave up pretending I would travel abroad. It seemed that England would never let me go.

"I returned to London. There, my sense of desolation grew ever worse. Existence, which in Greece had seemed so various and rich, in England now seemed drained of all color. What is happiness, after all, but excitement?—and what is excitement, but the frigging of the mind? But I was starting to find that I had spent my passions—when I drank, or gambled, or made love now, it grew ever harder to recapture the spark, that *agitation* which is the object of life. I returned to my poetry, to my memories of Haidée—and my fall. I struggled to make sense of the thing I had become. All night, I would scribble furiously, as though the rhythms of my pen might help me recapture what was lost—but I was fooling myself, writing only squandered my energies the more—dissipated them, like seed on barren ground. In Greece, blood had heightened all my pleasures—but in London, I drank it for its own sweet sake, and felt it gradually blotting out my taste for all else. And so, by dimming my other appetites, my vampire nature fed upon itself. More and more, I felt my mortality die—more and more, I felt myself a thing alone.

"It was in the depths of my weary desperation that my sister, Augusta, arrived in town. I had still not seen her since my return from the East—I had known what her blood would do to me. But when I received her note, asking if I would care to meet, it was this very knowledge which excited me, and by stirring up my muddy spirits, made the temptation impossible to resist. I sent a letter back, written in red ink, asking if she would care to be my guest at a meal.

I waited for her at the appointed place. Before I had even seen her, I had smelled her blood. Then she came into the room, and it was as though a world of grayness had been lit up by a thousand fiery sparks. She joined me. I kissed her softly, on the side of her cheek, and the delicate tracery of her blood seemed to sing.

"I paused—and was tempted—then decided to delay. We both sat down to eat. The pumping of Augusta's heart, the rhythm of her veins, sounded in my ears throughout the meal. Yet so also did the soft music of her voice, which charmed me as I had never been charmed before. We spoke of nothing, as usually only the oldest friends can do—we joked and giggled—we found we understood each other perfectly. Dining, talking, laughing with her, the great pleasures of mortality seemed to come back to me. I caught a glimpse of myself in the silverware. Life, in a warm flush, was rising in my cheeks.

"That night, I spared Augusta—and the next. She was not beautiful—but she was lovable—the sister I had longed for, and never known. I began to escort her out. My fever for companionship competed with my thirst. Sometimes, desire for her blood would empty me, and in a dark rush, the scent would cloud my eyes, and I would bow my head. Gently, my lips would caress the smooth skin of her neck. My tongue would dab—I would imagine biting deep, and draining the golden blood. But then Augusta would start, and look at me, and we would both begin to laugh. I would stroke my incisors with the tip of my tongue, but when I reached for her throat again, it was to kiss her and feel the pulse of her life, rich, and deep, and sensuous.

"One night, at a small waltz, she met my kiss. We both broke away at once. Augusta lowered her eyes, embarrassed and upset, but I had felt the passion soaring through her blood, and when I reached for her again, she did not push me away. Shyly, she raised her eyes. The perfume of her blood clouded me. I opened my mouth. Augusta shivered. She tossed her head back, and struggled to break free; then she shivered again, and moaned, and as I lowered my head, she met my lips. This time, we did not break away. Only when I heard a muffled sob did I look up. A woman was running down the passageway toward the waltzing hall. I recognized the back of Lady Caroline Lamb.

"Later that evening, as I walked into supper, Caro confronted me. She had a dagger in her hand. 'Use your sister's body,' she whispered, 'but at least take my blood.' I smiled at her wordlessly, then walked past—Caro choked and staggered back—when some ladies tried to take the dagger from her, she slashed the blade across her hand. She held up the wound to me. 'You see what I would do for you!' she screamed. 'Drink my blood, Lord Byron! *If you won't love me, then at least let me die!*' She kissed the gash, so that the blood was smeared across her lips. The scandal, next morning, was the toast of the gossip sheets.

"Lady Melbourne, furious, came to visit me that night. She held up a newspaper. 'I do not call this discretion,' she said.

"I shrugged. 'Is it my fault I'm pursued by a maniac?'

"'Since you mention it, Byron, yes, it is. I warned you not to destroy Caroline.'

"I stared up at her languidly. 'But you didn't warn me sufficiently, did you, Lady Melbourne? Remember? Your reluctance to tell me about the effect of a vampire's love?' I shook my head. 'Such coyness.'

"I smiled, as a faint lividness touched Lady Melbourne's cheeks. She swallowed, then composed herself. 'I gather,' she said icily, 'that the latest victim of your love is to be your sister.'

"'Caro told you that?'

"'Yes.'

"I shrugged. 'Well—I can't deny it, I suppose. It's an interesting scrape.'

"Lady Melbourne shook her head. 'You're impossible,' she said at last.

"'Why?'

"'Because her blood . . .'

"'Yes, I know,' I said, interrupting her. 'Her blood is a

torture to me. But so is the thought of losing her. With Augusta, Lady Melbourne, I feel I'm a mortal again. With Augusta, I can feel that the past is dissolved.'

"'Of course,' said Lady Melbourne, unsurprised.

"I frowned. 'What do you mean?'

"'She shares your blood. You are drawn to each other. Your love can't destroy her.' She paused. 'But your thirst, Byron—your thirst will.'

"I stared at her. 'My love can't destroy her?' I repeated slowly.

"Lady Melbourne sighed, and reached out to stroke my hand. 'Please,' she whispered. 'Do not allow yourself to fall in love with your sister.'

"'Why not?'

"'I would have thought that was evident.'

"'Because it's incest?'

"Lady Melbourne laughed bitterly. 'We are hardly fitted, either of us, to take a stand on issues of morality.' She shook her head. 'No, Byron—not because it is incest—but because she shares your blood, and you are drawn to it. Because her blood is irresistible to you.' She took my hand, and squeezed it tightly. 'You will have to kill her eventually. You know that. Not now, maybe—but later, as the years pass—you know you will.'

"I frowned. 'No. I don't know that at all.'

"Lady Melbourne shook her head. 'You do. I'm sorry—but you do. You have no other relative.' She blinked. Were there tears in her eyes?—or was it just the glint of a vampire's stare? 'The more you love her,' she whispered, 'the harder it will be.' She kissed me gently, on the side of my cheek—then noiselessly, she left the room. I did not try to follow her. Instead, I sat in silence. All that night, I pondered her words.

"Like a splinter of ice, they seemed embedded in my heart. I admired Lady Melbourne—she was the shrewdest, wisest woman I knew—and her certainty had been frightening. From then on, I was in agonies. I would part from Augusta, but at once existence would seem dull and gray, and I would hurry back to her, to her companionship, and the perfume of her blood. How perfect she was for me—how kind and goodhearted—with no real thought but to give me happiness—how could I even think of killing her? And yet I did, of course, all the time—and more and more, I saw how right Lady Melbourne had been. I loved—and I thirsted—and there seemed no escape. 'I have tried, and hardly, too, to vanquish my demon,' I wrote to Lady Melbourne, 'but to very little purpose.'

"Yet oddly, such torment did serve to stir me. After all—better agony than dullness; better an ocean storm than a placid pond. My mind, scorched by contradictory desires, sought to lose itself again in fierce excess; I re-entered Society, wildly and fervently, and found myself drunk on dissipations to which before I had grown immune. Yet my gaiety was like a fever; in Italy, it is said, in times of plague, orgies were held in charnal houses, and my own pleasures too, even at their height, were dark with the shadow of my fantasies of death. The image of Augusta fading in my arms, drained a lovely white, haunted me; and the conjunctions of life and death, of joy and despair, of love and thirst, began to disturb me again, as they had not done since my revelings with Lovelace in the East. For a long while now, I had seen my victims as little more than walking sacks of blood; but now, for all that my thirst was as desperate as before, I mourned again for those I had to kill. 'That will comfort them,' Lady Melbourne sneered mockingly; and I knew that she was right, that *pity,* in a vampire, was just another word for *cant.* Yet still—my self-disgust returned. I began to kill with less savagery—to be conscious of the life that I was draining with the blood, to feel its uniqueness, even as the spark was snuffed out. Sometimes, I would fantasize that my victim was Augusta; my guilt would be heightened—so too would my pleasure. My revulsion and delight began to seem intertwined.

"It was therefore with a certain tortured hope that I began to correspond with Annabella again. In the crisis that tortured me that long, cruel year, her moral strength—yes, her moral *beauty*—seemed more and more to offer a hope of redemption—and I was desperate enough to grasp at it. Ever since my first glimpse of her, in that evening in Lady Melbourne's salon, Annabella had held a fascination for me; 'I know you for what you are,' she had whispered—and indeed, in a strange way, it seemed that she did. For she had sensed the pain in my soul—the longing for a sense of absolution—the blighted love of higher things, and better days. As she wrote to me, appealing not to the creature I was, but to the man I might have become, I found she was renewing feelings in me I had thought were lost—feelings that a vampire should never entertain—feelings entwined within that single word, *conscience*. It was an unsettling power, then, that she had—and there was awe in the homage she drew from me. Like a spirit herself, she seemed—but of light—seated on a throne apart from the surrounding world, strong in her strength—all most strange in one so young.

"And yet I mustn't exaggerate. Morality was all very well—when I was feeling sorry for myself—but it couldn't hold a candle to the taste of living blood. Nor, of course, could my admiration for Annabella compare to my infatuation with my sister, a longing that now began to grow more cruel. For Augusta was pregnant, and I feared—I hoped—that the child might be mine. For weeks after its birth, I delayed in London; when I set out at last for Augusta's home in the country, it was with the horrified certainty that it was to kill my own child. I arrived; I embraced Augusta; she led me to where my daughter lay. I bent low over the bed. The child smiled up at me. I breathed in deep. The blood was sweet—but it was not golden. The baby began to mewl. I turned round to Augusta, a cold smile writhing on my lips. 'You must give my congratulations to your husband,' I said. 'He has given you a beautiful child.' Then I walked out, in a fury of disappointment and relief, and galloped across the countryside, until the moon rose pale and calmed my rage.

"Once my frustration had died, I was left with my relief. Augusta stayed with me for three weeks in a house by the sea, and in her company, I felt almost happy. I swam, and ate fish, and downed neat brandies—I didn't kill for the three weeks I was there. At last, of course, the craving grew too great—I returned to London—but the memory of those weeks was to stay with me. I began to imagine that my worst fears might be wrong, that I could live with Augusta, and conquer my thirst. I began to imagine that my very nature might be denied.

"But Lady Melbourne, of course, merely laughed at this idea. 'It is a great shame,' she said, one fateful night, 'that Augusta's child was *not* your own.'

"I looked at her, puzzled. She saw my frown. 'I mean,' she said, 'it is a shame that Augusta continues to be your only relative.'

"'Yes, so you keep saying,' I replied, frowning again, 'but I don't understand why. I have told you—I believe in the power of my will. I believe that my love is greater than my thirst.'

"Lady Melbourne shook her head sadly. She reached out to stroke my hair, and her smile, as she ran her fingers through my curls, was desolating. 'There is gray here,' she said. 'You are getting old.'

"I stared up at her. I smiled faintly. 'You are joking, of course.'

"Lady Melbourne widened her eyes. 'Why?' she asked.

"'I am a vampire. I will never grow old.'

"At once, a look of terrible shock crossed Lady Melbourne's face. She rose to her feet and almost staggered to the window. Her face in the moonlight, when she turned back to me, was as bleak as winter. 'He never told you,' she said.

"'Who?'

"'Lovelace.'

"'You knew him?'

"'Yes, of course.' She shook her head. 'I thought you had guessed.'

"'Guessed?' I asked slowly.

"'You—with Caroline—I thought you understood. Why

I begged you to have pity on her.' Lady Melbourne laughed, a terrible sound of pain and regret. 'I saw myself in her. And Lovelace in you. That, I suppose, is why I love you so much. Because I still love . . . I still love—him—you see.' Tears, noiselessly, began to slip down her face. Like drops of silver on marble, they gleamed. 'I will love him forever—forever and ever. You were kind, Byron, not to give Caroline the kiss of death. Her misery will come to an end.' She bowed her head. 'Mine never will.'

"I stayed frozen where I sat. 'You,' I said at last, 'you were the girl he wrote to.'

"Lady Melbourne nodded. 'Of course,' she said.

" 'But—your age—you have grown old . . .'

"My voice trailed away. I had never before seen a look so terrible as Lady Melbourne's then. She crossed to me, and held me in her arms. Her touch was icy, her breasts cold, her kiss on my forehead like that of death. 'Tell me,' I said. I stared out at the moon. Its brilliance, suddenly, seemed unforgiving and cruel. 'Tell me everything.'

" 'Dear Byron . . .' Lady Melbourne stroked her breasts, feeling the lines that furrowed them. 'You will grow old,' she said. 'You will age faster than a mortal. Your beauty will wither and die. Unless . . .'

"Still I gazed out at the blaze of the moon. 'Unless?' I asked calmly.

" 'Surely you know?'

" 'Tell me. Unless.'

" 'Unless . . .' Lady Melbourne stroked my hair. 'Unless you drink the golden blood. Unless you feed on your sister. Then, your form will be preserved, and you will never age. But it must be the blood of a relative.' She bent low, so that her cheek was resting on my head. She cradled me. For a long while, I said nothing at all.

"Then I rose, and crossed to the window, and stood in the silver wash of the moon. 'Well, then,' I said calmly, 'I must get a child.'

"Lady Melbourne stared at me. She smiled faintly. 'It is a possibility,' she said at last.

" 'It is what you did, I presume.'

"Lady Melbourne bowed her head.

" 'When?' I asked.

" 'Ten years ago,' she said eventually. 'My eldest son.'

" 'Good,' I said coldly. I stared back out at the moon. I felt its light refresh my cruelty. 'If you have done it—I can do it. And then I shall live with my sister again. But until then—to save her from the aspersions of the world—I shall marry.'

"Lady Melbourne looked at me, shocked. 'Marry?'

" 'Yes, of course. How else am I to get a child? You wouldn't have me fathering a bastard, I trust?' I laughed mirthlessly—then I felt despair rise up with the cruelty of my heart, and I brushed Lady Melbourne's embrace aside. 'Where are you going?' she shouted after me. I didn't reply. I swept from my rooms, out into the street. The horror screamed in my blood like wind against wire. That night, I killed often, and with the savagery of madness. I ripped throats open with my naked teeth, I drained blood until there was nothing of my victims but bundles of bone and white skin, I grew drunk on death. By the time the sun rose in the eastern sky, I was rosy with blood, and fat like a leech. My frenzy began to die. As the sun rose higher, I crept back to the welcoming darkness of my rooms. There, like a shadow of the night, I cowered.

"That afternoon, I wrote to Annabella. Our correspondence, I knew, had softened her heart. She had refused me before, but not this second time. She accepted my offer of marriage at once."

Chapter X

The principal insane ideas are—that he must be wicked—is foredoomed to evil—and compelled by some irresistible power to follow this destiny doing violence all the time to his feelings. Under the influence of this imagined fatalism he will be most unkind to those he loves best, suffering agonies at the same time for the pain he gives them. He then believes the world to be governed by a Malignant Spirit, & at one time conceived himself to be a fallen angel, though he was half-ashamed of the idea, & grew cunning & mysterious about it after I seemed to detect it . . . Undoubtedly I am more than any one the subject of his irritation, because he deems himself (as he has said) a villain for marrying me on account of former circumstances—adding that the more I love him, & the better I am, the more accursed he is.

LADY BYRON, STATEMENT TO A DOCTOR
ON THE SUPPOSED INSANITY OF HER HUSBAND

hy did I marry her?" Lord Byron paused. "Yes—to father a child—but why her?—why Annabella? She was to prove nearly fatal to me. Lady Melbourne, when I told her who my bride was to be, had prophesied as much. She understood me, better, perhaps, than I did myself. For she saw the poison of anguish in my soul; saw how violently it blazed, deep below the ice of my outward form; saw how this was dangerous. 'You are wounded,' she told me, 'and so you are turning to Annabella in the hope she will offer you a cure.' I laughed at this scornfully, but Lady Melbourne shook her head. 'I have warned you before, Byron. Beware of my niece. She has quite the worst kind of moral virtue— strong and passionate.'

"'Good,' I answered. 'That will increase the pleasure of destroying it.'

"But I was lying to myself—and Lady Melbourne had been shrewder by far than I cared to admit. The turmoil of my feelings for Augusta, my self-disgust, my dread at what the future would hold—all made me desperate for a sense of peace. I knew of no one else but Annabella who might offer me this—and though it seemed a vain hope, I had no choice, eventually, but to acknowledge it. I had traveled north to her parents' home. I waited for her by the fire in the drawing room. I had been left alone. Annabella came to me and stood, for a moment, frozen in the doorway. She stared into my eyes. A shadow passed across her face, and I saw how she recognized the death-chill in me—how sullied I had become, how coarsened, since our last meeting. I did not look away from her gaze, but it was so clear and beautiful that inwardly I shrunk, as evil spirits, it is said, must always do in the presence of good. And then she crossed the room; she held my hands; and I felt her compassion for me, rising and intermingling with her love. I bent my head and kissed her, softly. As I did so, the hopes I was placing in her welled up into thought, and I could no longer stave off recognizing them. I knew then I would do it—I would marry her.

"And yet so nearly I didn't. I stayed with Annabella two weeks, and didn't drink once; instead, I felt myself grow withered and cold. The winds were freezing; the food appalling; the parents frigid and tedious. Damn it, I thought to myself, I'm a vampire, a lord of the dead—I don't have to put up with this. When I escaped at last, back south, killing seemed like freedom again, and in the passion of my blood lust, I could almost forget my need to have a child. As the date of the wedding drew near and then passed, I continued to linger in my London haunts, and when I set out at last, the prospect of marriage seemed as chilling as before. I passed the road to Augusta's house; on a compulsion, I followed it; when I arrived, I wrote a letter, breaking the engagement off. But I couldn't sleep with Augusta that night; her husband was with her and my torment of frustration was enough to persuade me to rip my letter up. Reminded of why I was marrying, I set out at last, meeting up with Hobhouse on the way, and then traveling slowly north, towards my anxious bride. It was now the dead of winter. Snow was thick on the ground, and the whole world seemed frozen. My own soul too seemed turned to ice.

"We arrived at our destination late in the evening. I paused outside the gates. Ahead, I could see lights twinkling. Set against them, the darkness and the gleaming snow seemed like freedom. I longed to run like a wolf, wild and cruel. I longed to kill. Blood would look beautiful, splashed across the snow. But Hobhouse was with me—there was no escape—we rode up the path. Annabella received me with undisguised relief.

"I married her in the drawing room of her parents' house. I had refused to enter a church—enough to send her mother into hysterics, as we took our vows, at the thought of what her daughter might be marrying. But Annabella herself, as I slipped the ring onto her finger, stared at me with her customary calm, mournful and sublime, and I felt her eyes stilling my restlessness. There was no reception. Instead, once the new Lady Byron had changed into her traveling dress, we climbed into a carriage, and set off, on a wintry journey of forty miles, to a remote country pile named Halnaby Hall. There we were to pass our honeymoon.

"On the way, I studied my wife. She smiled calmly back. Suddenly, I hated her. I looked away, staring out at the frozen fields. I thought of Haidée, of blue skies, and warm pleasures—I thought of blood. I glanced back at Annabella. Suddenly, I laughed. I was a creature dangerous and free—and yet this girl thought to chain me with sniveling vows? 'I will be even with you yet,' I whispered. Annabella looked back at me, startled. I smiled coldly, then stared out again at the passing streets. We were in Durham now, and the sight of so many people aroused my thirst. Bells were ringing from the cathedral tower. 'For our happiness, I suppose?' I said mockingly. Annabella stared at me in silence, her face pale with pain. I shook my head. 'It *must* come to a separation,' I hissed. I thought of the fate in store for her child. 'You should have married me when I first proposed.' Before I had met Augusta. Before I had learned the full horror of my fate—which now would surely engulf us both.

"Suddenly, I felt a terrible shame. Annabella still hadn't answered me, but I could feel her anguish, in a way I had never felt a mortal's pain before. She had so much—and so little—of the child—and yet always, behind her eyes, there seemed to wait that eternal depth. We arrived at Halnaby Hall at last. As we climbed out of the carriage, she squeezed my arm, and I smiled at her. We kissed. Later, before dinner, I had her on the sofa. Her eyes still gleamed as she looked up at me, but it was with passion now, no longer with pain. It was good to give her pleasure—and good as well to feel my power over her—to feel her body obey me, if not her mind. At dinner, her pippin face stayed happy and flushed. I wondered what conjunction might have happened in her womb—what spark of something new might be growing there.

"The thought aroused me. The darkness seemed to be calling to my thirst, and I told Annabella I wouldn't be sleeping with her. But pain burned in her eyes again, and she touched my hand so softly that I couldn't resist her appeal. That night, I had her again behind the crimson curtain of our four-poster bed. Then, for the first time in a long while, I slept. I had a terrible dream. I imagined I was in a laboratory. A pregnant woman was lying on a slab. She was dead. Her stomach had been ripped wide open, and a figure in black robes was bending over it. I walked closer. Surely it was the Pasha. I could see now that he was slicing out a child, cutting the dead fetus from its mother's womb. Wires were attached to the tiny creature's head. They burned and sparked; the fetus moved; it opened its mouth, and wailed with life. Slowly, the Pasha bent forward his head. 'No!' I screamed. The Pasha bit; I saw the baby stiffen, then slump, and blood began to drip from it, spreading impossibly fast, until it seemed like a flood that was filling the room. I held the Pasha's shoulder, and pulled him round. I stared into his face. But it was not the Pasha's. No. It was my own.

"I screamed. I opened my eyes. Light from the fire was shining through the red cloth. 'Surely I am in Hell!' I muttered. Annabella stirred, and sought to hold me, but I brushed her aside. I left the bed, and sat staring out at the soft mask of snow across the moors. I rose, and left my body, to wander on the winds of that freezing night. I found a shepherd, alone, searching for a lamb. He was never to find it. His blood fell in a shower upon the snow, pitting it like gleaming rubies. When I had drunk my fill, I dropped my victim, and returned—to my body—and to my bed. Annabella, sensing my misery, reached out to hold me, and rested her head upon my chest. But her love did nothing to soothe my spirits, only agitated them the more. 'Dearest Bell,' I said, stroking her hair, 'you should have a softer pillow to lie on than my heart.'

"The next morning, I stayed in bed till twelve. When I rose at last, I found my wife in the library. She looked up at me. I saw that there were tears in her eyes. I reached for her, felt her body against mine. I breathed in her scent. I frowned, then stroked her belly. I frowned again. She was not pregnant. I could tell. There was no stirring of another creature's blood in her womb, no infant life. I sighed. I clung to my wife, as though to protect her against her fate. 'Believe me,' I whispered, almost to myself, 'I am more accursed in this marriage than in any other act of my life.'

Bell stared deep into my eyes. 'Please,' she said at last, in a soft, desperate voice, 'what is this agony you are guarding from me?'

"I shook my head. 'I am a villain,' I whispered. 'I could convince you of it in three words.'

"Bell said nothing for a while. She pressed her cheek against my chest again. 'Does your sister know of it?' she said eventually.

"I stepped back. I was shaking. 'For God's sake,' I whispered, 'don't ask about her.'

"Bell continued to stare at me. Her eyes seemed to be reaching to the depths of my soul. 'There is no secret,' she said at last, 'no matter how terrible, which will destroy my love. No secret, B.' She smiled, a quiet smile of pity and contemplation, and then her face was, as usual, still, not stern, and touched by love. I choked, and turned away from her.

"Bell did not follow me—and neither in the weeks to come, did she press me about the secret which she knew I bore. But I, like a man with a wound, kept touching it, and half-exposing it to her view, for her calmness infuriated me, and I was often raging to see it destroyed. In such moods, I would loathe her. I would hint at the miseries awaiting us, as though my doom was an antidote to my married state— husband, not vampire, seemed the more dreadful word—I would almost be in love with my fate again. But then the horror would return and with it the guilt—and Annabella's love would still be there. At such times, when I could trust myself to her, I would almost feel happy, and my dreams of redemption would come back to me. But my mind was a tumult, and my feelings changed like the flames of a fire. It was not an easy honeymoon.

"And all the time, my thirst was growing worse. Bell was permanently about me—and it maddened me. We returned to her parents' home—bad food again, and worse conversation. I craved vice. One evening, my father-in-law told a story for the seventh time. My patience snapped. I announced I was leaving for London at once. Bell demanded to go with me. I refused. We had a furious row. There seemed something strange about Bell—something almost priggish—a quality her virtue hadn't suffered from before. She repeated her arguments again, in front of her parents, and I had no choice but to bow to them.

"I left with my wife, then—but my rage against her now was icy and cruel. 'We will visit Augusta,' I announced suddenly. 'We have time on our way back to London.'

"Bell did not complain. On the contrary, she seemed pleased. 'Yes, I'm looking forward to meeting your sister,' she said. She paused and smiled faintly. 'About whom I have heard so much.'

"Oh—but she was to hear more—much more. After three months apart from Augusta, my hunger for her was desperate, and my passion a maelstrom of conflicting desires. Our carriage pulled up outside her house. Augusta descended the stairs to welcome us. She greeted Bell first; then she turned to me. She brushed her cheek against my own, and I felt a spark that ran to the depths of my soul. 'Tonight,' I whispered, but Augusta looked shocked, and turned away. Bell stood waiting for me, to take my hand. I walked past her without a glance.

"That night, Bell went early to bed. 'Are you coming, B?' she asked.

"I smiled coldly, then glanced at Augusta. 'We don't want *you* here, my charmer,' I sneered, reaching out to take Augusta's hand. Bell's face grew pale; she stared at me, but after several seconds' silence, she turned and withdrew without a further word.

"When she had gone, Augusta rose to her feet. She was angry and upset. 'How could you treat your wife like that? B, how *could* you?' She refused my demands to sleep with her. 'There was no harm in it before, but not now, B—not now. Go to Annabella. Be kind to her. Comfort her.' Then she pushed me away, and I saw that she was crying as she ran from the room.

"I wandered out into the garden. I hated Augusta, then— but I loved her too, her and Bell, I loved them both madly. And yet it was their very pain which had most aroused me, the glimpse of the almost-tears in their eyes, their own love fighting and mingling with their fear. I raised my face up to the blazing moon. I felt its light replenish my cruelty. I glanced up at the room where Augusta slept. Her perfume came to me on the sighing wind. Suddenly, with my nails, I slashed across my wrist. Blood welled up. I drank it. Lightness, like quicksilver, rippled through my veins. I rose, and my own desires bore me on the wind, and I entered softly into Augusta's dreams. Her husband was snoring by her side—but I lay with her, my sweet sister, and felt her flesh warm against my own, her blood, blood of my blood, sighing with mine, moving with its flow. A cloud passed from the moon . . . and its light spilled across the bed. 'Augusta,' I whispered, as her throat was touched with silver. I bent my head and my teeth pressed gently. Like the skin of a peach, the throat began to give. I pressed further. Still the skin gave. So easy it would be, to puncture it. I imagined the flood of ripeness and taste, the golden liquid, rising to welcome the touch of my lips, feeding me with youth, eternal youth. I tensed—and then I pulled myself back. Augusta gasped, clutching at the sheets, and I moved with her, until, damp-limbed, she lay still in my arms. I stared into her face, tracing my own in her lineaments. For hours I lay. I began to hear the first songs of half-awakened birds. Like a star, I faded on the coming light.

"Bell was awake when I returned to her. Her face was haggard, and her eyes full of tears. 'Where have you been?' she asked.

"I shook my head. 'You don't want to know.'

"Bell reached for me. I shrunk from her touch. She froze. 'Do you hate me?' she asked at last.

"I stared at her. Guilt, frustration, pity, and desire, all rose up within me, fighting for supremacy. 'I think I love you,' I said at last. 'But I am afraid, dearest Bell, it may not be enough.'

"Her eyes looked deep into my own, and as ever, I felt them healing me and calming my rage. She kissed me softly on my lips. 'If love is not enough,' she said at last, 'then what can redeem us?' I shook my head. I held her in my arms. For the rest of that night, her question tortured me. If not love—then what? I didn't know. I didn't know.

"For we were both, Annabella and myself, chained on the rack of my destiny. Love pulled us one way, my thirst the other. I was frightened by how nearly I had killed Augusta, how easy it had seemed, and I felt a fresh desperation to save her from myself and get a child. But for a long time, the horror of my situation numbed me. I couldn't do it—not implant a meal of blood in Annabella's womb—not when that meal would be her flesh, and mine. And so Augusta continued to torture me—and the effort of sparing her— and Annabella's womb—drove me into rages that were close to insanity. I could no longer bear to sleep with Bell.

Instead, I haunted the crossroads and fields, slaking my thirst, venting my rage, with attacks of furious savagery. But fresh blood now could barely stave off my frenzy—within hours, my need would be as desperate as before. One night, returning to Augusta's home, her scent almost overpowered me again, and it was all I could do, standing by her bed, not to slice across her naked throat. With a desperate effort, I controlled myself, and I melted away on the rhythms of her breath. I paced in the garden, up and down—then, for the first time in a week, I returned to my bed.

"Wordlessly, Bell raised her arms to greet me. Like bright poison, my blood seemed then. Bell shuddered, then screamed, a desperate, animal sound. 'Your eyes are full of hell-fire,' she gasped. I smiled; the fire seemed to be in hers as well, and her cheeks were flushed, her lips bright red. Suddenly, she snarled; she pulled my mouth to hers; her purity seemed burned away. There was nothing of Annabella now in her whorish, heartless face; nothing of Annabella in what she did with me that night. She began to scream, writhing like a woman possessed, as my sperm flooded through her, bearing its tiny, fatal seed of life. Her whole body buckled; she raised her arms; her fingers reached up to stroke my face. Then she began to weep.

"'You have conceived,' I whispered. 'Our child is growing within your flesh.' Annabella looked up at me; then her face twisted, and she looked away. I left her. She lay where she was, sobbing noiselessly.

"The fruits of that night were both life and death. Yes—a child was born—already, I could nuzzle my cheek against Annabella's stomach, and recognize the faint golden scent from within her womb. But there was death in such a perfume—and death too in Annabella herself. Something in her had died that night—the infinite in her seemed burned away. She grew colder, harsher—the eternity behind her eyes began to dim—what before had been passion now seemed priggishness. She still loved me, of course—but like Caro, that was to be her torture and her doom. There seemed no hope of redemption for either of us now—

and with Bell's destruction, I felt my own last hope was dead as well.

"For now began the true torture. We left Augusta and headed for London. I had rented a new house, on one of the most fashionable streets in town—number Thirteen, Piccadilly. A place of ill luck? No—we brought the ill luck there ourselves. Bell's symptoms now were clearly gestatory. I could smell the child in her early morning vomit, or in the sweat that glistened oily across her swollen belly. I could scarcely bear to be parted from the smell. And so Lord and Lady Byron were always to be seen, arm in arm, the model married couple—the devoted husband and his pregnant wife. But Bell at least, seeing the desire in my face, was wise enough to know that it wasn't for her.

"'You look at me with such longing,' she said one night, 'but there is no love in your eyes.'

"I smiled. I stared at her belly, imagining—below her dress, below her underclothes, deep within her flesh—the golden fetus ripening.

"Bell watched me, and frowned. 'Your face, B—it puzzles me.'

"I looked up. 'Indeed?' I said.

"Bell nodded. She studied me again. 'How can any face so beautiful look so hungry and cruel? You look at me—or rather'—she clasped her stomach—'you look at this, in the same way that you used to look at Augusta. I remember how your eyes used to follow her round the room.'

"I stared at her, my face passionless. 'And why does that puzzle you, Bell?'

"'It puzzles me,' she said, 'because it also frightens me.' Her eyes narrowed. They glittered, cold and stern. 'I am afraid, B, of what you will do to my child.'

"'Our child?' I laughed. 'Why, what could I do?' Suddenly, my face froze. 'Do you think I might strangle it at birth and drain its blood?'

"Bell stared at me. Her face seemed more drawn than I had ever seen it before. She rose to her feet. She clasped her belly—then she turned, and wordlessly, she left the room.

"The next week, Augusta arrived to stay with us. She had come at Annabella's invitation. This disturbed me. I wondered how much Bell either knew or guessed. Certainly, the scent of Augusta's blood distracted me; I grew savage again with conflicting desires; I ordered her to leave. All this Annabella watched with cold, suspicious eyes, and she began to clutch her stomach as though guarding it from me. From then on, I tried to be more careful. As Lady Melbourne warned: 'Do not lose the wife before you have the child.' And so I began to leave Bell alone at nights. I would dine, get drunk, visit the theater—and then, swathed in black and violent cruelty, I would prey once again in the city's vilest haunts. I would feed until my skin was rosy and sleek—I would feed until I was absolutely gorged on blood. Only then would I return to Piccadilly. I would join Bell in bed. I would hold her in my arms—and, of course, I would feel her belly's swelling curve. Softly, remorselessly, the beating of a tiny heart would sound in my ears. Despite myself, I would press my wife's belly again. It would seem to stir and ripple to my touch. I would imagine I had only to press, and the skin and flesh would part like water. I would imagine the fetus, viscous and blue, with its unbearably delicate network of veins, waiting for my touch—waiting for my taste. I would bite it so gently—I would suck the blood out like water from a sponge. These longings would become so intense that I would start to shake. I would imagine killing my wife where she lay—slicing open her belly, parting the muscles and organs and flesh—and there it would be—curled and waiting—my child—my creation. I would remember my dreams of the Pasha's tower. I would long for his knife, his dissecting slab.

"I would wake from these fantasies shuddering with disgust. I tried to cauterize them, to seal them from my brain. But it was in vain. Nothing could rid me of their presence—nothing—they were a part of the poison that ran in my blood—the mingled fire of sensation and thought. I could no sooner escape such rottenness than I could escape myself. The Pasha was dead—but just as syphilis survives the infected whore so too did his evil live on, consuming my veins, and all those I loved. 'I wish the child were dead!' I would scream, when its blood beat particularly golden in my ear, and my fantasies seemed to be melting me. Bell would stare at me in horror. I would try to calm myself. 'Oh Bell,' I would sob. 'Dearest Bell.' I would stroke her hair. Frightened, she would shrink back, then, hesitantly, reach out to hold my hand. Sometimes, she would press it against the swelling of her stomach. She would look up and smile, with doubtful hope, searching in my face for the father of her child. But she never found him. Dead-eyed and frozen, she would turn away.

"One night, late in her pregnancy, she shuddered at my look, then gasped.

"'Bell,' I said, kneeling down beside her, 'what is it? Bell!' I tried to embrace her, but she pushed me away. She gasped again—and the scent of my child, in a sudden golden flood, dizzied my eyes and dissolved the room. Bell groaned. I reached for her hand. Still she pushed me away. I rose to my feet. I called for attendants. When they came, they too seemed to shrink from me, so fierce and cold was the darkness in my eyes. Bell was lifted from the floor, and taken to her bed. I stayed below. The perfume of my child's blood hung heavy in the air. All that night, and into the morning, the scent grew ever more beautiful.

"At one o'clock in the afternoon, the midwife came down to me.

"'Is it dead,' I asked, 'the child?' I laughed at the midwife's look of shock. I had no need of her answer. I had only to breathe in the living blood. The house seemed full of rich blossoms and colors. Unsteadily, I climbed the stairs. Like Eve I felt, approaching the fruit of the forbidden tree. My limbs shuddered, I gasped for breath, I felt the sickness of a deep and ecstatic thirst. I walked into the room where my wife had been confined.

"A nurse came across to me. 'My Lord,' she said, holding up a small white bundle, 'our congratulations. You have a daughter.'

"I looked down at the bundle. 'Yes,' I choked at last. The scent of blood seemed to burn my eyes. I could scarcely make out my child, for when I looked, I could only see a golden haze. 'Yes,' I gasped again. I blinked. Now I could see my daughter's face. 'Oh God,' I whispered. 'Oh God.' I smiled faintly. 'What an implement of torture have I acquired in you.'

"The nurse backed away from me. I watched as she laid my child back in her cradle. 'Get out!' I screamed suddenly. I looked around the room. 'Get out!' The attendants stared at me, frightened, then they bowed their heads and scurried away. I crossed to my daughter. Again, she seemed enveloped by a halo of fire. I bent low over her. In that moment, all feeling, all sense, all thought was lost to me, melted into a blazing mist of joy. The richness in my child's blood seemed to rise to meet my lips, scattering gold like a comet's tail. I kissed her, then I took her in my arms. I bent low again. Tenderly, I placed my lips upon her throat.

" 'Byron!'

"I paused—and then slowly I looked round. Bell was struggling to sit up from her bed. 'Byron!' Her voice was hoarse and desperate. She rolled from her bed, and tried to cross to me.

"I looked down at my child again. She held her hand up to my face. How tiny her fingers were, how exquisite her nails. I bent my head closer, to study them.

" 'Give her to me.'

"I turned round to face Bell. She staggered, as she held out her arms, and almost fell.

" 'I have been waiting a long time for her,' I said softly.

" 'Yes,' gasped Bell, 'yes, but now—I am her mother—she is mine—please, B,' she choked—'give her to me.'

"I stared at her, not blinking. Bell struggled to meet my gaze. I glanced back at my child. She was very beautiful, this creation of mine. She raised up her tiny hand again. Despite myself, I smiled at the sight.

" 'Please,' said Bell. 'Please.'

"I turned from her, and walked to the window. I gazed

out at the cold London sky. How warm and soft my child felt in my arms. I felt a touch on my arm. I glanced round. The expression on Bell's face now was terrible to see.

"I looked away from her, back out at the sky. Darkness was rising in the east, and the clouds already seemed pregnant with the night. London, in a great mess, stretched away to meet them. I felt chilled with a sense of the vastness of the world. All this, and more, the Pasha had shown me in the flight of his dreams, but then—I had not understood—*I had not understood.* I closed my eyes—I shivered—I felt the measureless nature of things. What, in such a universe, was human love? A bubble, nothing more, on the breaking surge of eternity. A spark, brief and flickering, lit against the dark of a universal night. Once it was gone—then the void would come.

"'You are to remember this moment,' I said, without looking round. 'You must leave me, Bell. No matter what I say—no matter how strongly I appeal to you later—*you must leave me.'*

"I turned round to look at her at last. Bell's eyes, so cold for so long, were damp with tears. She reached up to try to stroke my cheeks, but I shook my head. 'She is to be called Ada,' I said, placing our daughter in her arms. Then I turned, without a further word, and left the room. I did not look round again.

"'You are insane,' said Lady Melbourne, when I told her what I'd done. 'Quite insane. You marry the girl, you get her pregnant, she gives you the child—and now this. Why?'

"'Because I can't do it.'

"'You must. You must kill her. If not Ada—then Augusta.'

"I shrugged and turned away. 'I don't think so,' I said. 'Pleasures are always sweetest when anticipated. I shall continue to anticipate.'

"'Byron.' Lady Melbourne beckoned to me. Her pale face gleamed with pity and contempt. 'All the time,' she whispered, 'you are getting old. Look at me. I waited. I was foolish—I gave in at last. We all do. Get it over with now.

Drink your daughter's blood while you still have your youth. You owe it to us.'

"I frowned. 'Owe it?' I asked. *'Owe it?* To whom do I owe it?'

"Lady Melbourne's brow creased only slightly. 'To all our kind,' she said at last.

"'Why?'

"'You are the slayer of Vakhel Pasha.'

"I stared at her in surprise. 'I never told you that,' I said.

"'We all know.'

"'How?'

"'The Pasha was a being of extraordinary powers. Amongst the vampires, who are the lords of death, he was almost our king. Did you not realize that?' Lady Melbourne paused. 'We all felt his passing.'

"I frowned. Suddenly, half-formed from the shadows of my mind, the Pasha's shape seemed to pass before my eyes, pale and terrible, his face frozen with unbearable pain. I shook my head—and the phantom was gone. Lady Melbourne watched me with a faint smile on her bloodless lips. 'Now that he is dead,' she whispered in my ear, 'you are his heir.'

"I stared at her coldly. 'Heir?' I repeated. Then I laughed. 'How ridiculous. You forget—I killed him.'

"'No,' said Lady Melbourne, 'I do not forget.'

"'Then what do you mean?'

"'Why, Byron,' Lady Melbourne smiled again, 'that he had to choose you first.'

"'Choose? To do what?'

"Lady Melbourne paused and her face froze back into icy stillness. 'To scale the mysteries of our kind,' she said at last. 'To find meaning in the face of eternity.'

"'Oh, well.' I laughed shortly. 'Nothing difficult, then.'

"I turned away scornfully, but Lady Melbourne followed me and took my arm. 'Please, Byron,' she said, 'kill your child—drink her. You will need all your strength.'

"'For what? To become a thing like the Pasha? No.' I brushed Lady Melbourne away. 'No.'

"'Please, Byron, I . . .'

"'*No!*'

"Lady Melbourne shuddered at my glance. She lowered her eyes. For a long while she stood in silence. 'You are so young,' she said at last. 'But already, you see what power you have.'

"I shook my head. I took Lady Melbourne in my arms. 'I do not want power,' I told her softly.

"'Because you have it already.' Lady Melbourne looked up at me. 'What more can you want?'

"'Rest. Peace. To be mortal again.'

"Lady Melbourne sniffed. 'Impossible dreams.'

"'Yes.' I smiled faintly. 'And yet—so long as Ada and Augusta live—then perhaps'—I paused—'then perhaps there is a part of me which *is* mortal still.' Lady Melbourne began to laugh. But I quieted her and held her; like a trapped victim, she stared deep into my eyes. 'You ask me,' I said slowly, 'to fathom the mysteries of our vampire breed. The mystery, however, is not to know, but to escape what we are. Vampires have power—knowledge—eternal life—but all these are nothing while we also crave blood. For as long as we have such a thirst, we shall be hunted and loathed. And yet—knowing this—I still find my own thirst growing daily more fierce. Soon, blood will be my only pleasure. All other joys will taste like ash in the mouth. That is my doom—our doom—Lady Melbourne, is it not?'

"She made no answer. In her eyes I saw my face reflected, ardent and harsh. My passions were crossing it like the shadows of clouds.

"'I will find an escape,' I said at last. 'I will search for it, if needs be, across eternity. And yet'—I paused—'the journey will grow harder, the pilgrimage more cruel, the more my humanity is lost to me. I had not understood this before—but I see it now. Yes.' I nodded. 'I see it now.' My voice trailed away. I looked into the dark. A shadowy figure seemed to be watching me. For the second time, it seemed to wear the Pasha's face. Then I blinked, and there was nothing. I turned my gaze back to Lady Melbourne. 'I shall leave England,' I told her. 'I shall leave my sister and my child behind. I shall not drink their blood.'

"I turned. Lady Melbourne did not try to stop me this time. I crossed the room, and walked out, my footsteps echoing, into the hall. Caroline Lamb was there. She was horribly thin, and her smile, as I walked past her, was like that of a skull. She rose and followed me. 'I hear you are leaving England,' she said. I didn't reply. She held my arm. 'What will you tell your wife?' she asked. *Vampire.*'

"I turned to face her. 'Listening at keyholes, Caro?' I asked. 'That can be dangerous.'

"Caro laughed. 'Yes, it can,' she said. Her expression was bitter and strange, but though she struggled, she couldn't bear the fierceness of my eyes. She fell back. I walked on down the hall.

"'Take me with you!' Caro suddenly screamed. 'I will make beds for your favorites! I will walk the streets to win you victims! Please Byron, please!' She ran after me, and threw herself at my feet. She took my hand, and started kissing it. 'You are fallen, but oh, my Byron, you are an angel still. Take me with you. Promise. Swear to me.' Her whole body began to shake. 'A vampire's heart is like iron,' she muttered, more to herself than to me. 'It softens when heated with the fires of lust, but afterwards it is cold and hard.' She looked up into my face, and began to laugh wildly. 'Yes, cold and hard. Cold like death!'

"I shrugged her away.

"'You wouldn't dare leave me!' said Caro disbelievingly. 'Such love—such hate—you wouldn't dare!'

"I walked on.

"'I will damn you! I will damn you, damn you, damn you!' Caro's voice choked and fell. I paused. I glanced back at her. Caro, still sunk on her knees, shuddered, and then the fit seemed to pass, and she dabbed a tear away. 'I will damn you,' she said again, but softly now. 'My dearest, dearest love, I will'—she paused—*'save you.'*

"Three weeks later, unknown to me, she visited Bell. I had not, of course, been able to leave. Augusta had been

staying with us—and Ada's blood—oh—Ada's blood—
Ada's blood was even sweeter than hers. And so I had
stayed, and the temptation grew in me, and I knew that
Lady Melbourne had been right—I would surrender to it.
One night, standing by the cradle, I would have fed, if Bell
had not interrupted me. She looked at me strangely, and
held the baby to her breast. She told me she wanted to leave
London—return to the country—perhaps stay with her
parents for a while. I nodded distractedly. Soon after that,
she left. I had told her I would follow on. By the carriage
that was to take her, she held our daughter to my lips. Then
she kissed me herself, passionately, and held me until I
thought she would never let go. She broke free at last.
'Goodbye, B,' she said. Then she climbed into the carriage,
and I watched as it rolled down Piccadilly. I was never to
see her, nor my child, again.

"Some two weeks later, the letter came. It demanded a
separation. The same afternoon, I was visited by Hobhouse.

"'I thought you should know,' he said, 'the most incredi-
ble rumors are flying round town. They say your wife wants
to separate from you—and much worse.'

"I tossed Hobby the letter. He read it, his frown deepening all the time. At last, he dropped it and looked up at me.
'You will have to go abroad, of course,' he said.

"'Why,' I asked, 'are the rumors that bad?'

"Hobby paused—then nodded.

"'Tell me.'

"Hobhouse smiled. 'Oh—you know,' he said, waving his
hand. 'Adultery, sodomy, incest . . .'

"'And worse?'

"Hobhouse stared at me. He poured out a drink, and
handed it to me. 'It's that bitch, Caroline Lamb,' he said at
last. 'She is telling people . . . well, you can guess.'

"I smiled faintly, and downed the drink—then smashed
the glass onto the floor. Hobhouse shook his head. 'You will
have to go abroad,' he said again. 'Please, old man. You
really don't have any choice.'

"Of course I didn't. And yet still I couldn't bear to leave.

The more I was damned in the newspapers, or hissed at in the streets, the more desperately I longed for my stolen mortality, to deny what it seemed the whole world now knew. But my doom was fixed—Caro had done her work too well. One night, I went to a dance with Augusta on my arm. As we walked into the hall, the whole room fell still. All eyes were on me—and then they looked away. No one came up to us. No one spoke to us. But I heard the single word whispered from behind our backs—*vampire*. That night, I thought I heard it everywhere.

"I knew then my exile was irrevocable. A few days later, I sent Augusta away. Through everything, she had stood by me, and her love had never failed. Without her, my life would be a solitude. And yet there was relief too when we parted, for I could be certain now I would never drink her blood. I renewed my travel plans. My despair became mixed with a wild sense of freedom. The world hated me—well, I hated it. I remembered my old intentions. I would travel— and I would search. As Lady Melbourne had put it—I would chart the nature of my vampire state. I ordered a carriage to be made, based on the design of Napoleon's. It contained a double bed, a wine cellar and a library. In the wine cellar, I stored bottles of Madeira mixed with blood— in the library, books on science and the occult. I also hired a physician, a young man who had written on properties of the blood. He had a reputation for dabbling in the darker fringes of medicine. Such knowledge, I thought, might prove stimulating. I gave him samples of my own blood to study. The name of this doctor was John Polidori.

"The departure date grew nearer and nearer. My house in Piccadilly was steadily packed up. I roamed the echoing, empty corridors. In the nursery, and Augusta's room, a faint, mocking tang of blood still hung. I tried to ignore it. I rarely went out now—my face and name were notorious— but I was fully occupied with business and friends. I had also taken a lover. Her name was Claire, and she was only seventeen. She was pretty enough, I suppose, but odd-headed—she had thrown herself at me—I used her to keep my mind off things. One afternoon, she brought her sister with her. 'This is Mary,' she said.

"The sister was pretty too—solemn though, less wild than Claire. She flicked through the books I was packing for my trip. She picked one up, and read the title from the spine: *'Electricity and the Principles of Life.* My husband is interested in such things,' she said, fixing me with her deep, serious eyes. 'He is a poet too. Perhaps you know him?' I raised an eyebrow. 'Shelley,' Mary said. 'Percy Shelley. I think you might enjoy his company.'

" 'Sadly,' I said, gesturing at my trunks, 'you see that I am about to travel abroad.'

" 'So are we,' said Mary. 'Who knows? Perhaps we will meet up on the Continent.'

"I smiled faintly. 'Yes—perhaps we will.' But I doubted it. I could see, from the gathering madness in Claire's eyes, that her brain was being turned by her passion for me. From then on, I discouraged her visits. I would not have her cracking, and following me. If she did—well—that would be too bad for her.

"On my last night in London, I stayed in Augusta's room. The scent of blood now was almost gone. I lay on her couch, breathing in its last faint traces. The house was dark and still; emptiness hung in the air like dust. For hours I lay there alone. I felt hunger and regret contending in my veins.

"Suddenly, I thought I heard a footfall. At once, I sensed the presence of something not human in the house. I looked up. There was nothing. I summoned all my power to compel the creature to show himself, but still the room was as empty as before. I shook my head. My loneliness was deluding me. Suddenly, the emptiness seemed unbearable, and though I knew it would be a phantom, I longed to see Augusta's face again. From her fading perfume, I conjured up her form. She stood before me. 'Augusta,' I whispered. I held out my hands. She seemed impossibly real. I tried to stroke her cheek. To my shock, I felt the glow of living flesh.

" 'Augusta?'

"She said nothing, but desire and love seemed to glow in

her eyes. I bent to kiss her. As I did so, I realized for the first time that I couldn't smell her blood. 'Augusta?' I whispered again. She pulled me gently to her. Our cheeks brushed. We kissed.

"And then I screamed. Her lips seemed to be alive with a thousand moving things. I stepped back—and saw how my sister was covered in a shimmering, twisting white. I reached out to touch her again—and the maggots fell, and coiled along my finger. My sister raised her arms, as though appealing for help, and then slowly, her body crumbled away, and the floor was carpeted with writhing worms.

"I staggered back. I felt something behind me. I turned. Bell was holding up Ada to me. I tried to brush her away. I saw Ada start to bleed and melt; I saw Bell's flesh freeze and shrivel on the bone. All around me were the forms of people I had loved, imploring, beckoning, reaching for me. I pushed past them; they seemed destroyed by my touch— and then they rose again and ghoul-like, followed me. They held me with their soft, dead fingers; I looked despairingly around; I thought I saw a figure, ahead of me, cloaked in black. He turned. I looked into his face. It seemed very like the Pasha's. But if it was, it had changed. It was perfectly smooth, and the paleness was touched with a livid, hectic yellow. But I saw it only for the fraction of a second. 'Wait!' I shouted. 'What are these visions you are conjuring for me? Wait, I order you to wait!' But the figure had turned and was gone, so soon that I thought it had surely been a fantasy, and I realized that the other phantoms had disappeared as well, and I was alone again. I stood on the stairway. All was silent. Nothing moved. I took a step forward. And it was then I realized I was still not quite alone.

"I smelled her blood before I heard her faint sobs. It was Claire. I found her hiding behind one of the chests. She was dumb with fear. I asked her what she had seen. She shook her head. I held her with my eyes. Her terror was arousing me. I knew I needed blood. The visions, the dreams I had had—I knew that only blood would keep them away.

"I reached for Claire's throat—I touched it—and then I

paused. I could feel the life beating deep within her. I placed my finger below her chin. Slowly, I guided her lips towards my own. I shook—I closed my eyes—I kissed her. Then I kissed her again. She stayed solid in my arms. I took her. I gasped. Still she was alive. I folded her in my dissolving embrace. I flooded her. 'I give you life,' I whispered. I rose up from her. 'Go now,' I told her. 'And for both our sakes— never try to see me again.' Claire nodded, wide-eyed; she straightened her clothes; she left me, still without saying a word. It was now almost morning.

"Hobhouse came an hour later, to see me off. Polidori was with him. By eight o'clock, we were on the road."

Chapter XI

Many and long were the conversations between Lord Byron and Shelley, to which I was a devout but nearly silent listener. During one of these, various philosophical doctrines were discussed, and among others the nature of the principle of life, and whether there was any probability of its ever being discovered and communicated . . . Perhaps a corpse would be reanimated; galvanism had given token of such things: perhaps the component parts of a creature might be manufactured, brought together and endued with vital warmth.

Night waned upon this talk, and even the witching hour had gone by before we retired to rest. When I placed my head on my pillow I did not sleep, nor could I be said to think. My imagination, unbidden, possessed and guided me, gifting the successive images that arose in my mind with a vividness far beyond the usual bounds of reverie. I saw—with shut eyes, but acute mental vision—I saw the pale student of unhallowed arts kneeling beside the thing he had put together. I saw the hideous phantasm of a man stretched out, and then, on the working of some powerful engine, show signs of life, and stir with an uneasy, half-vital motion. Frightful must it be; for supremely frightful would be the effect of any human endeavor to mock the stupendous mechanism of the Creator of the world . . .

MARY SHELLEY, INTRODUCTION TO *Frankenstein*

21 nd so ended," said Lord Byron, "my vain attempt to live like a mortal man." He paused; and his face, as he studied Rebecca, seemed lit by a mingling of defiance and regret. "Henceforth," he said, "I was to be myself, a thing alone.

"Alone?" Rebecca hugged herself. Her voice, after such a long silence, seemed to intrude on her ears. "Then who . . ."

"Yes?" Lord Byron raised a mocking eyebrow.

"Who . . ." Rebecca stared, transfixed, into the paleness of her ancestor's face. "Whose descendant am I?" she whispered at last. "Not Annabella's?—not Ada's?"

"No." He stared through her, into the darkness beyond. Again, there seemed defiance and pain on his brow. "Not now," he said faintly.

"But . . ."

His look seemed to stab her. "I said, not now!"

Rebecca swallowed, but though she tried, she couldn't conceal her frown. It was not his sudden anger that had shocked her—rather, the way he seemed disturbed by it himself. After so long, she thought—so long to grow accustomed to the thing he had become—his loneliness still seemed to take him by surprise. And she felt pity for him, and Lord Byron, as though reading her thoughts, stared suddenly at her and started to laugh.

"Do not insult me," he said.

Rebecca frowned, pretending not to understand.

"There is a great freedom in despair," said Lord Byron.

"Freedom?"

"Yes." Lord Byron smiled. "Once reached, even despair can be a paradise."

"I don't understand."

"Of course not. You are mortal. How can you know what it is to be damned? I knew, that morning of my flight from England's shores—and yet, somehow, hopelessness seemed sweeter by far than hope had ever done. I stood below the fluttering sail, and watched the white cliffs of Dover disappear behind the waves. I was an exile. I had been driven, a damned thing, from my native land. I had lost my family, my friends, and all I had loved. I would never be otherwise than what I was—the wandering outlaw of my own dark mind. And yet my despair, like my face, wore a guarded smile." Lord Byron paused. He stared deep into Rebecca's eyes, as though willing her to try to understand. He sighed at last, and looked away, yet his smile remained, touched with mockery, and proud.

"I kept to the deck. Again and again the white cliffs would rise, then disappear. "I am a vampire," I said to myself. The wind shrieked, the mast quivered, and my words seemed lost on the breath of the storm. And yet they were not. For they, like me, belonged on the tempest's roar. I clung to the sides of the ship, as the waves heaved and bounded like a horse that knows his rider. I had a bottle in my hand. It was uncorked. I breathed in the scent of mingled wine and blood. I longed to hurl the bottle out into the sea. The blood would arc and be scattered on the winds; I would rise with it, then soar, as free and wild as the storm itself. I felt a laughing exhilaration fill my blood. Yes, I thought, I would keep my promise, I would search out the secrets of my own vampire nature—I would become a pilgrim of eternity. All I had to do was ride the storm.

"I drank from my bottle, then I lifted it, ready to hurl it at the winds. Blood from the rim was splashed across my hand. I tensed—and then I felt a touch on my arm. 'My Lord.' I looked around. 'My Lord . . .' It was Polidori. He scrabbled with a folder he held under his arm. 'My Lord—I was wondering if you would look at my tragedy?'

"I stared at him in cold disbelief. 'Tragedy?' I said at last.

"'Yes, My Lord.' Polidori nodded. He held out a sheaf of papers. '*Cajetan,* a tragedy in five acts, being the Tragical History of Cajetan.' He fumbled with his folder. 'I'm particularly stuck with this line. "So, groaning, did the mighty Cajetan—"'

"I waited. 'Well,' I asked, 'what did the mighty Cajetan do?'

"'That's the problem,' said Polidori. 'I'm not sure.' He handed me the sheet of paper. The wind snatched it from his grasp. I watched it as it fluttered above the ship, then out across the waves.

"I turned around. 'I am not interested in your tragedy,' I said.

"Polidori's eyes, which bulged at the best of times, seemed ready to burst from his skull. 'My Lord,' he spluttered, 'I really think . . .'

"'No.'

"His eyes popped again with indignation. 'You're a poet,' he complained. 'Why can't I be one?'

"'Because I pay you to carry out medical research, not to waste your time on scribbling trash.' I turned back to stare out at the waves. Polidori spluttered something else, then I heard him turn and leave. I wondered if it was too late to send him back. Yes, I thought, and sighed—it probably was.

"And so I tried hard, in the days that followed, to improve our relationship. Polidori was vain and ridiculous—but he was brilliant as well, with a searching mind, and his knowledge of the frontiers of science was profound. As we traveled south, I would ask him about theories of the nature of life, of creation, of immortality. To these topics at least, Polidori brought a wealth of expertise. He knew about all the latest experiments, of the search for cells that would endlessly reproduce, of the *potential*—he would use no stronger word—for the spontaneous electrical generation of life. Often, he mentioned texts I had seen in the Pasha's laboratory. I began to wonder about these. Why had the Pasha been so interested in galvanism and chemistry? Had he too been seeking a scientific explanation of his immortality? Had he too been searching for a principle of life?—a principle which, once found, might obviate the need to survive on blood? If such had indeed been the case, then perhaps Lady Melbourne had been right after all—I shared more with the Pasha than I had ever thought.

"Once or twice, as I had done in London, I imagined I saw him. It was always only the faintest glimpse, and his face, as before, had a hectic yellow gleam. Yet I never had the sense, which I knew I possessed, of being close to another creature of my kind—and the Pasha, anyway, I knew was dead. I began to ask Polidori about the workings of the mind, of hallucinations, and the nature of dreams. Again, Polidori's theories were daring and profound. He had written a thesis, he told me, on somnambulism. He offered to mesmerize me. I laughed, and agreed, but Polidori's mortal eyes could gain no hold on mine. Instead, it was I who invaded Polidori's brain. Appearing in his dreams, I whispered to him to give up poetry, and show the due respect which his employer was owed. When he woke, Polidori's response was a lengthy sulk. 'Damn you,' he muttered, 'even in my subconscious you insist on lording it.' For the whole day, he scarcely spoke a further word. Instead—pointedly—he sat working on his tragedy.

"By now we were in Brussels. I was keen to see the fields of Waterloo, where the great battle had been fought a year before. The morning after he had begun his sulk, Polidori was sufficiently recovered to accompany me. 'Is it true, My

Lord,' he asked, as we rode out, 'that you like to be known as the Napoleon of rhyme?'

"'It is what other people have called me.' I glanced at him. 'Why, Polidori? Is that why you're coming with me now?—to see me at Waterloo?'

Polidori nodded stiffly. 'Certainly, My Lord, I believe you have been unchallenged as a poet for far too long. I think'—he coughed—'no, I believe—that my tragedy may prove to be your Wellington.'

"Again, I laughed, but I made no further reply, for by now I was starting to smell stale blood. I cantered forward. Ahead of me, the gently rolling hills seemed deserted and calm. But yes—I breathed it in again—the scent of death was heavy on the air. 'This is the site of the battle?' I called back to our guide. He nodded. I stared around, then galloped on. Mud sucked at my horse's hooves, and as it was churned, so it seemed to ooze with blood. I rode to where Napoleon had camped on the day of his fatal defeat. I sat in my saddle, and stared out at that plain of skulls.

"The fields of corn swayed in a gentle breeze. I could almost imagine they were whispering my name. I felt a strange lightness filling me, and I rode forward, to try to shake it off. As I did so, the mud I was passing through seemed to suck more and more. I cantered across to a stretch of grass. Still the mud oozed. I looked down. It was then I saw that the grass was staining red. Wherever my horse trod, bubbles of blood welled up from the earth.

"I looked around. I was alone. There was no trace of my riding companions, and the sky seemed suddenly purple and dark. All sounds had fallen and faded away—the birds, the insects, the rustling of the corn. The silence, like the sky, was cold and dead. Across the whole wide plain, not a living thing moved.

"And then, from beyond the crest of a distant ridge, very faint, I heard a sound. It was the beating of a drum. It paused—and then, louder than before, it began again. I rode my horse forward. The drum beat quickened. As I rode up to the ridge, it seemed to echo through the skies. I reached the ridge. I reined in my horse. I sat and stared at the scene below.

"Blood was seeping up from the fields, as though the soil were a bandage laid across an unstanchable wound. The earth began to melt, and blend with the pools of gore, so that across the battlefield, clots of dirt and blood began to form. Soon, I could recognize human forms, staggering free from the hold of their graves. Lines of them began to form, and I could see the rotting shreds of their uniforms. I was staring at regiments—battalions—armies of the dead. They met my gaze with idiot eyes. Their skins were putrid, their noses collapsed, their bodies rank with blood and slime. For a second, all was still. Then, as though swayed by a single mind, the soldiers took a pace forward. They took off their hats. With a terrible slowness, they waved them in the air, saluting me. *'Vive l'Empereur!'* they shouted; 'Long live our Emperor!—the Emperor of the Dead!'

"I turned in the saddle. I remembered my last night in Piccadilly. I was certain that this was another such vision, conjured up for me. I searched for the creature that bore the Pasha's form. I saw him, on horseback, silhouetted against the purple sky. He was watching me. 'Vakhel Pasha?' I whispered. I narrowed my eyes. 'Can it really be you?' He raised his hat, mimicking the salute of the dead soldiery. He began to gallop away, but I followed him, to destroy him, and wrest back control of my dream. The creature turned. There was a frown of surprise on his face. Suddenly, before I had seen him move, I felt his fingers about my throat. I was taken aback by his strength. It was a long time since I had confronted a being with powers like my own. I fought back. Again, I saw surprise and doubt cross the Pasha's face. I felt him weakening. I slashed across his face. He stumbled back, rolling on the ground. I stepped forward. At that same moment, I heard a scream.

"I glanced around. Polidori was watching me. He stared into my eyes, then screamed again. I looked back at where the Pasha lay—he was gone. I swore under my breath. I could hear birds again now, and looking out at the battlefield, there was only grass, and untrampled crops.

"I glanced back at Polidori. He was still asleep, moaning and writhing on the ground. Our attendants were crossing to him. Good, I thought. They were welcome to him. I wheeled my horse around and crossed the battlefield. Peasants tried to offer me broken swords and skulls. I bought a few. Otherwise, I rode alone, meditating on Napoleon's fall and the fatal transience of mortality.

"As we journeyed back to Brussels, Polidori continued to watch me silently. His eyes were suspicious and full of fear. I ignored him. Only later that night, once I had killed and fed, and was warm with blood, did I deal with him. He was asleep. I woke him roughly. I gripped him around the throat. I warned him never to read my dreams again.

"'But I saw you in a trance,' Polidori choked. 'I thought it might be interesting to read your thoughts. Indeed'—he puffed out his chest—'as your physician, I believed it was my duty to.'

"I stroked my finger down the side of his cheek. 'Do not try it again,' I whispered.

Polidori stared at me aggressively. 'Why not, My Lord?' he asked. 'Do you think my mind is not the equal of yours?'

"I smiled. 'No,' I whispered very softly. Polidori opened his mouth, but when he saw my eyes, his face turned white, and he could only make a gabbling sound. At last, he bowed his head. He turned and left me. I hoped—I thought—he had understood.

"But there was no restraining his vanity. Polidori continued to brood. 'Why,' he asked me suddenly, a few days later, 'did the soldiers salute you as the Emperor?'

"I stared at him in surprise, then I smiled coldly. 'It was only a dream, Polidori.'

"'Was it?' His eyes bulged, and he nodded his head excitedly. 'Was it?'

"I looked away, staring out through my carriage window,

admiring the beauty of the passing Rhine. I advised Polidori to do the same. For a few miles, he did. We rode in
silence. Then Polidori began to jab his finger at me.

" 'Why you?' he exploded again. *'Why?'* He patted at his
chest. 'Why not *me?*'

"I looked at him, and laughed.

"Polidori choked, he was so furious, then he swallowed,
and tried to compose himself. 'And pray tell me, My Lord,
what can you do that I can't do better?'

"I smiled faintly. 'Apart from write poetry that sells?' I
leaned forward. 'Three things.' I reached for my pistol and
cocked it. Polidori shrunk back. 'I can hit a keyhole at thirty
paces.' I gestured out at the Rhine. 'I can swim across that
river. And thirdly . . .' I placed the barrel of my pistol under
Polidori's chin. I captured his eyes and invaded his mind. I
conjured up an image for him, of himself pinned out and
flayed on his own dissecting table. I watched as the color
drained from Polidori's face. I laughed and sat back.
'Thirdly,' I repeated, 'as you see—I can fill you with a terror
that would drive you insane. So, Doctor . . . do not tempt
me.'

"Polidori sat shivering and gulping for air. We relapsed
into silence again. He said nothing further until the carriage
stopped for the night. Then, as we climbed out, he looked at
me. 'Why *should* you be an emperor?' he asked. 'Why
should the dead have appeared to you?' Resentment and
envy darkened his face. Then he turned and ran from me
into the inn.

"I let him go. His questions were good ones, of course.
The Pasha's heir, Lady Melbourne had called me—and the
Pasha had been something very like a king. I did not want
such power—the king times were over—and though I was a
vampire, I could still value liberty. But the dead at Waterloo
had paid homage to me—had they been conjured up, then,
as a mockery? And by whom? The Pasha himself? But the
Pasha was dead—I was sure of it—I had punctured his
heart—*I had felt him die, I knew I had.*

"It couldn't have been his face, then, which I had glimpsed at Piccadilly, or seen livid and pale against the sky at Waterloo. I began to guard my thoughts. I would not let them be surprised again. If some creature was abroad who wanted to challenge me—well—let it—but I doubted its powers would be equal to mine. We journeyed on, past Drachenfells and then into Switzerland. The Alps, wintry and vast, began to tower above us. All this time, I saw nothing strange. My dreams were uninvaded. The creature—whatever it was—seemed left behind. I was pleased, but not surprised. I remembered slashing its face at Waterloo. It would have been foolish to have dared contend further with me. As we approached Geneva, I began to relax." He paused. "Which turned out to be a bad mistake, of course."

Rebecca waited. "The Pasha?" she asked eventually.

"No, no." Lord Byron shook his head. "No, it was quite a different order of shock than that. We arrived at the Hôtel d'Angleterre. I left my carriage and walked into the hall. As I did so, I breathed in a scent. It was familiar, deadly, irresistible. I froze, then looked around, half-expecting to see Augusta. But there was only Polidori and the hotel staff. Numbly, I signed the register. Age, it asked. Suddenly, I felt a terrible, weary despair. One hundred, I wrote. Then I retired to my room, trying to empty out my mind. But it was impossible. Everywhere hung the tang of golden blood.

"An hour later, a note was sent up to me. I ripped it open. 'My dearest love,' I read, 'I am sorry you are grown so old; indeed I suspected you were two hundred from the slowness of your journey. I am here with Mary, and with Shelley too. I hope we shall all see you soon. I certainly have much to tell you. But for now, Heaven send you sweet sleep—I am so happy.' It was signed, simply, 'Claire.'

" 'Bad news?' Polidori asked, with his usual tact.

" 'Yes,' I said slowly. 'You could say that.'

"Polidori grinned. 'Oh dear,' he said.

"I managed to avoid Claire for two more days. But she

pestered me all the time with notes, and I knew she would track me down in the end. After all she had crossed half Europe to be with me, so her madness was clearly not to be denied. She found me one afternoon, as I rowed with Polidori out on the lake. She stood waiting for me, two companions by her side. I was trapped. As I drew closer to her, so the perfume in my nostrils grew more and more intense. I scrambled from the boat, and walked slowly up to her. She held out her hand—reluctantly, I took it; I gave it a kiss. As I did so, I felt dizzy with thirst. Hurriedly, I dropped Claire's hand and turned my back on her—on her, and the fetus of our unborn child.

"'Lord Byron?' One of Claire's two companions had walked forward to greet me. I stared into his face. It was delicate and pale, framed by long golden hair—a poet's face—almost, I thought, a vampire's face. 'Mr. Shelley?' I inquired.

"He nodded.

"'I am very glad to meet you,' I said, taking his hand. I shook it, then glanced at the third member of the group. Shelley, following my eyes, took his companion by the arm. He led her forward. 'You have already met Mary, Claire's sister, I believe?'

"I smiled and nodded. 'Yes, I have met your wife.'

"'Not my wife.'

"I stared at Shelley in surprise. 'Oh, I do apologize, I thought . . .'

"'Shelley does not believe in marriage,' said Mary simply.

"Shelley smiled at me shyly. 'I hear you don't have much time for the married state yourself.'

"I laughed, and the ice was broken. Claire ran up to me, angry at being ignored, and tried to take my arm, but I shrugged her away. 'Come and dine with me tonight,' I whispered in Shelley's ear. 'Do not bring Claire.' And then, with a bow to the two sisters, I went back to the boat.

"Shelley did come that night, and he came alone. We

talked until the early hours. His conversation enchanted me. He was an incorrigible infidel. It was not just marriage he damned—he damned priests and tyrants and God as well. 'This is the winter of the world,' he told me. 'Everything is gray and burdened with chains.' And yet this recognition had not bred despair—instead, his faith in the future burned like a flame, and I, who had forgotten what passionate hope could be, listened, entranced. Shelley believed in humanity; believed it could attain a higher state. I mocked him, of course, for many of his speculations—he was talking of things he couldn't possibly know. And yet I was intrigued as well when he spoke of opening his mind to the universe, of tautening his perceptions like the strings of a lyre, so that his visionary senses might be immeasurably increased. 'There are strange forces in the world,' he told me, 'invisible to us, but as real, for all that, as you or me.'

"'And how do you make contact with such forces?' I asked.

"'Through terror,' said Shelley at once. 'Terror and sex. They can both serve to open up the world of the unknown.' My smile broadened. I stared into Shelley's eyes. I thought again what a beautiful vampire he would make.

"I decided I would stay in Switzerland. Shelley and his ménage were already settled in a house by the lake. I rented a large villa some two hundred yards away—at the distance where the scent from Claire's womb became faint. Claire herself was still importunate, and there were times when she refused to stay away. Mostly, though, I avoided her successfully, and the torture she bore me in her flesh was kept at bay. Shelley, of course, I saw all the time. We boated, and rode, and talked late into the nights.

"After a few weeks, the weather took a marked turn for the worse. There were endless fogs, and storms, and heavy rains. We kept to my villa day and night. In the evenings, we would gather in my front room. A fire would blaze in the giant hearth, while outside, the wind would scream across the lake, and buffet the glass of the balcony doors. Often, we would stand by them and watch the play of lightning over the icy mountain peaks. The sight would inspire me to renew my questionings about galvanism, and electricity, and whether there existed a principle of life. Shelley too was fascinated by such issues, and at Oxford, it seemed, had even conducted experiments.

"'Successful?' I asked.

"Shelley laughed, and shook his head. 'But I still believe it might be possible to generate life,' he said. 'A corpse, perhaps, might be reanimated.'

"'Oh yes,' said Polidori, butting in, 'my Lord Byron would know all about that, wouldn't you, *My Lord?*' His face began to twitch. 'Emperor of the Dead,' he spat. I smiled faintly, and ignored him. Polidori was jealous of Shelley. He had good cause. Shelley and I continued to talk. After a few more interruptions, Polidori swore at us, and stormed away.

"He brought out his tragedy, and began to read it aloud. I heard Claire giggle. Polidori broke off and flushed. He stared around the room. We all fell silent. 'You,' said Polidori suddenly, pointing at Shelley. 'My poem. What do *you* think of it?'

"Shelley paused. 'You're an excellent doctor,' he said at last.

"Polidori shook. 'Are you insulting me?' he asked in a low, tremulous voice.

"Shelley looked surprised. 'Dear me, no,' he said. He shrugged. 'But I'm afraid I don't think your poem is worth very much.'

"Polidori slammed his manuscript down onto the floor. 'I demand satisfaction,' he shouted. He crossed to Shelley. 'Yes, sir, you, I demand satisfaction!'

"Shelley burst into laughter.

"'Oh for God's sake, Polidori,' I drawled, 'Shelley is a pacifist. If you must fight a duel, then do it with me.'

"Polidori glanced at me. 'You mock me, My Lord.'

"I smiled. 'Yes, I do.'

"Suddenly, Polidori's shoulders slumped. Crestfallen, he

turned back to Shelley. 'In what way, do you think, my poem fails?'

"Shelley thought. At that moment, lightning stabbed across the Jura, and the whole room was lit up silver with its glow. 'Poetry,' Shelley said, as the roll of thunder faded away, 'must be'—he paused—'must be a spark of fire, an electrical charge, giving life to a dead world, opening eyes which have been shut for too long.'

"I smiled at him. 'Like terror, then?'

"Shelley nodded, his eyes wide and solemn. 'Yes indeed, Byron—like terror.'

"I rose to my feet. 'I have an idea,' I said. 'Let us try to see if Shelley's theory is right.'

"Mary frowned at me. 'How?' she asked. 'What do you mean?'

"I crossed to a shelf, and held up a book. 'I shall read you ghost stories,' I said. 'And then, each one of us will take it in turn to come up with a story of terror of our own.' I walked around the room, dimming the lights. Only Shelley helped me. Polidori watched sniffily, while Mary and Claire looked uncertain and afraid. I gathered them around me as we sat by the fire. As I began, there was a satisfying rumble of thunder from outside. But I had no need of the storm—my voice alone, I knew, would cast a spell of fear. I seemed, to the others, to be reading from the book, but of course, I had no need of it—the tales of horror I told them were my own. There were two stories I composed that night. In the first, a lover clasped his newly-wed bride—he kissed her—and felt her turn into the corpse of all the girls he had betrayed. And in the second . . ." Lord Byron paused. He smiled at Rebecca. "The second told the story of a family. Its founder, for his sins, was doomed to give the kiss of death to all his descendants" Lord Byron paused *"to all of his family who shared his blood.* Yes," he nodded seeing how Rebecca sat frozen in her chair, "I remember Claire enjoying that one as well. She began to clutch her belly, just as Bell had done. And then—well—the scent of her terror encouraged me. I told them my own story—disguised, of course—the story of two friends who traveled to Greece—and what happened to one of them there. There was silence when I finished. I noted with pleasure how strongly Shelley was affected. His eyes were wide and staring, drawn almost from the sockets by the convulsion of the muscles, so that it seemed as though his eyeballs had just been placed within a mask. His hair seemed to glow, and his face had a paleness that was almost like light.

"'And that was . . . just a story?' he asked eventually.

"I raised an eyebrow. 'Why do you ask?'

"'The way you told it'—his eyes widened even further—'it seemed—well—you spoke it as though it contained some terrible truth.'

"I smiled faintly, but as I opened my mouth to answer, Polidori interrupted me. 'My turn now!' he said, jumping to his feet. 'Be warned, though, ladies,' he added, bowing gallantly to Mary, 'it may well turn your blood to ice.' He posed with a candle, cleared his throat, and began. The story was ludicrous, of course. A woman, for some unexplained reason, had a skull for a head. She went spying through keyholes. Something shocking happened to her, I can't remember what. Eventually, Polidori got stuck, and had her finished off in some tomb, again for no reason that I could see. The evening, which before had indeed seemed electric with fear, now declined into hilarity.

"Then suddenly, at the height of our laughter, Mary screamed. The balcony doors swung open—the wind swept through the room—all the candles were blown out. Mary screamed again. 'It's all right!' Shelley shouted, as he rushed to close the doors. 'It's only the storm!'

"'No,' said Mary. She pointed again. 'There's something on the balcony. I saw it there.' I frowned, and walked with Shelley out through the doors. The balcony was empty. We tried to peer into the dark, but rain was driving in across the lake, and blinded us. I could smell nothing.

"'I saw a face,' insisted Mary, as we began to light the candles again. 'Hideous, evil.'

" 'Was it pale?' I asked. 'Did it have burning eyes?'

" 'Yes.' She shook her head. 'No. His eyes . . .' she looked at me—'his eyes, Byron, they were very like yours.'

"Shelley glanced at me. His expression was strange. Suddenly, I laughed.

" 'What is it?' Shelley asked.

" 'Your theory seems proved,' I said. 'Look at us. All in a state of nerves. Polidori, my congratulations.' Polidori smiled, and bowed. 'Your story can't have been as laughable as I had thought it was. We all seem to be hallucinating.'

" 'I didn't imagine it,' said Mary. 'There is some—thing—out there.'

"Shelley crossed to her and took her hand. But all the time, he continued to stare at me. He was shaking.

" 'I want to go to bed,' said Claire in a low voice.

"I looked at her. 'Good.'

"She rose to her feet and stared around the room, then ran out.

" 'Shelley?' I asked.

"He frowned. His pale face was bathed in sweat. 'Some power is here,' he said, 'some awful shadow of unseen power.' Deeper and deeper, I knew he was sinking into the darkness of my eyes. I stared into his thoughts, and saw how in love he was with his ecstasy of fear. Like moonlight on a tempestuous sea, I cast the gleams of a remoter world upon his soul. He shuddered, welcoming his terror as it rose. He turned to Mary. He tried to still his fear. But he was not escaping so easily. Again my power rolled through his mind. When Shelley looked at Mary, he saw her naked, and her side seemed pale, and hideous, and deformed; her nipples were closed eyes; suddenly, they opened, and their gleam was like a vampire's, mocking him, calling to him. Shelley shrieked, then stared at me. The skin of his face was drawn into countless wrinkles—the lineaments of a terror that could not be contained. He put his head in his hands and ran out from the room. Polidori glanced at me, then hurried after him.

"Mary too rose to her feet. 'This evening has been too much for all of us,' she said, after a long pause. She glanced out at the night. 'I trust we may sleep here?'

"I nodded. 'Of course.' Then I smiled at her. 'You must anyway. We still haven't heard your story.'

"'I know. I am very bad at invention. But I shall try to think of something.' She bowed her head, then turned to go.

"'Mary,' I called after her.

"She turned to look at me.

"'Do not worry about Shelley. He will be well enough.'

"Mary stared straight at me. She smiled faintly. Then, without a further word, she left me alone.

"I stood on the balcony. The rain had stopped, but the storm was still violent. I sniffed the winds, for the scent of the thing that Mary had seen. There was nothing. She must, after all, have imagined it. It was odd, though, I thought, that her hallucination should have been so like my own. I shrugged. It had been a strange, intoxicating night. I stared out again at the raging of the storm. In the distance, the mountains gleamed like fangs, and the moon, behind the clouds, I knew was full. Knowledge of my own power screamed in my blood. From distant Geneva, the clocks struck two. I turned, and closed the balcony doors. Then, silently, I passed through the villa to the Shelleys' room.

"They lay naked and pale in each other's arms. Mary moaned as my shadow crossed her; she turned in her sleep; Shelley too stirred, so that his chest and face were upturned toward me. I stood by his side. How beautiful he was. Like a father stroking his sleeping daughter's cheeks, I scanned his dreams. They were lovely and strange. I had never met such a mortal before. He had spoken of wanting the secret power, the power of the world that lay beyond man, and his mind, I knew, was worthy of it. That evening, down in the drawing room, I had given him a glimpse of what lay beyond mortality. And yet I could give him more—I could create him in my own image—I could give him existence for eternity.

"I felt a sudden desperate pain. How I longed for a companion of my own kind I could love! We would still be vampires, it was true, cut off from all the world, but not wretched and alone as I was now. I bent low over Shelley's sleeping form. It would be no sin to make him a being like me. It was life I would give him, and life, after all, was the gift of God. I laid my hand on his chest. I felt his heart beating, waiting to be opened to my kiss. No. It would not be a slave I was creating, not a monster, but a lover for all time. No. No fault, no sin. I ran my finger across Shelley's chest.

"He didn't stir, but Mary moaned again, as though struggling to wake up from some terrible dream. I glanced at her—and then beyond—and slowly, I raised my lips from Shelley's chest.

"The Pasha was watching me. He stood by the door, cloaked in shadow, no expression on his smooth, pale face. His eyes, though, seemed to pierce like light into my soul. Then he turned and disappeared. I rose from Shelley's bed, and glided after him.

"But he was gone. The house seemed empty, and there was still no scent of his presence in the air. Then a door slammed, and I heard the wind screaming down the passageway. I hurried along it. The door at the end was swinging in the gale. Beyond it waited the garden. I passed outside, and searched for my quarry. All was dark and tossed by the storm. Then, as lightning stabbed above the mountain peaks, I saw a black form lit up against the waves of the lake. I hurried on the wind, down toward the shore. As I approached him, the dark form turned and looked at me. His face still blazed with a yellow gleam, and his features seemed even more cruel than I remembered them. But it was him. I was certain now. It was him.

"'From what depths of Hell, what impossible abyss, have you returned?'

"The Pasha smiled, but said nothing.

"'And now—damn you—*damn you*—of all times—to

reappear now . . .' I thought of Shelley, still asleep in the
house. 'Would you deny me a companion? Am I not to
create, as you created me?' The Pasha's smile broadened.
His yellow teeth were unbearably foul. Anger, as fierce as
the wind at my back, swept me forward. I took the Pasha by
the throat. 'Remember,' I whispered, 'that I am your
creature. Everywhere I see bliss, from which I alone am
excluded. I was human; you have made me a fiend. Do not
mock me then for desiring happiness, nor try to frustrate
me when I search for it.' Still the Pasha grinned mockingly.
I tightened my grip. 'Leave me,' I whispered, 'my creator—
and because of that—my eternal—*enemy.*'

"The Pasha's neck snapped in my grip. His head lolled,
and blood from his throat began to pump across my hands. I
dropped the corpse onto the ground. I stared at it—and saw
that the Pasha now had Shelley's face. I bent down beside
him. Slowly, the corpse reached up for me. It kissed me on
the lips. It opened its mouth. Its tongue was a worm, fat and
soft. I shrunk back. I saw I had been kissing the teeth of a
skull.

"I looked away—and when I glanced down again, the
corpse was gone. I heard a wild laughter deep within my
mind. I stared wildly around. I was alone now on the shore,
but still the laughter rose, until the lake and mountains
seemed to echo with it, and I thought that it would deafen
me. It reached a peak and then was silent, and at the very
same moment, the glass in the balcony windows was
smashed—the doors flew open—books and papers were
scattered on the gale. Like a plague of insects they were
swept out across the lawns to the shore where I stood,
fluttering and landing all about me, trapped in the mud, or
sinking slowly into the waters of the lake. I picked up a book
which lay sodden at my feet. I looked at its spine. *Galvanism
and the Principles of Human Life.* I remembered it. I had
read the same title in the Pasha's tower. I gathered up more
books, more scattered sheets—the debris of the library I
had brought with me. I piled them in a mound on the
pebbles of the shore. When the storm was dead, I lit a fire.

Dully, the pyre began to burn. As the sun rose, it was greeted by a pall of black smoke across the lake."

Lord Byron paused. Rebecca stared at him. "I don't understand," she said at last.

Lord Byron hooded his eyes. "I had felt mocked," he said quietly.

"Mocked?"

"Yes. My hopes—they had been taunted."

Rebecca frowned. "You mean your search for the principle of life?"

"You see"—Lord Byron smiled bitterly—"how empty, how melodramatic such words must always sound?" He shook his head. "And yet I had thought I was exempt. I was a vampire, after all—who was I to say what was impossible? Yet standing by the lake that morning, as the ash was scattered from my pyre of books, I felt nothing but impotence. I had great powers, yes—but I knew now there were others, with greater powers still—and beyond us all—fathomless—the universe. How could I presume to find the spark of life? It was a hopeless ambition—an ambition better suited to some Gothic tale—some science fiction or fantasy." Lord Byron paused, and twisted his lips into a smile. "And so my hatred for the Pasha—my creator who it seemed I could not destroy—blazed more fiercely than ever before. I longed for one final, fatal confrontation. But the Pasha, like a true god, now stayed hidden from me.

"My restlessness began to gnaw at me again. I thought of leaving for Italy, but my reluctance to part from Shelley was too great, and we set off instead on a tour around the lake. I still longed for him—to give him my blood—to make him a vampire lord like myself—but I was no longer willing to impose this by force. My loathing of the Pasha was a warning to me; I did not want what he had—an eternity of his creation's hate. And so I tempted Shelley—hinted at what I could give to him—whispered of dark secrets and strange mysteries. Did Shelley understand? Perhaps—yes, perhaps—even then. It happened once, we were boating on the lake. A storm blew up. Our rudder broke. It seemed we would be swamped. I stripped my jacket off, but Shelley sat still and just stared at me. 'Don't you know?' he said, 'I can't swim.'

" 'Then let me save you,' I shouted, reaching for him, but Shelley shrunk back. 'I am afraid of any gift of life from you,' he said.

" 'You will drown.'

" 'Rather that than . . .'

" 'Than'—I smiled—'than what, Shelley? *Life?'*

"He gripped the sides of the boat, and stared into the waters, then up again, into my eyes. 'I am afraid,' he said, 'of being dragged down, down, *down.'* And he sat where he was, his arms folded, and I knew then I had failed, for that summer at least. The storm abated—the boat was safe—and so were we. Neither of us mentioned what had passed between us. But I was ready now to leave for Italy.

"And yet still I stayed on. It was the blood of my unborn child, of course, which kept me there. As before, it tortured and tantalized me. The danger was growing steadily worse. I refused to have Claire alone with me. Shelley too I felt uneasy with now, and Polidori, of course, was insufferable. Of all that group, I saw Mary the most. She was writing a book. It had been inspired, she said, by the nightmares she had had during the terrible storm. Her novel told the story of a scientist. He created life. His creation hated and was hated by him. Mary called this novel *Frankenstein*.

"I read some of it in manuscript. It had a profound and terrible effect on me. There was much—too much—in it I recognized. 'Oh Frankenstein,' the monster told his maker, 'I ought to be thy Adam, but I am rather the fallen angel, whom thou drivest from joy for no misdeed.' I shuddered at these words. From then on, I encouraged Shelley to leave, to take Claire with him and look after her child. At last, they did. Now I was ready. I would hunt down my own Frankenstein. And yet"—Lord Byron paused—"no—the Pasha wasn't wholly a Frankenstein—and the effect of the book didn't lie altogether in its truth. The novel, for all its power, was fiction still. There was no science capable of generating life. Creation remained a mystery. I was struck again by how ridiculous my ambitions had been. I was glad I had watched my library burn.

"I dismissed Polidori. I had no need of him now. I paid him off handsomely, but he took my decision with typical bad grace. 'Why should it be you,' he said, counting through the money, 'who has the power to do this? Why not me?'

"'Because I am of a different order than you.'

"'Yes.' Polidori narrowed his eyes. 'Yes, My Lord, I think you are.'

"I laughed. 'I have never denied you your great insight, Polidori.'

"He leered back at me, then took out a tiny vial from his pocket. He held it to the light. 'Your blood, My Lord.'

"'What of it?'

"'You have been paying me to carry out tests on it. Remember?'

"'Yes. What have you found?'

"Again, Polidori leered. 'Do you dare,' he chuckled lowly, *do you dare* despise me, when I know what I know?'

"I stared at him. Polidori began to shudder and mutter beneath his breath. I invaded his mind, filled it with blank terror. 'Do not menace me,' I whispered. I took the vial of blood from his hands. 'Now go.' Polidori rose to his feet. He stumbled from the room. The next day, without having seen him again, I left.

"I rode high up the road that passed across the Alps. Hobhouse had come to join me. We traveled together. The further we went, the more dizzying rose the walls of toppling rock. Above us, crags of ice towered, and vast ravines; over peaks of snow, wide-winged eagles soared.

"'This is like Greece,' Hobhouse said. 'You remember, Byron? In Albania . . .' His voice trailed away. He looked over his shoulder, as though in involuntary fear. I too looked around. The track was empty. Above it stretched a wood of withered pines. Their trunks were stripped and barkless, their branches without life. Their appearance

reminded me of me and my family. On the other side of the
path, a glacier stretched like a frozen hurricane. Yes, I
thought—if he comes at all—it will be here. I braced
myself. I was ready for him. But still the path was as empty
as before.

"Then, around twilight beyond the Grindenwald, we
heard horse's hooves. We looked around and waited. A
man, alone, was coming up behind us. His face, I saw, had a
yellow gleam. I drew out my pistol—and then, as the
horseman drew up to us, I slipped it back again. 'Who are
you?' I shouted. It was not the Pasha.

"The traveler smiled. 'Ahasver,' he said.

"'What are you?' asked Hobhouse, his own pistol cocked
and still ready in his hand.

"'A wanderer,' said the horseman. His accent was
strange, but of the most beautiful and soul-searching melo-
dy. He smiled again, and bowed his head to me. 'I am a
wanderer, like your friend here, Mr. Hobhouse, just a
wanderer.'

"'You know us?'

"'*Ja, natürlich.*'

"'You are German?' I asked.

"The traveler laughed. 'No, no, *milord!* It is true, I love
the Germans. They are a race of such philosophers, and
without philosophy—who would there be to believe in me?'

"Hobhouse frowned. 'Why shouldn't they believe in
you?'

"'Perhaps, Mr. Hobhouse, because my existence is an
impossibility.' He smiled and turned back to me, as though
feeling the gleam of my eyes. 'What are you?' I whispered.
The traveler met me with a stare as deep as my own. 'If you
must call me anything, *milord,* let it be'—he paused—'Jew.'
He smiled. 'Yes—Jew. For, like the members of that extraordinary and estimable race, I belong to all countries—
and yet, to none of them.'

"Hobhouse frowned. 'The man's a damned lunatic,' he
hissed in my ear. I motioned him to be quiet. I studied the
traveler's face. It was an extraordinary blend of age and

youth. His hair was long and white, but his eyes were as deep and brilliant as mine, and his face quite unwrinkled. He was not a vampire—at least he seemed not to be—and yet there was an air of remarkable mystery about him, which I found both repugnant and awe-inspiring. 'Do you wish to ride with us?' I asked.

"Ahasver bowed his head.

" 'Then let us press on,' I said, wheeling around my horse. 'We still have an hour till we reach the next inn.'

"For the length of the ride, I studied him. We talked. He spoke in English, but he would slip occasionally into other tongues, some modern, some ancient, some which I failed to recognize at all. I soon found out that he had been in the East. At supper, he dined with us, then retired early to bed. I did not sleep. I kept watch on his room. At two, I saw him slip out through the inn. I followed him.

"He climbed the crags with impossible speed. He bounded over crevices of ice and up snaking glaciers. Ahead, jagged, like a city of death, the mountain peaks waited, as though in scorn of the works of man, but Ahasver was no mortal thing to be repelled by their walls. No. I knew what he was. I remembered the phantoms in Piccadilly, how they had changed their form before my very eyes. I remembered snapping the Pasha's neck, and finding I held a skeleton. What powers he had, and how changed, I didn't know—but I was certain of one thing—it was the Pasha I pursued up that mountain face.

"He stayed within my eyeshot all the way. Was he leading me deliberately? I didn't care—one of us would die—I scarcely minded which. I reached the summit of a cliff. My quarry had been just ahead. I looked around. Suddenly, the rocks were empty and bare. I stared down below me, at the mists as they boiled round the glaciers. Then I heard a footstep behind me. I turned. There, facing me, the Pasha stood.

"Like thought, I flew at him. He stumbled, and I saw sudden panic on his face as he began to slip. He reached for me and pulled me down, so that we rolled together by the precipice edge, the gulf seeming to beckon us. I felt the Pasha changing and melting in my arms, but I held on, smashing his head against the rocks, until blood and brains were flowing everywhere. Still I smashed the skull. The Pasha's struggle began to fade. At length he lay motionless—I paused—his eyes were still open, but they had the glaze of death. Then slowly, the shattered face changed. Now it was Ahasver staring up at me. I scarcely noticed. I stabbed him through his heart, again and again. I kicked his body. I watched as it plunged into the gulf below.

"In a slow ecstasy, I walked along the cliff. I felt thirsty. I would return to the road, and have a traveler, drain him dry. Ahead, springing out from a gash in the rock, a torrent was falling—like the tail of a white horse streaming in the wind—the pale horse, on which Death is mounted in the Apocalypse. 'Death.' I whispered the word, to hear the sound it made. 'Death.' It was as though I had never heard it before. Suddenly, a frightening, strange, unfamiliar sound. 'Death!' The rocks of the mountain echoed to my scream. I turned. Ahasver was smiling at me. His face was as smooth as before. Slowly, he bent his knee.

" 'You are worthy to be Emperor.'

"I stared at him, where he stood, by the torrent's fall. 'The Pasha . . .' I said. I frowned. Then I began to shake. 'You are not him. He is dead.'

"Ahasver's expression didn't change. 'Whatever, wherever he may be . . . you are Emperor now.' He smiled suddenly and saluted me. *'Vive l'Empereur!'*

"I remembered the shout from Waterloo. 'All this time,' I said slowly, 'since I left England—you have been pursuing me, mocking me. Why?'

"Ahasver shrugged, then bowed his head in assent. 'I get bored,' he murmured. 'Eternity drags.'

" 'What are you? You are not a vampire.'

"Ahasver laughed derisively. *'Vampire?* No.'

" 'Then what?'

"Ahasver stared at the mists where they curled like distant seas. 'There are forces in this world,' he said at last, 'full of power and strangeness and sublimity. You yourself, *milord,* have evidence of this. In you, the twin poles of life and death are confounded—what man falsely separates, you unite. And you are great, *milord*—terribly great—but there are powers and beings even greater than you. I tell you this, both to warn and help you in your agony.'

"He stroked my cheeks, then kissed me. 'Ah, *milord,'* he said, 'your eyes are as deep and beautiful and dangerous as mine. You are extraordinary—extraordinary.' He took me by my arm, led me along the top of the cliff. 'I appear to men sometimes, to torture them with thoughts of eternity, but to vampires—who would understand me better, and therefore be more truly appalled—never. You, though— you are different. I had heard the rumors, that the Lords of the Dead had a new Emperor. Then your fame began to fill the world. Lord Byron—Lord Byron—your name seemed to hover on every tongue. I was intrigued. I came to you. I tested you.' Ahasver paused and smiled. *'Milord,* I can promise you this—you will be an emperor such as the vampires have never known.

"'And therefore I warn you. If I have been mocking your hopes, then it is to remind you that you cannot escape your own nature. To imagine otherwise is to torture yourself. Do not trust in mortal science, *milord.* You are a creature beyond its power to explain. Do you truly expect it to save you from your thirst?' Ahasver laughed, and gestured with his hand. 'If the abysm could vomit forth its secrets . . .' He waited. Below us, the chasm was as silent as before. Ahasver laughed again. 'Deep truth is imageless, *milord.* What I know, you cannot. So be content with the immortality you have.'

"'Do you drink blood?'

"Ahasver stared at me. He didn't reply.

"'Do you drink blood?' I repeated bitterly. 'No. How then can you tell me to be *content?* I am cursed. How can you understand that?'

"Ahasver smiled faintly. In his eyes, I thought I saw a gleam of mockery. 'All immortality, *milord,* is a curse.' He paused, and took my hands. 'Accept it, though—accept it as it is—and it becomes a blessing'—his eyes widened—'a chance, *milord,* to walk among the gods.' He kissed me on my cheek, then whispered in my ear. 'A curse must live off its victim's self-hate. Do not hate yourself, *milord,* and do not hate your immortality. Welcome the greatness which is ready to be yours.'

"He pulled away from me, then gestured at the mountains and the sky. 'You are worthy to rule—more worthy than any of your breed before. Do it, *milord.* Rule as Emperor. This is how I help you—by telling you to abandon your ridiculous guilt. See!—the world is at your feet! Those who surpass or subdue mankind must always look down on the hate of those below. Do not fear what you are. Exult in it!' Below us, the clouds boiled white and sulfury, like foam from the ocean of Hell. But then, as I stared, I saw them thin and part, and the deep abyss was opened to me. My spirit, like lightning, seemed to dart across the void. I felt the rich pulse of life fill the heavens. The very mountains seemed to stir and breathe, and I imagined the blood in their stony veins, so vividly that I longed to tear the rocks apart, and feed on them, and all the world. I thought this passion would overwhelm me—this passion of immortality—and yet it did not—for my mind had grown colossal, expanded by the beauty of the mountains and my thoughts. I turned to Ahasver. He was changed. He stretched away, high beyond the peaks, into the sky, a dark form of giant shadow, meeting with the dawn as it rose above Mont Blanc. I felt myself rise with him, moving on the wind. I saw the Alps stretched out far below. 'What are you?' I asked again. 'What nature of thing?' I felt Ahasver's voice repeat within my thoughts: 'You are worthy to rule—exult in it!'

" 'Yes!' I shouted, laughing. 'Yes!' Then I felt rock beneath my feet. The wind moaned and cut across my back. The air was cold. I was alone again. Ahasver was gone.

"I returned to the road. I killed the first peasant I met, and emptied him. I felt how dread I was, how fathomless and alone. Later, with Hobhouse, I rode back past my victim's corpse. A crowd was gathered round it. A man was bent over the dead man's chest. As we passed, he glanced up and looked into my face. It was Polidori. I met his stare until he looked away. I shook out my reins. I laughed, to think that he was following me. I was a vampire—didn't the fool understand what that meant? I laughed again.

"'Well,' said Hobhouse, 'you seem damned cheery all of a sudden.'

"We descended into Italy. On the way, I killed and drank remorselessly. One evening, outside Milan, I captured a handsome shepherd boy. His blood was as tender and soft as his lips. As I drank it, I felt a touch on my back.

"'Zounds, Byron, but you always did have a good eye. Where'd you find such a pretty trull?'

"I looked up and smiled. 'Lovelace.' I kissed him. He was as golden and cruel as he had been before.

"He laughed as he embraced me. 'We have been waiting for you,' he said. 'Welcome, Byron. Welcome to Milan.'

"There were other vampires gathered in the city. They had come, Lovelace told me, to pay their respects. I did not find this strange. Their homage, after all, was nothing but my due. There were twelve of them, the vampires of Italy. They were deathly and beautiful, and their powers were great, like Lovelace's. But I was greater than them all—I could feel it so easily, as I had not done before—and even Lovelace now seemed daunted by me. I told him, in strange hints, of my meeting with Ahasver. He had never heard of such a being before. This pleased me. Where before he had been the teacher, now I commanded instinctively. He, and all the vampires, respected my order to leave Hobhouse alone. Instead, we hunted other prey, and our banquets ran red with living blood.

"It was our habit, before such meals, to attend the opera. I went one night with Lovelace and a third vampire, as beautiful and cruel as either of us, the Contessa Marianna Lucrezia Cenci. As she descended from our carriage, and smoothed down the skirts of her crimson gown, she smelled the air—her green eyes narrowed—she turned to me.

'There is someone out there,' she said. 'He has been following us.' She stroked her gloves along the length of her arm, much like a cat when she cleans herself. 'I will kill him.'

"I frowned. I too could smell our pursuer's blood.

"'Later,' said Lovelace, taking Marianna's arm. 'Let us hurry, or we will miss the opera's start.'

"Marianna glanced at me. I nodded. We took our places in our private box. The performance that night was of Mozart's *Don Giovanni*—the man who seduced a thousand women, and abandoned them all. As the opera started, our eyes began to gleam—it was a story written, it seemed, to appeal to us. Lovelace turned and smiled at me. 'You will see shortly, Byron, how the rogue is confronted by his wife. He had left her, don't you know, because he had the itch of unrestrainable villainy.' He grinned again.

"'A man after my own heart,' I replied. The wife entered—the Don ran away—the servant was left to handle things. He began to sing to the wife, describing his master's conquests around the world. 'In Germany, two hundred and thirty-one; a hundred in France; in Turkey, ninety-one.' I recognized the song at once. I turned to Lovelace. 'This was the same tune you hummed,' I said, 'when we hunted in Constantinople and Greece.'

"Lovelace nodded. 'Why, yes sir, but my own list of victims is longer by far.'

"Marianna turned to me, stroking back her long black hair. '*Deo,* but this gives me a killing thirst.'

"At that very moment, there was a disturbance. The door to our box swung open. I looked around. A haggard young man was staring at me. It was Polidori. He raised his arm and pointed at us. 'Vampires!' he shouted. 'They are vampires, I have seen them—I have proof!'

"As the audience turned in their seats to stare, Marianna rose to her feet. '*Mi scusi,*' she whispered. Soldiers came into the box. She whispered to them. They nodded, then took Polidori roughly by the arms. They dragged him away.

"'Where have they taken him?' I asked.

" 'The cells.'

" 'For what offense?'

" 'One of the soldiers will claim he was insulted.' Marianna smiled. 'That is how it is always done, My Lord.'

"I nodded. The opera continued. I watched as Don Giovanni was dragged to Hell. 'Repent!' he was commanded. 'No!' the Don screamed back. 'Repent!' 'No!' I admired his spirit. Marianna and Lovelace both seemed moved as well.

"Out in the dark streets again, their eyes burned bright and eager with thirst. 'Are you coming, Byron?' Lovelace asked.

"Marianna shook her head. She smiled at me as she took Lovelace by the arm. 'My Lord has other business tonight.' I nodded. I called my carriage up.

"Polidori was waiting for me. 'I knew you would come,' he said, shivering as I walked into his cell. 'Are you here to kill me?'

"I smiled. 'I have a policy of trying not to kill my acquaintances.'

" 'Vampire!' Polidori spat suddenly. 'Vampire, vampire, vampire! Damned, loathsome vampire!'

"I yawned. 'Yes, thank you, you have made your point.'

" 'Leech!'

"I laughed. Polidori shuddered at this. He pressed himself flat against the prison wall. 'What are you going to do with me?' he asked.

" 'You are being expelled from the territory of Milan. You will go tomorrow.' I tossed him a bag of coins. 'Here—take these, and never try to follow me again.'

"Polidori stared at the coins in disbelief. Then suddenly, he flung them back at me. 'You have everything, don't you?' he screamed. 'Wealth, talent, power—and now, even generosity. Oh, wonderful! The demon who was kind. Well, damn you, Byron, damn you to Hell. You're a damned cheat, that's all you are. I despise you, I despise you! If I were the vampire, *I* would be the lord!'

"He slumped, and fell sobbing at my feet. I reached out to

him. Polidori shrunk away. 'Damn you!' he screamed again. Then he fell forward, and leaned his head against my knees. Gently, I stroked the locks of his hair.

" 'Take the money,' I whispered, 'and go.'

"Polidori stared up. 'Damn you.'

" 'Go.'

"Polidori kneeled in silence. 'I would be a creature of terrible power,' he said at last, 'if I were a vampire.'

"There was silence. I stared down at him with mingled pity and contempt. Then suddenly, he sniveled. I pushed him back with my foot. Moonlight was spilling in through a window in the cell. I kicked Polidori so he lay in the light. He started to whimper as I stripped off his shirt. My blood was starting to burn me now. I put my foot on Polidori's chest. He stared at me wordlessly. I bit into his throat, then ripped with a dagger down across his chest. I drank the blood as it pumped up from the wound, while I tore at the bones, until the heart was exposed. It was still beating, but faintly, and growing ever more faint. His nakedness was horrible. I had lain stripped in the same way—deprived of dignity, life, humanity. The heart twitched, like a fish on a riverbank—and then was still. I moved on the corpse. I gave it the Gift."

Lord Byron sat in silence. He stared at something in the darkness, which Rebecca couldn't see. Then he ran his fingers through the curls of his hair.

"The Gift," Rebecca said at last. "What was it?"

"Something terrible."

Rebecca waited. "Indescribable?"

Lord Byron stared at her. "Until you have received it— yes."

Rebecca ignored the implications of the word *until*. "And Polidori," she asked, "he—he was all right . . . ?" She knew how inadequate her phrase was to the question. Her voice trailed away.

Lord Byron poured another glass of wine. "He awoke from death, if that is what you mean."

"How?—I mean . . ."

Lord Byron smiled. "How?" he asked. "His eyes opened—he breathed hard—a convulsive motion agitated his limbs. He looked up at me. His jaws opened, and he muttered some inarticulate sounds, while a grin wrinkled his cheeks. He may have spoken—I didn't hear—one hand was stretched out to detain me, but I couldn't bear the sight of him, this corpse, this hideous monster to which I had given existence. I turned, and left the cell. I paid the guards. They escorted Polidori to the frontier at once. They were found several days later, ripped apart and drained white of their blood. It was all kept quiet."

"And Polidori?"

"What of him?"

"Did you see him again?"

Lord Byron smiled. He stared at Rebecca with burning eyes. "Haven't you guessed?" he asked.

"Guessed?"

"The identity of the man who sent you here tonight? The man who showed you the papers? The man on the bridge?" Lord Byron nodded. "Oh yes," he said. "I was to see Polidori again."

Chapter XII

Lift not the painted veil which those who live
Call Life: though unreal shapes be pictured there,
And it but mimic all we would believe
With colours idly spread—behind, lurk Fear
And Hope, twin Destinies; who ever weave
Their shadows, o'er the chasm, sightless and drear.
I knew one who had lifted it—he sought,
For his lost heart was tender, things to love,
But found them not, alas! nor was there aught
The world contains, the which he could approve.
Through the unheeding many he did move,
A splendor among shadows, a bright blot
Upon this gloomy scene, a Spirit that strove
For truth, and like the Preacher found it not.

PERCY BYSSHE SHELLEY, *Sonnet*

*P*olidori? That . . . man?" Rebecca sat numbed in her chair.

Lord Byron smiled at her. "Why are you so shocked? I was sure you had guessed."

"How could I have done?"

"Who else had an interest in sending you here?"

Rebecca stroked back her hair and patted at it, as though hoping that way to calm her racing heart. "I don't know what you mean," she said.

Lord Byron stared at her, his smile slowly curling and growing more cruel. Then he laughed and raised an eyebrow. "Very well," he said mockingly, "you don't understand."

Rebecca listened to the sound of her heart in her ears, beating blood—Ruthven blood—Byron blood. She licked her lips. "Polidori still hated you, then?" she asked slowly. "Even once you'd given him what he had asked you for? He felt no gratitude?"

"Oh, he loved me." Lord Byron folded his hands. "Yes, he always loved me. But in Polidori, the love and the hate were so dangerously mixed that it was very difficult to tell them apart. Polidori couldn't, certainly, so how the devil was I to? And once he was a vampire—well . . ."

"You were afraid of him?"

"Afraid?" Lord Byron stared at her in surprise. He shook his head, and then suddenly all was silence, and Rebecca put her hands up to her eyes. She saw herself sliced with a thousand cuts, hanging from a hook, her blood dripping like the finest rain. She was dead, drained white. Rebecca opened her eyes. "Have you not understood, the power I have?" Lord Byron smiled. "I, afraid? No."

Rebecca shuddered, and tried to stagger to her feet.

"Sit down."

Again her mind was invaded by fear. She struggled against its hold. The terror grew worse. She could feel it melting her courage away. Her legs collapsed. She sat down. At once the terror drained from her. As she stared, despite herself, into Lord Byron's eyes, she felt an unnatural calm returning to her mind.

"No, no," he said. "Fear?—no. Guilt, though. Yes, there was guilt. I had made of Polidori what the Pasha had made of me. I had done what I had sworn I would never do. I had added to the ranks of the living dead. For a while, I was quite wretched about it, and like all complaining persons, I couldn't help telling my companions so. I had no wish to see Polidori again—not after what I had seen in the cell—but the Contessa Marianna, who loved me, tracked the Doctor down. She found him in the hall of a tourist's hotel. He was laughing hysterically, as though quite insane, but he knew Marianna as a vampire at once, and with her beside him, he seemed to calm down. He had been hired, he explained, by an Austrian count. The Count had caught a chill. 'He asked me'—and here Polidori had begun to splutter again—'he asked me—ha, ha, ha!—he asked me *to bleed him!* Ha, ha, ha, ha! Well—I did as he asked. He's upstairs now. And I have to say—his chill has got worse.' Here, Polidori had collapsed into mirth—then he began to cry—and then his face froze totally. 'Tell Byron,' he whispered, 'I want the money after all. He'll understand.' His eyes were bulging by now. His tongue was like a mad dog's, hanging foamy and flaccid. His whole body shook. He turned his back on Marianna, and ran into the streets. She didn't bother to follow him.

"Her advice to me later was simple. 'Kill him. It will be for the best. There are those, *milord,* who cannot take the Gift. Especially not from you. Your blood is too strong. It has unbalanced his mind. There is nothing for it. You must put him down.' But I couldn't bear to. That would merely have compounded my fault. I sent him the money he had asked me for. I made only one condition—that he return to England. I had decided by now I would live in Venice. I didn't want Polidori bothering me."

"And he went?"

"When he received the money—yes. We heard reports of him. He had been hired by a succession of Englishmen. They all died. No one suspected Polidori, though. It was merely said of him he was overfond of applying the leech." Lord Byron smiled. "He got back to England at last. I knew, because he started pestering my publisher with unreadable plays. The news of that caused me some amusement. I warned my publisher to keep his windows locked at night. Otherwise, I gave Polidori very little thought."

"He really kept away from you, then?"

Lord Byron paused. "He would not have dared come near me. Not while I was in Venice."

"Why not?"

"Because Venice was my stronghold—my lair—my court. In Venice, I was unassailable."

"Yes, but why Venice?"

"Why Venice?" Lord Byron smiled fondly. "I had always dreamed of the city—I had expected much—I was not disappointed." Lord Byron stared back into Rebecca's eyes. "Why Venice? You need to ask? But I forget it has changed. When I lived there, though . . ." Lord Byron smiled again. "It was an enchanted, sadness-haunted island of death. Palaces crumbled into the mud—rats played among the maze of dark canals—the living seemed outnumbered by ghosts. Political glory and power had been destroyed—no reason for existence was left her but pleasure—Venice had grown into a playground of depravity. Everything about her was extraordinary, and her aspect like a dream—splendid and filthy, graceful and cruel—a whore whose loveliness concealed her disease. I found in Venice, in her stone and water and light, an embodiment of the beauty and vileness of myself. She was the vampire of cities. I claimed her as my right.

"I stayed in a great *palazzo* by the Grand Canal. I was not alone in Venice. Lovelace was with me, and other vampires too—it was the Contessa Marianna who had first persuaded me to come. She lived across the Lagoon, in an island palace, from which she had preyed on her city for centuries. She showed me her dungeons. They were as damp as tombs; coils of chain still hung from the walls. In former times, she explained, victims had been fattened and prepared in them. 'It is harder now,' she said. 'Everyone talks of these absurd things, rights—*droits.*' She spat the word in French, the language of the Revolution which had overthrown the old order in Venice. She laughed derisively. 'I feel sorry for you, *milord*. All the true pleasures of aristocracy are dead.' Yet in Marianna herself, the spirit of the Borgias still seemed to survive, and her entertainments were cruel enough. Her victims were carefully selected or bred; it amused the Contessa to garnish them, to dress them as cherubs, or arrange them in tableaux. These banquets would be served by the Contessa's slaves—mindless revenants, such as the Pasha had possessed.

"Lovelace, when he was drunk, would taunt me about these. ''Tis fortunate, Byron, the Contessa did not find you before you grew her King. See yonder Tom-turd-man?' he would ask, gesturing towards one of the blank-eyed slaves. 'He was once a rhymester, much like yourself. He scribbled libels against *ma donna* the Contessa. What think you, does he play the satirist now?' But to Lovelace's regret, I would merely smile, for I watched the zombies and the meals they served, not indifferently, but with a sense of numbness. I ruled, as Ahasver had ordered me to rule—but did not prescribe. Marianna's cruelty was as much a part of her as her beauty, or her taste, or her love of art—I did not seek to change it. But later, once I had crossed the lagoon back to my own *palazzo,* memories of what I had seen would return to me, and give me much to wonder and philosophize about.

"For I was still much perplexed by myself and my breed. I had a gondola, black, edged with gold. I would haunt the canals, gliding along them like the fever-mists, preying on the human filth of the city, the whores and pimps and murderers. I would drain them, then toss them overboard, leave them floating as food for the rats—I would order my gondola out from the canals—I would abandon the city and cross the lagoons. There, in the purple stillness of the marshes, I would contemplate my own emotions, and all I had done and experienced that night. My feelings, it seemed, were becoming dull. Freshness was gone. The deeper in blood I waded, the colder grew my soul. I was a vampire—and more, greatest of the vampires—Ahasver had taught me his lesson well. I could not deny what I was— and yet still I regretted what was dying in me. I fought against it. I remembered the opera of *Don Giovanni.* When I wasn't feeding, I was making love as Don Giovanni had done, compulsively, to reassure himself of his humanity. Countesses, prostitutes, peasant girls—I had them all—an endless stream—in gondolas—at masques—or bargained for with their parents in the street—against walls—on tables—or under them. It was life—yes—*it was life*—and yet . . ."

Lord Byron paused. He sighed, and shook his head. "And yet always, at the very height of pleasure and desire— worldly, social or amorous—there mingled a sense of sorrow and doubt. This grew. I fucked numbly—like the rake who is growing old—whose powers can no longer keep pace with his desires. My wildness was really nothing but desperation. In the lagoons, at night, I would admit this to

myself. I had no pleasures now but the drinking of blood—
my mortality was dead—I could scarcely remember the
person I had been. I began to dream of Haidée. We would be
in the cave above Lake Trihonida. I would turn to her, to
kiss her—but her face would be rotten, enslimed with mud,
and when she opened her mouth, she would choke up water.
In her eyes, though, there would be reproach, and I would
turn away, and the dream would fade. I would wake up,
trying to remember the person I had been, in that lost,
precious hour before the Pasha had come. I began a poem. I
called it *Don Juan*. Its hero was named in mockery of
myself. He was no monster—he did not seduce, he did not
prey, he did not kill—instead—*he lived*. I used the poem to
record, while I could, all my memories of mortality. But it
was also a farewell. My life was spent—it was nothing now
to me but a dream of what once had been. I continued to
write my great epic of life, but without any illusions that it
would rescue me. I was what I was—the vampire lord—
and my realm was that of death.

"I began to feel loneliness again. Marianna and Lovelace
were about me—and other vampires—but I was their
Emperor, and I did not choose to reveal to them my
melancholy. They would not have understood—they were
too deep in blood, their callousness was too exquisite and
sharp. I began to long again for a companion, a partner of
the soul with whom I might share the burden of eternity. It
could not be anyone. If needs be, I would have to wait. But
if I found a person who was suitable—I would persuade
him—and then I would have him—I would make him a
vampire as mighty as myself.

"Two years after my arrival in Venice, I learned that
Shelley was traveling to Italy. Claire was with him, and with
her a baby—the infant daughter I had fathered on her. I had
been told already of the birth of this child. I had ordered her
to be christened Allegra, after a whore of whom I had been
fleetingly fond—and now Allegra was being brought to me,
bearing inside her, like a casket of perfume, her fatal load of
blood.

"Shelley arrived in Italy—I wrote to him, asking him to visit me in Venice. He refused. This disturbed me. I remembered Switzerland, and his suspicions of me there, his fear. Then he wrote, inviting me to stay with him. I was sorely tempted. Allegra—and Shelley—to see them both—yes, I was tempted. But I was reluctant as well—because I was afraid to smell the golden blood again—and because I wanted Shelley to come, to be drawn like a fly to me. I waited where I was. I did not leave Venice.

"Then, in early April, I received a shock. I learned that Lady Melbourne was dead. The same afternoon, she arrived at my *palazzo*. My look of surprise amused her greatly. 'You had escaped England already,' she said. 'Do you really think I was going to stay there alone? And besides—people were starting to talk—they were wondering how I managed to stay so well preserved.'

"'And now?' I asked. 'What will you do?'

"'Anything.' Lady Melbourne smiled. 'I can do anything. I have become a true creature of the dead. You should try it, Byron.'

"'I couldn't—not yet—I enjoy my fame too much.'

"'Yes.' Lady Melbourne stared out across the Grand Canal. 'We have all heard, in London, of your debaucheries.' She glanced around at me. 'I have grown quite jealous.'

"'Stay here, then. You will enjoy Venice.'

"'I'm sure.'

"'Will you stay?'

"Lady Melbourne stared into my eyes. Then she sighed and looked away. 'Lovelace is here.'

"'Yes. What of it?'

"Lady Melbourne stroked the furrows on her face. 'I was twenty,' she said in a distant voice, 'when he saw me last.'

"'You are still beautiful,' I said.

"'No.' Lady Melbourne shook her head. 'No, I couldn't bear it.' She reached up for my own face. She stroked my cheeks, and then the curls of my hair. 'And you?' she whispered. 'You, too, Byron, are getting old.'

" 'Yes.' I laughed lightly. 'The crow's-foot has been lavish with its indelible steps.'

" 'Indelible.' Lady Melbourne paused. 'But not inevitable.'

" 'No,' I said slowly. I turned away.

" 'Byron.'

" 'What?'

"Lady Melbourne said nothing, but the silence was rich with unspoken meaning. I walked to my desk, and took out Shelley's letter. I tossed it to Lady Melbourne. She read it, then handed it back to me. 'Send for her,' she said.

" 'Do you think so?'

" 'You look forty, Byron. You are growing fat.'

"I stared at her. I knew she was telling the truth. 'Very well,' I said. 'I will do as you suggest.'

"And I did. My daughter was sent for and arrived. I had refused to see Claire again—the bitch was still too dangerously in love with me—so Allegra came in the company of her Swiss nurse, Elise. Of Shelley, to my disappointment, there was no sign.

"Lady Melbourne had stayed with me, hidden in my palace away from Lovelace, to make certain that my daughter truly arrived. 'Kill her,' she said, that first evening, as we watched Allegra playing on the floor. 'Kill her now, before you grow to feel affection for her. Remember Augusta. Remember Ada.'

" 'I will,' I assured her. 'But not now—not with you here. I must be alone.'

"Lady Melbourne bowed her head. 'I understand,' she said.

" 'You will not stay here, in Venice?' I asked again.

" 'No. I will cross the ocean to America. I am dead now. What better time to visit a New World?'

"I smiled and kissed her. 'We will meet again,' I said.

" 'Of course. We shall have all eternity.' Then she turned, and left me. I watched her from my balcony. She sat in her gondola, her face cloaked. I waited until I could see her no more—then I turned, and studied my own face in a mirror, tracing again the marks of my age. I glanced down at Allegra. She smiled at me, and held up a toy. 'Papa,' she said. *'Bon di,* papa.' Then she smiled again. 'Tomorrow,' I muttered. 'Tomorrow.' I left my palace. I found Lovelace. I preyed that night, with particular savagery.

"The next day came, and I did not kill Allegra. Nor the next day—nor the next day after that. Why not? I see the question in your face. But do you need to ask? There was too much of the Byron about her—of me—and of Augusta. She frowned and pouted quite like us. Deep eyes—a dimple in her chin—a scowl on her brow—white skin—sweet voice—a liking for music—a fondness for having her own way in everything. I would raise her to my mouth, part my lips and she would smile at me, just as Augusta had always smiled. Impossible. Quite impossible.

"And yet, as ever, the torture of the blood was unbearable—worse, indeed—or was it just that I had forgotten how desperate the craving could be? Elise, I saw, was growing suspicious—not that I cared—but I was worried about what she might write to Shelley. She began to guard Allegra more closely—and all the time, my love for her, my little Byron, was growing—until at last, I knew, I couldn't do it—not kill her—not see her wide eyes close in death. It was a pointless agony to have her round my rooms. I sent her away, to be looked after in the home of the British Consul. A vampire's palace, after all, I thought, was hardly the place to bring up a child.

"And yet there were others for whom the knowledge that Allegra was in the care of strangers proved all too upsetting. One summer afternoon, as I was breakfasting with Lovelace, and making our plans for the evening ahead, Shelley was announced. I rose to greet him, delighted. Shelley was affectionate enough, but came to the point at once—Claire was worried about Allegra, and had made him promise to visit me. I tried to set his doubts at rest. We talked about Allegra, her future and her present health—Shelley seemed pacified—and then, so anxious I grew to ease his doubts, almost surprised. Lovelace too, watching me with his emerald eyes, was smiling faintly, and when I invited Shelley to stay for the summer, he actually laughed. Shelley turned, a look of hostility on his face. He glanced at Lovelace's breakfast, an uncooked steak—he shuddered—and looked away again.

" 'What's the matter?' Lovelace asked. 'Do you not enjoy the taste of—meat?' He grinned at me. 'Byron—do not say he is a vegetarian!'

"Shelley stared back at him in fury. 'Yes, I am a vegetarian,' he said. 'Why are you laughing? Because I will not pimp for the gluttony of death? Because the bloody juices and raw horror of your meal fill me with disgust?'

"Lovelace laughed even more; then he froze. He stared into Shelley's face, which was pale and framed by golden hair like his, so that it seemed to me, who was watching them, that life and death were both mirroring the beauty of the other. Lovelace shuddered, then grinned again, and turned to me. *'Milord,'* he bowed. He slipped away.

" 'What was he?' Shelley whispered. 'Surely not a man?' He was shaking, I saw.

"I took his arm, and tried to comfort him. 'Come with me,' I said. I pointed to my gondola, moored by the palace steps. 'We have much to discuss.'

"We crossed to the sandy bank of the Lido. I had horses there. We climbed into our saddles, then rode together along the dunes. It was an eerie place, matted with thistles and amphibious weeds, oozing with salt from the tides, quite solitary. Shelley began to grow less upset. 'I love these wastelands,' he said, 'where everything seems boundless. Out here, you can almost believe that your soul is the same.'

"I glanced at him. 'You still dream then, do you,' I asked, 'of possessing secret visions and powers?'

"Shelley smiled at me, then he spurred his horse forward, and I joined him, galloping through the sea. The winds drove the living spray into our faces, while the waves, lapping against the shore, harmonized our solitude with a feeling of delight. At length, we slowed our gallop, and began to chat again. The mood of happiness lingered on. We laughed a lot—our conversation was amusing, witty, and frank. Only gradually did the talk darken, as though shadowed by the purple clouds of evening, which deepened above us as we turned to ride home. We began to talk of life and death, of free will and destiny—Shelley, as was his custom, argued against despondency, but I, who knew more than my friend had yet dared imagine, took the darker side. I remembered Ahasver's words to me. 'Truth may exist,' I said, 'but if it does, it is imageless. We cannot glimpse it.' I glanced at Shelley. 'Not even those beings who have penetrated death.'

"A flicker of something passed across his face. 'You may be right,' he said, 'that we are helpless before our own ignorance. And yet—I still believe—Fate, Time, Chance, and Change—all are subject to eternal Love.'

"I scoffed. 'You talk of Utopia.'

"'Are you so sure?'

"I reined my horse in. I stared at him. My eyes, I knew, had grown suddenly cold. 'What can you know of eternity?'

"Shelley would not meet my look. By now, we had reached the end of our ride. Still not answering me, he slipped from his saddle, and took his place in the gondola. I joined him. We began to slip across the lagoon. The waters, caught by the sun's dying rays, seemed a lake of fire, but the towers and palaces of Venice, white in the distance against the dark of the sky, were like phantoms, beautiful and deathly. My own face, I knew, was just as pale. We passed the island where Marianna's palace stood. A bell was ringing. Shelley glanced at the bleak walls, and shuddered, as though scenting, across the waters, emotions of despair and pain. 'Is there truly an eternity,' he asked me in a distant voice, 'which lies beyond death?'

"'If there were,' I replied, 'would you dare to desire it?'

"'Perhaps.' Shelley paused. He trailed his fingers through the waters of the lake. 'So long as I did not have to lose my soul.'

" 'Soul?' I laughed. 'I thought you were an infidel, Shelley. What's all this talk about losing a soul? You're sounding rather Christian to me.'

"Shelley shook his head. 'A soul, which I—and you— and all of us—share with the soul of the universe. I believe—I hope . . .' He glanced up. I raised my eyebrows mockingly. There was a long silence. 'I might dare,' he said at last, nodding. 'Yes, I might.'

"We talked no more, not until we reached the *palazzo* steps, where we started to joke and banter again. I was content enough. Shelley could not be forced, he had to come to me—come to me and ask. I was prepared to wait. He stayed all summer, not in Venice, but across the lagoon on the Italian shore. The city, I knew, disturbed him—he could see the filth and degradation, he told me once, crawling beneath the outward show of beauty—in this, Venice was like Lovelace and Marianna, both of whom he had met, and been instinctively revolted by. He was revolted as well, I could see, by my own moods and habits, and the contempt and desperation he recognized as their source—and yet, all the time, I fascinated him too—as I was bound to do—for he had never met a being such as myself. We talked much, riding as before along the bank of the Lido. I pushed and tantalized him all the time. He would stare at me, horror mingled with yearning and respect. He was ready to fall, I could sense it—ready to succumb. One night, we stayed up late, discussing again the worlds that were veiled from mortal view. I spoke from experience—Shelley from hope. I was almost ready to speak the naked truth but by now it was five—and dawn was unshadowing the Grand Canal—the night was almost gone. I begged Shelley to stay. 'Please,' I asked. 'There is much . . .'—I smiled—'much I could *reveal* to you.'

"Shelley stared at me—he trembled—I thought he would agree. But then he rose. 'I must get back,' he said.

"I was disappointed, but I did not protest. There was plenty of time. I watched his gondola until it disappeared from view. Then I too crossed the Venetian lagoon. I visited

Shelley in his dreams. I did not feed, but I tempted him. I showed him Truth—a mighty darkness filled with power, radiating gloom as the sunbeams give forth light, formless, an abyss of death, it seemed—and yet as well, imbued with life—where immortality might be searched for and found. I walked into that darkness. Shelley stared, but he could not yet follow me. I glanced back. I smiled. Desperately, Shelley was holding out his arms to me. I smiled again, and beckoned. Then I turned, and was swallowed up by the dark. Tomorrow, I thought—tomorrow night—he would be able to follow me. Tomorrow, it would happen.

"The next afternoon, I was disturbed at my breakfast by Lovelace. He sat down with me and dawdled at the table. We chatted of nothing for a while. 'Oh,' said Lovelace, grinning at me suddenly, 'your friend—the vegetable-eater—didst know he is gone?'

"My face froze, while Lovelace's grin broadened. 'Why, I thought he must have informed you last night. Did he not?' And then he laughed, and I pushed the table over in my fury, and screamed at him to leave me alone. Lovelace did so, a smile still playing on his lips. I ordered my servants to cross the lagoon, to visit Shelley's home, to make certain— absolutely certain—that he was not still there. But even as they left, I knew that Lovelace had been telling the truth— Shelley had fled me. For several weeks, I was plunged into despair. I knew how close he had been to becoming mine. This realization, which for a long while was a torment, at last grew to comfort me. He would come back. He wouldn't be able to stay away. He had so nearly fallen—surely now I had only to wait?

"And yet even as I reawoke from my despair, I found my longing for companionship unappeased. My love affair with Venice was coming to an end. Its pleasures bored me—I knew now for certain that I was beyond the reach of human delights—I needed something more. Blood thrilled me as it had always done, but even my hunting now began to seem dull, and Lovelace in particular sickened me. I knew that his glee over Shelley's departure had been an expression of his jealousy, but even understanding that, I found it hard to forgive him, and I deliberately avoided his company. I began to be haunted in my dreams by Haidée again, so vividly that I sometimes thought of leaving Venice for Greece. But Haidée was dead—I was alone—what point was there? I stayed where I was. My misery grew worse. The other vampires seemed afraid of me.

"It was Marianna who best understood my loneliness. This surprised me, though it should not have done, for the cruel rely for the subtlest pleasures upon their sensitivities. She asked about Shelley. I told her, in a mood of self-mockery at first, then, recognizing her sympathy, with truthfulness. 'Wait,' she advised. 'He will come. It is best if the mortal desires the Gift. You remember what happened with Polidori.'

"'Yes.' I nodded. 'Yes.' I could not risk turning Shelley's mind. But I had known that already . . .

"'And in the meantime,' Marianna smiled at me, 'we must find you another companion.'

"I laughed derisively. 'Oh yes, Contessa, of course.' I glanced at her. 'Who?'

"'A mortal.'

"'I will destroy her mind.'

"'I have a daughter.'

"I looked at her in surprise. 'And you haven't drained her?'

"Marianna shook her head. 'I had promised her to the Count Guiccioli. Do you remember him? You met him in Milan.'

"I nodded. He had been among the vampires who had come to pay their respects to me. A shriveled, evil old man with greedy eyes. 'Why to him?'

"'He wanted a wife.'

"I frowned.

"'Do you not know?' Marianna asked. 'The children of our kind are highly prized. They can endure the love of a vampire, and not be driven mad by it.' She paused. 'Teresa is only nineteen.'

"I smiled slowly. 'And married to the Count Guiccioli, you say?'

"Marianna stretched out her fingers, as though her nails were claws. 'It will, of course, be a privilege for him, *milord*, to surrender up his bride to you.'

"I smiled again. I kissed Marianna long on her lips. 'Of course it will,' I murmured. 'Of course it will.' I paused. 'See to it, Contessa.' And Marianna did.

"The Count, of course, was not happy at all—but what did I care?—wasn't I his Emperor? I ordered him to bring Teresa to a masque. He did so, and introduced me to her. I was enchanted. She was voluptuous and fresh, with plump, full breasts and rich auburn hair. There was something of Augusta in her. Her eyes melted when I looked at her, but though she could not resist my spell, she did not seem disturbed or unsettled by her passion. 'I'll have her,' I whispered to the Count. He grimaced, but bowed his head in mute acceptance. I let him live with us for the first few months, but after a while, I found him cramping, and I ordered him away.

"Teresa was delighted. If she had been in love before, she was besotted now. 'A Peer of England, and its greatest poet—my lover!' She would kiss me, then clap her hands with delight. 'Byron, *caro mio!* You are like a god of the Greeks! Oh Byron, Byron, I will love you forever! Your beauty is sweeter than my sweetest dreams!' I was fond of her as well. She had restored to me a portion of my past. We left Venice, that vampire city, behind. We moved instead to a palace near Ravenna.

"I was happy there—happier than I had been since the hour of my fall. I lived almost as a mortal. I had to prey, of course, but Teresa, if she suspected my habits, did not seem to care—she was cheerfully immoral in everything. I watched her carefully for signs of madness or decline, but she continued the same—impulsive, beautiful, fascinating—adoring me, and adorable. I tried, as far as I could, to banish all reminders of my vampire state. Allegra, whom I had brought with us from Venice, was growing older now. Her blood was sweeter and more tempting every day. In the end, I sent her to a convent. Otherwise, I would have killed her, for I couldn't have held out against her blood much longer. I hoped I would never need to see her again. Haidée too, or rather her ghost in my dreams, I attempted to banish. Ravenna, at this time, was near revolution. The Italians, like the Greeks, dreamed of liberty. I supported them with money and my influence. I dedicated my part in this struggle to Haidée—to her passion for freedom—to the first and greatest love of my life. My dreams of her began to fade, and when she did visit me, the reproach in her eyes seemed less full of pain. I began to feel free.

"And it was in such a spirit, as the year went by, that I waited for Shelley. I knew he would come. He wrote to me sometimes. He would speak of vague schemes, of utopias, of communities that he and I could form. He never mentioned that last night in Venice, but I could sense, unspoken in his letters, his yearning for what I had offered him then. Yes, I was confident—he would come. In the meantime, though, I lived with Teresa alone. We had little contact with either vampire or man. Instead, I filled our house with animals— dogs and cats, horses, monkeys, peacocks and guinea hens, an Egyptian crane—living creatures whose blood, I found, no longer tempted me." Lord Byron paused and glanced around the room. "You will have seen for yourself that I still like to keep such pets." He reached down to stroke his sleeping dog's head. "I was happy," he said, "in that palace with Teresa, as happy as I had been since the day of my fall." Lord Byron nodded and frowned with surprise. "Yes"—he frowned again—"I was almost happy."

He paused. "And then one evening," he said at last, "I heard Teresa scream." He paused a second time, as though the memory unsettled him. He drank from his wine. "I reached for my pistols. I hurried to Teresa's room. The dogs on the stairway were barking with fright, and the birds were flapping against the walls.

"'Byron!' Teresa ran out to me. She clasped her breast. A

wound, very thin and delicate, had been slashed across the skin.

"'Who was it?' I asked.

"She shook her head. 'I was asleep,' she murmured between her sobs. I walked into her room. At once I smelled the vampire scent. But there was something else as well, much sharper in the air. I breathed it in and frowned. There was no mistaking the smell. It was acid."

"Acid?" Despite herself, Rebecca leaned forward in her chair.

Lord Byron smiled at her. "Yes." His smile faded. "Acid. The letter came the following week. It claimed that Polidori was dead. Suicide. He had been found, seemingly lifeless, his dead daughter beside him and a half-empty bottle of chemicals by his side. Prussic acid, to be precise. I read the letter through a second time. I tore it up and threw it on the ground. As I did so, I smelled the bitter tang again.

"I turned around. Polidori was watching me. He looked vile—his skin was greasy, his mouth lolled open wide. 'It's been a long time,' he said. As he spoke, the stench made me turn away.

"He smiled horribly. 'I do apologize for my unpleasant breath.' Then he peered at me and frowned. 'But you don't look too well yourself. Getting old. Not quite so beautiful now, *My Lord.*' He paused, and his face twitched. 'Little daughter still not killed yet, then?'

"I stared at him with hatred. He lowered his gaze. Even now, he was my creature, and I his lord. Polidori staggered back. He gnawed at his knuckles, staring with his bulbous eyes down at my feet. Then he shuddered and giggled. 'I killed *my* daughter,' he said.

"He began to shake. I watched him, then I reached out to touch his hand. It was sticky and cold. Polidori let me take it. 'When?' I asked.

"His face was suddenly twisted by grief. 'I couldn't fight it,' he said. 'You never told me. No one ever did. I couldn't fight it, not the calling of the blood.' He giggled and bit on his knuckles again. 'I tried to stop myself. I tried to kill myself. I drank poison, My Lord, half a bottle of the stuff. It had no effect, of course. And then I had to kill *her*—my little girl'—he chuckled—'my *sweet* little girl. And now'—he breathed in my face—'I will always have this poison in my mouth. Always!' He screamed suddenly, *'Always!* You never told me, My Lord—you never said—but thank you—thank you—I have found out for myself—*you stay as you are when you drink the golden blood.'*

"I felt pity for him, yes, of course I did. Who better was there to understand his pain? But I hated him as well—hated him as much as I have hated anything. I gave him my hand a second time—tried to calm him—but he stared at it wildly, then spat at it. I flinched—instinctively, I reached for my pistol—I placed it under Polidori's chin. But he laughed. 'You can't harm me now, My Lord! Haven't you heard—I am officially dead!'

"He giggled and spluttered. I waited until he was silent again. Then I smiled coldly, and pushed him back with the pistol barrel. He fell against the wall. I stood over him. 'You always were ridiculous,' I whispered. 'Do you still dare to challenge me? Look at the thing you are now, and learn restraint. I could make your condition, wretched as it is, much worse by far'—I stabbed into his mind, so that he screamed with pain—'much worse. I am your creator. I am your Emperor.' I lowered my pistol, and took a step back. 'Do not provoke me again, Doctor Polidori.'

"'I have power too,' he stammered. 'I am a thing like you now, My Lord.'

"The sight of him, his bulbous eyes staring, his mouth hanging wide, made me laugh. I slipped my pistol back into my belt. 'Go away,' I said.

"Polidori stayed frozen. Then he shuddered, and began to mutter to himself. He reached up for my hands. 'Care for me,' he whispered. 'Care for me. You are right—I am your creature now. Show me what that means. Show me what I am.'

"I stared at him. For a moment, I hesitated. Then I shook

my head. 'You must steer your own course,' I told him. 'We are all lonely, we who wander the Ocean of Time.'

"'Lonely?' His cry was unexpected and terrible—a shriek, a sob, an animal sound. It froze my blood. 'Lonely?' Polidori said again. He started to laugh uncontrollably. He choked, then spluttered, and stared at me with burning hate. 'I do have power,' he said suddenly. 'You believe yourself miserable, but I can make you so wretched that even the gleam of the moon will be hateful to you.' He leered horribly, and wiped at his mouth. 'I have already fed on the blood of your whore.'

"I took him by the throat. I held him close to my face. Again I stabbed deep into the whorls of his brain, until he screamed with mindless agony, and still I stabbed, and still he screamed. I dropped him at last. He wept, and whimpered and groveled at my feet. I stared at him with contempt. 'Touch Teresa, and I will destroy you,' I said. 'Do you understand?'

"Polidori spluttered something, then nodded.

"I held him by his hair. Like his skin, it was sticky and greasy to the touch. 'I will destroy you, Polidori.'

"He sniveled. 'I understand,' he said at last.

"'What do you understand?'

"'I will not'—he sniffed—'I will not . . . I will not kill those you love,' he sniffed at last.

"'Good,' I whispered. 'Keep your word. And then—who knows?—I may grow to love even you.' I dragged him to the stairway. I pushed him. He bumped and clattered down the steps, startling a flock of guinea fowl. I returned to my balcony. I watched Polidori leave across the fields. That evening, I rode along the boundaries of the palace estate, but there was no scent of him—he was gone. I wasn't surprised—I had instilled a terrible fear in him—I doubted he would return. But I warned Teresa, all the same, to beware the smell of chemicals.

"And it was not only Teresa I was worried for now. Shelley had just written to me, proposing vaguely that we meet—I wrote back at once, inviting him to stay, and to my surprise, one night he arrived at my gates. I had not seen him for three years. I kissed him on the side of the neck and bit him gently, drawing blood. Shelley tensed—then held my cheeks—and laughed with delight. We stayed up, as we always did, late into the night. Shelley was full of his usual talk—wild schemes and utopias—impious jokes—visions of liberty and revolution. But I began to grow impatient—I knew why he had really come. The clock chimed four. I crossed to the balcony. Fresh air cooled my face. I turned back to Shelley. 'Do you know what I am?' I asked.

" 'You are a mighty and troubled spirit,' he replied.

" 'What I have—my powers—I can give them to you.'

"Shelley said nothing for a long while. Even in the shadows, his face shone pale as mine, his eyes burned almost as bright. 'Space,' he said at last, 'wondered at the swift and fair creations of God when he grew weary of vacancy—but not as much, Lord Byron, as I wonder at your works. I despair of rivaling you, as well I may. You'—he paused—'an angel in the mortal paradise of a decaying body—while I . . .' His voice trailed away. 'While I—am nothing.'

"I drew him to me. 'My body need not decay,' I said. I stroked his hair, pressed his head against my chest. I bent my head low. 'Nor need yours,' I whispered.

"Shelley looked up at me. 'You age.'

"I frowned. I listened to my heart. I could feel my blood crawling slowly through my veins. 'There is a way,' I said.

" 'It cannot be true,' Shelley whispered. He seemed almost to be challenging me. 'No, it cannot be true.'

"I smiled. I bent down beside him. A second time, I bit into his throat. Blood, in a single ruby drop, gleamed on the silver of his skin. I touched the drop, felt it melt across my tongue, then I kissed the wound, and licked at it. Shelley moaned. I drank, and as I did so opened his thoughts—dissolved their mortal bounds—so that fragments of vision might glimmer in his dreams. My lips kissed again—and then left the touch of his skin. Slowly, Shelley turned to stare at me. His face seemed lit by another world's fire. It burned gently. For a long while, Shelley said nothing at all. 'But to kill,' he murmured eventually, 'to track things that laugh, and weep, and bleed. How can this be done?'

"I turned away from him, to stare back out across the fields. 'The life of the wolf is the death of the lamb.'

" 'Yes. But I am not a wolf.'

"I smiled to myself. 'Not yet.'

" 'How can I decide?' He paused. 'Not now.'

" 'Wait if you wish.' I turned again to face him. 'Of course you must wait.'

" 'And in the meantime?'

"I shrugged. 'You grow philosophical—I grow bored.'

"Shelley smiled. 'Move from Ravenna, Byron. Come and live with us.'

" 'To help you decide?'

"Shelley smiled again. 'If you like.' He rose to join me by the balcony. We stood in silence for a long while. 'Perhaps,' he said at last, 'I would not shrink from killing . . .' He paused.

" 'Yes?' I asked.

" 'If . . . If my path through the wilderness could be marked with the blood of the oppressor and the despot . . .'

"I smiled. 'Perhaps.'

" 'What service I—you and I—together—could give the cause of liberty.'

" 'Yes. Yes. To share the burden of my rule. To consecrate it to freedom. To lead—not to tyrannize. What could we not do?'

" 'The dawn is coming.' Shelley pointed. He glanced at me. 'Greece is in revolt—its fight for liberty is begun—had you heard?'

"I nodded. 'I have heard.'

" 'If we had the power . . .' Shelley paused. 'The power of other worlds—like Prometheus we could bring it—the secret fire—to warm despairing humanity.' He held my shoulders. 'Byron—could we not?'

"I stared past him. I thought I saw, conjured from the dawn's play of light and dark, the figure of Haidée. It was only for a second—a trick of my eyes—and she was gone. 'Yes,' I said, meeting Shelley's look, 'yes, we could.' I smiled. 'But first—you must wait—you must think—and decide.'

"Shelley stayed another week, then returned to Pisa. A short while after, I followed him. I did not like stirring myself, but for Shelley—I did it. There was a good deal of English Society in Pisa—not the worst kind—but literary—so bad enough. Shelley rarely came to see me alone. We rode, though, and practiced with our pistols, and dined—we were always the twin poles, opposite and yet alike, around which the world of our gatherings spun. I waited—not patiently—I never had patience—but with a predatory sense of expectation. One day, Shelley told me he had imagined he had seen Polidori. That disturbed me— not that I was afraid of Polidori himself—but because Shelley might recognize the truth, and be alarmed by the creature the Doctor had become. I tried to press him to make up his mind. I came to him one night. We talked long and late. I thought he was ready. 'After all,' he said suddenly, 'what is the worst that can happen? Life may change, but it cannot fly. Hope may vanish, but it cannot be destroyed.' He stroked my cheeks. 'But first let me talk to Mary and Claire.'

" 'No!' I said. Shelley looked surprised. 'No,' I repeated, 'you mustn't let them—guess. There are mysteries, Shelley, which have to be kept.' Shelley stared at me. His face was expressionless. I thought I had lost him.

"But then, at last, he nodded his head. 'Soon,' he whispered. He pressed my hand. 'But if I cannot tell them, at least give me time—a few more months—to be with them in my mortal form.'

"I nodded. 'Of course,' I said. But I did not tell Shelley the truth—that a vampire must say farewell to all mortal love—and nor did I tell him of a truth darker even than that. I felt troubled by this need for silence—of course— and even more so when Claire, through Shelley, began to pester me, demanding that I move Allegra from the convent, and return her back to her mother's care.

"'Claire has bad dreams,' Shelley tried to explain. 'She imagines that Allegra will die in that place. She is quite convinced of it. Please, Byron—her nightmares are terrible. Take Allegra back. Let her come and live with us.'

"'No.' I shook my head. 'Impossible.'

"'Please.' Shelley caught my arm. 'Claire is almost frantic.'

"'So what?' I shrugged impatiently. 'Women are always making scenes.'

"Shelley tensed. The blood left his face, and I saw him clench his fists. But he controlled himself. He bowed. 'You know best, of course, My Lord.'

"'I'm sorry,' I said. 'Really, Shelley, I am. But I can't remove Allegra. You will just have to tell Claire that.'

"And Shelley did. But still Claire's nightmares grew worse, and her fears for her daughter ever more wild. Shelley, who had looked after Allegra as a baby, was sympathetic to Claire, I knew, and I could sense that the issue was coming between us. But what could I do?— nothing. I couldn't risk seeing Allegra now. She was five— her blood would be irresistible to me. So I continued to reject all Claire's appeals, while hoping that Shelley would soon make up his mind. But he didn't. Instead, I watched him grow distant and cold.

"And then the news came that Allegra was ill. She was faint and feverish—she seemed to be suffering from a loss of blood. Shelley came to me that afternoon. He told me that Claire was full of wild plans, to rescue Allegra, to steal her from the convent. I was appalled. I hid my agitation, though, and only let Teresa glimpse how unsettled I was. That night, we dined with the Shelleys, as we normally did. We broke up early. I went for a long, long ride. Then, toward dawn, I returned to my room. I paused on the steps . . ." Lord Byron's voice fell away.

He swallowed. "I paused on the steps," he said a second

time. "I staggered. I could smell the most delicious scent. It was more beautiful than anything in the world. I knew at once what it was. I tried to fight it—but I could not—I went to my room. The scent filled me now, every vein, every nerve, every cell. I was its slave. I looked around. There, on my desk, was a bottle . . . I crossed to it. It was uncorked. I shook. The room seemed to melt into oblivion. I drank. I tasted wine—and mixed with it—*and mixed with it . . ."* Lord Byron paused. His eyes seemed to gleam with a feverish light. "I drank. The blood—Allegra's blood— it . . . What can I say? It showed me a glimpse of paradise. But a glimpse was not enough. A glimpse, and nothing more, would drive me mad. I needed more. I had to have more. I filled the bottle with wine again. A second time, I drained it to its dregs. The thirst seemed even more terrible. I stared at the bottle. I smashed it on the ground. I had to have more. *I had to have more."* He swallowed, and paused. He closed his burning eyes.

"Where had it come from?" Rebecca asked quietly. "Who had left it there?"

Lord Byron laughed. "I didn't dare to think. No—that's wrong—I was too intoxicated to think. I only knew that I had to have more. I struggled with temptation all the next day. News came from the convent—Allegra was worse— weaker—she was still losing blood—no one knew how. Shelley frowned when he met me—he looked away. The thought of losing him steeled me—I would not do it—I would not succumb. The afternoon, and then the evening, came and went. Again I rode. Again I returned to my rooms late at night. Again"—Lord Byron paused—"again, a bottle stood waiting on my desk. I drank it. I felt life like silver flood my veins. I saddled my horse. As I did so, I heard a low laugh, and the smell of acid came to me on the wind. But I was mad with need. I didn't pause. I galloped all night. I came to the convent where Allegra lay near death. A guilty thing, I slunk through the shadows, unseen, unsuspected by the nuns. Allegra sensed me, though. She opened her eyes.

They were burning. Her fingers reached for me. I held her in my arms. I kissed her. Her skin seemed to scald my lips. Then I bit. Her blood . . . Her blood . . ."

Lord Byron tried to speak on, but his voice choked, and died. He clasped his fingers, and stared into the dark. Then he bowed his head.

Rebecca watched him. Did she feel pity? she wondered. She remembered the tramp by Waterloo Bridge. She remembered the vision of herself on the hook. "It gave you what you wanted," she asked. Her voice sounded cold and remote in her ears.

Lord Byron looked up. *"Wanted?"* he asked.

"Your aging—your daughter's blood froze it for you?"

Lord Byron stared at her. The fire had left his eyes; they seemed quite dead. "Yes," he said at last.

"And Shelley?"

"Shelley?"

"Did he . . . ?"

Lord Byron glanced up. His face was still numb, his eyes still dead.

"Did he guess?" Rebecca asked quietly. "Did he know?"

Slowly, Lord Byron smiled. "I told you, I think, about Polidori's thesis."

"On somnambulism."

"Somnambulism and the nature of dreams."

"I see." Rebecca paused. "He invaded Shelley's dreams? He was able to?"

"Shelley was mortal," said Lord Byron shortly. His lip curled in a sudden flickering of pain. "From the day of Allegra's death, he began to avoid my company. He spoke to friends of my 'detested intimacy.' He complained of suffering from unnatural terror. Walking by the sea, watching the effect of moonlight on the water, he had visions of a naked child rising from the waves. All this was reported back to me. I thought of searching Polidori out, of annihilating him utterly, as I had promised I would do. But that, I knew, would not be enough. It was Shelley now who was my enemy. It was Shelley I had to confront and persuade. He had bought a yacht recently. I knew he was planning a voyage down the coast. I had to face him before he left.

"It was swelteringly hot the day before Shelley was due to sail. As I rode to his house, prayers were being offered in the streets for rain. It was twilight when I reached my destination, and still the heat was unbearable. I kept to the shadows, waiting for the household to retire. Only Shelley did not go to bed. He was reading, I could see. I came to him. Unnoticed, I sat in the chair by his side. Still Shelley did not look up. He was shaking, though. His lips sounded the words he read—from Dante—*The Inferno*. I spoke a phrase of verse with him: 'Nessun maggior dolore'—'there is no greater sorrow.' Shelley looked up. I completed the line: 'Than to remember happiness when miserable.'

"There was silence. Then I spoke again. 'Have you decided?' I asked.

"Shelley's look of shock froze and darkened into hate. 'You have a face like Murder,' he whispered. 'Yes. Very smooth, but bloody too.'

"'Bloody? What are you saying, Shelley? None of this cant. You knew I was a creature of blood.'

"'But I did not know everything.' He rose to his feet. 'I have been having strange dreams. Let me tell you about them, *My Lord*.' He spoke the title as Polidori did, with scalding bitterness. 'Last night—I dreamed that Mary was pregnant. I saw a foul creature bending over her. I pulled the creature away—I looked into its face—that face was my own.' He swallowed. 'Then I had a second dream. I met myself again, walking on the terrace. This figure, who looked like me, and yet was paler, with a terrible sadness in his eye, stopped. "How long do you mean to be content?" he asked. "How long?" I asked him what he meant. He smiled. "Have you not heard?" he said. "Lord Byron killed his baby girl. And now I must go to kill my own child." I screamed. I woke up. I was in Mary's arms. Not yours, Lord Byron—not ever yours.'

"He stared at me, his deep eyes fierce with revulsion. I felt a desperate loneliness sweep across my soul. I tried to hold him, but he backed away. 'The dreams were sent by an enemy,' I said.

"'But were they false, the warnings they gave?'

"I shrugged despairingly.

"'Did you kill Allegra, My Lord?'

"'Shelley . . .' I held out my hands. 'Shelley—do not leave me alone.' But he turned his back on me. He walked from the room. He did not look around. I did not pursue him—what point would there have been? Instead, I returned to the garden, and mounted my horse. I rode back through the burning night. The heat, if anything, was growing more cruel.

"For the first time in several months, I slept. Teresa did not disturb me. My dreams were unpleasant—heavy with guilt—sullen with foreboding. I woke at four. The heat was still stifling. As I dressed, though, I heard a distant roar of thunder, rolling in from the sea. I stared out through my window. The horizon was darkening into a purple haze. I rode to the shore, then along the sands. The sea was still crystalline, brilliant against clouds which had deepened now to black. Thunder rolled again and then lightning, in a silver sheet, illumined the sky, and the sea, suddenly, was a chaos of boiling surf, as the gale swept in across the bay. I reined in my horse, and stared out to sea. I glimpsed a boat. It rose and plunged, and rose again, and then it disappeared behind mountains of waves. The wind shrieked in my ears. 'I cannot swim.' Shelley's words, from all those years before, seemed to rise up in my mind. He had refused my offer to save him then. I stared out again at the boat. It was laboring. Then I saw it turn and start to capsize.

"I slashed my wrist. I drank my blood. I rose up on the gale. I became the breath of darkness, sweeping out across the sea. I saw the wreckage of the boat as it was pounded by the waves. I recognized it. I searched desperately for Shelley. Then I saw him. He was clinging to a shattered board. 'Be mine,' I whispered to his thoughts. 'Be mine, and I will save you.' Shelley stared around wildly. I reached for him. I held him.

" 'No!' Shelley screamed. 'No!' He slipped from my grasp. He struggled in the water. He looked up to the sky, and seemed to smile, and then he was swept away, and the waves pounded over his head. Down he went, down, down, down. He did not rise again."

Chapter XIII

But I have lived, and have not lived in vain:
My mind may lose its force, my blood its fire,
And my frame perish even in conquering pain;
But there is that within me which shall tire
Torture and Time, and breathe when I expire;
Something unearthly, which they deem not of,
Like the remember'd tone of a mute lyre.
Shall on their soften'd spirits sink, and move
In hearts all rocky now the late remorse of love.

LORD BYRON, *Childe Harold's Pilgrimage*

His body was washed up ten days later. The exposed flesh had been eaten away; what was left had been bleached by the sea; the corpse was unrecognizable. It might have been the carcass of a sheep for all that I could tell. I thought of Haidée. I hoped that her body had never been found, a rotten mess in a Hessian sack—I hoped that her bones still lay undisturbed beneath the water. Shelley's corpse, stripped of its clothes, was a nauseous and degrading sight. We built a pyre on the beach, and burned it there. As the flames began to spread, I found the scent of dripping flesh unbearable. It was sweet and rotten, and stank of my failure.

"I wandered down to the sea. I stripped to my shirt. As I did so, I glanced around and saw, standing on the hill, the figure of Polidori. Our eyes met; his puffy lips thinned and spread into a sneer. A billow of smoke from the pyre passed between us. I turned again. I wandered into the sea. I swam until the flames were extinct. I did not feel purified. I returned to the pyre. There was nothing but ash. I scooped the dust up and let it run through my fingers. An attendant showed me a charred lump of flesh. It was Shelley's heart, he explained—it hadn't burned—perhaps I would like it? I shook my head. It was too late now. Too late to own Shelley's heart . . ."

Lord Byron paused. Rebecca waited, a frown on her face. "And Polidori?" she asked.

Lord Byron stared at her.

"You hadn't won Shelley's heart. You had lost. And yet— when you saw Polidori—you didn't confront him—you let him go. And he's still alive now. Why? Why didn't you destroy him, as you had said you would?"

Lord Byron smiled faintly. "Do not underestimate the joys of hatred. It is a pleasure fit for eternity."

"No." Rebecca shook her head. "No, I don't understand."

"Men love in haste—but to detest—leisure is needed— and I had—I have"—he hissed the word—"leisure."

Rebecca's frown deepened. "How can I tell if you're being serious?" she asked with sudden anger and fear. She hugged herself. "You *could* have destroyed him?"

Lord Byron stared at her coldly. "I believe so," he said at last.

Rebecca felt her heart slow. She was afraid of Lord Byron—but not as afraid as she had been the night before, when Dr. Polidori had surprised her by the Thames, with madness in his face, and poison on his breath. "Only believe?" she asked.

Lord Byron's eyes were still cold as he replied. "Of course. How can we be certain of anything? Polidori is infused with a part of myself. That is the Gift—that is what it means. Yes," he said with sudden vehemence, "I could destroy him—yes—of course I could. But you ask why I don't, and why I didn't in Italy, after Shelley drowned. It is the same reason. Polidori was given my blood. He was my creature. He, who had bequeathed me my loneliness, had become by that act almost precious to me. The more I hated him, the more I understood that I had no one else. Perhaps

Polidori had intended such a paradox. I don't know. Even Jehovah, when he sent the flood, could not bear the total destruction of his world. How could I have outraged Shelley's ghost by behaving worse than the Christian god?"

Lord Byron smiled grimly. "Because it was Shelley's ghost, you see, and Haidée's, which haunted me. Not literally—not even any longer as visions in my dreams— but as a blankness—a desolation. My days were listless— my nights restless—and yet I could not stir myself, nor do anything but kill, and brood, and scribble poetry. I remembered my youth, when my heart overflowed with affection and emotions; and yet now—at thirty-six—still no very terrible age—I could rake up all the dying embers in that same heart of mine, and stir scarcely even a temporary flame. I had squandered my summer before May was yet ended. Haidée was dead—Shelley was dead—my days of love were dead.

"And yet from torpor, those same memories aroused me at last. All that long, ditch-water year, the revolt in Greece had been gathering apace. The cause of which Haidée had dreamed—the revolution which Shelley had longed to lead—the lovers of freedom, among which, once, I had counted myself—now looked to me. I was famous—I was rich—would I not offer the Greeks my support? I laughed at this request. The Greeks didn't realize what they were asking for—I was a deathly thing—my kiss polluted all it touched. And yet, to my surprise, I found I was moved—a thing I had come to believe quite impossible. Greece— romantic and beautiful land; freedom—the cause of all those I had loved. And so I agreed. I would not just support the Greeks with my wealth—I would fight among them. I would leave Italy. I would tread, once again, upon the sacred soil of Greece.

"For this, I knew, might be my last chance—to redeem my existence, perhaps, and exorcise the ghosts of those I had betrayed. And yet, for myself, I had no illusions. I could not escape what I was—the freedom I fought for would not be my own—and though I fought for liberty, I would still be more bloodstained than the cruelest of the Turks. I felt a terrible agitation when I glimpsed the distant coast of Greece again. I remembered my first sight of it, all those years before. What an eternity of experience I had undergone since then! What an eternity of change . . . These were the same scenes—*the very soil*—where I had loved Haidée—and last been mortal—and free of blood. Sad—so sad—to look upon the mountains of Greece, and think of all that was dead and gone. And yet there was joy too, intertwined with my misery, so that it was impossible to distinguish between the two. I did not try. I was here to direct and lead a war. Why else, after all, had I come to Greece, if not to occupy my stagnant mind? I redoubled my efforts. I sought to think of nothing but the fight against the Turks.

"And yet when it was proposed that I should sail to Missolonghi, the shadows of horror and regret returned, blacker than ever. As my ship crossed the lagoon toward the harbor, the guns of the Greek fleet boomed out to welcome me, and crowds were gathered on the walls to cheer. But I barely noticed them. Above me, distant against the blue sky, was Mount Arakynthos; beyond it, I knew, was Lake Trihonida. And now, waiting for me—Missolonghi—where I had ridden to after killing the Pasha—and rejoined Hobhouse—not a mortal any longer—but—*a vampire.* I remembered the vividness of my sensations that day, fifteen years before, watching the colors of the swamps and the sky. The colors were just as rich now, but when I looked at them, I saw death in their beauty—disease in the greens and yellows of the swamps, rain and fever in the purples of the clouds. And Missolonghi itself, I could see now was a wretched and squalid place—built on mud, surrounded by lagoons, fetid and crowded and pestilential. It seemed a doomed place for heroism.

"And so it proved to be. Hemmed in by the enemy as we were, the Greeks seemed more interested in fighting one another than the Turks. Money flowed like water through my hands, but to little purpose that I could see, beyond funding the squabbles of which the Greeks were so fond. I sought to reconcile the various leaders, and discipline the troops—I had the money, after all, and the power of compulsion in my eye—but any order I imposed was fragile and brief. And all the time, the rains fell and fell, so that even if we had been ready to attack, we could have done nothing, so dismal and hopeless the conditions had become. Mud was everywhere—swamp mists hung over the town— the lagoon waters began to rise—the roads were soon nothing but an oozing morass. And still it rained. I might just as well have moved back to London.

"As a cause, then, liberty began to lose its gloss. For a long time, since arriving in Greece, I had reduced my number of killings to a minimum—now I began to feed wantonly again. Each day, through the cold winter rains, I would leave the town. I would ride the oozing path along the edge of the lagoon. I would kill, and drink, and leave my victim's corpse among the filth and reeds. The rain would wash the corpse into the mud of the lagoon. Before, I had tried not to prey on the Greeks—the same people I had come to save— but now I did it unthinkingly. If I hadn't killed them, after all, the Turks would have done.

"Then one afternoon, as I was riding by the lake, I saw a figure muffled in rags by the path. The person, whoever it was, seemed to be waiting for me. I was thirsty—I had not yet killed—I spurred my horse on. Suddenly, though, the horse rose up and whinnied with fear—it was only with an effort I could bring him under control.

"The figure in rags had stepped onto the path. 'Lord Byron.' The voice was a woman's—cracked, hoarse, but with a hint of something strange, so that I shivered, caught between horror and delight. 'Lord Byron,' she called again. I saw the glint of bright eyes beneath her hood. She pointed a bony hand at me. It was bunched and gnarled. 'A death for Greece!' The words sliced through me.

"'Who are you?' I shouted, above the drumming of the

rain. I saw the woman smile—suddenly, my heart seemed to stop—her lips had reminded me—though I knew not how—of Haidée. 'Stop!' I shouted. I rode toward her—but the woman was gone. The lagoon bank was empty. There was no sound but the pelting of the rain upon the lake.

"That night, I was seized by a convulsion. I felt a terrible horror come on me—I foamed at the mouth—I gnashed my teeth—all my senses seemed to fall away. After several minutes, I recovered, but I was afraid, for I had felt, during my fit, a state of self-revulsion such as I had never known before. It had been heralded, I knew, by the woman who had met me on the path by the lagoon. Memories of Haidée—torments of guilt—longings for what was impossible—all had risen like a sudden storm. I recovered. Weeks passed—I continued to marshal my troops—we even launched a brief attack across the lake. But all the time, I remained tense—filled with a strange foreboding—waiting to glimpse the strange woman again. I knew she would come. Her demand echoed in my brain: 'A death for Greece!'" Lord Byron paused. He stared into the dark, and Rebecca heard—or did she imagine it?—the sound of something from behind her again. Lord Byron too seemed to have heard the noise. He repeated his words, as though to silence it. His words hung like the pronouncement of a doom. "'A death for Greece.'"

He looked away from the darkness, back into Rebecca's eyes. "And she did indeed come again—two months later. I was riding with companions, reconnoitering the ground. Some miles from the town, we were overtaken by heavy rain, slanting down in heavy sheets of gray. I saw her, squatting in a pool of mud. Slowly, as before, she pointed at me. I shuddered. 'Do you see her?' I asked. My companions looked—but the road was empty. We returned to Missolonghi. By now, we were soaked. I had a violent perspiration, and a fever in my bones. That evening, I lay on my sofa, restless and melancholy. Images of my past life seemed to float before my eyes. Dimly, I heard soldiers squabbling in the street outside, shouting violently as they always did. I had no time for them. I had no time for anything but memories and regrets.

"The next morning, I tried to shake off my misery. I rode again. It was April now—the weather, for a change, was fine—I joked with my companions, as we galloped down the road. But then, in an olive grove, she appeared to me again, a phantom huddle of dirty rags. 'Ahasver?' I screamed. 'Ahasver, is it you?' Then I swallowed. My mouth was dry. The syllables hurt my throat to pronounce. 'Haidée?' I stared. Whatever she had been, she had vanished now. My companions led me back to the town. I was raving, calling after her. The fit of horror and self-disgust returned. I was taken to my bed. 'A death for Greece. A death for Greece.' The words seemed to beat in my ears with my blood. Death—yes—but I could not die. I was immortal—or at least—*for as long as I fed on living blood.* I imagined I saw Haidée. She stood by my bed. Her lips were parted—her eyes bright—on her face, intermingled, were love and disgust. 'Haidée?' I asked. I reached for her. 'Are you truly not dead?' I tried to touch her—she melted away—I was alone, after all. I took a vow. I would drink no more. I would defy all agonies, defy all thirst. A death for Greece? Yes. My death would achieve far more than my life. And for myself? Release—extinction—nothingness. If I could have it indeed, I would welcome it.

"I kept to my bed. The days passed. I was feverish already—now my pain grew infinitely worse. I fought it, though—even when my blood began to burn—when it seemed that my limbs were shriveling up—when I felt my brain, like a drying sponge, glue to my skull. The doctors gathered—flies on rotting meat. Watching them buzz and fuss, I longed for their blood, to drain them all. I fought the temptation—I banished them instead—my strength and health continued to decline. Slowly, the doctors began to buzz back. Soon, I lacked the energy to keep them away. I had been worried that they might save me—but hearing them now, talking among themselves, I knew I had been wrong—with something like relief, I encouraged them. The pain now was terrible—blackness was starting to burn up my skin—my mind was drifting. Still, though, I would not die. It seemed not even the doctors could finish me off. And then they asked to bleed me again.

"I had refused a first request. What blood I had in me was already almost gone—to be drained would have made the agony worse—I hadn't been able to face the pain. Now though, I was desperate. Weakly, I agreed. I felt the leeches being applied to my brow. Each one burned like a drop of fire. I screamed. Surely such agony couldn't be borne.

"The doctor, seeing my pain, held my hand. 'Do not worry, My Lord,' he whispered in my ear. 'We will soon have you well.'

"I laughed. I imagined the doctor had Haidée's face. In my delirium, I screamed at her. I must have fainted. When I came to, I was staring at the doctor's face again. He was cutting my wrist. A tiny trickle of blood flowed out. I wanted Haidée. But she was dead. I screamed out her name. The world began to swirl away. I called out other names— Hobhouse, Caro, Bell, Shelley. 'I will die,' I shouted, as darkness lapped out from the leeches on my brow. I imagined my friends were gathered around my bed. 'I will be as you are,' I told them, 'mortal again. I *shall* be mortal. I *shall* die.' I began to sob. Still the darkness spread. It dimmed my pain. It dimmed the world. Is this death, I wondered—and then, like a final candle in a universe of black, the thought was snuffed out. There was nothing else. Darkness was all.

"I woke to moonlight. It was bright against my face. I moved my arm. I felt no pain. I stroked my brow. There were craters where the leeches had been. I lowered my hand, and the moonlight shone upon the wounds again. When I touched them a second time, the craters seemed less deep— a third time, and the wounds were entirely healed. I stretched my limbs. I rose to my feet. Against the stars, I could see a mountain peak.

"'There is no physic, My Lord, like Our Lady the moon.'

"I stared around. Lovelace smiled at me. 'Are you not glad, Byron, I have saved you from those cozening Missolonghi quacks?'

"I stared at him hard. 'No, damn you,' I said at last, 'I had been trusting in their skills to finish me.'

"Lovelace laughed. 'Not the poxiest mountebank could kill you off.'

"I nodded slowly. 'So I find.'

"'You are in need of a good restorative.' He gestured. I saw two horses. Behind them, a man had been bound to a tree. He struggled as I looked at him. 'A dainty dish,' said Lovelace. 'I thought—bold Greek warrior that you are—you might appreciate the blood of a Mussulman.' He grinned at me. Slowly, I crossed to the tree. The Turk began to writhe and twist. He moaned beneath his gag. I killed him with a single slash across the throat. The blood—after so long—yes, I had to admit—it tasted good. I drained my victim empty. Then, with a faint smile, I thanked Lovelace for his thoughtfulness.

"He stared into my eyes. 'Do you think I would have left you in agony?' He paused. 'I am vicious and cruel, a most accomplished villain, but I love you well enough.'

"I smiled. I believed him. I kissed him on his lips. Then I glanced around. 'How did you get me here?' I asked.

"Lovelace jiggled a purse of coins in his hand. He grinned. 'There is no one like your Greek for the taking of a bribe.'

"'And where have you brought me?'

"Lovelace bowed his head. He made no reply.

"I looked around. We were in a hollow of rocks and trees. I stared up at the mountain peak again. That shape—the silhouette against the stars . . .

"'Where are we?' I asked again.

"Slowly, Lovelace looked up at me. The moonlight burned on the pallor of his face. 'Why, Byron,' he asked, 'do you truly not remember it?'

"For a moment, I stood frozen—then I moved through the trees. Ahead of me, I saw a glint of silver. I left the trees behind. Below me, a lake—moon-stained—its waters breathed on by the faintest of breezes. Above—the mountain—that familiar silhouette. Behind . . . I turned—and there it was. Slowly, I walked to the entrance of the cave. Lovelace had come and was standing by my side. 'Why?' I whispered. Fury and despair must have blazed up in my eyes, for Lovelace staggered back, as though appalled, covering his face. I pulled away his arm, forcing him to meet my stare. 'Why, Lovelace?' My grip tightened. *'Why?'*

"'Leave him.'

"The voice that spoke from the cave was faint—almost inaudible. But I recognized it—recognized it at once—and I realized, hearing it now, that its echoes had never truly faded from my mind. No—they had always been with me. I loosened my grip. Lovelace shrank back. 'It is him,' I whispered. I didn't ask—merely stated a fact—but Lovelace nodded. I reached for his belt—I slipped out his pistol—I cocked it.

"'Hear him,' Lovelace said. 'Hear what he has to say to you.'

"I made no answer. I stared about me, at the moon and the mountain, the lake and the stars. How well I remembered them. My grip tightened around the pistol butt. I turned and walked into the darkness of the cave.

"'Vakhel Pasha.' My voice echoed. 'They told me you had been buried in your grave.'

"'And so I was, *milord.* So I was.' The voice, still faint, came from the back of the cave. I looked into the shadows. A figure, prostrate, was huddled there. I walked toward it. 'Do not look at me,' the Pasha said. 'Do not come any nearer.'

"I laughed contemptuously. 'It was you who had me brought here. It is too late now to give out such commands.' I stood above the Pasha. He was pressed against the rocks. Slowly, he turned to look up at me.

"Despite myself I breathed in. The bones beneath his cheeks had collapsed—his skin was yellow—pain was stamped on his every look—but it was not his face which horrified me. No—it was his body—which was naked—do you understand?—*naked*—stripped of clothing, yes—but of skin too—in places, even of muscle and nerve. The wound to his heart was still open and unhealed. Blood, like water from a tiny spring, bubbled faintly with each tortured breath he took. His flesh was blue with rottenness. I watched as he brushed at a gash to his leg. A worm, white and bloated, dropped from the wound. The Pasha crushed it between his fingers. He wiped his hand across a rock.

" 'You see, *milord*, what a thing of beauty you have made of me.'

" 'I am sorry,' I said at last. 'I had thought to kill you.'

"The Pasha laughed, then choked, as blood in a froth swelled up between his lips. He spat it, so that it dribbled down his chin. 'You wanted revenge,' the Pasha said at last. 'Well—see what you have achieved—a horror much worse than any death.'

"There was a long silence. 'Again,' I said eventually, 'I am sorry. I did not intend it.'

" 'Such pain.' The Pasha stared at me. 'Such pain, stabbing into my heart, on the point of your sword. Such pain, *milord*.'

" 'You seemed dead. When I left you there, in the ravine, you seemed dead.'

" 'And so I nearly was, *milord*.' He paused. 'But I was greater than you knew.'

"I frowned. 'How?'

" 'The greatest of the vampires—such as I, *milord*'—he paused—'and you—cannot be killed so easily.'

"My knuckles whitened as I gripped the pistol. 'But there is a way, then?'

"The Pasha struggled to smile. His effort collapsed in a grimace of pain. When he spoke again, it was not to answer me. 'I have lain years, *milord*, in the dirt of the grave. My flesh melting into sludge—my fingers ringed with worms— every foul thing that the soil can breed leaving their tracks of slime across my face. And yet—I could not move—such was the weight of earth above my limbs, between me and the healing light of the moon, and all those living creatures which might have restored me with their blood. Oh yes, *milord,* the wound you gave me was grievous indeed. A long time it took me, to recover my strength, to pull myself at last from the embrace of the grave. And even now—you see'— he gestured at himself—'how far a way I have still to go.' He clasped his heart. Blood, in soft bubbles, seeped across his hand. 'The wound you struck still flows, *milord.'*

"I stayed frozen. The pistol seemed melted into my hand. 'You are recovering then?' I asked.

"The Pasha inclined his head a fraction.

"'And you will be whole again, eventually?'

"'Eventually.' The Pasha smiled. 'Unless—the way that I mentioned . . .' His voice trailed away. Still I didn't move. The Pasha reached up to take my hand. I let him hold it. Slowly, I bent, and knelt beside his head. He turned to stare into my eyes. 'Still beautiful,' he whispered, 'after all these years.' His lips twisted. 'Older, though. What would you not give to have your former loveliness restored?'

"'Less than to have back my mortality.'

"The Pasha smiled. I would have struck him then, had it not been for the ache of sadness in his eyes. 'I am sorry,' he whispered, 'but that can never be.'

"'Why?' I asked, with a sudden sense of rage. 'Why me? Why did you choose me for your—for your . . .'

"'Love.'

"'For your curse.'

"Again he smiled. Again, I saw the sadness in his eyes. 'Because, milord . . .' The Pasha reached up to stroke my cheek. The effort made his whole body shake. His finger, against my flesh, felt bloody and raw. 'Because, *milord'*—he swallowed, and unexpectedly his face seemed lit up with desire and hope—'because I saw the greatness in you.' He choked violently, but not even the pain could dim his sudden desperate passion. 'When we first met, even then, I recognized what you might become. My faith has not been misplaced—already you are a creature more powerful than me—the greatest, surely, of all our breed. My wait is over. I have an heir—to take up the burden, and continue the search. And where I have failed, *milord—you will succeed.*'

"His arm dropped. His whole body shook again, as though with the pain of the effort of his speech. I stared at him in astonishment. 'Search?' I asked. 'What search?'

"'You spoke of a curse. Yes. You are right. We are cursed. Our need—our thirst—it is that which makes us an abomination—loathed, and feared. And yet, *milord,* I believe'—he swallowed—'we have a certain greatness . . . If only . . . If only . . .' He choked again, so that blood was spattered across his beard.

"I stared at the crimson flecks, and nodded. 'If only,' I whispered, completing his words, 'we did not have our thirst.' I remembered Shelley. I closed my eyes. 'Without thirst, what then could we not achieve?'

"I felt the Pasha squeeze my hand. 'Lovelace tells me that Ahasver came to you.'

"'Yes.' I looked at him with sudden wonderment. 'You know of him?'

"'He has had many names. The Wandering Jew—the man who mocked Christ on His way to Calvary, and was sentenced, for his crime, to eternal restlessness. But Ahasver was already ancient when Jesus was slain. Ancient, and eternal as all his kind are.'

"'His kind?'

"'Immortals, *milord.* Not like us—not vampires . . . True immortals.'

"'And what,' I asked, 'is true immortality?'

"The Pasha's eyes burned very bright. 'Freedom, *milord,* from the need to drink blood.'

"'It exists?'

"The Pasha smiled faintly. 'We must believe so.'

"'So you have never met these immortals, then?'

"'Not as you have done.'

"I frowned. 'Then how can you know they exist at all?'

"'There are proofs—faint—often doubtful—but proofs

of *something*, nevertheless. Twelve hundred years, *milord*, I have sought them. And we must believe. We must. For what other choice or hope do we have?'

"I remembered Ahasver, how he had come to me, and the strangeness of all he had revealed. And I remembered more. I shook my head, and rose to my feet. 'He told me there was no hope for us,' I said, 'no escape.'

"'He lied.'

"'How can you know?'

"'Because he must have done.' The Pasha struggled to raise himself. 'Do you not see?' he asked with feverish passion. 'There is a way, somehow, to win immortality. True immortality. Would I have searched all these years, if I hadn't had hope? It exists, *milord*. Your pilgrimage may have a chance of an end.'

"'If mine, why not yours?'

"The Pasha smiled, the fever burning again in his eyes. 'Mine?' he asked. 'Mine too has the chance of an end.' He reached for my arm. He pulled me down beside him again. 'I am tired,' he whispered. 'I have borne the hopes of our kind for too long.' His grip tightened. 'Take up the burden, *milord*. I have waited, for centuries, for such a one as you. Do as I ask now—release me. Give me peace.'

"Gingerly, I stroked his brow. 'So it is true,' I whispered, 'I can give you death after all?'

"'Yes, *milord*. I have been powerful, a king among the Kings of the dead. Extinction for vampires such as you and I is hard—for a long time, I believed, impossible. But it is not just life I have been searching for these long centuries. Death too has its secrets. In libraries, in the ruins of ancient towns, in secret temples and forgotten graves, I have hunted.'

"I stared at him. 'Tell me, then,' I asked slowly, 'what did you find?'

"The Pasha smiled. 'A way.'

"'How?'

"'It must be you, *milord*. You and no one else.'

"'Me?'

"'It can only be a vampire I have made. Only my creation.'
The Pasha beckoned to me. I bent my ear close to his lips.
'To end it,' he whispered, 'to free me . . .'"

"No!" Rebecca almost screamed the word.

Slowly, Lord Byron narrowed his eyes.

"Don't say it. Please. I beg you."

A cruel smile wrinkled Lord Byron's lips. "Why do you
not want to know?" he asked.

"Because . . ." Rebecca gestured with her arms as her
voice trailed away. "Surely you can see?" She slumped back
in her chair. "Knowledge can be a dangerous thing."

"Yes, it can." Lord Byron nodded mockingly. "Certainly
it can. And yet also—do you not think?—it is a base
abandonment, to resign our right of thought? Not to dare—
not to search—but to stagnate, and rot?"

Rebecca swallowed. Dark fears and hopes were mingled
in her mind. Her throat seemed dry with doubt. "You did it
then?" she said eventually. "You did as he asked?"

For a long while, Lord Byron made no reply. "I promised
him I would," he said at last. "The Pasha thanked me—
simply, but with courtesy. Then he smiled. 'In return,' he
said, 'I have been keeping something in wait for you.' He
told me of his legacy. Papers—manuscripts—the distilla-
tion of a millennium's work. They were waiting for me,
sealed, at Aheron."

"Aheron? The Pasha's castle?"

Lord Byron nodded.

"Why there? Why hadn't he brought them to give to
you?"

"I asked him the very same question, of course."

"And?"

"He wouldn't answer."

"Why not?"

Lord Byron paused. He glanced again into the shadows
that lay beyond her chair. "He asked me," he said at last, "if

I remembered the underground shrine to the dead. I did, of course. 'There,' he told me, 'you will find my parting gift to you there. The rest of the castle has been burned to the ground. The shrine, though, can never be destroyed. Go, *milord*. Find what I have left for you.'

"Again I asked why he hadn't brought his papers with him. Again the Pasha smiled, and shook his head. He took my hand. 'Promise,' he whispered. I nodded my head. He smiled again, then turned his face against the wall of the cave. For a long while, he lay in silence. At last he turned back and looked up at me.

"'I am ready,' he whispered.

"'It is not too late,' I said. 'You can be healed. You can carry on your search with me by your side.'

"But the Pasha shook his head. 'I have decided,' he said. He reached for my hand. He placed it over his naked heart. 'I am ready,' he whispered in my ear again.''

Lord Byron paused. He smiled at Rebecca. "I killed him," he said. He leaned forward. "Do you want to know how?" Rebecca didn't answer. "The secret. The deathly, deadly secret." Lord Byron laughed. It seemed to Rebecca, sitting frozen in her chair, that he had not been talking to her at all. "I sliced open his skull. I ripped apart his chest. And then . . ." He paused. Rebecca listened. She was sure there had been a noise—the same scrabbling she had heard before coming from the darkness by her chair. She tried to rise, but Lord Byron's eyes were on her, and her limbs seemed made of lead. She stayed where she was. The room around her seemed silent again. There was no sound now but the thumping of her blood.

"I ate his heart and brains. Simple, really." Again, Lord Byron was staring past her chair. "The Pasha died without a moan. The mess I had made of his head was revolting, but on his face, beneath the gore, was a look of rest. I called Lovelace. I met him by the entrance to the cave. He stared at me, astonished. Then he smiled, and reached out to stroke my face. 'Oh, Byron,' he said, 'I am glad. You are really quite the beau once again.'

"I frowned. 'What do you mean?' I said.

"'That you are beautiful. Beautiful and young as you used to be.'

"I touched my cheeks. 'No.' But they felt smooth and unlined. 'No,' I said again. 'I can't be.'

"Lovelace grinned. 'Oh, but you are. As lovely as when I met you first. As lovely as when you were created a vampire.'

"'But . . .' I smiled, meeting Lovelace's grin, and then I laughed in sudden ecstasy. 'I don't understand . . . How?' I laughed again. 'How?' I choked with disbelief. And then suddenly I did understand. I looked back into the cave, at the Pasha's mangled corpse.

"Lovelace too, for the first time, saw what I had done. He walked up to the body. He stared down at it, appalled. 'Dead?' he asked. 'Truly dead at last?' I nodded. Lovelace shivered. 'How?'

"I reached for him and stroked his hair. 'Do not ask,' I said. I kissed him lingeringly. 'You do not want to know.'

"Lovelace nodded. He bent by the corpse, and stared at it in wonder. 'And now?' he said at last, looking up at me. 'Do we burn his corpse, or bury it?'

"'Neither.'

"'Byron, he was wise and mighty; you cannot leave him here.'

"'I don't intend to.'

"'Then what?'

"I smiled. 'You will take the corpse to Missolonghi. The Greeks must have their martyr. And I . . .' I walked to the cave mouth. The stars had disappeared, blotted out beneath black cloud. I smelled the air. A storm was coming. I turned back to Lovelace. 'I must have my freedom. Lord Byron is dead. Dead in Missolonghi. Let the news be proclaimed across Greece and all the world.'

"'You wish'—Lovelace gestured with his arm—'that— *thing*—to be taken for you?'

"I nodded.

"'How?'

"I tapped on Lovelace's bag of coins. 'There is no one like your Greek for the taking of a bribe.'

"Lovelace smiled slowly. He bowed his head. 'Very well,' he said. 'If that is what you wish.'

"'It is.' I reached across and kissed him, then walked from the cave and untethered a horse. Lovelace watched me. 'What will you do?' he asked.

"I laughed, as I climbed onto the horse's back. 'I have a search to make,' I said.

"Lovelace frowned. 'Search?'

"'A last request, if you like.' I spurred my horse forward. 'Goodbye, Lovelace. I will wait to hear the cannons over Greece proclaim my death.' Lovelace swept off his hat in an extravagant bow. I waved to him—I wheeled my horse round—I galloped down the hill. The cave was soon lost behind rocks and groves of trees.

"The storm broke above me on the Yanina road. I paused for shelter in a tavern. The Greeks there muttered they had never heard such thunder. 'A great man has passed away,' they all agreed.

"'Who might it be?' I asked.

"One of them, a bandit I guessed from the pistols in his belt, crossed himself. 'Pray to God, it is not the Lordos Byronos,' he said. His companions nodded in agreement. I smiled. Back in Missolonghi, I knew, the soldiers would be wailing and sobbing in the streets.

"I waited for the storm to pass. I rode all night, and into the day. It was twilight when I reached the road to Aheron. By the bridge, I found a peasant. He screamed as I gathered him onto my horse. 'The *vardoulacha!* The *vardoulacha* is back!' I cut his throat—I drank—I tossed his body into the river far below. By now, the moon was gleaming brightly in the sky. I spurred my horse on through the gorges and ravines.

"The archway to the Lord of Death stood as before. I rode under it, past the cliff, and then, rounding the promontory, toward the village and the Pasha's castle on the crag. Before, it had loomed against the sky—but now, when I looked, it seemed melted away. I rode through the village. There was nothing of it left, save for odd mounds of rubble and weed, and when I passed the castle walls, they too seemed swallowed up into the rock, so that no one would have known they had ever been there. But it was when I reached the summit, where the castle had stood, that I sat frozen with astonishment. Strange twisted stones gleamed against the azure gloom, as though molded like sand by streaks of rain. Slowly, I dismounted. Of the mighty edifice that had once been there, nothing recognizable remained. Cypress and ivy, weed and wallflower grew matted together over the stones—nothing else grew. The whole place was blasted and overthrown. I wondered if it was I who had destroyed it, I who had brought the curse upon the place, when I had stabbed my sword through the heart of its lord.

"I searched for the great hall. There was no trace of the pillars or the stairways, nothing but the strange twists of rock everywhere, and I felt a mounting sense of hopelessness. Then, just as I was nearing despair, I recognized a fragment of stone behind some weeds. It too had melted, but I could just make out a trellis pattern. I remembered it from the kiosk, the one that had led to the temple of the dead. I cut my way through the weeds. A darkness opened up ahead. I stared into it. There were stairs, leading deep into the earth. The entrance had been almost totally concealed. I brushed the remaining weeds away. I started my descent into the underworld.

"Down I went—down, down, down. The darkness began to be lit by red flames. As they grew stronger, I recognized frescoes painted on the walls, the same I had seen on my descent all those years before. I paused by the entranceway. I saw the altar and the chasm of fire, unchanged. I breathed in the heavy air. And then, at once, I tensed. I swept back my cloak. There was a vampire, ahead of me, I could smell its blood. What was such a creature doing here? I nerved myself. Cautiously, I walked into the shrine.

"A black-cloaked figure stood against the flames. It had its back to me. Slowly, it turned around. It lifted the hood that was covering its face. 'You killed him then,' said Haidée.

"For an eternity, it seemed, I didn't reply. I stared into her face. It was wrinkled and dry, aged before her time. Only her eyes had the freshness I remembered. But it was her. It was her. I took a step forward. I held out my arms. I laughed with relief, and joy, and love. But Haidée, watching me, backed away.

" 'Haidée.'

"She turned.

" 'Please,' I whispered. She made no answer. I paused. 'Please,' I said again. 'Let me hold you. I had thought you were dead.'

" 'And am I not?' she said softly.

"I shook my head. 'We are what we are.'

" 'Is that so?' she asked, turning to look at me again. 'Oh, Byron,' she whispered. 'Byron.' I saw tears begin to line her eyes. I had never seen a vampire weep before. I reached for her, and this time, she let me take her in my arms. She began to sob, and kiss me, her dry lips pressing almost desperately, and still she sobbed, and then she began to hit me with her fists. 'Byron, Byron, you fell, you fell, you let him win. Byron.' Her body shook with her anger and tears, and then she kissed me again, even more urgently than before, and held me as though she would never let me go. Her body still shuddered as it pressed against my own.

"I stroked her hair, now lined with gray. 'How did you know,' I asked, 'to wait for me here?'

Haidée blinked her tears away. 'He had told me what he intended to do.'

" 'That if I agreed—he would send me here?'

"Haidée nodded. 'He *is* dead? Truly dead?'

" 'Yes.'

"Haidée looked into my eyes. 'Of course he is,' she whispered. 'You are beautiful and young once again.'

" 'And you,' I asked, 'he gave you the Gift as well?'

"She nodded.

" 'So you could have done what I did. You could have—'

" 'Had my beauty restored?' She laughed bitterly. 'My youth?'

"I made no answer, but bowed my head.

"Haidée took her arms away from me. 'I try not to drink human blood,' she said.

"I frowned in disbelief. Haidée smiled at me. She opened her cloak. Her body was shriveled and lined, an old woman's, touched by black. 'Sometimes,' she said, 'lizards, crawling animals—I will drink from them. Once, a Turk who tried to force himself on me. But otherwise . . .'

"I stared at her appalled. 'Haidée . . .'

" 'No!' she screamed suddenly. 'No! I am not a *vardoulacha!* I am not!' She shuddered, and clutched at her body, as though she longed to rip her vampire flesh away. She shook, and when I tried to touch her again, she beat me back. 'No, no, no . . .' Her voice trailed away, but no tears would rise now to her burning eyes. She clutched herself as she stared at me.

" 'The Pasha, though,' I whispered, 'he was a killer, and a Turk.'

"Slowly, Haidée began to laugh, a terrible, heart-rending sound. 'Did you not realize?' she asked.

" 'What?'

" 'He was my father.' She stared at me wildly. 'My father! Flesh of my flesh—*blood of my blood.*' She started to shake again, and moved even further back from me, so that her head was now framed by the wall of fire. 'I couldn't,' she whispered, 'I couldn't, no matter what he had done, I couldn't, I couldn't! Don't you see? Surely you wouldn't have had me drink my own father's blood? Not the man who had given me life?' She laughed. 'But of course, I was forgetting—you are the creature who has killed his own child.'

"I stared at her in horror. 'I never knew,' I said eventually.

" 'Oh yes.' Haidée smoothed back her hair. 'He had bred me. It seems that was something he had always done—fathering on his brood-mare peasants in the village. But I was different. For some reason, I touched his heart. In his own way, perhaps, he even loved me. He let me live. He fed on me, of course, but he let me live. His daughter. His beloved daughter.' She smiled. 'He had intended to give me to you, all along. Isn't that amusing, isn't that strange? You were to be his heir—and I your vampire bride. No wonder he was upset when we fled from him.'

"I swallowed. 'He told you this himself?'

" 'Yes. Before he . . .' Her voice trailed away. She hugged herself tight, and rocked to and fro. 'Before he made me a monster.'

"I stared into her burning vampire eyes. 'But after that?' I asked. I shook my head in passionate disbelief. 'Afterward, you never tried to follow me?'

" 'Oh yes.'

"Her words were cold. They settled in the pit of my stomach like ice. 'I never saw you,' I said.

" 'Didn't you?'

" 'No.'

" 'Then perhaps it was because I couldn't bear you to.' She turned from me, to stare into the flames. For a long time, she seemed to trace patterns in the fire. She turned back to me. 'But think,' she said with sudden passion. 'Are you certain? Think, Byron, think.'

" 'Was it you at Missolonghi?'

" 'Oh yes, of course, there was Missolonghi too.' Haidée laughed. 'But how could I have resisted catching a glimpse of you then? After so long—to hear your name, the messiah from the West, on everyone's lips. And I hoped— perhaps—a tiny part of the reason you had come . . .' She paused. 'You had memories of me?'

"I stared into her eyes. There was no need for me to make a reply.

" 'Byron.' She reached for my hands. She held them tight. 'So beautiful you looked. Even old, even coarsened, riding by the swamps.'

"I remembered her pointing, and the words she had cried. 'Why did you want me dead?' I asked.

" 'Because I love you still,' she said. I kissed her. She smiled sadly at me. 'Because I am old and ugly, and you—you, Byron, are a *vardoulacha* too, who was once so brave and good.' She paused. She bent her head, then looked up at me. 'But . . . as I said—it was not the first time I came after you.'

"I stared at her. 'When?' I asked.

"She lowered her head.

" 'Haidée—tell me—when?'

"Her eyes met mine again. 'In Athens,' she said quietly.

" 'Very soon, then, after . . .'

" 'Yes—a year after that. I followed you. I watched you kill. I was wretched. But perhaps I would still have revealed myself to you . . .' She paused.

" 'Except?' I asked.

"She smiled at me—and suddenly, I knew. I remembered the street, the woman holding the baby in her arms, the scent of golden blood. 'It was you,' I whispered. 'The child in your arms, it was ours—yours, and mine.' Haidée didn't answer. 'Tell me,' I said. 'Tell me that I'm right.'

" 'So you do remember, then,' said Haidée at last. She took a step toward me, away from the flames. I held her in my arms. I stared over her shoulder into the fire. 'A child,' I whispered. 'From that last hour—a child.' A thread, however delicate, wound from our final act of mortal love. A memory, preserved in human form, stamped with the imprint of what we had been. A link, a last link, to all that we had lost. A child." Lord Byron shook his head. He stared at Rebecca, and slowly, he smiled.

"It was a boy. Haidée had had him sent away. She had not been able to bear his scent. I too, of course, was dangerous to him. He had been kept at school in Nafplio. I could not go and see him with my own eyes, of course, but when we left Aheron together, Haidée and I, we made provision for our son. I had him taken from Nafplio, and sent to London. He was educated there as an Englishman. Eventually, he even took an English name." He smiled again. "Can you guess what it was?"

Rebecca nodded. "Of course," she said dully. "It was Ruthven." She sat frozen. She had heard the noise from the darkness again. She met Lord Byron's stare. Gently, she moistened her lips. "And you?" she asked. "Did you stay away from England, and your son?"

"From England, yes—in the main. I had the Pasha's manuscripts. With Haidée, I continued the search, across continents and hidden worlds. But Haidée soon was growing old—too old to walk—too old to be seen."

Rebecca nodded, appalled. She understood. "Haidée then—she is the—thing—I saw in the crypt?"

"Yes. She has still not drunk. She stays down there, in that place of the dead. The Pasha's body too is near her, beneath the tombstone in the church. For two long centuries they have rotted there together, the Pasha dead, Haidée still alive, and waiting in vain for my search's end."

"So"—Rebecca swallowed—"you have not found it yet?"

Lord Byron smiled grimly. "You have seen that I have not."

Rebecca twisted a curl of her auburn hair. "And will you ever succeed?" she dared to ask at last.

He raised an eyebrow. "Perhaps."

"I think you will."

"Thank you." He inclined his head. "May I ask why?"

"Because you still exist. You could end it, but you do not. As the Pasha promised—there must be hope after all."

Lord Byron smiled. "You may be right," he said. "But to die—it would be at Polidori's hands—and that I couldn't bear." His brow darkened. "No. Not destroyed by an enemy. Not by one who has killed all I loved." He stared at Rebecca. "You understand, of course, that your own presence here is due only to his hate. Each generation of Ruthvens he has sent to me. You, Rebecca, I am afraid, are not the first, but only one of a very long line."

Rebecca stared at him, at the ice and pity mingled in his eyes. She understood now that she was doomed. Her fate, after all, had already been sealed. "Polidori, then," she asked, in a steady voice, "he doesn't know that you can be destroyed."

Lord Byron smiled faintly. "No. He doesn't."

Rebecca swallowed. "Whereas now, I do."

Again, he smiled. "Indeed."

Rebecca rose to her feet. Slowly, Lord Byron did the same. Rebecca tensed, but he passed her, watching her all the time, and walked into the shadows. The scratching from the darkness was insistent now. She searched the gloom but could make nothing out. Lord Byron, though, was watching her. His pale face gleamed like a flame of light. "I am sorry," he said.

"Please."

Slowly, Lord Byron shook his head.

"Please." She began to back toward the door. "Why have you told me all this, if only to finish it by killing me?"

"So that you might understand what your death will achieve. So it can be easier." He paused, and glanced into the shadows. "For both of you."

"Both?" Again, there was the scrabbling. Rebecca stared wildly into the dark.

"There is no other way," Lord Byron whispered. "It must be done." But he was not speaking to Rebecca anymore. He was gazing at a shadowy form, crouched down beside his feet. His arm shaking, he stroked its head. Slowly, it crossed into the candlelight.

Rebecca stared at it. She moaned. *"No. No!"* She clasped her fingers over her eyes.

"And yet once, Rebecca, she was very like you. Yes. Very strangely like you." Lord Byron stared at her with mingled pity and desire. Softly, he crossed to her. "Do you dare look into her face again? No? And yet I tell you"—Rebecca felt the soft touch of his lips upon her own—"she had your face, your form, your loveliness. It is as if . . ." His voice trailed away.

Rebecca opened her eyes. She stared into the dark depths

of Lord Byron's stare. She saw him frown, and traced misery and hope as they crossed his face. "Please," she whispered. "Please."

"You are her very image, you know."

"Please."

He shook his head. "She must have you. She must drink her own blood at last. Two hundred years have passed, and now . . . here you are—with a face like the one that used to be her own. And so . . ." Again he kissed Rebecca softly on the lips. "I am sorry. I am sorry, Rebecca. But I hope, perhaps now, you can at least understand. Forgive me, Rebecca."

He took a step backward. Rebecca stared, transfixed, at the soft flame of his face. She saw him glance down at the creature waiting twisted at his feet. She too stared down at it. Suddenly, red eyes, bright as coals, met her look. Rebecca began to shake. She turned. She pushed against the door. It opened, and she stumbled out, and slammed it shut again.

She began to run. A long corridor was stretching away from her. She didn't remember it from before. It was badly lit, and she could scarcely make her way. Behind her, the door stayed closed. Suddenly, Rebecca stood still. She thought she could see something, hanging, just ahead. It was swinging slightly, and creaking. Then Rebecca heard the splash of liquid on the floor.

She breathed in deeply. Slowly, she walked toward the hanging thing. It was pale, she could see now, gleaming in the dark, and then suddenly her blood froze solid in her veins, for she saw that the gleam was that of flesh, human flesh, a carcass hanging by its heels from a hook. Again there was the drip of liquid on the floor. Rebecca stared down. A thick droplet of blood was forming in the corpse's nose. It fell, and again there was the splash on the floor. Rebecca saw now why the body was so gleaming white. Not knowing what she did, she touched the corpse's side. It was cold, and virtually drained of its blood. Again, there was the splash. Rebecca crouched down on her heels. She stared into the corpse's face. She tried to scream. No sound came out. She looked again at her mother's face. Then she rose and began to shudder, and run.

All the way down the corridor, further corpses had been hung by hooks. Rebecca had to pass them as she stumbled on her way, and they would swing against her face, clammy and smooth as she tried to brush them away. On and on, she staggered; more and more, the corpses of the Ruthvens blocked her way. At last, Rebecca fell to her knees, sobbing with hatred and fear and disgust. She turned around, looked at the row of butcher's hooks she had passed, and moaned. Back down the corridor, beyond her mother's corpse, waited a gleaming, empty hook. Rebecca found her voice at last; she screamed. The hook began to swing. Rebecca buried her face in her hands; again she screamed; she waited, prostrate, on the corridor floor.

At last, she dared to look up again. The corridor was empty. The row of her ancestors had disappeared. Rebecca stared around. Nothing. Nothing at all. "Where are you?" she screamed. "Byron! Where are you? Kill me if you must but no more tricks like these!" She pointed at where the carcasses had been, and waited. Still the corridor continued empty as before. "Haidée!" Rebecca paused. "Haidée!" No answer. Rebecca rose to her feet. Ahead of her, she saw a single door. She walked toward it. She pushed it open. Beyond, she saw a candle flame. She walked through the door; then she froze. She was standing in the catacomb.

The tomb was just in front of her; on the far wall were the steps that led up to the church. Rebecca crossed to them. She climbed the steps, and pushed at the door. It was locked. She pushed again. It wouldn't shift. Rebecca sat on the top step, pressed against the door, waiting. All was silent now. The door behind the tomb was still open, but Rebecca couldn't face returning to the corridor. She waited several minutes. Still silence. Gingerly, she descended a single step. She paused. Nothing. She walked down the remaining steps. She stared around the crypt. The fountain bubbled noiselessly, otherwise all was still. Rebecca looked ahead, at the door behind the tomb. Perhaps she would make it. If she ran, and found a door onto the street—yes—she might make it after all. Quietly, she crossed the floor of the crypt. She stood by the tomb. She nerved herself. She knew, if she went, she would have to go—now.

The claw seized her around her throat. Rebecca screamed, but the cry was muffled by a second hand, holding her mouth and stifling her. Dust choked her eyes; it smelled of living death. Rebecca blinked. She looked up at the centuries-old thing that was Haidée. Two red eyes burning; open, toothless mouth; shriveled insect-head. Rebecca struggled. The creature seemed so frail, but its strength was implacable. Rebecca felt its grip around her throat start to strangle her. She choked. She saw the creature raise its other hand. Its claws were long like scimitars. The thing stroked a single finger down her throat. Rebecca felt a welling of blood from the wound. Then she struggled to turn her head away. The thing was lowering its lips; the stench of its breath was terrible. Rebecca felt the claw touch her neck again. She waited. The lips, she knew, were just above the wound. She shut her eyes. She hoped that death, when it came, would be quick.

Then she heard the rattle of the creature's breath. She tensed—and nothing happened. She opened her eyes. The creature had lifted its lips from her neck. It was staring at her with its burning eyes. It was shaking. "Do it," Rebecca heard Lord Byron say.

The thing still stared at her. Rebecca peered beyond its head. Lord Byron was standing beside the tomb. Slowly, the creature looked at him.

"Do it," he said again.

The creature made no answer.

Lord Byron stretched out to touch its hairless skull. "Haidée," he whispered, "there is no other way. Please." He kissed her. *"Please."*

Still the creature was silent. Rebecca saw Lord Byron study her. "She knows the secret," he said. "I have told her everything." He waited. "Haidée, we agreed. She knows the secret. You cannot let her go."

The creature shook. Its thin, skinless shoulders moved up and down. Lord Byron stretched out to comfort it, but he was brushed away. The creature stared into Rebecca's eyes again. Its own face was twisted, as though with tears, but its burning eyes were as dry as before. Slowly, it opened its mouth—then shook its head. Rebecca felt the grip lift from around her throat.

The creature tried to rise. It staggered. Lord Byron captured it in his arms. He held it, kissing it, rocking it. Disbelievingly, Rebecca rose to her feet.

Lord Byron stared at her. His face was icy with pain and despair. "Go," he whispered.

Rebecca couldn't move.

"Go!"

She held her hands over her ears, the cry was so terrible. She ran from the crypt. On the stairway, she paused, to look back down. Lord Byron was bent over his charge, as a parent holds his child. Rebecca stood, frozen—then she turned, and ran, and left the crypt behind.

At the top of the stairs was a passageway. She followed it. At the far end, she reached a door; she turned the handle, and opened it, and gasped with delight when she saw the street beyond. It was dusk. The sunset was streaking the muggy London sky, and she stared at the colors with wonderment and joy. For a minute she paused, listening to the distant city roar, the sounds she had never thought to hear again—the sounds of life. Then she turned, and began to hurry down the street. She glanced around once. The front of Lord Byron's house was still dark. The doors were all shut. No one seemed to be following her.

Had she paused, though, and hidden to make absolutely sure, she would have seen a figure slip out from the dark. She would have seen him tracing the way she had just gone. She would have smelled, perhaps, a distinctive tang. But she didn't pause, and so she didn't see her follower. He passed, as she did, and left the street behind. The faint smell of acid in the air was soon dispersed.

Postscript

The face of the corpse did not bear the slightest resemblance to my dear friend—the mouth was distorted & half open showing those teeth in which poor fellow he once so prided himself quite discoloured by the spirits—his upper lip was shaded with mustachios which gave a totally new character to his face—his cheeks were long and bagged over the jaw—his nose was quite prominent at the bridge and sank in between the eyes—his eye brows shaggy & lowering—his skin like dull parchment. It did not seem to be Byron.

JOHN CAM HOBHOUSE, *Diaries*

**POCKET BOOKS
PROUDLY PRESENTS**

SLAVE OF MY THIRST

Tom Holland

**Coming Soon
in Hardcover
from Pocket Books**

The following is a preview of
Slave of My Thirst. . . .

London,
15 December, 1897.

To those whom it concerns—

If you are reading this letter, then you will no doubt suspect the danger you are in. The lawyers you have approached are under instructions to deliver to you a body of papers. The story they reveal is a terrible one. Indeed, only recently did I understand its full extent when a copy of Moorfield's book was sent to me from Calcutta, together with a bundle of letters and journals. Start with Moorfield's book, at the chapter titled 'A Perilous Mission'—I have left three letters where I found them within the pages of the book. Otherwise the papers are arranged by myself. Read them in the order in which they have been placed.

My poor friend. Whoever you may be, whenever you may read this—do not doubt, please, that what is recorded did occur.

May God's hand protect you.

Yours in grief and hope,

ABRAHAM STOKER.

Letter, Dr John Eliot to Professor Huree Jyoti Navalkar.

———

Surgeon's Court,
Hanbury Street,
Whitechapel,
London,

5 January 1888.

My dear Huree,

You will see that I am now securely established in London. I trust you will note the address and perhaps, despite the nature of our parting, take advantage of it to write to me. I do not have much opportunity now for the type of arguments we used to enjoy. I have never been of a particularly convivial nature; and yet sometimes I find myself lonelier in this mighty city of six millions than I ever was amongst the Himalayan heights. Of my two oldest friends, one, Arthur Ruthven, is dead—the victim, it would seem, of a cruel and pointless murder. The other, Sir George Mowberly, you may have read of in the newspapers, for he is now a Minister in the Government.

I cannot regret my isolation too greatly, though. My practice is exceedingly vast, so vast that I find myself almost numbed by it. My rooms, you must understand, are situated in the most outcast corner of this great city of outcasts. There is no form of wretchedness or horror that its streets do not breed. Why did I feel I had to travel to the East to relieve the burden of human suffering when here, in the richest city in the world, there is misery on a scale so terrible?

To you, I can confess my response to this place. With others, however—yes, and with myself as well—I am as cold as ice. There can be no other way. How else shall I survive what I see on my rounds? A man dying of smallpox in a cellar, his wife eight months pregnant, their children creeping naked in the filth. A small girl, dead for two weeks, found buried beneath the ordure of her brothers and sisters. Not even amongst the slums of Bombay did I witness such scenes. Emotion, in these conditions, would be like a candle-flame in the gale. But fortunately I am by nature a passionless creature; logic and reason have always been the predominant features of my mind. For all your efforts, Huree, I remain untouched by the teachings of the East.

What of those things I glimpsed in Kalikshutra? Do I think I can explain them logically? Not yet, I admit—but one day I will, I am confident. One thing for sure, Huree, I do not accept your explanations. Demons? *Vampires?* What has science to do with such fantastical ideas? Nothing. The physician who dabbles in such things must soon sink to the level of a medicine man. I will not become a witch doctor performing ghastly rituals to appease horrors and spirits he cannot understand. The memory of poor Paxton's son still haunts me, you see—the pain in his eyes, the blood that spurted from his skewered heart. What had he become, Huree? The victim of a terrible and inexplicable disease, yes—but not a ghoul, not a creature to be destroyed as he was. No doubt he *was* beyond the reach of my help; and yet I am haunted by the knowledge that I did not seek to cure him, but to kill him instead—to *murder* him. When I did so, I betrayed my entire life's work.

Write to me again. You will have noticed from this letter how keen I am to continue our arguments. Reply soon, and be as rude as you like.

JACK.

Letter, Lady Rosamund Mowberley to Miss Lucy Ruthven.

———————

2, Grosvenor Street,
Mayfair,
London.

13 April 1888.

My dearest Lucy,

I trust you will forgive me for writing to you at a time when I know your attentions will be fully focused upon your impending first night, but I am in a state of such distress that I cannot refrain from making contact with you. This morning I received a letter. It was hand delivered. My name had been printed in capitals on the envelope, and the writing inside was in capitals as well. The letter was unsigned. I therefore have no way of knowing who sent it to me. And yet its message was an extraordinary and terrifying one. 'I HAVE SEEN G. MURDERED,' it read. When I tell you that my dear George has been missing for a week now and that furthermore, even before his disappearance, he had seemed the likely target of a dangerous conspiracy, then you will understand why I fear the worst. I have asked a man to investigate this mystery for me. You will remember him, I am sure; his name is Dr John Eliot, and he may very well shortly be visiting you. I therefore feel it would be for the best if I give you a full account of my meeting with him this morning.

The weather then was more than usually icy and raw, and even those most prosperous stretches of London seemed unwelcoming. Beyond the City, however, I seemed to have entered a circle of Hell, and not even the most blissful of climates, I think, would have ameliorated the scenes of horror I witnessed there. George had warned me that Dr Eliot had what he once mocked as 'the missionary spirit'— yet surely even missionaries must shrink before entering such a place, where shivering creatures huddle in rags and young girls bare themselves without a hint of shame. I was greatly relieved when at length we attained our destination.

I pushed the door fully open, walked inside and looked around. It seemed a virtual chemist's laboratory. Test-tubes and pipings were everywhere, and a flame was rising from a burner on the desk. Crouched over this same desk, with his back to me, was the figure of a man. He must have heard my entrance, but he did not look around. Instead, I observed with some surprise that he was aiming a syringe into his arm. He jabbed the needle down, and the syringe began to fill up with a flow of purple blood. Then, gently, the needle was removed again and the blood added to some substance on a dish.

'Please take a seat,' said Dr Eliot, still not turning round. I did as he instructed. Five minutes I sat there as he studied his dish and scribbled down notes. At length, I heard him mutter impatiently and push back his chair. 'It is no good,' he said, turning to face me for the first time. 'I am sorry to have kept you waiting,' he said. He turned off the bunsen flame, and at once it was as though the flame behind his face and eyes had been extinguished too. He crossed to me and slumped into the armchair opposite.

'Now,' he said, 'what can I do for you?'

I swallowed. 'Dr Eliot, I am the wife of a dear friend of yours.'

'Ah.' He widened his eyes at this. 'Lady Mowberley?'

'Yes,' I said. I smiled nervously.

'You were in India, were you not?'

He nodded with just the faintest inclination of his head. 'Until six months ago. There is some problem?' he asked. 'Lady Mowberley, tell me, is George not well?'

I struggled to compose myself. 'I fear that George may be dead.'

'Dead?' His voice scarcely registered the shock he must

have felt. 'But you only fear it,' he said at last. 'You are not certain?'

'He has been missing, Dr Eliot.'

'Missing? For how long?'

'For almost three weeks now.'

'You have reported this to Scotland Yard?' he asked.

I shook my head.

'Why ever not?'

'There are circumstances, Dr Eliot. Very particular . . . circumstances.'

He stared deep into my eyes, then nodded slowly. 'And so—because of these circumstances—you have come to me?'

'George spoke very highly of your powers.'

Dr Eliot frowned. 'By powers,' he said, 'I suppose George meant those tricks of observation with which I used to impress him and poor Ruthven at university? I have no use for them now,' he said. 'No, no! They are a childish waste of time!'

'Why do you say that? I have heard stories of you, heard how you solved mysteries that had baffled the policy.'

'Please,' he answered, 'do not be upset. I have merely been warning you, Lady Mowberley, that my ability to aid you must be doubtful in the extreme.'

It seemed to me that his reticence might in truth be vanity and that all he needed was some chance to display his powers. 'What can you read from my appearance now?' I asked him suddenly.

'Oh, merely that you are from a wealthy but non-noble family, that your much-loved mother has recently died, and that you hardly ever venture out from your home, having a morbid fear of High Society. All that is clear enough. In addition, I would hazard the suggestion that you have journeyed abroad within the past year or so, possibly to India.'

I laughed. 'Until your last comment, Dr Eliot, I was afraid that you were cheating and that my husband had written to you describing me.'

'You have not been abroad?'

'Never.'

He slumped back in an attitude of despair. 'You see then what I mean? My powers have faded hopelessly.'

'Not at all,' I assured him. 'Your previous descriptions

were utterly correct. But before you explain them to me, I would be interested to know why you thought I had been abroad?'

'On your neck,' he replied, 'I noticed a couple of blemishes which seemed to me very like mosquito bites. I have often observed that such bites, if they were ever septic, will endure as faint marks on the skin for a couple of years. Obviously, if my diagnosis had been correct you would at some stage have had to have been abroad. India I guessed because of your necklace and earrings. They are of a very distinctively Indian make.'

'Hearing such an explanation,' I replied, 'I almost feel that I should have been abroad. However, the blemishes are merely an allergy to the filthy London air.'

'You were brought up away from the metropolis, then?'

'Yes,' I replied, 'near Whitby, in Yorkshire. I spent my first twenty-two years there, and have only been in London since my marriage to George some eighteen months ago.'

'I see.' He was studying the marks on my neck again. 'And the jewellery?'

'The jewels were given to me,' I said, 'by my dearest George. But the previous points you made,' I asked, 'could you tell me how you arrived at them?'

'Oh, they were simple,' he replied.

'My lack of noble blood is evident then, I suppose?'

Dr Eliot chuckled to himself. 'Your breeding, Lady Mowberley, is exquisite in every way. One thing, however, betrays you. You wear a brooch with the Mowberley coat of arms, and a bracelet round your wrist with the very same design. Clearly the ornaments have not been recently made. Therefore they must be heirlooms, a part of George's inheritance and not your own, and yet you seem most attached to the memory of your own family. Why then do you not wear jewels inherited from them? Probably, I would suggest, because such jewels do not bear a coat of arms, and you are seduced by the novelty of wearing ornaments that do.'

'Dear me!' I lamented. 'You seem to have a low opinion of my character.'

'Not at all,' laughed Dr Eliot good-humouredly. 'But was my reasoning exact?'

'Perfectly,' I replied, 'though I blush to confess it. However, I do not understand how you knew of my attachment to my family's memory.'

'You will permit me to compliment you again, Lady Mowberley, when I observe that your dress perfectly reflects your wealth and taste. Your umbrella, however, seems out of place. It is clearly old, for its handle has a couple of cracks which have been expensively repaired, and the initials carved into the wood are not your own. It is ridiculous to assume that you cannot afford a new umbrella—therefore the one you carry must have some sentimental value, and when I observe the faint strip of black still tied in mourning round the handle, the probability is hardened into fact. Whose umbrella had it been, then? A woman's clearly, and someone older than you, for the umbrella itself seems almost antique. I deduced, therefore, that it must have been your mother's. Your mother never saw you married?'

I shook my head. And then—I was feeling a little emotional, perhaps—I told him the full story of my marriage to George: of how we had been pledged to each other since he was sixteen and I was twelve.

'But—forgive me if I seem to pry—you were content with this arrangement yourself?'

'Oh yes, indeed!' I replied. 'You must understand, Dr Eliot, that George has been my sweetheart for as long as I can recall. When my mother died, to whom else could I turn?'

'But George, surely, had left Yorkshire a long time before? Had you seen him at all since then?'

'Not for six or seven years.'

'A period which you had spent entirely near Whitby?'

'Yes. My mother, Dr Eliot, had grown very sick in that time. She needed me to attend on her, for she was nervous and infirm.'

'Very well then,' he said. 'Give me the facts surrounding George's disappearance.'

'My husband,' I told Dr Eliot, 'had always had great ambitions to rise in politics.'

'Ambitions,' Dr Eliot murmured, 'but not the application, as I recall.'

'It is true,' I admitted, 'that George sometimes found the day-to-day business of political life tiresome. But he had hopes, Dr Eliot, and noble dreams. But although George struggled manfully, his hopes always seemed doomed to frustration, and I know he felt his failure very keenly. He would never admit it to me, but I know that his despair was compounded by the parallel success of your mutual friend and contemporary, Arthur Ruthven. Arthur's career in the India Office, I need hardly tell you, had been a glittering one.

'Arthur Ruthven,' I continued, 'was a very good friend—you will hardly need me to tell you that. He was perfectly aware of George's desire to rise in the Government, and I am sure that he did his best to help. Do not misunderstand me, Dr Eliot. Arthur was always the soul of propriety. He would have done nothing unworthy of his position of trust. But he may have had words with his Minister, he may have dropped the occasional hint. Nothing more than that, I am certain—nothing more. Suffice it to say, however, that some two years ago, shortly before our wedding, George finally entered the Government.'

'In the India Office?' Dr Eliot asked.

'Yes.'

'What were his responsibilities?'

I frowned. 'I am not certain. Does it matter?'

'If you don't tell me,' he replied sharply, 'how can I possibly decide?'

'I do know,' I said slowly, 'that he has a Bill to pilot through the House this summer. I believe it is related to the Indian frontier.'

'Do you know if he was working on it with Arthur Ruthven? George as the Minister and Arthur as the diplomatist?'

'Yes.'

'Good.' He folded his hands again. 'Then that is suggestive.'

I frowned. 'I don't understand you,' I said.

He gestured disdainfully. 'Clearly, Lady Mowberley, if Arthur Ruthven's fate *has* overtaken your husband, then we shall need to establish what it is which might link the two men. They were both working on this Bill and it is concerned with the Indian frontier. That is a topic of some sensitivity, I would have thought. You see, Lady Mowberley, what a fruitful line of inquiry at once opens up?'

I swallowed. 'You are seeking for something which links

the two men. Well, Dr Eliot, there is something. It was just over a year ago,' I said slowly, 'when Arthur came round to our home for a light evening meal.' I then described to Dr Eliot what we had discussed that night, chiefly, dear Lucy, it had been you and your determination to go back to the stage. You will remember how opposed your brother had been; and yet by the end of that evening he was laughing admiringly at your enthusiasm. Arthur had said, 'Lucy clearly will not be turned aside. For obsessions are irrational and almost daemonic things.'

'Indeed,' murmured Dr Eliot. 'I remember at college Ruthven had a famous obsession of his own.'

'And what was that?' I inquired.

'He was a great collector of ancient Greek coins.'

'And so he still was when I knew him. Indeed, he often claimed within my hearing that his collection was quite unsurpassable.'

'Arthur himself readily admitted that there was an absurd aspect to his enthusiasm, especially in one otherwise so sober and reserved. "But there is nothing I would not do," he told us that night, "in pursuit of a coin from the age of the Greeks. I have the honour of my collection to uphold. Indeed, it seems that I have grown notorious, for see"—he reached in his bag—"I have only today received a personal challenge."'

'"A challenge?" I remember George exclaiming. 'What the devil do you mean?"

'Arthur placed on the table a red wooden box. Inside was a small card with writing on it. "What is it?" I asked in astonishment.

'"See for yourself," said Arthur, handing it to me.

'I took it. The card was of the highest quality but the writing was clumsy, and the ink of a strange quality, for it was a dark purple and flaked when touched. The message was even more strange. *Sir you are a fool,* it read. *Your collection is worthless. You have allowed the greatest prize of all to slip through your hands.* It was signed simply, *A rival.*

'George took the message from my hands and read it for himself. He began to laugh, and soon we had all joined in.

'Two weeks later, Arthur Ruthven disappeared. A week after that, his corpse was found floating in the Thames off Rotherhithe, naked and wholly drained of its blood.'

I paused. Dr Eliot, his eyes half-closed, and laced his

fingers together as though in prayer. 'Your account,' he said at last, 'implies a link between Arthur's disappearance and his earlier receipt of the peculiar box.'

'When Arthur was pulled from the water, his hand was clenched. A Greek coin was discovered in his palm.'

'Suggestive,' observed Dr Eliot, 'but not conclusive.'

'The coin was certified to be of great value.'

Dr Eliot stared at me impassibley. 'You informed the policy?'

'I did.'

'And their response?'

'They were very polite, but . . .'

'Ah.' Dr Eliot smiled faintly. 'You did not have the box, then?'

'It was never found.'

'Ah,' Dr Eliot nodded again. 'That is a shame.' He narrowed his eyes. 'But perhaps, Lady Mowberley, since you obviously feel it worth your time to be here, you have some further evidence yourself?'

I lowered my eyes. 'I do,' I whispered.

'Tell me.'

'Some months ago a parcel came, addressed to our house. Inside there was a box . . .'

'And the box was the same as that which Arthur had received?'

'In almost every way.'

'Remarkable,' said Dr Eliot, rubbing his hands. 'There was a piece of card too, was there then, addressed to George?'

'No, sir,' I replied. 'It was addressed to me.'

'Ah. Intriguing. What was its message?'

'"Madam, you are blind. Your husband does not love you. He has countless women apart from you."' I choked, and sat in silence. At length I opened my eyes again.

'Do you have the message and box with you now?'

He smiled faintly and opened the box to take out the card. As he studied it, his smile faded and grew into a frown. 'Whoever wrote this,' he said at last, 'is a better pensman than she pretends to be, for the cursives are quite inappropriate to what is otherwise a clumsy hand. I say she, for the style of writing is a feminine one. Also, the ink—you will have guessed, of course—it is clearly an admixture of water and blood.'

'Blood?' I exclaimed.

'Undoubtedly,' he replied. 'There is clearly an intention expressed here to frighten you. You showed this to your husband, I presume?'

I nodded wordlessly.

'What was his response?'

'Outrage. Utter outrage.'

'He denied the message's accusation?'

'Absolutely.'

'And you—forgive me for asking this—you believed him?'

'Yes, sir, I did. Why should I not have done? George had always been the best of husbands, and the most transparent of men. If he had been betraying me, I would have known of it.'

'Good,' Dr Eliot murmured. He sank back into his chair. 'What happened next?'

'Three days after the receipt of the box, George too disappeared.'